BETWEEN WORLDS

MICKY O'BRADY

Table of Contents

CHAPTER ONE

Panic Attack

The second I put my foot onto the threshold of the Berlin Reichstag, I know this is not going to be a good day.

At all.

Like a steam train accelerating to crush me, a sense of doom hits me right in the face, smacking all conscious thought away. I freeze in the middle of a step, the panic too strong for me to move, too strong for me to breathe, too strong for me to do anything.

Two or three of my classmates bump into me from behind. "Move it, Noa." They're chatting, laughing, and completely unaware of what's going on inside my head as they push through the narrow glass doors into the historic building until they become one with my distorted vision. Everything melts into a grey mass around me.

My hands start shaking, a sure sign that I'm about to lose it for real.

Oh, please no.

I can't have a panic attack. Not another one. Not another one *in front of everybody*. At this rate, that's social suicide, and the kind there's no coming back from.

The second that thought shoots through my mind, my throat constricts even more. If I weren't so focused on keeping it together, I might roll my eyes. As if anybody cared about my social standing at this point.

I squeeze my eyes shut as tightly as I can. Must force it down—can't let it get the upper hand.

Sounds that aren't there, images I can't make sense of, scents I can't place.

It's an all-out assault on my senses, tearing reality out of my grasp bit by bit, leaving me in limbo and about to fall.

Something rushes across my field of vision, too fast and blurry for me to recognize. All I get is a vague impression of a tall human body in a weird outfit.

A hard shoulder rams into my back. "Keegan, move it. You're blocking the way. What's wrong with you, freak?"

The force of the impact snaps my head into my neck, frees my mind from its spell, and propels me over the threshold into the building. Only sheer luck keeps me from sprawling belly-first onto the squeaky-clean linoleum floors, and as much as I want to turn around and introduce my fist to Kevan Buttrago's face, I don't. I never do.

Instead, I ignore him. I've become a master at that. Plus, he's done me a favor. Thanks to him, I'm back to normal.

My heart still races as if I just finished a marathon, but my vision has lost the cloudy grey layer and haze that surrounded my every thought. It's gone, and so is the feeling of dread.

I swallow dry.

Close call.

Buttrago strides past me, snickering, and while it shouldn't hurt, it still does. After all, he's my oldest friend—or rather, he used to be. Not anymore, not for a long time. It must have been in eighth grade when I couldn't ward off a panic attack at somebody's fancy planetarium-birthday party, and he was privy to the whole thing. So was his phone, and then a couple of hours later almost everybody in school was, too. The videos of me pressed into a corner, rocking back and forth, trying to keep my senses together brought me many new names, *freak* being one of the nicer ones.

One week later I went and, in the ballsiest decision I've ever made in my life, got myself a nose stud at some really shady piercing studio downtown that didn't believe in checking IDs.

George and Elaine were *delighted.* Meaning, they nearly had matching heart attacks. Their obedient and quiet daughter with a nose stud? To my parents, nothing could be worse than sticking out, than being different.

As if my panic attacks didn't already take care of that.

Kevan joins the rest of the group, getting a couple of high fives from his buddies. For what, I don't have a clue.

Brushing my sweaty hands off my jeans, I make my best attempt to appear as if nothing happened and follow the rest of the herd to the lobby. Everybody's chatting and taking selfies with their phones, feeling on top of the world for a change, courtesy of being an ocean and a continent away from home. This class trip has been in the making for almost six months, and now we're finally here. Seeing most of Europe in three weeks.

It sounds like a fun vay-cay, but the whole trip has education written all over it in broad Sharpie letters. In truth, it's nothing but school in disguise for moderately rich kids whose parents won't even notice or mind them gone for almost a month. I bet in Kevan's case, they're actually happy he's gone, not like mine, who gave me a hug with *that* look on their faces—*that* look that said if things went wrong, I might not see them again. Or might return to only one parent still alive.

I blink rapidly a couple of times.

They're going to be fine. Yes, Andrew died of complications from his leukemia, but that doesn't mean a simple cold will kill George and Elaine like it killed my brother, or that it's going to happen while I'm gone. Everybody's cancer is different, right?

I blink again before my eyes turn watery.

All I want is to go back home and make sure they're okay. FaceTime doesn't count.

One more day. Only one more day until we fly back home to Chicago, ending this trip from hell. Judging by the hidden glances and giggles aimed at me, I haven't shot up the ranks in popularity recently—to absolutely nobody's surprise. That'd be a tough task to pull off anyway, with my free tuition thanks to my mom working as the principal's secretary.

I blow my white-blonde hair out of my face, annoyed by the strands that always defy my attempts to keep them behind my ear. I've given up trying to wear anything that would even vaguely resemble a hairstyle other than a ponytail. My hair is the only part of me that actually has a mind of its own and is not afraid to show it.

"All right, class. Gather tight." Ms. Saunders claps twice, an enthusiasm in her voice Andrew would have loved, just like this trip.

Well, he always was the better one of us… that much is clear.

I stuff my hands deep inside my jeans pockets and follow the herd to where Ms. Saunders waits for us next to a German-looking man in a suit, and by German-looking, I mean tall and blond.

"Hello, everybody. My name is Günther Hochmeister, and welcome to the Berlin Bundestag." He doesn't even try to pronounce his name in English, instead making that hissing-slash-throat-clearing sound the Germans do for a *ch*.

"I'm glad so many of you are interested in the history of Germany and Europe, and I hope I can add a couple of facts to your repertoire that you haven't heard about in class so far." He turns around, motioning the group to follow him.

Like a herd of sheep led to slaughter, we fall in line behind him. Our noisy steps echo through the halls and make it almost impossible to listen to Mr. Hochmeister, which will be a problem for the unavoidable quiz or essay afterward. Oh, well. I'll have to read up on it later.

While he talks, I take a good look around. The Bundestag-slash-former-Reichstag is a pretty nice building, modern and clean, with wide hallways and blue-framed doors and windows. It looks nothing like the pictures we saw during class, with Nazi flags hanging from the walls and roof and Nazi officers and soldiers standing everywhere.

In fact, there's not much here at all reminding me of the time during the 1930s and 40s besides the walls. To quote my homework, *traces of historical events were retained during remodeling after Germany's reunification*, and if I had to guess, I'd say I'm looking right at that. These must be the original walls from the last century, all weathered and worn down, pockmarked by bullet holes where they haven't been fixed with obviously newer materials.

One big stretch of a curved wall catches my attention, and it's not because of the beautiful but partially destroyed reliefs close to the ceiling. It's because it's covered with words and sentences carved into it like an early version of graffiti, all of them written in the Cyrillic alphabet. I.e., undecipherable for me.

All but one, that is, and it's jumping right at me:

Love.

I drag a finger over the letters that would mean nothing to me if I weren't a romantic at heart. How must it have been during those years, when the Nazis thought they were the kings of the world, before the Allied forces defeated them? How much different must life have been? Yes, technically, I know all the facts: the number of deaths, the horror of living under the Nazis, their experiments on innocent people, their complete disregard for life, but… it feels so far away. So unbelievable and inconceivable that my brain refuses to make sense of it.

"Noa Keegan. Today, please?"

Ms. Saunders' annoyed voice cuts into my brain like a knife through butter. I jerk my hand away from the wall and hide it behind my back as if I had done something forbidden, which I'm pretty sure I haven't.

"'Course," I mumble, scrambling to catch up with the others through the blue-framed glass door my teacher holds open for me, a stern look on her face.

"Pull yourself together, Noa. We're guests here."

"I didn't do—"

"Just saying, Noa. Just saying."

She sighs and lets the door fall closed behind us, her attention already back on our tour guide's words.

"The elevator holds a maximum of five people, so we'll go up to the dome in small groups." Mr. Hochmeister stops in a narrower area in a side wing of the building.

"Thank you. We're so excited." Ms. Saunders is back to wearing her happy face.

I huff once, wrinkling my nose. Should have opted for one of my other nose studs today. The silver butterfly—that would've been it. A butterfly could spread its wings and fly away without a care in the world, without any baggage, and just *be*.

I pat my right front pocket, glad I carry my usual stack of replacement studs. Force of habit, I tend to wear my heart on my sleeve, or rather, my mood on my nose. I fish for the little stud that's easily discernible from the others by its edges. One quick plug, pull, and push, and the flower is gone, replaced by the stylized outline of a butterfly.

I straighten up, as if I could take flight myself. That's more like it.

Slowly but steadily, the group in front of me dwindles down as student after student takes the elevator to the Reichstag's glass dome rising high above the seat of the German parliament. Must be cool sitting in one of those seats and doing politics, knowing what historic significance this place once held.

Well, cool or frightening. Both are an option.

"Room for one more," Mr. Hochmeister calls over from inside the elevator, one arm extended to keep the doors from closing.

For a short moment, Ms. Saunders weighs her responsibilities against the call of history. As if she really considered staying down with us. Puh-lease. We're sixteen, she trusts Kevan, her favorite student, and she's a history nerd. It's really no contest.

And right I was. She all but jumps forward and squeezes herself between my classmates, which leaves only me and… yeah. Ugh, Kevan.

"We'll send it down right away and I expect you up without any delay. Understood?" Ms. Saunders orders. The doors close on her and the elevator takes off.

So much for thinking this day couldn't get any worse. Even the reflection thrown back at me from the elevator's shiny metallic doors doesn't do me any favors: My little frame looks like a child's next to Kevan's well-developed one. How my parents can be tall while I ended up on the shorter side of things is beyond me.

I straighten up even more. I don't want to think about George and Elaine.

He jabs an elbow into my ribs, distracting me. "You and me, freak."

I roll my eyes. "Awesome, Kevan, awesome. Oh, and so mature."

He snickers again and turns toward me. "You know me. I've always been a big boy."

I harrumph once and stare straight ahead, trying to ignore him looking at me. He'll stop bothering me if I don't react. They always do.

His finger grazes my cheek, brushing a strand of blonde hair out of my eyes. "You know, if you'd do something with your hair and maybe took out that stupid nose stud… you'd be pretty, Noa. I could help you with that, tit for tat, and you—"

My stomach freezes over in an instant. "What?"

"I said, if—"

"I heard you the first time." With a quick twist of my upper body, I swat his hand away and create some distance between those fingers and myself. He lost the privilege to touch me in any way when he turned one-eighty on me and sent that video.

A flicker of annoyance crosses Kevan's face, like he couldn't believe I did that.

Neither can I.

I drop my gaze to the floor and step off to the side. "Leave me alone, Kev." My cheeks burn, and not only because I did the unheard of and actually reacted to Kevan's stupid comment, but mostly because of the comment itself.

"If you'd do something with your hair and maybe took out that stupid nose stud, you'd be pretty."

Come on. I'm not ugly, seriously. I'm not the type to go around and throw myself at guys, but to Kevan and probably every male in school, that means I'm too unnoticeable, too unexciting in every way besides my, uh, *freak-side*.

No need to remind me of it.

I swallow down a lump inside my throat.

Tit for tat. He actually had the audacity to drop the whole you-could-be-pretty-line on me and then ask for something in return? *Ass.*

They've been pulling that one for years: Noa, help me with my homework, and I'll invite you to my next party. Noa, give me some lunch money and you can sit with us.

Fool me once, shame on you. Fool me twice…

I chew on the inside of my cheek so hard, it hurts.

Thankfully, the elevator finally arrives and we enter, pressing D for dome. The cabin moves up a mere second after the doors close.

Unfortunately, it's not fast enough to escape Kevan. He leans against the wall across from me despite me looking anywhere but at him.

"I meant it." He crosses his arms in front of his chest.

Deep breath. He's not getting to me. He's not. "Kev, you—"

That's when I feel it. Like reality isn't as thick around me anymore, like something reaching for me, trying to pull me in and under to drown me. I almost choke on my next breath when the sense of doom from earlier is back, bringing with it the sure knowledge that something bad is about to happen.

I stumble a step forward, my knees about to give in under me.

The elevator shoots up, each foot adding another layer of horror. My fingers tingle first, only to turn numb a second later. My heart races yet doesn't pump any blood.

A raspy breath leaves my throat.

Oh no, no, no, *no.*

Not so soon after.

I've never had them this close together, and never this bad.

And I can't have *another* one in front of Kevan.

"Stop the elevator," I wheeze, bent over, one hand clawing at my tight black shirt around my neck to loosen it—to no avail.

Air. I need air.

"What?"

"Stop… elevator," I croak. My arms and legs cramp up from my body's response to the threat it's perceiving. I have to get out of here; maybe it's claustrophobia.

"Shit, Noa," Kev curses when I stumble and almost fall. "Is it…?" He doesn't need to finish that sentence.

I nod, wheezing in short and fast breaths. Now he can get his phone out and continue what he started.

The elevator slows down and opens without a sound—and the very same moment that I catch a glimpse of the huge glass dome above me I'm hit square in the chest with what must surely be the force of lightning. Holy cow, it's never been that bad.

I lean forward, my arms tightly wrapped around my body. A groan leaves my throat. *Must hold it together. Must.*

Kevan goes ahead, supporting me by the elbow. "Get out, come on. It'll be better here."

Oh my god, no, it won't. Whatever I do, I can't move forward. "No," I breathe, cold sweat running down my neck.

"You have to," Kev answers, and with one strong pull, he drags me out of the elevator with him.

My feet touch the soft blue carpet of the walkway surrounding the gallery above the German Parliament, and if Kevan didn't have such a good grip on me, I'd fall.

He guides me forward toward a more secluded area and away from our peers, something I would normally recognize as surprising, but not right now. As it is, I'm fighting to keep myself from finding another corner and rocking in it.

By now, my vision is almost gone, the view of the blue seats below us and the German Eagle sign hanging above it replaced by something white and sterile. A stinging scent hits my nose that's too reminiscent of a hospital. Sounds that are impossible to be heard here assault my ears, and it's the last straw.

I'm losing it, and there's no way around it.

I have to leave. I have to get back to safety, to downstairs, where

I was normal.

"Let go." With all the power I've left, I tear myself loose. Getting back to the elevator and to ground level is my one and only priority if I want to break free before it's too late, and I'm not even sure it isn't already. Swaying, I take a couple of steps away from Kevan—and then, without a warning, a vortex opens beneath me.

It sucks me down into a darkness that's somehow still light. It pulls and pushes me, twisting my body and flattening it at the same time. My vision grows black, then white. My breathing stops, my body contorts into unnatural positions, and forces I can't make sense of whip my head around.

I scream as reality kicks me out of its realm, the sensation of loss so profound and painful it hurts like a knife to the heart.

A short flash lights up my vision, the temperature drops by several degrees, all followed by the loud howl of a siren.

My body collapses under me.

I hit cold tile floor and—

CHAPTER TWO

Confusion

Before I even open my eyes, I notice the smell.

Like during the panic attack, the air has a sterile, almost medical, quality to it, as if somebody used too much disinfectant in a hospital.

I groan. My head hurts. As if that realization had triggered something, my senses slowly wake up, extending their tendrils beyond the limits of my body.

That's when I hear the breathing.

And that's also when I feel the warmth right above me.

My eyes fly open, taking a second to make sense of the olive-colored background with dark circles in it until I recognize it as a face hovering a mere couple of inches above me.

"Whoa!" Wide awake. I propel myself backward until I smack into a cold wall. *Too close.* That glowering face… too close.

"Where…?" *Where am I?* A cot. Small room. Walls made out of something black and polished that reflects the bright ceiling lights with a greenish sheen, like the inside of a shell. The black color is even on the ceiling; it's everywhere… besides the front of the room.

That's where the bars are.

Now wait a second.

That can't be real.

I can't be in a cell.

My heart beats so fast, I can't catch a breath at all. It's not getting any better when the man moves closer again, staring at me with a hostility that freezes me to the core.

"How did you get here?" His voice is calm and controlled but carries a thinly veiled threatening undertone. He's not happy. Not at all.

My voice, on the other hand, is gone—completely. All I can do is stare.

The man is dressed in some kind of black uniform complete with what must be rank insignia on the collar of his shirt. A German police officer? I mean, we saw them before, but their uniforms looked different. I *think*. It's not like I was paying special attention to them, but I'm pretty sure that they all wore German flags on their upper arm, not a black one with… *circling dots?*

"I repeat: How did you get here?" He takes another intimidating step closer, leaving almost no room between himself and me in the corner of my cot.

"I-I don't know." I push myself against the cold wall until I'm sure I can't get any farther away from him. I probably shouldn't be afraid, but how can I not be? I'm in a cell with a police officer—no, not police, but who then? Private security? A soldier? Guarding a cell? Guarding *me?* That doesn't make any sense.

Everything about him screams military, though, from the straight posture and cold stare to the muscular and tall body. His face would be interesting if he didn't scare the bejeezus out of me with his glare: light-colored eyes framed by olive skin and dark, buzz-cut hair. Not African-American, not Caucasian, but something in-between, with a little teardrop-curve to the eyes.

"W-Where am I?" I'm surprised I found my voice and even more so that it doesn't break since my guard isn't inviting any questions, that much is clear.

The soldier doesn't even so much as acknowledge my question. "How. Did. You. Get. Here?"

Okay, now I'm sure I did something wrong. I must have. Don't have a clue what, but I must have. They wouldn't treat me like this if

I didn't.

Can they hold me responsible if I broke something during the panic attack? That's a medical emergency. I shouldn't be accountable, right? Judging by the deadly stare, I'm not so sure about that anymore.

"I don't know." I swallow hard, my gaze darting left and right, trying to find a way past that man and away from him, but there's nowhere to go. It's a cell, all right, albeit one with weird walls.

Like lightning, he thrusts his arm forward and grabs my hair, jerking my head back until it hits the wall. A surprised grunt tears from my throat.

"I expect answers, and I expect them now," he says, his voice a low, menacing growl. "The area is restricted, but here you are. You have exactly three seconds to come up with a good explanation as to how you got in and tell me how many others there are, or I can make this much worse for you, *Ghost*." With that, he bangs my head against the wall behind me.

I cry out. Both hands fly up to my head in an attempt to protect it and lessen the pull of the soldier's hands on my hair.

His eyes narrow to slits. "Three. Two. One."

I squeeze my eyes shut, bracing myself for whatever is coming, giving in, like I was raised to do. All the fight I ever had is in my nose stud.

"Your loss." The man hauls me up by my hair so brutally, I scream. His other hand wraps around my throat as he slams my body into the wall behind me as if I weighed nothing. His face hovers above mine so close, I have to cross my eyes to look at him.

He squeezes.

The pressure on my throat cuts off my air with a choking wheeze. Like a bobble-head figure, my eyes pop out of their sockets from the pressure building behind them. Blood swooshes in my ears, desperate to find a way out of my skull and back into my body.

Help. I need help. I need this to stop, or—

"You will start to feel very uncomfortable in a matter of seconds. Then I might let you get some air, or maybe not. I want answers, and

I want them now: How. Did. You. Get. Here?" Cocking his head to the left, he observes me as I'm sure my face turns purple.

My throat hurts, my vision dims, and my lungs burn and sting from my need to breathe. I gag, I gasp, I try to pry his fingers away from my throat, but to no avail. He's stronger than me by a mile. I claw at him, but my movements turn sluggish from my heart beating so fast that it has used up all my oxygen in no time.

A shadow falls into the cell.

"That's enough, soldier." The voice that booms over us from behind my attacker is commanding, deep and authoritative. Like a switch flipped, the hands in my hair and around my throat are gone, leaving me to fall forward onto all fours onto the cot, barely catching myself with my outstretched hands.

Coughing and gagging, I rub my throat, my rough breathing filling the silence.

Air. Finally.

"Sir, I—"

"Leave."

There's a hissing sound, then footfalls enter the cell.

"But, sir, the regulations—"

"Don't apply in this case. Leave. This is Minister-only." The steps stop in front of my cot. "*Now,* soldier."

"Yes, sir." Heels click together, then quick, crisp steps lead out of my cell. There's another hiss and then I'm left alone with the man who saved me. I'm still on all fours—well, threes actually, since I'm still massaging my burning throat—and all I see are black combat boots and black military-style tactical pants.

I blink once. The tears the attack brought to my eyes drip onto the plastic surface. What have I gotten myself into? I didn't do anything, I swear.

A hand finds my arm and gently pulls me up to sitting. "Are you okay?"

Am I? I breathe in deeply, while I lift my head up, and—

My eyes connect with the ones in front of me and the breath I just took hitches in my throat.

Amber.

Mesmerizing bright, clear amber eyes of an intensity I've never seen before, and they're looking straight at me. No: they're *evaluating* me. Heavy dark brows scrunch together ever so slightly as he cocks his head to the left, the shadows falling on his face emphasizing his high cheekbones and full lips.

"Are you okay?" he repeats when all I do is stare.

"Y-Yeah," I croak. My legs fold under my body until I sit on my butt, my breathing still kind of raspy.

He straightens himself up to standing and nods, his gaze roaming over me, assessing me. "Interesting." Deep and full, his voice is perfect for his size, and for whatever reason, it resonates through my body, tugging on some kind of string inside my chest I never knew I had.

I swallow dry as I take him in completely.

He's even bigger than the guy who choked me, if that's possible. Bigger and… more intimidating, even though he's still young, maybe twenty-one at the most. He doesn't quite reach Brock Lesnar proportions, but he's a solid LeBron James with a good touch of The Rock Dwayne Johnson, because he must be hiding a bodybuilder's figure under this tight black uniform similar to my guard's, but not quite the same. Whereas the guard looked like one of a million others in the same uniform, the new guy rocks black cargo pants and a tight black Lycra shirt that emphasizes his size. Whoever first called black slimming was wrong. On him, it brings out every muscle, underlines every inch of his width.

It also matches his dark hair, which is a tad too unruly to be tidy, although it would still be considered short.

He takes a step back, his arms folded in front of his chest. "Who are you?"

"Noa Keegan," I squeak, wishing I sounded stronger. "You?"

A small smile tugs at the corners of his lips. "That's not what I meant, and you know it, Noa Keegan. Who sent you?"

Who sent me? "N-Nobody. I don't even know where I am. I mean, I-I just woke up here." Where is everybody? They can't leave me alone, can they? At least Ms. Saunders should be here. I'm still underage, and—

"Fair enough," he says, "although I am sure you know where you are. But let me humor you. You are in Germany. Berlin. The Unification Building, to be precise."

"Unification Building?" I thought I did my homework well. Where do they have a Unification Building? Close to the Berlin Wall that used to separate the city and the country?

"How'd I get here?" Ambulance? But why was the other guy basically trying to choke the life out of me? That doesn't make sense.

"That's what I would like you to answer. Are there others?"

"Others?" I cough twice when my voice breaks. "Of course. My whole high school year." And thanks for leaving me alone, everyone. Not that I expected otherwise, but it still stings.

He steps closer again. "How many, and where?"

I push myself deeper into the wall that is my only reassurance this all is real. How can I be in a cell? I didn't do anything, and if my parents find out—

I hold back a groan. Once they find out—because there is no doubt in my mind they will—it won't be a pleasant conversation. It doesn't matter what got me in here. All they ever preached to my brother and me is to live our lives quietly, to walk a straight line. Andrew was always good at that, but I was never good enough, thanks to my panic attacks.

Drawing my legs in, I let my head sink down onto my forearms. "I don't know," I whisper into my arms. "I woke up in here and then got choked." Something stings behind my eyes, but it can't possibly be tears.

A muscle in his jaw twitches. I'm sure he's losing patience with me, like the other one did. "All right then. Let me repeat my question. Where are the others? Are they Ghosts as well, and if so, how many are there?"

It's the second time somebody mentions Ghosts. "Ghosts?"

His massive chest heaves up and down once, amber eyes never leaving mine, not missing a thing. He tilts his head to the left again, as if trying to figure me out.

"I see," he says, drawing the words out. "I see."

Big Guy walks toward the bars that must have closed after the other soldier exited and presses one hand against an area with a bluish glow to it. The bars slide apart with the slightest whooshing sound.

"Come." He steps out of my cell without looking back to check on me.

I scramble to get off the cot and out of here. "Come where?"

He stops and turns around. "To see the Minister. He will decide what to do with you."

The Minister? Oh, holy cow, I'm in deeper trouble than I thought.

I groan and rub a palm over my forehead.

That moment when I stepped across the threshold of the Reichstag and knew this wasn't going to be a good day?

Yeah.

I hate it when I'm right.

CHAPTER THREE

Different

For a moment, I consider running for it.

Maybe I could make it past Soldier. I'm small, I could duck under him and then… Yeah, and then what? Whom am I kidding? I don't have the guts to run, and even if I did, I don't know where I am or where to go.

"Come," he says again, walking away from the cell without looking back at me, expecting me to follow as if I were a little puppy called by its master.

And of course I do because that's how I was raised. Obedient.

I hurry out of the cell that I hope to never ever see again—this one, or any other cell, for that matter. I'm surprised Soldier didn't put me in cuffs, but then he probably looked at little pitiful me and knew I wouldn't stand a chance even if he pointed me in the direction I needed to run.

Something cramps on the inside of my chest, but I ignore it.

Our steps make almost no sound on the floor as we walk down the empty narrow hallway toward a bigger door that doesn't swing open but slides open completely silent once we approach it. Fancy, those Germans.

Soldier turns left into another empty sterile hallway, trusting me to keep up with him. I speed up until I'm next to him, my heart beating like crazy. "Excuse me, why… why the Minister?" We could drop that visit and call it a day? Maybe?

"You are his responsibility."

There goes that hope out the window.

"I am?" Isn't that overreaching a little bit?

"You are. All intruders are."

Now wait a second, he must have it wrong. "I'm not an intruder."

He stops and gives me a raised eyebrow. "Yet you were in a Level One restricted area."

"I wasn't. I was up under the Dome—"

"Exactly."

He resumes walking toward another door that slides open, then turns left into a much bigger and busier hallway than before. There are blue-framed windows on the opposite side that are somewhat familiar-looking.

I shake my head once to clear it. Restricted area? I would never trespass… unless Kevan dragged me somewhere. Oh, I'm so going to kill him if he did that to me.

Well, I won't. But I'll have to get back at him somehow, or it'll get even worse. I know that much.

Balling my hands into fists, I stuff them deep into my pockets. If this is Kevan's next prank on me, I don't care what my parents say—I will make him pay for it. Or at least I'll try.

I'm so focused on my blossoming wrath it takes me a while to recognize the intricately decorated reliefs on the walls and ceiling, but eventually even my brain makes the connection. "Is… Is this still the Reichstag?"

I'm asking more myself than Soldier, but still, he stops again for a second, looking at me, maybe trying to figure out if I'm pulling his leg. "I told you we're still in the Unification Building."

Meaning the Reichstag? Why can't people stick to one name, especially in a foreign language—

Oh.

Wait a second. Soldier here speaks perfect English—not English with a German accent. This is American English with a slight local dialect I can't quite place. What is an American soldier doing in Germany, and why is one of my own people holding me? If he's from the Embassy, shouldn't he help me?

I'm about to gather all my courage and ask when somebody bumps into me accidentally, apologizing under their breath before passing on.

That's when I realize something else is off, but blinded by my usual habit of keeping my head down, I didn't lift my eyes off the floor enough to actually *see*.

Now I do.

First, this hallway is much busier than it was before.

Second, none of the people roaming the hallway wear suits or business attire like earlier today. Almost all are dressed in lab coats, some even with protective goggles pushed up into their hair. The few who don't sport lab coats have definitely read different fashion magazines than what we have in Chicago, or I missed the latest craze over… whatever this material and style is.

What happened to the Germans?

My head turns left and right, trying to take it all in and make up my mind. It's the Reichstag, all right, only with very strange employees. The area Soldier leads me through actually looks vaguely familiar. If I'm not mistaken we might have passed—

Oh, holy cow.

Not caring about the people I almost run over, I dart toward the wall on my left, my finger finding the same spot inside the curved wall under the same relief as before.

It's gone.

My hand glides across the smooth stone that shows no sign of wear or tear, no graffiti, no nothing. The one word I could identify in Cyrillic isn't here, yet I'm sure it *was* right here a mere hour ago, maybe even less.

It is the same spot, and yet it isn't. How can that be? They can't have fixed it that quickly, I mean, it was *carved into the stone*.

What's going on here?

My fingers leave sweat prints on the cold wall, and suddenly, it's really, really hot in here.

Me in a cell, guarded by an American soldier.

No graffiti, although it's the right piece of wall.

No people in suits, but people in lab coats and weird clothing.

My gaze falls to the left, the sinking feeling in my stomach getting even worse.

No glass doors leading to the elevators, but a large open doorway instead.

It must be the wrong location—

"Are you coming?"

I'm so startled by the voice, I turn around out of reflex and bump right into Soldier, almost bouncing off his chest.

His *very muscular* chest.

I drop my hands as if they'd touched a hot stove and shove them into my pockets. "Uh, there was graffiti there. I thought. I mean, when I was here last." I hate that I sound as if I'm defending myself, as if I've done something wrong.

Soldier gives me a long look that I can't quite interpret. "We don't tolerate vandalism of any kind," he finally says, turning to leave again.

I suck in my lower lip and bite on it. It would be nice if the pain could either wake me up or clear my mind. Right. No vandalism, no graffiti.

But it was right there.

A ball of ice forms inside my stomach despite the heat that makes me break out in a sweat. I must be confusing things. We're most likely in a completely different wing. Of course. That's what it must be.

Cursing under my breath, I fall into step with Soldier, mentally comparing our path with where I walked earlier this morning. If I'm not completely wrong—although I kind of hope I am—the elevators should be around the next corner.

They are.

But not how I remember them.

Instead of one small elevator, three empty glass tubes with the diameter of maybe one and a half yards lead from the floors beneath us to the ones above us. Each has a man-sized cutout at ground level, but no doors.

Just when I'm about to ask, a man rushes past us toward the left tube and steps into its opening—without even looking down.

Before I can shout a warning, something transparent and disk-like appears right under his feet, lifting him up and out of view within two or three seconds.

I stare after him open-mouthed, frozen in my tracks.

Soldier realizes I've stopped again, sighs, and takes my elbow, dragging me toward the tube thingy.

I don't even realize he's doing it.

That man, he stepped into nothingness, and then—

Another person appears from below in the tube on the left, first the head, and within a second or two, the rest of his body. Recognition hits me like a fist to the gut. My stomach muscles tighten and I hold my breath.

The guy who choked me.

I brace myself for another hostile glance or worse, only this time, he doesn't pay me the slightest bit of attention. Once he reaches the floor level, he steps out of the tube without missing a beat, staring down onto his left wrist and never taking his eyes off of it, as if it were the most interesting thing in the world.

I crane my neck over my shoulder at him while Soldier guides me forward—and directly into one of those tubes. A surge of panic shoots through me right before the strangest sensation of tingling and pulling hits my body, and *something* appears under me, whisking me up instead of letting me drop.

My mouth falls open as I look down to my feet.

There's nothing there.

I lift up one, then the other foot, but still, there's no surface, no propelling mechanism or anything. An elevator without a motor? Or a floor?

"Exit the next floor." Soldier takes my elbow again. Might be my deer-caught-in-headlight-stare that makes him take that precaution.

With a big step, he guides me out of this elevator-thingy and onto the blissfully solid tile surface right under the dome—the same dome I remember before I blacked out, only it looks completely different now.

Completely.

What was a wide, open area designed for visitors with a view of the parliament below is now one solid floor filled with lab equipment and people working in lab coats. I'm no expert, especially not in anything physics or science-related, but this stuff… I don't think it's only everyday supplies. Wide, gate-shaped constructions rise from the floor, wires poking out all over like everything is still under construction. Dozens of tables are spread around the area, covered with thick square metal things with liquids dripping out of them and fumes rising up. A huge, man-sized metal ring stands in the middle of the room, some kind of blueish energy zapping from one end to the other. About a million other things line up against the walls or peek out from their storage underneath the tables, most I can't even begin to identify.

If somebody told me I'd stepped into a madman's laboratory, I'd believe them.

All this stuff makes me feel uneasy. On the edge. Like my body knew more, but my mind hadn't quite caught up with everything. Every breath turns raspy, and the sensation of doom I only know too well blossoms in my stomach.

Right.

Because I see a science lab, and I picture being the guinea pig or what? *Get a grip, Keegan.*

I almost trip over my own feet as I follow Soldier along a barely cleared path toward a door in the wall cutting off a smaller part of the dome from the lab.

Jacob Canyon, Minister for TA.

By now I wish the plaque on the door read *Police* rather than *Minister.*

I swallow hard.

I'll… play it by ear. I didn't do anything, right?

Still, I can't shake the feeling that I'm missing something, something big. It's staring me right in the face, but my brain refuses to make sense of it.

Soldier places his hand onto another blueish thingy like the one down in the cell and the doors slide apart. He leads me into a wide office with floor-to-ceiling windows on the left and straight ahead. They seamlessly melt into the glass dome above, giving this room the impression of being out in the open. The same material I saw before, the shiny green-blackish stuff, covers the floor and the walls, like in my cell. Looks a tad… sinister somehow. If it weren't for the light shining in through the glass dome, it'd be downright spooky. The only furniture is the large, sturdy desk at the far end of this room together with three comfy-looking chairs in front of it, but that's it. Rather minimalistic.

The moment the doors close behind us, I can breathe easier again. That is until Soldier clears his throat. "Sir. It's a single intruder and under control. No Ghosts as far as we know, but—"

"Why is she not in a cell?"

I barely suppress a double-take when I find the source of the angry snarl. Instead of the middle-aged man I expected judging by the voice, a thin, white-haired figure stands in front of one of the windows on our left, looking outside. His back is hunched over, and one of his hands rests on a cane that seems to support almost all of his bodyweight. He looks ancient.

"You of all people I expected to follow protocol." The snide and strength in his voice is the absolute contrary to the fragility in his posture.

Soldier steps next to me, almost protectively. "That would be because she met Paragraph-One-criteria, sir."

For a moment, it's dead silent.

Then the old man turns around with a speed that belies the fragility of his body. "Paragraph One? Are you sure that—"

His voice trails off without finishing the sentence. Instead, he stares at me, one hand on his cane, the other one still extended as if to point at me.

"Now look at that," he whispers about five seconds later, shaking his head ever so slightly. What am I, an exotic zoo animal?

Creepy.

Completely creepy.

Gramps blinks a couple of times, the hand on his cane shaking in the same rhythm. He must be well over eighty—heck, ninety—with his snow-white hair, all the wrinkles in his face, and hunched-over body. His eyes, though, his eyes are blue, clear, and alert—and scaring me more than the guy who choked me.

Subconsciously, I take a step back half into Soldier, but no farther. A large, warm palm in my lower back keeps me right where I am—and I'm close enough to feel his voice reverberate through me when he speaks.

"Sir? Is everything all right? Should I—"

The old man shakes himself loose from staring at me, and it feels like a weight has been lifted off of me. "No, it's all right, Sentinel. You saw it, right?"

Soldier hesitates before he answers. "Yes, sir, but it's weaker than expected."

"But still, it's there."

What is there? What the heck are they talking about?

The old man's focus returns to me. "What's your name, sweetheart?"

Sweetheart? This is getting better by the minute. A stronger person would have shown him the middle finger, but not me. Never me.

"Noa Keegan," I say as evenly as I can, which more or less only means I don't sound completely afraid.

"Noa Keegan." Grandpa repeats my name as if expecting a different answer. "Of course. Well, Noa Keegan, my name is Jacob Canyon. I'm the Minister for T.A. Welcome."

"Uh, thank you." It doesn't feel like a warm welcome, that much is for sure.

The Minister points his cane at me, luckily not falling over without it. "Noa, why don't you join me over here for a second, will you please?"

I hesitate for a moment until Soldier gives me the softest nudge and a slight nod.

"Okay." I wipe my palms on my thighs and cross the five yards to where the Minister is looking out the window—the window that shows a Berlin unlike the one I remember from our tour.

This view is taking my breath away.

As if it could change the scene in front of me, I'm right up against the window, both hands pressed against the cold glass, stunned by a city that is Berlin—yet isn't.

It bears a certain resemblance to what we saw during our sightseeing tour, but not much. Gone are the greys, gone are the neon signs and billboards, and the traffic on the four-lane streets. Instead, Berlin is green everywhere—covered with trees, bushes, grass—where before busy roads crisscrossed the town. Even from up here, I can make out a couple of people walking, but no cars.

What I remember to be medium-sized high-rises or large apartment complexes are gone, replaced by white, half-round structures at least forty stories high. Dozens of them stand scattered throughout the green, like a giant had played golf and lost his balls. A flock of birds flies by, and farther in the distance, something bigger lifts off one of the golf-ball things, almost a helicopter, but not quite, too fast and smooth.

No matter where I look, though, the whole scene below me radiates a tranquility beyond anything I've ever seen before.

"Wow." My breath fogs up the glass.

The Minister's cane touches the window next to me twice. "I take it you like the city?"

Do I like the city? It's breathtaking. Green, beautiful, and... *wholesome* somehow.

Canyon looks over to me. "I assume your Berlin looks closer to what ours did in the 1940s?" Without waiting for an answer, he jabs his cane repeatedly at something on the outside. "We put most traffic underground since then. Safer, better controlled, less destructive to the environment. It suits the planet."

"You *what?* *M-My* Berlin?" I try to add one and one yet arrive at nothing. Our class took the bus here. I *saw* the traffic, just as busy as in Chicago, all around the Victory Column, the same one that is still proudly standing in the distance. *Without* any traffic around it.

The Minister walks over to his desk. "Have a seat," he says while settling down behind it. I follow, although I have a hard time tearing myself away from that view. Once I reach the chair closest to the window, my knees give in of their own accord.

I have a bad feeling about this. Very bad, actually, and despite George's frequent loathing of anything politics-related, me sitting in front of an actual minister is not my main concern anymore.

I force myself away from the view of a Berlin I don't recognize. The theory about Kev playing a trick on me is once and for all out the window, quite literally.

The Minister turns to Soldier next to the desk. "Are we off?"

Soldier never moves from his stance, his legs spread shoulder-width apart, his arms crossed behind his back. He nods once. "Yes, sir. Off and secured."

"Good. Well, Noa, I have news for you."

"Okay." My voice is a squeak and nothing more, maybe because I lack the air thanks to my heartbeat turning more into a weak flutter. This whole thing is seriously starting to freak me out. Majorly. I'm waiting for the sensation of overwhelming doom, of panic, but nothing. At least something is working in my favor for a change.

Canyon smiles again, like a grandfather at his grandchild, although I wouldn't know, having been completely grandparent-less for all my life.

"This might sound strange to you, even crazy, but you're not home anymore. Well, you are in a way, but not home as you know it." He chuckles and leans his cane against the desk.

"There is no way to sugarcoat it," he continues, "so bear with me. You've stepped through a breach between universes and ended up in ours. This is not your home. It might look similar, but it's not. Welcome to our universe. Welcome to Terra, little Earthling."

CHAPTER FOUR

New World

I stare at the old man in front of me with my mouth open. I didn't hear that right, did I?

He's pulling my leg.

He *must* be pulling my leg.

A different universe? Impossible.

Canyon gives me that grandfatherly smile again, while Soldier stays next to the desk in his wide stance, his arms behind his back.

Neither man says anything.

Just like down in the hallway when I felt something was wrong but couldn't put a finger on it, a ball of ice forms inside my stomach while the rest of my body breaks out in sweat.

This must be a dream. An aftershock of my panic attack. A sedative-induced state of mind. *Something* other than the real deal.

I did *not* cross into another universe.

Nope. Impossible. It's much more likely my brain finally went the whole mile and turned completely crazy on me.

But then… *Something* is off, and I knew it from the moment I woke up: the smell. The way I feel. This metal on the wall down in the cell and here, that's stuff I've never seen before. That I was in a cell and not in a hospital or some kind of nurse's office, and let's not even mention the non-existent graffiti, the elevator tube, the lab under the dome, or that Berlin isn't Berlin anymore.

Everything about this is off, odd, and weird, but still, my brain refuses to believe what it heard.

Another look out the window and I'm about to throw up. "Impossible," I repeat to myself in a small whisper. "Completely impossible." I twirl my butterfly nose stud with shaking fingers.

Canyon looks at me with a certain pity in his eyes. "I know what it sounds like, but it's true. Our world has known about the existence of parallel universes for a while, but for somebody from a less developed world…" He shrugs. "It must sound crazy."

That's putting it mildly.

The problem is that part of me fears Canyon is right—and that can't be. It can't possibly be.

The Minister taps his fingers on his desk. "Well, I thought it would be rough on you. It should be; it's a major change to your belief system, if I'm correct."

He leans forward, folding his hands in front of him. "How old are you, Noa?"

"Almost seventeen." And apparently not very mature, or I wouldn't give my age like a kindergartner.

"All right then. I assume you have some kind of physics class in the school you are attending?"

"I do." Not quite my favorite, but I don't hate it, either.

"Good." He nods. "Now, you have probably heard of Einstein, have you not? Compared to him, we've taken physics and relativity to a whole new level. See, at any given point in time, there are an infinite number of universes existing parallel to each other. For every possible outcome of a situation, a new universe births into existence. Most of the time, though, no true split-off happens, at least none that would matter." He pauses to check if I'm getting it so far.

I narrow my eyes, following his mental exercise. "Like, if I turned left down the street versus right?" Seems like not a very good reason to make a whole new universe out of my decision.

Canyon nods again. "Exactly. But let's say you do exactly that, turn left versus right. That changes only a minuscule part of the universe you're in, especially when the outcome is the same—for example, you arrive at school. Now, if the outcome changes—in one universe you get killed by a vehicle, in the other you don't—that changes everything. Events that ripple down the event horizon create separate universes from each other. From here on, we have two universes: one in which you're alive, doing what fate has in stock for you, and another one in which you will be absent, your timeline deleted. No continuation of any kind."

The shaking of my hands intensifies, so I push them under my thighs, hiding them. "There might be universes out there where I'm... *not there?*" I really don't want to say *dead*. It's a word my family doesn't like to use.

"Millions or more," Canyon says. "You were born in countless other universes, but your path differs from the timeline you did grow up in. In many other universes, you weren't even born, depending on what caused the split-off from the original timeline before your birth. Something could have changed your parents' path, or that of your grandparents. Speaking of..." He lifts a hand while the other opens a drawer. "If you wouldn't mind." He pushes a small rectangular device across the desk over to Soldier.

"Of course, sir."

Soldier takes the smooth black box and squats down in front of me, taking my hand in his.

The moment his skin touches mine, I all but jump up from the sudden surge passing through me all the way down to the center of my chest.

He looks up, his eyes finding mine, completely misinterpreting my twitch. "It won't hurt."

Praying I'm not blushing, I nod, willing myself to not focus too much on the weight and warmth of his hand on top of mine as he flattens it onto the device, pressing down ever so slightly.

"What is this?" I'm glad I sound strong, the stupid flutter inside my chest not betraying me.

Canyon answers. "A GeneScreen. We'll compare your genetic data to the data of all humans currently alive on Terra. That way we'll see if there's another version of you in this universe."

Another version of me? My mouth drops open. Of course, it would make sense, but—

"If there is no match with your gene data, the system will automatically search for relatives, giving us an idea of where you're coming from."

Right.

A small scraping sensation on the underside of my palm distracts me from the crazy thought of meeting an alternate-reality family before I can digest that thought completely.

Soldier lets go of my hand, and for a moment, I regret it, missing the warmth.

"Done, sir." He places the box on Canyon's desk and takes the same position next to the desk again: arms behind his back, wide stance, seemingly relaxed, although I doubt he truly is. This man is trained to fight, and it oozes from every pore: the smooth, fluid movements, the confident posture, the authority in his voice. Everything.

Everything but his eyes. They're too warm for a mere fighter, too intelligent. Maybe it's the amber, maybe it's something else, but his eyes fascinate me.

Canyon clears his throat, breaking the spell that has me staring at Soldier like a mesmerized doll.

My hand still burns where he touched it.

"Well, now, back to my explanation of rudimentary Universe Division Theory. What I was hinting at is that depending on the magnitude of the event, there will be a split off or not. Imagine time and our universe as a long string of wool, with little fibers sticking out here and there. If they're small, they either break off or get smoothed in farther down the way. The timeline will correct itself and find its balance, aligning with the original one as if nothing had ever happened. That would be the case for any minor difference between universes—but for something major, something that affects many little strings…" He makes a twirling motion with his fingers. "It connects all those smaller strands, forming a new one."

My brain works frantically to make sense of it, and surprisingly, it does. I mean, I've wondered before, like everybody probably has: What if? So instead of my *what-ifs* being all teenage girl dreams, in a different universe, they could have happened. My parents could be healthy instead of sick. Andrew could still be alive. Kevan could not have taken that video of my panic attack, or maybe in a different universe, I wouldn't even have them.

A small beep comes from the GeneScanner-thingy. Canyon looks at it—and then looks at it again. He makes a small huffing sound and shakes his head. "Now that it explains it," he murmurs.

"Explains what?" How I ended up here?

His gaze flies to mine, a quick smile appearing on his face. "Nothing. It's nothing. Scientific mind, always trying to figure things out, you know?" He circles a finger at the side of his head, like gears in motion. "No match, though. You're unique, at least in our universe."

A weight falls off my shoulders. Meeting myself, seeing what could have been… I don't know. It would have been odd.

On the other hand, why am I not here? Did something happen to me? Did something happen to my parents already, before they had me? Or their parents?

As if that thought had connected two dots, all of a sudden I finally understand my situation. Completely.

I'm in a foreign universe.

And my parents are still in my original one.

If fate ever played jokes, this must be the cruelest one.

"I need to get home," I whisper, my shaking finger swiping a strand of hair behind my ear, as if clearing my sight could clear my mind. I need to get home as soon as possible. What if—

No. Nothing is going to happen to them. They're fine. All tests looked stable before I went. They're *fine*.

"I really need to get home." This time I say it louder, my hammering heart emphasizing each syllable.

Canyon pushes the GeneScreen to my Soldier—not *my* Soldier, *the* soldier. "Keep this until we're back at Central." Then his attention is back on me, and so is his mild smile. "I know, Noa. Of course you want to go back home. I completely understand." He pauses, folds his hands in front of him, and rests them on the desk. "Unfortunately, though, it's not in my power to send you back."

His smile contradicts the words he just dropped on me like a bomb.

"You… You can't send me back?" I repeat, barely whispering. That can't be. "Then how did you get me here?" A burning pricks behind my eyes, but I refuse to give in. I'm not crying like a little girl. I'm not.

The Minister shakes his head. "It wasn't us who brought you here. Probably some kind of… accidental connection. I can't offer you a way back." Canyon leans back into his chair, twiddling his thumbs. Soldier breaks his stance for the first time, throwing a glance at his boss, then at me, and back.

I'm staring straight ahead at the old man in front of me because if I don't, I'm afraid the tears might fall of their own accord, and then I'll be bawling about a second or two later.

Not going to happen.

Canyon pushes his chair back. "And I'm sorry, but I need to leave. Urgent matters of the State, my dear." He fishes for his cane. "I'll have my Sentinel take you to our guest facilities and get you set up with everything you need." I get a small wink that turns into a nod toward Soldier. "She's yours. You know what to do. Priority Alpha protocol applies." He pushes off the desk, standing up slowly.

Soldier straightens, the poster boy of chin up, chest out, shoulders back, and stomach in. "Of course, sir. I'll assign Holloway to you then."

"Thank you."

Soldier hesitates. "Sir? A modulator, if I may suggest?"

The old man's head whips around with heat in his eyes that would made me shrink away if it were directed at me.

"I didn't ask for your opinion, Sentinel. You have your orders. Now leave," he hisses, the blue in his eyes dark and menacing.

A muscle twitches in Soldier's jaw. Nothing more and nothing less. "Yes, sir." Like the dress-down was not even worth mentioning. He turns toward me, every move crisp. "Noa?"

My name rolls off his tongue like honey drips off a spoon. I never liked Noa quite that much, given all the idiotic one-liners I've heard too many times over the years, from it being a boy's name to being asked where I'd parked my Ark.

When *he* says my name, I want to stay put so he has to say it again. It sounds *that* good.

Only, well, I do get up, not wasting a single look back at Canyon. No matter if he is Soldier's boss or not, you don't talk to anybody like that. George always says the measure of a good person is how well he treats his subordinates.

George. *Dad.*

I have to swallow hard to get that thick lump out of my throat. Has somebody called my parents by now to tell them that I've gone missing? What story did Kevan come up with? That I vanished into thin air? Maybe he's the one getting pumped full of sedatives this time around; it would serve him right.

I only hope I'll make it home again. In time. Fate has been mean to us already, giving three out of four family members cancer and killing one, but she surely can't be *that* mean.

I need to be home before either of my parents dies.

As much as we disagree on anything that's worth arguing over, I couldn't live with that.

CHAPTER FIVE

Avery

As quickly as we made it up to the dome, Soldier leads me down the same—and only slightly less scary—glass tubes. This time, we descend farther and exit into a much bigger wide area without windows that reminds me of a subway station, only there are at least thirty or more reflective glass doors in the wall in front of us, all a wee bit rounded, like little wannabe-Hobbit doors.

To our left and right, people arrive from similar tubes, entering or exiting one of the Hobbit holes. A busy buzz fills the air, courtesy of everybody's fast pace and the occasional hushed chat between people. The ones who travel alone either focus on their wrists in front of their faces or stare ahead into nothingness, as if they weren't quite there.

I wonder if they're on drugs or something.

Soldier guides me to one of the round doors labeled '13' that opens automatically toward a cylindrical glass capsule of sorts, complete with two seats facing each other, fitted tightly into a dark tunnel with only occasional ceiling lights.

"Sit," he says, pointing to one of the seats while his other hand enters something into a touch-screen installed next to the door.

My butt hits the thin cushion a half-second before the glass cylinder shoots forward, all without a single jostle, drag, or pull I can pick up on. I mean, the ceiling lights in this tunnel blur together into one, so we must be fast, but… I don't feel it. At all.

Traffic underground.

Wide eyes stare back at me through the reflection in the glass walls, the white-blonde of my messy ponytail glowing under the harsh artificial light.

A different universe.

Trapped.

Soldier still stands behind me, hunched over because of his size. Within seconds, a brighter light appears at the far end of the tight tube, and *boom*, just like that, we've come to a complete stop in front of another glass door that opens on its own.

A bell sound chimes. "Bellevue Palace." Different universe, same subway announcements.

We exit the pod and enter a smaller version of the subway station we just came from.

Unbelievable. The same two miles that took our class twenty minutes this morning, we travel within twenty seconds.

I glance left and right as we walk up a couple of stairs and out into what I recognize to be the Berlin Tiergarten, Berlin's inner-city park we walked through this morning before coming over to the Reichstag. We visited everything: the Bellevue Palace, the Victory Column, all the touristy stuff clearly visible from here.

Only it doesn't hold any resemblance to this morning.

Bellevue Palace looked nice before, a three-winged large, white building, and while obviously built to impress, it was still practical. Typical German. This, though, *this* Bellevue Palace is beautiful. Old, but beautiful. It's higher, larger, and much more intricately decorated than what I remember.

They say the grass is always greener on the other side, but here it's true. The lawn in front of the palace grows in the juiciest green I've seen in my life, and how they landscaped those trees and bushes into these perfect sculptures, I have no idea.

Next to the building's main entrance, two flags ripple in the wind, one German, and one black-and-golden, the same as on

Soldier's uniform.

With a click, my mind aligns the flag with something in my science book: an atom. Terra's flag is the symbol of an atom with electrons circling around its core.

Soldier's strides never slow down, not even up the wide stairwell toward the palace. I'm so busy not falling behind while checking out this place, I almost run into the man opening the door for us.

"Whoops, sor—" The word gets stuck in the memory of two hands around my throat squeezing the living daylights out of me.

The guy from the cell, the one who didn't like me at all.

I squeak and take one big jump to Soldier's right side.

Better safe than sorry—although I needn't have worried. Like at the tube-elevators, the guy ignores me. Can't say I mind it.

I stumble after Soldier into the building. *Whoa. Nice.* Baroque furniture decorates every corner, and together with the high ceilings and chandeliers, it looks like I truly stepped into a palace, and not into the functional, practical seat of the German President.

Most doors we approach open on their own, but for the last two, Soldier presses his hand against some kind of reader, his hand—no, *the reader*, I think—glowing blueish, like it did before. We're basically alone here. Compared to the Reichstag, this building is empty.

Eventually, he stops in front of a door that's not glass for a change, but solid. "These will be your quarters. If you have any questions, I'll be here. Guard duty."

Soldier takes up a wide stance next to the door with his back to the wall and arms folded behind his back. On first glance, he seems relaxed, although I doubt he truly is.

The door in front of me hisses open when I get closer to it, retracting into the wall to the left. Judging from the experience of a whole two hours, that seems to be the way most doors work in here.

I take a tentative step into the room, then hesitate. "Guarding it *for* me, or *because* of me?" Either should worry me, but still I want to know.

Soldier's eyes meet mine, and—*boom*—guarded doors, Canyon and the different universe, Terra and Earth, none of that is important anymore. The little tug on the inside of my chest is. The little tingle down my spine. The warmth that lights up my face, as if his amber eyes had set me on fire.

I suck in my lower lip and bite down on it.

Something softens in his expression. "You're afraid," he says, completely matter–of-factly.

I let go of my lip. "Not at all." No way I'm admitting anything.

The corners of his mouth move up ever so slightly, adding a layer of warmth to his eyes I don't think he realizes he has. "Yes, you are. And… it's a wise precaution."

With that, he turns around, back to his soldier-stance, his short, slightly tousled dark hair illuminated by the ceiling lights behind him like a halo.

I swallow once.

"You never told me your name." And I did ask; it was my first question for him. He just never answered.

Soldier cocks one eyebrow and looks at me over his shoulder, still silent.

I roll my eyes ever so slightly, giving it all the spunk I have left after today, or ever. "What if I say *please?*"

I could swear something sparks behind those mesmerizing golden eyes of his, but it's gone as quickly as it appeared.

"Avery," he finally says. "Avery McTighe."

That's all I get before he focuses on the wall in front of him. I get the hint and enter my room, the doors closing right behind me.

"Avery," I whisper to myself.

Avery McTighe.

CHAPTER SIX

History Lesson

Several hours later, I've almost come to terms with where I am, although I still feel kind of hazy, like in a dream.

More like a nightmare, actually.

I've been gone from my world since early this morning. By now, my parents will most likely know that I'm missing, and I can only imagine what it'll do to them.

What it'll do to them if I never come back.

I bite the inside of my cheek. The day Andrew died, it almost killed my mom right with him. How one family can be so fragile and have three people with different types of cancer at the same time…

I huff once. Nothing is fair in life, and especially not this: My room is a full-blown luxury suite. Never in my life have I seen anything like it, but then, we never had the money to afford anything better than a Motel 6, so no wonder. My parents would deserve this, getting a lucky break once in a while. Not me, the only healthy one. How's that fair?

Despite my blue mood, eventually, curiosity kicks in and I start exploring. The large bed against the far end of the room next to a window completely freaks me out when I collapse onto it for the first time.

"*Analyzing*," it says in this weird synthetic, yet strangely human voice. *"Body type analyzed. Adjusting to maximize REM-sleep."*

Parts of the mattress tighten under me while others loosen up, making me all but sink into the comfy warm material. Heaven. Freaky, but heaven.

I almost give in right there and then. Sleeping, forgetting about what happened… it sounds fantastic, but it won't help me. For one, I'll probably have a nightmare and for another, I won't learn anything about my new… what? Home? No, *temporary* home. There must be a way back to my universe. There *must*.

I make it out of bed and to the no-less impressive bathroom. The general gist of things is as I know it: a toilet, a sink, etc., but everything is motion sensitive or scanning me or something… At least, I hear *"Analyzing"* quite a few times. I really hope the toilet won't ever say that. It would be a tad too weird for me.

I find clothing behind a door that I correctly assume is a closet and a fridge in the kitchen. The problem is that the thing won't open. Nothing, not even a little budge. How very frustrating, especially because my last meal was in the morning and in a different universe.

Okay, that does sound weird.

Whenever I wrap my hand around the fridge handle and pull, I get the same annoying and vexing answer. *"Analyzing. No data available. Please contact your closest B.I. Administrator."*

All right, then. I'll do that. Or not. Whatever.

Frustrated by my lack of success and growing hunger, I change into a set of clothes from the closet. Time to get rid of the smell of hours-old anxiety.

The moment I put on the shirt and pants, they shrink down, adjusting to a perfect fit.

Nice.

Zip-zip, and I'm sprouting a not-too-shabby outfit consisting of a pair of loose, comfy black pants and a white, moderately tight shirt. Before I forget it, I transfer my nose studs from my jeans pocket to the new outfit. *After* exchanging the butterfly for a star. Talking about universes, a star seems fitting.

By the time I'm done with everything, it's dark outside. Usually,

I like darkness. It opens up my mind and lets it drift. It's only that today I don't want it to. All I can think of is my home that's here, several thousand miles away, and yet isn't.

My stomach growls again. Plus, I'm feeling very much alone and a little bit lost.

Maybe it's the lack of sugar.

Yeah, that's what it must be.

My eyes drift over to the door. I wonder if Avery is still outside. Avery McTighe.

On a whim, I walk toward the doors and stop dead in my tracks when the previously brown wood flickers and becomes translucent at the exact level of my eyes.

I whistle through my teeth. "Fancy," I murmur to myself while leaning forward, casting a glance through the newly formed plate-sized spyhole. To the right of the door, Avery's shoulder is visible, but otherwise, the hallway with its white, bright walls and light is empty. Everything's a bit hazy, maybe because the outside of the door is still not transparent, so whoever was waiting in front of it wouldn't see me checking up on them.

I jerk back. Ugh, I *hope*, or otherwise Avery is going to think I'm a stalking freak. I press my right hand to the doorframe like I've seen Avery do, and a split second later, the doors slide apart. All right then, I figured out at least something in this wonderland.

Avery stands exactly where I last saw him, a lone figure morphed into the shadows.

"Avery?" It feels odd calling him by his first name, but what else am I supposed to do? I won't call him "Sentinel," like Canyon did, whatever exactly that means. It feels derogatory somehow.

"Noa." He doesn't even look my way, keeping his hands behind his back and posture straight.

I scan him over from head to toe. "Have you moved at all since I went inside?"

"No."

That seems uncomfortable. "Why not?"

"Because it's my job."

I hesitate for a moment. Should I ask or should I not…? "Do you… Do you want to come inside?" It's odd to have somebody guard my door, standing there without anywhere to sit, while I have all the comforts I can imagine. Minus a fridge I can't handle.

"That's not my job," he replies, and although he says it completely level, I could swear his eyebrow went up by maybe a millimeter.

"Oh." I rub my nose stud. "Of course." *Way to go, Noa.*

Awkward silence stretches between us.

I shouldn't have come out, but then, in that moment… I sigh. Only one way to save this. "Well, I… I do have some difficulties with the fridge-thingy in there." There we go. True story.

"The fridge?" His eyebrow creeps even higher, up to the hairline.

"Yeah?" I give him a shy smile. Here's to hoping he doesn't think I'm an imbecile who can't even open a fridge. "Help?"

Avery hesitates for a second before he unfreezes from his position. "Of course." He follows me inside, the doors closing behind him with a *swoosh*.

The moment they do, a shiver runs down my spine. It's dead silent in here, so silent I think I can hear Avery breathe behind me. My steps falter for a moment.

Stupid, so stupid. Avery might be big, but he's not dangerous. He's my guard; there's no need to be nervous. Part of my brain thinks it's funny I'm trying to convince myself *that's* the reason why I'm nervous, and not because my brain did the math and realized I'm alone in my room with a guy—a guy like Avery.

Ignoring the heat building up in my cheeks, I lead the way to the fridge and grab the handle.

"*Analyzing. No data available. Please contact your closest B.I. Administrator.*"

I throw a glance at Avery, giving the handle a good pull for emphasis. "See?"

He cocks his head before he nods to himself once. "Ah, of course." He takes one step and his bigger body is right next to me, heat radiating off of him. He grabs the handle right above my hand, accidentally brushing my skin ever so slightly.

A tiny gasp escapes me, but thanks to the talking fridge, Avery doesn't pick up on it.

"Analyzing. A meal of 75% carbohydrates and fiber combined with 20% polyunsaturated fatty acids is recommended. You may choose your vegetables. 5% of your meal also remains for free choosing."

My hand drops off the handle at the same time my jaw drops open. "What…?"

The fridge beeps and opens, finally revealing a view of the inside.

"How'd you do that?" I stare at Avery, who shrugs, sifting through the fridge until he finds what he's looking for and loads it into my arms.

"I'm sorry. Should've told you this wouldn't work since you're not Augged," he says, grabbing some boxes before giving the door a gentle nudge with his shoulder to close it.

"Excuse me, I'm not what?"

He carries the food over to the table in front of the window with a more-than-stunning view, despite the dark. The Spree River is lined by trees, all of them illuminated, emphasizing their turning leaves even in the darkness.

"Augged." He repeats the word that makes absolutely no sense to me.

"Augged, okay." I slide into a chair and give the other one a little shove as a hint to Avery, who's already back to the same stance he was in front of my door. That man doesn't relax. At all.

He opens his mouth and closes it again, then sits down. "Augged means 'enhanced.'" He takes a box out of my hands that I'm apparently too stupid to open. He fiddles with it, and a second later the lid pops up.

"All of us are. We're born, gene screened, aptitude tested, and then augmented accordingly. There are standard Augs everybody has, and advanced ones, depending on profession."

The finger I poked into the mass of brownish, rice-like stuff freezes. "Wait, like plastic surgery?" Is that why he looks like a million bucks, and most people I've come across so far seemed young? Besides Canyon, obviously.

Confusion flickers across his face. "Surgically? No, why would we? Genetically, of course. Or bio-medically, depending on." He gives my prodding hand a small slap and hands me a napkin.

"See my palm?" He holds it up, showing a normal palm with maybe, *maybe*, a little bit of a rougher texture. "I have sensors integrated. Gives me an advantage for my Sentinel duties. It's also a biofeedback sender and receiver. That's what the nutrition dispenser was looking for, the information about what your body needed at this moment." Avery pulls a fork from the box in front of me that I could swear wasn't there a second before.

"That's also part of how I knew you weren't from here." He pushes the fork into my hands when I make absolutely no move to grab it because I'm kind of busy hanging on his every word. "You don't show." He taps his forehead.

"I don't show?" Show what?

A small smile appears on his face. "Identification. Every citizen of the Great Union has their ID information in a chip implanted in the forehead. It's invisible, pain free, and can be updated remotely without physical access. As a Sentinel, my eyes are Augged so I can see everybody's ID. For security reasons. It's like a holographic image hovering in front of their head." He draws a circle with his finger where he'd expect the image to be.

Wow. Like in a trance, I take a bite of my food, chewing without tasting, torn between awe and a certain queasiness. "So nobody is normal here?" *Oops.* Not what I meant. Luckily for me, Avery doesn't seem to mind.

"Depending on the point of view. Augs have been done for close to fifty years. This *is* our normal. There is a small percentage who refuse to be Augged, but they're not part of our society, which is built on the modifications. I couldn't do my job as well as I do if I didn't have them." He shrugs and opens a second box for me, this one with a fruit salad.

I want to ask all about it, what the Augs do, what kind of Augs he has, if he could add on new ones or exchange them like I do with my piercings, but I don't. I get the feeling it's something personal. So instead, I opt for another question.

"So why does everybody speak English?" Avery does. Canyon did. Even the furniture talks back to me in English.

"It's the common language of the Great Union."

I lift one eyebrow. "The Great Union."

"A united people under a single leader. Instead of keeping the planet divided into hundreds of countries with separate governments, we unified the people of Terra into the Great Union. English was chosen as Terra's first language, although local dialects and mother tongues are still spoken around the world. Only two of my colleagues from Sentinel training spoke no English when we started. They learned quickly, though."

Okay, makes sense then. Sentinel training—he must've started young. Back home, if he wanted to be a police officer, he'd still be at the academy. "Have you always wanted to become a Sentinel?" I take a piece of fruit. *Mmm! Strawberry.*

Avery doesn't miss a beat. "Of course."

"Wow, *of course?*" I say. "Are you one of those who already knew in middle school what they wanted to be?" I've got two of that kind in my year, one working on admission to med school, the other taking college classes for acting. Part of me envies that they know who they are and what they want to do.

Avery cocks his head. "What do you mean? Of course I knew in… middle school."

Judging by the short hesitation, I take it they don't have middle school as I know it. I'll add it to the list and decide to not push that topic, either, citing cultural differences.

"Okay, so you're a Sentinel? Is that, like, private security?" I feel so much more comfortable around him now that he's sitting down and we're having something close to a normal conversation. He really isn't that much older than me.

"Sentinels are the security branch of the GU." Avery nods, his hands playing with a napkin on the table. "We used to have soldiers and armies during World War II, and of course also police forces. All of that merged together into the Sentinel Forces after Hitler was killed and the Great Union was formed, so—"

I don't think I heard that right. "When Hitler was *killed?*" I'm not an expert in history, but I know for a fact that didn't happen at home in my universe.

Avery taps his index finger onto the table. "June 23rd, 1940, right here. Well, next door in the Reunification Building, actually, which is why we made it the Ministry of Technological Advances once we became the GU."

The fork with the impaled strawberry hovers between my mouth and the box. 1940… They had five fewer *years* of a world war that killed millions of people and destroyed what, sixty percent of Europe?

Avery notices the fork. "What?"

I blink twice. "Nothing, just… We didn't have that. WWII lasted into 1945, killed millions, and Germany ended up occupied and divided into East and West, not as a center for a unified Ministry."

My appetite is gone. I wonder what made the difference. Why did they get quote-unquote lucky and kill Hitler, while in my world they suffered through so much more agony? Why didn't he get killed in my world as well? Maybe that's why there's no me in this universe. As far as I know, my grandparents were immigrants after the war. Maybe in this timeline, that didn't happen and they never met.

Creepy.

One person killed—and such a major impact and difference. *Millions* of people.

A shudder runs down my back, and I feel cold.

"You okay?" Avery reaches out for my arm but stops a hair's breadth before touching me. Skin-sizzling static passes between us. I can tell the exact moment when he notices it, too, because he quickly withdraws his hand and clears his throat. "I know it's a lot to take in. I recommend you lie down and recover. Tomorrow morning, I will pick you up at 0800 hours. The alarm will wake you an hour prior. I will let admin know to remote unlock your nutrition dispenser, so it shouldn't be a problem for your breakfast."

He pushes his chair back, getting up. "Good night, Noa Keegan," he says on his way to the doors.

"Good night, Avery McTighe," I whisper back, too softly for him to hear.

CHAPTER SEVEN

Deal

The next morning, I might look fresh, but I don't feel it. I wouldn't describe the night as a good one, either, thanks to too many nightmares to keep track of. At least everything worked as promised, the wake-up call *and* fridge. I also figured out the shower which of course *adjusted* to an ideal temperature before it even doused me with water.

At exactly 8 A.M., a short *beep* comes from the door and announces Avery—actually, a voice announces him, the same one that seems to live in all of my gadgets here.

"*McTighe, Avery, First Class Sentinel,*" she says.

First Class, look at that.

Maybe that's why he looks fresher than I do, although I'm pretty sure he didn't leave his post all night. I'm not above sneaking to the door and snooping through the rather convenient peephole between nightmares.

"Good morning, Noa." Avery's deep voice resonates all the way down to my chest, especially when his eyes sweep over me, stopping for a short moment at my nose stud before they move on.

This morning it's a turquoise stone that matches my eyes. Yay me for always carrying at least five or more replacement piercings. One never knows which mood might strike.

"Good morning, Avery." I give him a shy and probably wide-eyed smile, swiping the bangs out of my face.

"The Minister is waiting for you in the park." He straightens up and steps aside to make room for me. "Shall we?"

I don't know what I expected, but it wasn't another meeting with the Minister. A spark of hope lights up inside my heart. Maybe… Maybe the Minister has an idea for how to bring me home. Why else would he want to meet with me?

Avery leads us down the same hallways and past the same guard as before into a crisp autumn morning. None of the chilly breeze sneaks through the black jacket I grabbed from the closet in my room though. With the first gust of wind the jacket tightens, keeping the cold air out and me snuggly warm.

I whistle through my teeth. Nice.

Avery is quiet, and so am I. The closer we get to the bridge crossing over a small blue lake and the lone figure supported by a cane, the more nervous I become. The memory of Canyon hissing at Avery replays in my mind. Maybe that's why I feel like I have to keep my guard up. Call it the leftovers of a careful upbringing.

Once we're close enough, Avery breaks the silence. "Sir." He steps away to the side, his eyes searching our surroundings, a soldier doing his job.

Canyon turns around, one slow inch at a time. "Hello, Noa. I trust you had a good night?" His smile is so grandfatherly, I'm honestly waiting for him to produce some candy for me out of his pockets.

"Yes, thank you. Just… missing home." The moment I say it, I realize I didn't phrase it correctly. I don't miss home. I miss my *parents*. I'm okay with this place, with Terra. It feels right somehow. Like the better version of what we have. Only it's worth nothing without my parents.

Canyon pats my forearm. "I know, I know. Tell me about your life back there, child. Where do you live? Who are your parents?"

I choose to ignore the fact that he called me a child. "I'm from Chicago, and so are my parents. My mom works as a secretary for my school, and my dad is an architect. Well, was."

"Was?"

"He hasn't been working lately. Both my parents are ill." I focus on a tree at the far end of the lake.

Canyon's brows furrow. "What do you mean by that?"

I close my eyes and take a deep breath. No tears. "Cancer. Both of them. The doctors can't find a cure for it. They don't have much longer." Which is why I need to go home. They're my responsibility.

Canyon huffs once and rolls his eyes. "Cancer." He covers the exasperated eyeroll with a quick smile. "Such an ugly disease, I mean. It's become rare in the augmented population, and if it happens, it's curable ninety-nine percent of the time."

I can only wish. "Not for us." Not by a long shot.

"What are your parents' names?"

Now it's my turn to huff. "Why? Do you want to check if they exist here and get a bone marrow transplant for them or something?" I shouldn't be aggressive toward him, but he has me on edge. The whole topic has me on edge. I sigh and close my eyes. "George and Elaine. George and Elaine Keegan."

Canyon nods. "I see. Well, Noa, I'm sorry to hear about your parents, and I completely understand why you want to go home as quickly as possible."

Pause.

His eyes bore into mine. Only now do I notice how piercing their blue is. Although he must have been striking when he was young, the intensity of his stare makes me uncomfortable. It's too observant.

"I have a proposal for you. Mutually beneficial. See, I'm the Minister for T.A., for Technological Advancement. My job is to oversee all scientific research and progress the GU is conducting, and right now... Right now we've hit a rough patch."

"A rough patch?"

"Correct. We're a society that believes in bettering itself through science. Since we adopted this policy, we've had no more war, and almost no violence. We're a peaceful people, but we've become a bit too... *complacent* over the years. Lazy. Too pleased with where we are instead of striving to better ourselves. People are set in their ways. They will always choose the path of the least resistance." An irritated frown crosses his face.

Canyon pauses and leans slightly more forward, taking the weight off his cane. "I have a plan for this world, Noa. A good one. One that opens their eyes and lets them see not everything is about them. One that shows them the way and leads them to a better and safer future. One that might include crossing into other universes." He averts his gaze out to the lake.

My eyebrows fly up. "Really?" *Crossing back home.*

"Really. But connecting two universes and sending somebody through isn't child's play, as you can imagine. In research, just as in real life, everything comes down to… funding, to resources, and we never have enough of either."

Oh.

"I see," I whisper, pushing my hands as deep into my pockets as I can so nobody will see their shaking. "I see."

Intellectually, I understand it. Until yesterday, I didn't even know parallel universes existed, and I can't even begin to imagine how difficult it must be to send somebody across willingly. That doesn't mean I don't feel rejected and left alone.

I swallow a lump in my throat. What did I think was going to happen? That bringing me home would be a priority for him? Of course not. He's a minister; I'm still only a single sixteen-year-old girl whose fate is not important in comparison to what he must be seeing daily in his job, guiding millions of people through life.

Some things are the same, no matter which universe.

"But"—he shuffles his feet until he's facing me—"there might be an option."

Hope, you are a finicky little creature. "What option?"

Canyon's gaze bores into me. "Work with me. I want you to tip the scale. I want the people to see you, a child from a different universe, and I want them to understand what's at stake." A muscle in his jaw thrums, but then the smile is back. "If you stayed out of the public eye until I give my State of Technology speech and I unveiled you right there and then, it could give us the necessary boost for… progress. The people need tangible evidence and examples. They need a show. If we want to get this done, this is the way to go."

A show.

With me as the puppet dancing in the middle.

George always says politics is the dirtiest business one could go into. He never votes, and neither does Elaine. Both of them have an old, festered distrust of anything politics- or government-related, remnants of their pseudo-hippie years, I suppose.

In so many ways, I'm different than them, so much that I sometimes wonder if all their good genes went to perfect Andrew while I got the lousy leftovers. Aside from cancer, obviously. Once it comes to politics, though, we're on the same page. We don't get involved.

Not that anybody had asked me to so far.

As if Canyon had read my thoughts, he straightens up, extending the hand he doesn't need for his cane to steady himself on the balustrade. "Until then, I need to keep you a secret. Limited exposure, stay indoors, stay off the TC, mostly at least. Once we unveil you, both of us will benefit. I can get the push I need to become President again, and once that happens, I'll do all I can to get you back. Quid pro quo, Noa."

I stare at the hand extended to me as if I'd expect it to slap me.

Quid pro quo. Another fancy way of saying tit for tat. And it feels dirty.

In a flash, my guard is up—much more so than before. Tit for tat. It's like school all over, me going against my principles to get what I want or need, only the stakes are higher than in school. It's not about being invited to a party if I play along. It's about returning home. *Home.* "*Quid pro quo?*" The hand in front of me turns into a poisonous snake.

"Yes. *Quid pro quo.* A mutual alliance. I will have you sign a contract specifying the deal between you and me. Strictly to make things easier, of course. A couple of restrictions for your own safety, and an outline of what is expected of you in return for our support."

Something inside my stomach turns sour.

Canyon smiles at me, and while I have absolutely no objective reason to feel threatened or afraid, his smile makes me want to run in the opposite direction.

This is my only chance of getting home, though.

The hand is still extended, and it doesn't waver.

"I'll make sure you'll be in the universe you belong, Noa." Canyon's tone is so sweet, all the tiny hairs on my body raise in response.

But I don't have a choice, inborn distrust of authorities or no.

With the exact same nausea I always had agreeing to a deal with Kev and friends, I take the hand held out for me. "Tit for tat."

His fingers close around mine with a surprising strength.

It should feel good. After all, I'm taking action to get myself home, but… it rather feels like selling my soul to the devil.

"Wonderful." Canyon beams. "I will have the Sentinel get you up to speed and ready. Once we—"

Somebody clears their throat behind us. "Excuse me, sir."

A man dressed in the same uniform as Avery bows his head toward the Minister. He's tall and wide and holds himself with the same straight posture that seems to be part of a Sentinel's job description. Like Avery's, his eyes are amber, albeit not as bright. Plus, this guy's downward-turned mouth gives him a look of a permanent frown.

"I'm sorry to interrupt, sir, but matters have come up."

Canyon sighs. "Does it have to be now?"

The Sentinel nods. "Yes, sir. Ghost activity."

There we go again. What is it with these Ghosts—?

"I see. Of course." Canyon adjusts his cane. "Excuse me, sweetheart. My presence is required elsewhere. Sentinel." With a short nod at Avery, Canyon shuffles down the bridge.

The other Sentinel looks over at Avery, the trace of a smug grin on his face. "McTighe. Your duties have been upgraded to babysitting, I take it?" He jerks his chin at me.

"My duties are none of your concern, Holloway," Avery answers, completely calm. He takes a step forward so that I'm partially hidden behind him. "In fact, last time I checked, it was the other way around. And with the Sentinel Forces on high alert as it is, I'd expect you to be even more vigilant, and right now, your principal is getting away. You might want to rectify that."

Holloway looks over his shoulder at a surprisingly quickly retreating Minister and curses under his breath. He throws one more cold glance at Avery before he rushes off to catch up with Canyon in a few long strides. Only when they've turned around a corner in the park does Avery relax.

Well, *relax* is perhaps too strong a term. Only then does he step aside from his protective stance in front of me.

And somehow… somehow I wish he didn't.

A shudder runs down my spine as I stare after Canyon and that weird Sentinel. I can't shake the feeling of… I don't know, unease. That I'm missing something. I huff once. Something? Everything. My naiveté in this universe rivals that of a newborn puppy.

Some things are universal, though. "He doesn't like you." I stuff my hands into my pockets and look up at Avery.

For the longest moment, Avery stays quiet. "No. We trained together. We're both competitive. I came in first, him second. Holloway doesn't do well with losing, especially to me."

"Well, it's obvious." Anybody would've picked up on it. I twirl my nose stud. This universe is giving me a headache—a headache that might stay for quite a while: If Murphy's Law of whatever can go wrong will go wrong is any indication, this could become my home.

A home I know nothing about.

I rub the bridge of my nose and sigh. Baby steps. "Avery, what are those ghosts I've heard people mention? We're still parallel universes, and Earth is pretty ghost-free."

A corner of Avery's mouth moves upward the slightest bit. "Not real Ghosts. It's a group of non-conformists giving us trouble. They're against Augs and many of our innovations and would prefer a life free of technology. Which would be fine if they didn't sabotage many of our facilities, causing casualties and lots of damage."

That sounds familiar. I'm almost glad Terra isn't as perfect as I thought it was, but on the other hand, it's also sad. I wonder if there is a universe somewhere without any conflict at all and nothing but peaceful cooperation.

Yeah, right. Only if all humans were gone, maybe then.

"Why are they called 'Ghosts?' I assume they're not invisible?" Maybe sneaky or super-fast, like pseudo-ninjas.

The twitch of his lips turns into something that's almost— *almost*—a smile, and it makes me proud I did that, no matter how bad the joke.

"Not quite. The Ghosts formed maybe a decade after the GU was founded. They named themselves *Freigeist*, which is German and roughly translates to free thinkers, but with the caveat that *geist* also translates to *ghost*. So after a couple of years, the press started calling them by the more catchy title *Ghosts* instead of *Freigeist*, and it has stuck ever since."

No sneaky ninjas. Bit of a bummer.

I turn around and lean onto the railing, the weight of the world on my shoulders, and my parents' warning in my ears: *Don't trust the government.*

Somewhere in the distance, a couple ducks quack between diving down to catch some insects or whatever. Most of the trees have lost their green, bringing on beautiful fall colors of red, orange, and brown. Despite being in the middle of the city, it's quiet here, only the breeze rustling through the trees providing the background noise for the talkative ducks. It smells like wet earth and forest.

A shadow falls over me a second before Avery leans onto the same railing on my left. He folds his hands in front of him and looks out into the beautiful scenery like I do.

After a while, he shifts his weight but keeps staring at the lake. "I'm sorry about your parents."

Of course he would have heard; he was standing right there. Not that it matters. Back home, nobody knows, my parents forbade me to talk about it. They didn't want the pity or the attention. Here, it doesn't matter.

"Thank you." I take a deep breath of fresh air to clear my mind. I've never spoken to anybody about my parents. Not even Kevan knew, back when we were still friends. "They've been sick for a while. First my dad, then my mom. I'm the only one healthy left in my family, and… and they're not doing well. That's why I need to get back, you know? Nothing is more important. They can't—" My voice breaks at the end of the sentence. They can't lose another child. George and Elaine never got over Andrew's death, and they never will. He was their perfect child, not the disappointment I grew up to be, with panic attacks and never being quite as good as Andrew, no matter how hard I tried. Andrew's death put the first nail in their coffins. No available chemotherapy sealed them.

I sniff once and wipe my nose with the back of my hand. Thinking of my parents, it gets to me. "What the Minister said… Is it true? That you don't have cancer on Terra?" What a sick twist of fate to drop me here of all universes to choose from and show me a life that could have been but never will be for my parents, like a carrot dangling barely out of reach.

Avery shifts his weight onto his other foot, his hands still folded in front of him and resting on the railing. "Yes. Our genome is modified to produce immune cells that detect any abnormalities on a molecular level. It's part of our pre-birth modifications. Even the Ghosts do it." He huffs. "They take the advantages and benefits of the very technology they condemn so much."

"Can it be done after birth too?" *Please say yes. Please say yes.*

Avery looks over his shoulder at me. "I know what you're thinking," he says quietly, "and while yes, it can, it's not like a single-dose medicine one can take. It requires re-writing of somebody's genome. It's complicated. I'm sorry."

Me too.

I don't want the sting in my eyes, the tears building up. I don't want to be weak. Distraction. Now, please. I look over to Avery. "So… are you close to your parents?" I don't know if we're at that level of sharing already, but hey, he's not that much older than me.

Speaking of. "How old are you anyway?"

"Nineteen," Avery says, "and no, I'm not. None of us are."

Wow, only nineteen. Guys on Terra seem to develop differently than their Earth-counterparts. Then I pick up on the second part of his sentence.

"None of you? Your siblings?" Isn't there usually at least one child that's the favorite and closest, like Andrew was to my parents? That they taught me to call them by their first names while Andrew used the classic "Mom" and "Dad" is proof of that in and of itself.

"No. All of us. All First Class Sentinels," he says. "We're all Second Children, you know?"

"Oh, me too." I lift up my finger as if I were in school. "I have— *had*—an older brother, Andrew." Despite the rush of sadness I still have when saying his name out loud, I'm almost happy I found something in common with Avery.

He looks at me, puzzled. "Wait, you're a Second?"

"Yeah, I guess so." I shrug. I've been called worse.

"And still you're in school?" Now he sounds confused, but so am I.

"Of course, why wouldn't I be?"

"In school to become what?"

Oh, that's the question, isn't it? How should I know? Eileen wants me to join her or take over her job in the school's secretary office and stay out of trouble, and it's been an ongoing source of… *dispute* between us. I don't have a master plan for my life, but at least for once, after school, I'd like to feel as if the world were open to me and not a song orchestrated by my parents.

I feel bad for that thought.

They only mean well.

"I don't know yet," I say a bit more grumpy than intended. "I'll let you know once I figure it out." It's a sore topic.

"So you have a choice?"

I throw him an irritated glance. "Of course. If my grades are good enough, and they are, thank you very much." It's the one thing I can be proud of: good enough grades. Not stellar, but good enough to have a choice.

Avery blows out a puff of air through pursed lips, one hand finding the back of his neck and massaging it, seemingly lost in thought, before he gives a dry laugh. "You know, for us here in Terra, we have a one-child policy. A strict one. If a couple doesn't comply, the children born after the First are recruited for Sentinel duties." He looks at me. "All second-born children become Sentinels. We are modified in utero to fulfill our jobs as smoothly as possible and taken from our families at the age of six for Sentinel training."

Something dark in his eyes lights up that I haven't seen before. It's gone as quickly as it appeared, and a moment later, I'm not sure it was even there to begin with.

Avery balls and releases a fist without noticing it. "So no, I'm not close to my parents." His jaw sets firmly. "I never had a choice."

He tears his gaze away from me and stares out at the lake again, where the ducks are still working on filling up their stomachs with insect breakfast.

For several more minutes, we stand next to each other quietly, lost in our thoughts.

The universe might be a different one, but the crosses we bear are anything but.

CHAPTER EIGHT

Intruder

The rest of the day passes in no time.

Avery receives new orders from Minister Canyon for me and follows them to the T. I get the feeling he doesn't do anything less than a hundred percent correct.

First I get a checkup in the Reichstag's medical facility that is so much different from any physical exam I've ever had to endure it's almost ridiculous.

The doctor hands me a pill and a glass of water without any explanation, as if it were clear what it was for.

I don't swallow it until Avery gives me a small nod. Somehow his approval means it's okay. Maybe because he knows about my parents, which also equals knowing about me, or maybe because for a moment, he granted me a look behind the façade he keeps up for his job.

I could bet Avery misses his parents just as much as I miss mine.

After I've taken the pill, the doctor has me stand on a round platform with an overhead disk that hums and glows, then spits out the results of my body scan down to the cellular level.

It feels very *Star Trek*-y, to be honest.

The doctor declares me healthy and, after a moment of confusion resulting from my question, even verifies that there is absolutely no cancer in my body. It does make me happy, although it still doesn't change the guilt.

Once my health check is over, Avery accompanies me back to Bellevue Palace.

We walk for a bit through the green and clean streets of Berlin, so unlike those I remember. Once in a while, somebody walks past us, oftentimes their eyes glued to the back of their wrists, like the people I saw down in the subway.

"What's up with everybody checking out their hands?" I nod at one of the pedestrians passing us, a man in his forties with fancy pink highlights that match the pinstripes in his suit.

"That?" Avery lifts an eyebrow and taps the back of his hand. "The T.C."

"T.C.?" I ask. Canyon mentioned me staying off of it, whatever it is.

"The TerraCon, a worldwide connection of data, accessible by anybody with Augs in retinas and skin."

Huh. "The internet." But fancier.

Avery cocks his head. "Internet?"

I nod, checking out a woman on the other side of the street, leaning against a lamp post, her wrist in front of her face. First I want to chuckle, but well… I don't think I look much better doing the same thing with my iPhone.

I tear my gaze off her. "Yeah, for us, it's the internet. Free information, accessible for most people, and uploadable by anyone."

Avery's brows furrow. "Why would you do that?"

"What?"

"Grant access to just anyone? Or even allow anyone to add content."

"Because the internet is free. Everybody has a right to voice their opinion." At least in the Western world.

"But what if they're wrong?"

I laugh. "Happens all the time. You just gotta use common sense and know your sources." I think we all had our experiences with the wrong copy-and-paste article in search for an easy fix for our homework, and—

I stop in my tracks, one hand on his sleeve. "Wait. The T.C.

here… It's not free?"

"Of course it's free." Avery pulls his shoulders straighter so my hand drops off his arm. "You can apply for a license to start a site. The government only monitors the information displayed for accuracy, and that's it." He shrugs, like it's no big deal.

My mouth drops open, though. "They monitor it?"

A crisp nod. "To avoid spreading misinformation."

My eyes widen. Misinformation is one of George's favorite words, only he blames the government for it.

The shiny new world named Terra just turned a tad more matte for me.

It's late by the time I'm finally back in my room, and I'm exhausted from all the new input. Running a marathon would have drained me less.

Avery drops me off at my door. "You can sleep in tomorrow. Good night, Noa." He melts back into the shadows like he did last night.

I hesitate for a moment. "Are you going to stay here again?"

"Of course."

"Don't you ever sleep?" I'm pretty positive he didn't move away from his post last night, and neither did he leave me today.

His features soften the slightest bit. "I can handle prolonged periods of sleep deprivation. Right now, you're my responsibility. Sleep is not important."

I yawn. "That's what you say." I give him a tired smile and enter my room, the doors closing behind me. It's dark outside already, but the lights turn on automatically once I set a foot into the suite.

Oh boy, what a day. My head's spinning from the onslaught of new impressions. The whole Canyon-thing is still a stone weighing heavily inside my stomach, but what other option do I have? None.

I've been here for over twenty-four hours now. Twenty-four

hours that were nothing to me but will have made the world of a difference to George and Elaine. No pun intended.

I use the backrest of the comfy leather chair for balance as I slip out of my shoes, my bare feet touching a floor that seems to mold itself around the soles of my feet. Being here is like being in the future because Terra is so much more advanced compared to us. Wait, I won't disrupt a timeline or anything if I bring knowledge of all this back home, will I?

I answer my own question the moment I ask it. It's a different universe, not my own universe's future. Not that I'm an expert, but nothing I do should matter in the grand scheme of things.

Now that's a confidence booster.

Kicking my other shoe off, I almost roll my ankle over it as I make my way over to the bed. Nothing sounds better than sleep lulling me into a cocoon of blissful ignorance. I pull my shirt over my head and discard it carelessly onto the ground, about to let myself fall face-forward onto the bed, when out of nowhere, an arm wraps around my throat.

The cry about to leave my mouth turns into a choked croak.

What—

Out of reflex, my hands fly up to my throat, not that it does anything against the strong, masculine forearm cutting off my air supply.

"Shh," someone shushes into my ear. "No sound." The arm around my throat tightens, emphasizing his point. Air wheezes in and out through my constricted windpipe, rasping.

"Do you understand?" The arm squeezes again, harder this time.

I try to nod but only manage a slight tilt of my chin. That voice, is that—

He pulls me closer until I'm off-balance and supported only by his body. The arm. I can't breathe, I can't—

Little black spots dance in front of my eyes, the pressure on my carotids spreading a comfortable warmth through my body that's in stark contrast to the cold that numbs my brain.

He drags me backward with him, controlling my head and

therefore my body like a puppet. "I'm taking you out of here. It is in your best interest to—"

The little breath I can still take hitches in my throat.

No.

As if his words had triggered a switch, something breaks loose inside of me, an ice-cold fear that for once overrules the compliance drilled into me since I was little.

Out of sheer desperation, I turn my head into the hollow of his elbow and sink my teeth through thin fabric into muscular flesh.

The response is immediate.

"Shit!" The man curses under his breath, automatic reflexes creating room between his body and my mouth. It's not much, but enough for me to drop my weight and slide out of his hold.

I crumble to the floor in a heap of bones, my head swimming with dizziness, blood swooshing in my ears like a storming river. Even though my brain's foggy, my body knows its flight mechanisms. I push off on all fours, scrambling to get away before—

A hand grabs my leg and yanks me back, the twist on my leg flipping me over, sunny-side up.

Olive skin, dark, teardrop eyes, black uniform—my first guard, the guy I keep running into.

Oh, shit.

The guard grabs my arm and throws me over his shoulders in a modified fireman's carry as if I weighed nothing at all.

"I'm taking you with me," he growls under his breath. "Keep quiet—"

No, no, no.

Screw all the choking he could do to me.

"Avery!" I don't yell it, I *scream* it from the top of my lungs. The doors can't be soundproof. Avery must be able to hear me. "Help, I—Avery!"

The guard curses under his breath and sprints toward the window, one of his hands easily holding my arms and legs together, like a shouldered deer on its way to slaughter.

No, no, no.

"Let go of me, let *go*!" Anytime now, I'll space out, useless as always in the face of panic. My heart hammers like crazy, each beat trying to push blood up to my brain and failing miserably.

I'm useless.

A hiss, a few quick sprinting steps—and then I'm falling backward, still glued to the guard's shoulders. A split second before I would've hit the floor, two hands pry me off my attacker and cradle me to a hard, muscular chest with the slightest scent of fresh grass.

I scream out as the guard's nails dig into my skin, leaving scratch marks when he crashes to the ground without me.

Avery loses no time.

He spins into a kick, driving his foot into the other guard's face. My abductor drops his arms and covers his nose as blood splatters from it.

Like I was an oversized puppy, Avery gently lowers me to the floor behind him, never taking his attention off the guard.

"Leiva," he growls, taking position between me and the other man. "You might want to explain this to me." His hands are raised, the threat in his voice thinly veiled.

The guard's eyes flash with anger. "What do you think, McTighe? That Canyon could keep it quiet?" He laughs out dry. "We're well connected. And we won't let him get away with this."

The second the last word has left his mouth, he pushes off the ground and throws himself at Avery.

A surprised yelp echoes through the room, and only after a second do I realize it came from me. I frantically scoot back on my butt, scrambling to get away from the tangled mass of bodies and extremities.

I've seen school brawls.

I've seen Kevan beat up two punks who molested a girl a year under us.

But I've never seen anything like this.

This is a real fight. A fight to destroy.

And Avery is winning it.

The guard is fast and vicious, but Avery is better. For every punch he gets, he hands out two better-placed ones. His speed is so unbelievable, it's hard to keep track of his movements. Within moments, both men are grunting, trying to get the upper hand—one to subdue, the other to flee. Leiva glances over to the window time after time, distracting him, and I'm not the only one noticing it.

The next time he checks the window, Avery rams his elbow into Leiva's face with so much force, I hear bone crunch.

Like a light switched off, the guard drops to the floor, motionless.

Silence.

Except for Avery's harsh breathing.

Nothing else.

Avery stays in his fighting stance: hands raised, knees bent, body coiled and ready to fight. His shirt is torn in several places, revealing glimpses of a flat stomach with ridges and a solid six-pack. Every breath he takes is a mesmerizing play of muscles. A thin layer of sweat covers his skin in goosebumps.

After a moment, he lets his guard down and gives me the onceover. "Are you okay?"

I need a second to process the question. "Y-Yes." I think. My throat still burns from the second choking within two days, but in the grand scheme of things… I'm okay.

Avery nods once and squats. He pulls something that looks like handcuffs without a chain from his back pocket and tightens it around the other man's wrists before he turns him over to search his pockets.

Somehow, I get myself up and standing, despite my arms and legs working against me with all their shaking and wobbling. Thanks, adrenaline, for showing up late to the party. What a help.

I reach for the bed to support myself, inching closer to Avery and the guard. Leiva, I guess.

Why did he come for me? What did I ever do—?

Avery presses a finger into the base of Leiva's skull, close to his ear. A short glow of the tip of his finger, an almost inaudible beep— and then a small hole opens in the bone behind the ear.

My knees don't exactly feel stable. I plant my butt safely on the bed next to Avery on the ground.

"Holy smokes, what…?" What is that? A *hole* in Leiva's head? I wrap my arms around my shirtless body, the strap of my bra dropping down my shoulder.

"His port." Avery retrieves a narrow rod-like device from his pocket and inserts it into the slot that can't be bigger than one for a cellphone charger. "If we want any information, I need to access him now. I'm sure they equipped him with emergency destructive programming in case of capture." The match-thingy lights up blue and flickers once.

Whoa.

"Is he… a robot?" That would explain why he's so strong.

Avery keeps his attention on the guard. "No. A Second Class Sentinel. Which is probably why they were able to turn him."

I swallow dry. "The Ghosts?" Going out on a limb here.

"The very same," he says, pulling out the match, giving it a critical onceover. "Good. I was worried he had time to compromise the data." He stands up and pockets the device, then turns to me. "I should—"

Avery freezes in mid-sentence, breath hitching in his throat. His eyes drop to my arms crossed in front of my bra.

Uh… No shirt.

I'm not wearing a shirt.

And I'm not the only one realizing that.

A muscle twitches in Avery's jaw, but he doesn't look away.

And it sets me on fire.

My entire world—both universes—comes down to Avery in front of me. Nothing else exists. Nothing else is important.

I see *everything* about him.

The amber in his eyes with a lighter ring around the right pupil, but not the left.

The bruise that's forming on his left cheek, purple and blue.

The leather necklace I never noticed before, a little silver charm dangling from it.

My heart misfires and fills me with something warm, wholesome.

A spark of… *something* lights up in Avery's eyes. In one swift move, he straightens what's left of his shirt and covers the necklace with it.

The heat surging through my body… Oh gosh, how embarrassing. I totally stared at Avery.

I drop my eyes and suck in my lower lip.

I stared.

But how could I *not* have?

"Uh, I should have him taken away." Avery turns so quickly on his heels I wouldn't be surprised if he left skid marks on the floor.

He grabs Leiva by the shoulders and hauls him toward the door, dropping him in front of it. "Backup will be here in a minute."

He stays next to the unconscious guard, waiting, not quite keeping his back to me, but not looking at me, either.

Awkward silence.

I'm such an idiot.

Completely inappropriate. But then, fair game. He didn't look away from me, and neither did I from him. I slide off the bed and walk across the room to my closet, getting myself another shirt, dark blue this time. Once it's tightened to fit, I'm back on my bed, the shaking in my legs almost gone.

Almost.

And as much as I want it to, I know it's not from Leiva's attack.

It's from the look in Avery's eyes when nothing else mattered but him.

CHAPTER NINE

Eavesdropped

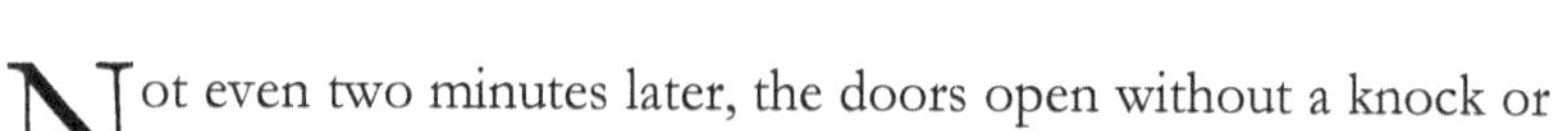

Not even two minutes later, the doors open without a knock or a beep.

Two Sentinels enter the room, both dressed in the same uniforms as Avery, their amber eyes assessing the situation. In a low voice, Avery reports what happened, and twenty seconds later, Leiva is gone, hauled off by the other two Sentinels. The moment the door closes behind them, the tension in the room is as palpable as before.

Avery's shoulders heave up and down once. "It's taken care of. You're safe." He crosses the room with long strides until he's in front of my bed.

In front of *me*.

My insides tighten.

"Why has he been following me?" I whisper, drawing my knees up to my chest. "What did he want with me? I'm no good for anything, I..." I rest my forehead on my knees. He couldn't even have gotten ransom from me without a family to blackmail.

Avery hesitates for a moment before he squats down and lays his large, warm hand on my shoulder. "He didn't follow you. He was sent here specifically for you by the Ghosts. They've been trying hard this year." He doesn't sound happy about that last part.

I lift up my head. "He *did* follow me. First he choked me in the cell, then I saw him when you brought me up to Canyon's office, then he was guarding the entrance at Bellevue Palace." So he had ample time to find out about me.

Something in Avery's eyes softens. He gives my shoulder a small squeeze. "I keep forgetting you don't know the basics of Terran society," he says gently. "Leiva is a Second Class Sentinel—opposed to a First Class. Remember I told you we're all Second Children?"

I nod. How could I not? I still feel sorry for Avery and every other First Class. Well, besides Holloway, maybe. He seems like an idiot.

Avery searches my eyes, satisfied with my nod. "While we Firsts are all naturally conceived humans, Second Class Sentinels are clones."

My jaw drops. "Clones?" I didn't hear that right.

"Clones. Designed for agility, speed, strength, and to follow orders. They have limited independent decision-making skills but are very useful as a force to be reckoned with. Seconds take care of all the base work for security, with us Firsts being their superiors."

A clone. Every time I thought I saw the same person, I most likely saw a different one. "But... how do you keep them apart?" I doubt they each have a different mole or other mark.

Avery taps his forehead again. "They show. All Firsts can read their info."

"Only Firsts?"

"Yes. That's our prerogative. They're ours to lead and to deal with." His jaw sets. "Which is why I had to take his information. This can't happen again."

I completely agree. "What was that? The thing you put into his... port?"

Avery drops his hand, stands up, and taps the bone behind his right ear. "All Sentinels have access ports. They're used for programming if necessary, or to retrieve information in case of emergencies."

He pulls up the heavy armchair that fell over during the fight as if it weighed nothing. "The combination of an organic brain with intelligent programmable synthetic components makes our duties easier." Two of his fingers move the curtain in front of my window to the left, barely enough to check something on the outside. "I added more security around your quarters. This will not happen again." He closes the curtain again. "I'll be outside if you need me. Good night, Noa."

He walks past me toward the door.

"Wait." I reach out and get a hold of his torn sleeve. "Please."

Avery stops, his gaze dropping to where my fingers twist into the fabric of his black shirt. "What is it?"

I lower my gaze to the ground. Heat flames to life in my cheeks. "I…" I don't want to sound needy, or even worse, creepy, but… To hell with it. I take a deep breath. "I don't want to be alone, not after this. Please don't leave." There, it's out. I bite my lip until it starts bleeding. There's no way I'm going to sleep after what just happened. I didn't even hear Leiva before he had an arm around my throat. Nobody suspected anything, and *boom*, suddenly he was here.

No, I really don't want to be alone.

Gently, Avery frees himself from my hold. "I can't," he says, much softer than I anticipated. "It's against protocol."

"Please." It's a pitiful whisper. An embarrassing pitiful whisper.

"It's against protocol."

This time I get it.

I close my eyes and nod. "Of course." Asking him to stay… I'll file it away as my second inappropriate action within five minutes.

For a good ten seconds, neither of us says anything. Then Avery sighs. His hand brushes over my cheek so quickly, I think I imagined it. "Go to bed, Noa."

My gaze flies up to meet his, hope in my chest.

"Go to bed," he repeats, then moves the heavy armchair to the space between the window and my bed.

A weight the size of a boulder drops off my shoulders. I clamber over the bed and slide under the covers, pulling them up to my chin. Within two or three seconds, the bed has adjusted itself around me, softened in some places and tightened in others. Even the blanket warms on its own.

Avery takes a seat in the chair. "Good night, Noa." His deep baritone vibrates in my chest and settles somewhere inside my heart. "Lights off."

The very last split second before the ceiling lights obey, I think I see a faint smile on Avery's face, but it's probably only my imagination.

"Good night, Avery," I whisper back, engulfed by a sensation of peace I didn't think possible a minute earlier.

I'm asleep in no time.

It must be hours later when the peacefulness ends.

Nightmares.

My parents die over and over again, and never am I there for them.

Leiva chokes me for fun until I can't breathe, and once I'm weak, he breaks every bone in my body.

Canyon lures me in with candy, only to bring me up on a stage and show me like a caged zoo animal.

No matter how much I toss and turn, I can't shake the dreams. If one leaves me alone, the next one takes over. Every time I manage to break free, another one pulls me under.

At one point, I think I feel a warm, slightly rougher hand on my cold and clammy one, but before I can analyze that piece of information, a soothing, deep voice lulls me into a deeper and finally dreamless sleep.

It must be hours before I finally drift up to the surface of reality again, disoriented as to where I am and confused by the voices coming from far away.

Then the memories of last night return with a jolt. I push myself up to sitting in my bed, my eyes scanning the dark in front of me as if I expected my nightmares to come true and Leiva to attack me again.

Nothing.

The room is so quiet, my heartbeat must be audible all the way to the bathroom. I let go of a big breath. No Leiva.

Good.

I look to the chair on my right, but there's no Avery, either.

Not good.

But there—the voices that woke me up, faint and muffled. I push my blanket off and tiptoe toward the door, my bare feet silent on the soft, squishy carpet. Is Avery out there? How long did he stay with me, did he—

The door turns translucent at eye level as soon as I'm close enough.

"You wouldn't have let me had I asked, Toshi!" Avery's loud voice booms through the door. I take a step back in surprise of the unexpected volume. My heart beats like crazy, as if I were doing something forbidden.

"You're damn right about that, Avery," an angry male voice shoots back. "Especially with who she is. And it's against protocol, you know that. If anybody else but me had come by and found you away from your post and *inside* your principal's quarters, you know what would have happened!"

My heart leaps into my throat. They're talking about me. I sneak closer, scanning the hallway in front of my quarters. Avery is on the left, in a new and untorn uniform shirt, glaring at another, significantly older and slightly shorter Sentinel with amber eyes and Asian features. Another First Class Sentinel.

"Look," says the other man, lifting both of his hands as if to calm himself and Avery down, "I'm not saying this went well. We—"

Avery huffs. "Not well, Toshi? There was a *Ghost* inside her quarters!" He points a quick finger right at the door I'm hiding behind. "They obviously know about her, and you can't tell me that this is going the way it's supposed to." He glares at Toshi.

"It's not our job to—"

"But it *is* my job to keep her safe!" Avery pauses, then works a hand through his hair as he takes and releases a deep breath. "Not even a modulator, Toshi. What's going on here?"

Toshi stays quiet for a moment. "I don't know, Ave. What I do know is that it's none of our business. You know how it goes."

"I want—"

"*You* want nothing, or you know the consequences, *Sentinel*," Toshi growls, much harsher than before.

Something freezes over in Avery's face. "Yes, sir," he replies stiffly.

Toshi pulls his shoulders back just the same. "I looked at your log. You haven't tethered her yet." He waits for an answer, but Avery stays silent, the muscles in his jaw working overtime. "I repeat. You haven't tethered her yet."

This time Avery responds. "It didn't seem right. No, actually. It seemed wrong."

The older Sentinel deflates visibly and frowns, then steps up so close to Avery, they're almost nose to nose. "Let me make this perfectly clear, *Sentinel*. She gets tethered as ordered. We follow the Minister's orders. We do not make our own, nor do we modify them. Do I make myself clear, or do I need to spell out the ramifications for you?"

"Yes, sir. No, sir." Avery is the picture-book example of standing at attention.

Toshi sighs and drops a hand on Avery's shoulder. "Stay out of this one, Ave. It's never worth it." His hand squeezes once, then he strides past Avery and down the hallway, his steps echoing back until he passes the door at the very end.

Glued to the floor, I stay exactly where I am, trying to control my breathing as if Avery could hear me if I didn't.

And who knows, he might. I have absolutely no clue if this window-in-door-thing works both ways, although I assume it doesn't for privacy reasons.

What was that about? Me, obviously, but why? Why was Avery so worked up, and why wasn't the other Sentinel? Modulator, tethers… My head spins with everything that happened today.

I stay rooted to my spot, replaying their conversation over and over in my head. It doesn't make any sense. Why would Avery ask what's going on? *Is* something going on? Should I be worried? I mean, more than I am after Leiva sneaking into my quarters and trying to do whatever he intended with me?

I mull it over again and again until I finally sneak back to bed and pull the warm covers up to my nose.

But no matter how hard I try, this time, sleep won't come.

CHAPTER TEN

Attack

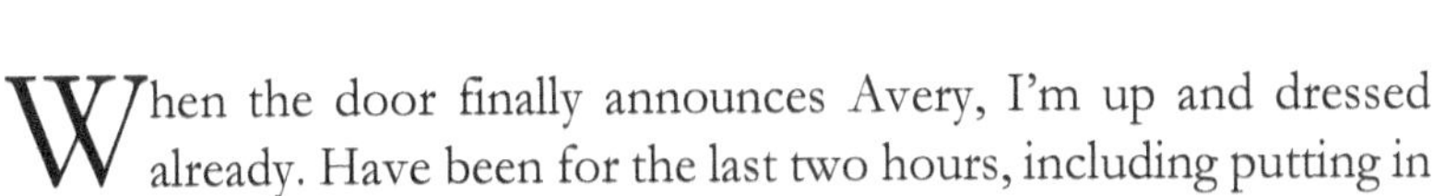

When the door finally announces Avery, I'm up and dressed already. Have been for the last two hours, including putting in my owl nose stud. It's an appropriate choice: She looks as wide-eyed as I've felt since last night.

"Good morning, Noa."

Judging by his calm tone of voice, yesterday was just another day at the office to Avery. If it weren't for the slightest purplish bruise on the right side of his jaw, he could've fooled me. He looks more rested than I do, although I know he didn't leave his post in front of my door to get some sleep.

I know because I checked every couple of minutes.

Well, it's not as if I could have fallen asleep again after all that happened, the argument with Toshi and the epic stare-down before that.

"Good morning, Avery." My heart does a silly little leap, courtesy of the memory of Avery's eyes on me. "How are you doing?" I circle a finger around my face in the area of his bruises.

Avery's jaw sets. "Well. Thank you." He stops in the middle between the door and me, his posture straight, his arms crossed behind his back. All business. A wall is up and palpable between us that wasn't there last night.

I wipe a non-existing strand of hair out of my face, my nervous phantom movement. "Uh, about last night, I... I wanted to say thank you, and—"

"Nothing to thank me for. It's my job to keep you safe."

If one can create a distance with a tone of voice, Avery is doing a great job. Like he didn't stay last night when I all but begged him to. Like he didn't defend me in front of his superior.

Like it meant nothing.

My face warms up like a lightbulb. "But—"

"But nothing, Noa." He doesn't even look at me when he clears his throat. "I suggest you check if there is anything you would need to take with you. If so, I also suggest getting it. Minister Canyon wants us back at his main office. We're leaving in thirty minutes."

"We're leaving?" My voice turns squeaky at the end. "To go where?" I don't want to leave. Leaving feels like giving up—it means letting go of the hope of accidentally crossing back over in the same location I crossed before. It's not quite logical, but come on, *something* pulled me over here, maybe all the machinery I saw under the dome close to Canyon's office. Who's to say it won't happen again in the other direction?

So yeah, leaving Berlin feels like giving up.

Avery nods, his eyes straight ahead. "Chicago. Once we're there, we'll get you situated and the Minister will… continue his efforts." He doesn't meet my eyes, instead looking at a spot somewhere behind my right ear.

Chicago. At least Chicago. It's completely irrational, but it makes me feel better. Closer, actually. Closer to my parents, and although we're still separated by a universe, we're at least in a town with the same name.

"I have nothing to pack." I pat my right front pocket that contains my piercings. That's all I need.

"Very well then." Avery opens the door, wordlessly leading the way down the hallway and out of Bellevue Palace, where another Second Class Sentinel opens the doors for us.

He looks exactly like Leiva.

For a moment it's all back: the surprise, the arm squeezing around my neck, the fear that paralyzed me, although at least it didn't turn into a full-blown panic attack.

A gentle hand pushes into the small of my back, breaking the spell.

"It's not him." Avery keeps his voice so low, nobody but me could hear him. Despite his reassurance, he still moves himself between me and the other guard.

It might not be Leiva, but the resemblance is enough to make me uncomfortable. Majorly.

We descend the stairs toward the pseudo-subway station in silence. The hobbit hole Avery directs me to is a tad bigger than the last one, and so is the capsule-shaped glass cabin awaiting us behind those doors.

It still only has two seats. Where is everybody else? Canyon?

"We go ahead. Understandably, the Minister wants you out of the Ghosts' way, so while he's still held up here, he sends us ahead. Sit." He enters commands into the touch screen next to the door, the same computer voice I've grown to love already talking back to him.

"*Chicago Ministry pre-programmed. Are you sure you want to chan—*"

Avery interrupts the computer's voice with a grumpy push of a button.

"*Code and new destination accepted,*" the computer voice announces. "*Your travel time will be one hour and thirty-five minutes. Please enjoy the ride.*"

My mouth drops open. "One and a half hours to Chicago?" From Germany? That can't be right. That wouldn't be enough to get me from downtown Chicago into the suburbs on most days.

To my surprise, Avery sits in the seat across from me that automatically adjusts to his wider frame. His legs aren't even half an inch away from mine. I imagine I can feel the warmth radiating from them.

"This line is the speed VacWay." He points with his chin out the front toward the tunnel we're already blazing through without the slightest sensation of movement. "Reserved for Government Officials. Otherwise, it would be about three hours."

I shake my head. "Doesn't matter. Both are amazingly fast. A trip on a plane is like eight hours for us to get there."

"A plane?" He tilts his head curiously. "But it's small."

Now I have to laugh. "Small? This is small. An international jet fits like five hundred people."

Avery raises an eyebrow. "The VacWay has pods leaving up to every two minutes, depending on connection. We have dozens or even hundreds of tubes parallel to each other all through the world, depending on location. By varying the intervals for the vacuum traction, we can reach high speeds, making fast travel possible. Plus, it's safe." A visible shudder runs over him. "Flying all this distance sounds dangerous to me."

For the first time since last night, a grin spreads over my face. "My, Avery. If I didn't know better, I'd say you were afraid of flying."

"I'm not." He crosses his arms in front of his chest and slides down into his seat. His legs bump into mine, and while it's a completely innocent touch, my heart skips a beat.

Avery's eyes widen so slightly I might have imagined it.

Then he straightens up again and swivels to the left, looking out the front instead.

Not awkward at all.

For a moment, it's so, *so* silent in this stupid pod that I hear my heart hammering way too loudly. I turn my chair forward as well, wishing Avery wouldn't be able to see my face burning. Alas, there's absolutely no privacy in this pod—*if* he looked, that is. Which he isn't.

Why would he?

Me, on the other hand… I can't help but check out his image in the glass. Even if I didn't want to, he's everywhere. The pod is made completely out of glass or something like it. Everything reflects everywhere with the lights on the inside of the pod and the ones integrated into the ceiling outside, morphing into a streak of brightness as we blaze by them.

Wherever I look, I can't escape Avery's dark, unruly hair, straight posture and wide shoulders. I remember what it felt like when he saved me from Leiva. I remember even better what he looked like with his shirt half torn off.

I meet his gaze via reflection without trying.

Avery stares straight ahead, as if there were no way he could have noticed me checking him out.

I shove my cold hands under my thighs.

Last night is still on my mind, whether I like it or not. *All* aspects of it, though granted, some I like to dwell on more than others, especially because the conversation with Toshi still gives me goosebumps.

After a couple of minutes, I break the silence. "Avery?" I sound like a child with my voice so thin. "What… What's a modulator?"

His head whips around, his whole body tense all of a sudden. "How do you know about a modulator?"

"I—" Judging by the look he gives me, this may not be the right time to bring up I heard him and Toshi last night. "Uh, you mentioned it up in Canyon's office?"

A little bit of the tension leaves his body. "I did." He turns forward again. "It's nothing for you to be concerned about."

Then why was he last night? And he was, I felt it. The way he said it to Toshi, it seemed like a big deal. I suck in and bite my lower lip, which has already taken quite the punishment over the last two days. "I feel like I'm missing something, Avery." If it weren't so quiet in here, he wouldn't have heard me. As it is, I'm not quite sure myself whether I said it out loud or just thought it.

Out of the corner of my eyes, I see his reflection and how he takes a deep breath.

In one abrupt movement, he turns his chair around, leaning forward to look at me. "Noa, I—"

Something flashes in the near distance, bathing our pod in bright white light for no more than a split second.

Avery's eyes pop open wide.

With a curse, he jumps up from his seat, almost hitting his head on the low ceiling as he dashes toward the control panel behind us. At the same time, the tube's ceiling lights turn from one longitudinal beam of light back into single lights until the pod slows down to a standstill.

"What's happening?" Malfunction? Out of gas?

Avery doesn't answer. Instead, he attacks the touchscreen close to the door. He curses and hits the wall with his palm in frustration. "Dead. Should have known, should have—"

"Avery, what—"

Movement catches my eye outside the window.

Oh, shoot.

People.

People clad in black with masks over their faces, like ninjas. They're coming at us, spilling out of a hole in the tube's ceiling like pepper from a shaker.

Avery reaches for something in his belt. "Ghosts," he growls, "Down, Noa."

I don't think. I do as he says.

Like a dog obeying an order, I drop to the floor and crawl closer to Avery and away from the front window.

Ghosts.

Again.

My throat constricts, shutting off all but a small wheeze of my air supply. It can't be much longer until my panic attack sets in full force and turns me into a useless mess.

Frantically, Avery hammers into the touchpad that still looks as dead as before.

I really don't like the word *dead.*

Crouched behind the seat, I try to swallow, but my mouth is too dry.

"Emergency systems rebooting," the computer voice announces. *Rebooting* doesn't inspire confidence, either.

Something thuds against the front window.

Avery swiftly turns on his heels, his body coiled and ready. "Whatever happens, stay with me. Don't run. Stay with me. Do you understand?" His voice is clipped, tight, but calm. Much calmer than mine.

"O-Okay," I squeak, my head bobbing like a doll's. He doesn't know I shut down with panic. He doesn't know. And I don't want to tell him.

Anytime now, it's going to happen. Anytime, I'm going to lose control over myself.

I'm already barely breathing as it is. It's a matter of seconds, I assume.

There's another thud, and this time I look.

I wish I hadn't.

At least twenty people dressed in black storm toward our pod from either side, the ones in the front holding a long device that looks way too much like a weapon.

Avery curses. "The vacuum generator shafts. That's how they get in. We should have known, damn it!"

The men in black lift that pipe-thing up together. It's at least a yard long and as thick as my arm.

My eyes go wide, a tight, heavy feeling gripping my chest. "Incoming!" I scream from the tops of my lungs, although Avery stands right next to me.

There's a short flash, and then something soft splatters across the window up front with the same thumping sound I heard before.

The gooey liquid spreading from the impact does its job.

Crumbling and melting at the same time, the window breaks down, and there's cheering coming in from the outside.

Avery moves in front of me, his deep voice a rock keeping me from gliding into panic. "Stay behind me. Stay close." He spreads his legs and raises his arms. A thick stick springs free from a device in his hand. The way he positions himself between the open window and me, he completely blocks me with his wide frame. For a moment, I wonder how he's going to fight off at least twenty men, but then I realize he's playing the tight pod to our advantage.

The first ninja climbs up but doesn't even make it in. Lightning-fast Avery, swings the stick, one end glowing blue when it hits the other man in the shoulder. The intruder cries out once, then falls backward, only to be pulled away by three others, replaced by five more trying to work their way inside.

They're fast. Their agility and numbers bring them closer and closer to reaching us, but Avery is faster. Wielding his stick like a sword of lightning, he strikes so incredibly quick, all I see is a blur. From where I'm crouched and hidden, it seems more like he's wearing this pod than standing in it, yet it doesn't restrict his movement. Each strike is precise, utilizing only as much space as necessary, but with each attacker he knocks down, three more appear.

Whump! Another thud comes from behind—a sound that's way too familiar. I jerk around, only to see the rear glass pane and door starting to melt away from the same goo they shot onto our pod's front.

Some of the ninjas high-five each other.

"Avery," I whisper when it becomes clear the material isn't going to hold much longer. Again, louder, I say, "Avery!"

We're trapped in here—worse so than before.

With one last growl, Avery mows down three more attackers trying to climb in at the same time before spinning toward me and yanking me up by one arm.

"Sitting ducks. Our advantage is gone." With that, he sneaks his left hand around my waist and lifts me up to his chest like a child cradling a stuffed animal. I squeak, my arms automatically clinging around his body, and not a second too early.

Avery adjusts his stick. A short, high-pitched whine bursts from it before he darts forward and jabs it like a spear at the melting rear wall of our pod.

I scream and brace myself for the impact—but there's nothing.

The knife-like tip on his stick I could swear wasn't there a moment earlier cuts the metal with ease, adding to the work of whatever is melting down the pod.

With four rapid slices, Avery opens a new hole in the wall in less than four seconds. He kicks the middle portion, shoving the glass panel out and onto our attackers, who barely scramble aside to avoid being trapped under it.

Before the next wave can get to us, Avery jumps out of the

broken pod. I cling to him like a baby monkey, my eyes closed, acid churning in my stomach and every breath burning as if it were my last.

We land smack in the middle of our attackers.

Boom.

His feet haven't even hit the ground, and Avery has taken down three ninjas with his stick as if they weighed nothing. Keeping me close to his chest, he sprints past the group of ninjas.

All the tiny hairs on my body rise to attention.

Avery lowers me to the ground, feet first. "Behind me."

It's an order, that much is clear.

He barely has time to get into a fighting stance. The first two ninjas storm toward him, shoulder to shoulder, filling out this narrow tunnel. Something metallic flashes in the right one's hand a split second before he rams it down at Avery.

I shriek—but the knife doesn't find its target.

In fact, it doesn't even come close.

Avery ducks out of the weapon's path and takes the attacker's legs out from under him with his stick, kicking the other ninja straight in the face at the same time.

Both his opponents drop like stones.

Two down, about a million more to go.

The other Ghosts must have realized the fight is back here now. They're spilling out of the pod from the front, lining up one behind the other inside the narrow tube, ready to fight, and slowly pushing us backward.

Oh, crap.

Fear shoots through my veins. It freezes my muscles and narrows my vision, painting the scene in stark detail.

We have nowhere to run, and they're dozens, only limited by the tight space in this subway tunnel.

This isn't going to end well.

Somebody steps into the broken rear window of our pod, a ninja who's a tad taller than the rest, standing straight, taking in the situation in front of him. "Change of status." His voice holds a bored arrogance. "Plan B."

Part of my brain, the part that's only barely functioning at this point, is wondering who'd ever come up with a cliché like a Plan B, but that thought comes to a screeching halt the moment three of the ninjas pull out guns—long, silver, and much more elegant than what I know as a gun, but still clearly guns.

My vision turns dizzy.

Growling under his breath, Avery takes one step back, his free hand subconsciously searching for me and nudging me farther behind him.

Before the tall Ghost can give the command to shoot, Avery is on the loose.

If he was fast before, he's lightning on his feet now.

The stick in his hand looks like a disk from the fast swirling and stabbing movements. He picks off the first five ninjas before anybody even has a chance to move. Muscles bulge under his shirt, stretching the black fabric to the max. He kicks left and right, mowing the other men down one at a time, leaving fewer than ten standing at this point.

More and more ninjas spill through the pod until Avery pauses, aiming his stick at it.

With a sizzling *buzz,* a bolt of lightning shoots out of the stick and hits the vessel, its blue fingers wrapping around everything metal. Five more Ghosts drop to their knees, twitching. Not the leader, though. He's the last one to jump ship before Avery's lightning bolt hits.

Still, the fight continues as if nothing happened, with one exception: No more Ghosts come charging to our side. Hope bounces in my chest. If these are the last ninjas standing, and looking at the way Avery is fighting… We may have a chance.

We *do* have a chance.

That is until one of the Ghosts racks up his gun, aims, and—

A loud, booming shot echoes down the tunnel.

I scream out, horror freezing me to my spot.

Avery twitches once and grunts but keeps on going.

Did they miss him? Did—

A second shot.

A third.

A fourth.

Every time Avery twitches, and *then* I see it.

His movements aren't so fast anymore.

His stick is losing speed.

His kicks are becoming sluggish.

The ninjas still hold their distance, waiting for him to collapse, only taunting him with their moves.

A *fifth* shot echoes through the tunnel, and Avery stumbles, barely catching himself.

"No!" I cry out, darting forward. Forgotten is my near-panic, forgotten is my fear of the Ghosts. They can't shoot him, they can't—

There's a *sixth* shot, and Avery freezes for a second before he sways, his stick for the first time missing a target.

The leader ninja nods toward the men with the guns. "Keep it up."

Before they can pull the trigger, I duck under Avery's arm and spread myself wide in front of him. "Stop it," I yell. Tears run down my face, burning my cheeks.

Boom, boom!

Something hot bites into my shoulder, and I cry out in pain.

Avery grunts a split second before his legs give way under him and he collapses to the ground.

"Av-y," I slur, the world suddenly so dark around me I could swear somebody switched off the lights.

My legs turn into pudding and I collapse on top of him.

Then, nothing.

CHAPTER ELEVEN

The Other Side

For the second time in about as many days, I wake up not knowing where I am, only this time my memory comes back much quicker. I kinda wish it didn't.

The pod. The ninjas shooting at Avery.

With a jolt, I wake up completely, sitting up so fast, I get dizzy. "What—"

I'm in a bed, complete with nice white blankets and a pillow, in the middle of a small, windowless room with a curved ceiling above me, a regular wooden door at the far end of it and—

"Welcome."

I jerk, almost hitting myself in the face when my hands fly up faster than ever. To my right, slightly behind me, seated in a chair is a… *guy*. A *young* guy.

I mean, he's definitely older than me, but not by much. His blond, curly hair is pulled back into a ponytail like mine, only for him it looks artsy and cool, while mine… yeah, not. Together with the green eyes, it gives him a soft look, especially because his cheeks are smooth, not a single bit of stubble anywhere.

He stands and pulls the chair closer to my bed, then falls down into it again, crossing his legs and folding his hands in his lap, like we were best buddies already. I scoot back against the head of the bed. Is he—?

"You must be Noa," he says, and I recognize the voice.

My throat tightens. "And you're the guy from the... pod." He's the leader ninja—leader Ghost, I correct myself. I'm with the Ghosts. Not that this was an unforeseeable turn of events after—

The guy bows his head slightly, his green eyes holding an amused sparkle. "Correct. What gave it away? My charming good looks?" He gestures to his face and down his body, winking.

My cheeks flush. "More like the arrogant posture." My eyes widen. *Whoops.*

The guy throws his head back and laughs out loud. Dimples pop out on both cheeks, emphasizing the light in his green eyes. "Point taken," he says, still grinning. "I'm Victor, by the way. Nice to meet you, Noa." He holds out a hand to me, and out of reflex I take it.

"Nice to meet you too," I murmur, not quite so big-mouthed anymore.

I'm with the Ghosts.

Repeat: *Oh, crap. I'm with the Ghosts.* Not that Victor was scaring me, but... they didn't quite send a friendly invitation for tea and cookies, either.

Victor nods, as if *of course* it was nice to meet him. I'm surprised the orders during the fight came from him. He can't be twenty yet.

Here at least, he's not quite as scary as the Ghosts were down in the tunnel. "What do you want from me and w-where... where am I?" It looks like some kind of basement room—of an old castle. Where else do you find curved ceilings, or gloomy, yellow, flickering ceiling lights?

"One of our Haunted Houses," Victor says, as if that would explain everything.

"Haunted House?" Seriously? I mean, it fits, but...

He grins. "Yup. We're the Ghosts. I'm sure they've told you about us already, am I right? Ghosts live in haunted houses. It actually is more of a nod to our name than anything else, but it stuck." He shrugs. "By the way, sorry you got hit. We were aiming at sedating the big guy, never at you, but when you threw yourself in front of him..." He shrugs again, as if that explained what happened.

Oh, shoot.

"Avery," I whisper hoarsely. "Where is Avery?" Why isn't he here with me? They shot him so many more times than me… I grasp my shoulder. Nothing but soreness. What did they shoot us with? "Where is Avery? Is he okay?" I repeat, this time stronger. He got like six of those shots, I only got one, and I was out for what must have been a long time.

Victor's eyes narrow. "He's still sedated, but fine." He watches me intently as I let go of a breath. "Why do you care?"

What kind of question is that? "Why wouldn't I care?"

He raises an eyebrow. "Because he's a Sentinel."

"So what?" *Ugh.* I got captured by the one group that would give George and Elaine's government paranoia a run for its money.

Victor smiles faintly, his gaze never moving away from me. "It doesn't matter now."

"Of course it matters." I glare at him. "Where is he?" Avery took all those hits to protect me. I need to make sure he's okay.

"He's where he belongs, together with all the other puppets Canyon controls," Victor says calmly.

What does that mean? "I want to see him." I push back the blanket, but Victor raises a hand, stopping me.

"First, tell me about yourself instead. You're from Earth." It's a statement, not a question. He leans forward, his green eyes boring into mine.

Just like Leiva said: The Ghosts know.

Well, and just because I woke up in a bed and not a cell this time doesn't automatically mean these guys are my friends. I want to run.

Instead, I cross my arms in front of my chest, which probably makes me look like a dumb kid, but I don't care. If I didn't, he might see the shaking. "Well, you obviously know that much. Then tell me why I'm here. What do you want from me?" He didn't answer when I asked before, so… not a good sign, right?

Victor's smile turns amused. "That's the question, isn't it?" He gets up and holds out a hand toward me to help me up. "As a citizen of Earth, you have obviously been there and know it intimately. You're an invaluable informant for us—for the Resistance. The fact that with you we have direct insight into Canyon's doing on Earth is worth your weight in gold, although…" He admires my rather petite stature when he helps me off the bed. "Although your weight in gold wouldn't be that much." He winks at me again.

Dammit, I don't want to blush.

I snatch my hand back and wipe it on my thigh. "What Canyon is doing on Earth?" I huff. "I don't think I'm going to be of much use to you then. Canyon isn't on Earth, whatever that's supposed to mean. He can't even bring me back. He told me. Can't connect the two universes unless he puts a ton of research into it." Which could take years before it works out. Years, in which my parents will surely die.

I swallow hard, almost missing the open-mouthed stare Victor gives me.

"What?" I ask.

I'm not a big fan of that look. Makes me feel like I'm missing something.

He catches himself. "Nothing. Let… Let me give you the tour and then introduce you to Tonya and the others."

I fidget at the little spiky stud in my pocket I so desperately need. My external confidence. "No."

Victor stops halfway to the door. "No?"

"No." I can feel a spine growing inside my back. It's a very unsettling sensation to not accommodate somebody after my parents drilled appeasement of others into me since the moment I was born. "I want to see Avery."

Victor's eyes grow wide. "The Sentinel? You want to see the Sentinel?"

I don't think that's so hard to believe. "Yes." I push my chin forward, trying to ignore the *other* unsettling sensation lurking at the corners of my mind, the one that wonders what they did to Avery.

He chuckles once. "Alrighty then. Why not? Something new." He shakes his head and opens the regular old door by its knob. Somehow that low-tech is way more comforting than anything else I've seen so far.

Victor leads the way down a windowless uneven hallway with a low curved ceiling that melts seamlessly into the walls. Thick electric cords run across the middle of the ceiling, connecting one low-hanging lightbulb with the next. Some of them dangle down precariously, as if they were about to fall sooner rather than later.

Overall, this place must have seen better days. Paint is chipped off the dirty white walls, revealing some kind of dull, black material underneath, and every couple of ceiling lights, one of the bulbs is out or flickers. Pretty spooky, all in all.

"What is this place?" I ask in a near-whisper while doing a slow turn, my neck craned and eyes wide. It's cold and smells stuffy, like a dungeon.

"I'll give you a hint," Victor says with a grin. "It's underground." He passes me by to lead the way. "I apologize for the state of our little lair here"—he points at the walls—"but as you can imagine, we don't have the resources or the luxury to get too attached to one place."

"Because you're working against the government?"

He chuckles again. "I see they tried to indoctrinate you already." He opens the door to a narrow stairway leading down into a basement. If I were alone, I'd surely not go down there: it screams spiders. It also screams claustrophobia, that's how narrow it is. The walls here aren't smooth, like in the hallway, but it looks like the stairs were hammered out of the ground, protruding rocks and all.

Victor holds the door open and glances toward me. "We might be working against the government, but mostly we're working *for* the people—the people of *two* worlds. You'll see that soon enough. Now come. Let's get this over with."

We walk down the uneven stairs into a large basement area with concrete walls and floors. It's much bigger than my room upstairs, but it gives the distinct sensation of an underground dungeon.

At the bottom of the stairs, a middle-aged and wide-shouldered man sits on an old, wooden chair, his arms crossed in front of his chest, his legs stretched out in front of him. Once he sees us, he gets up, still blocking the way.

"Victor. What brings you here?" He extends a hand that Victor shakes.

"Visiting hours," Victor answers, nodding his head.

The man tilts his head. "Is that…?"

"Yup," Victor says. "She wants to see the Sentinel."

"Huh, interesting. Well, good thing he's about to wake up completely. Didn't expect that for another couple of hours. He must have the metabolism of a horse." He steps aside, letting Victor and me pass.

We turn around the next corner, and there is Avery.

I stop mid-step, rooted to the ground.

To be fair, I didn't listen to the warning bells going off inside my head. I didn't think about what to *expect*, and instead I *assumed*.

I *assumed* he would be in a room similar to mine.

I *assumed*, since Victor seemed generally nice, that despite the rather unfriendly method of taking us in, certain standards would be kept up, especially since I myself woke up in a bed.

What I didn't *expect* was to see Avery in a cell, shackled to the wall, limp, and only barely conscious.

This place doesn't only feel like a dungeon, it *is* a dungeon. At least for Avery.

Somehow, I cross the distance to the bars in no time and wrap my fingers around the cold metal.

"Avery," I whisper, my heart cramping in my chest.

Two awful long seconds later, Avery slowly lifts his head up at the sound of my voice, his eyes unfocused and foggy. His chest heaves up and down in an unhealthy irregular rhythm, like he forgot how to breathe. He blinks heavily, his head falling back for a moment before he catches himself.

"Avery, I'm here." I reach one hand through the bars as if I could touch him at the opposite wall. He must be freezing cold with his back against the concrete wall, his black shirt torn in at least three different places.

Finally, some of the fog lifts. "Noa." It's a mere mumble, but I'll take it. His gaze darts to my right, his eyes narrowing to slits. "*Ghost.*"

Avery tries to straighten up, but the chains restrict his movement. He grunts once, flexing his arms to free himself, but to no avail. The skin on his wrists is chafed off already, either from his weight hanging in the shackles or from him subconsciously trying to free himself.

My eyes tear up seeing him like this, bound, obviously in pain. Well, obviously for me. I doubt the Ghosts would notice the dim in his golden eyes.

I do.

"Let him out of there," I whisper. "Please." My voice almost breaks at the end. I grip the bars. "Avery."

Victor shakes his head. "No way. He's not going to leave this cell for as long as he lives." He looks straight at me, pointing through the bars at Avery, who tries his best to shake off the fog. I wouldn't say he succeeds completely, but at least his eyes lose the haze—and they shoot fire at Victor.

Victor indicates the cell with a nod. "You don't know what you're asking. You have no idea whom you brought. This is not just any First Class Sentinel. This is Canyon's number one, his pet, his personal project." He laughs drily. "This one singlehandedly took down and imprisoned ten Ghosts last month when we tried to intercept a Rhodium transport. We'd be idiots if we let him go. Once the sedation has worn off and we access him, he's going to give us everything we need to know. He—"

A short, harsh laugh from inside the cell cuts him off. "What makes you think you're even going to get close enough to access me?"

I jump and spin to stare at Avery. He's straightened himself up against the wall as much as he can with those shackles. The small change in posture makes him seem so much larger than Victor, who has to crane his neck to look up to him, despite the distance between them.

Well, I guess that's the point.

But Victor is outside the cell, unbound, holding all the cards—and he knows it. He grins condescendingly. "Look at that. It speaks. Huh, let me see… For starters, because you're the one with his arms tied to the wall. It makes me pretty optimistic we'll get what we want, and even more, because you're awake. Then there's also the small matter of your principal here—"

"Leave her alone." Avery's voice is deep and low, like a lion's growl.

Victor laughs—he actually laughs and throws his head back, holding his stomach. "You're funny, Sentinel. I'd say you failed your task the moment Leiva was able to enter her room. It's kind of adorable you're still pretending you'd have a chance of getting her back to your master."

Yanking on his chains, Avery stumbles a step forward, his body still not quite following his commands. He almost falls when the chains snatch him back. "Noa, you—"

"No." Victor shakes his head. "She deserves to hear the truth, don't you think, Sentinel?"

A block of ice appears in my stomach that wasn't there before, despite my less-than-stellar situation. "What do you mean?"

Victor smooths one hand over his hair, then points at Avery. "Why don't you ask him? He's been keeping that from you, not me."

I look back at Avery. "What is he talking about?" I don't trust Victor. He's trying to play us, to get a rift between us so I'll cooperate with him. For what, I don't know, but I know I trust Avery much more than anybody else in this universe. Literally. He saved me from Leiva, and he tried his very best to save me from the Ghosts.

Avery's jaw tightens. "He's trying to get you to believe his conspiracy theories."

"Oh, if only they were just theories. It'd make my life much easier," Victor says nonchalantly, rocking back onto his heels. "Go ahead. Tell her what Canyon tells everybody, then tell her why you exist. I'm curious to see if she's still on your side after that."

The block of ice has reached my heart. "What is he talking about?" I repeat, never looking anywhere but at Avery. My lifeline in this universe.

Avery's face falls, and with it my hope. "Noa, I—"

Victor steps closer to the bars, huffing once. "Look at him. As if he had a mind of his own, or even feelings. Fascinating, isn't it?" He looks down at me, but I still refuse to meet his eyes. All I do is stare at Avery, who wordlessly pleads at me to listen.

Victor grabs the bars like I do. "If you think he's mad or sad because of you, you're mistaken. He's mad because he got an order, and he can't follow it. Isn't that so, Sentinel?"

Avery glares at Victor in response before his eyes dim again when they shift back toward me.

Victor smiles arrogantly. "And I doubt he even knows what sadness is because while he appears human, I'd go as far as to say he's not. How can you be, if you were made for one thing only? Made to be alone? Made for a battle that will never come because our *enemy* doesn't even know we exist? How very depressing it must be to not have a place in this world."

With every word, Avery's amber shines less brightly, like Victor sucked the life force out of his body. And he doesn't stop. "What he isn't telling you, Noa, is that he's been lying to you from the get-go. Isn't that so, Sentinel?"

There's a small twitch of Avery's jaw, but no response.

"Avery?" I need him to tell me all is well. I need *him*. Period.

But nothing.

Gently, Victor places a hand on my shoulder. "Noa, Canyon is a liar and criminal elected to be a minister. You said he can't bring you back home—but he can. Terra has been sending scientists over to Earth and back for decades, profiting from your unawareness and ignorance. Of course he can send you back, but he never intended to."

His hand on my shoulder weighs a ton. "And do you know why his pet was supposed to bring you to Chicago? Because that's his main research facility. Canyon didn't only want to keep you here. He wanted to do research on you, little Earthling."

His eyes shoot daggers at Avery. "And *this one* knew it all along."

CHAPTER TWELVE

Tit for Tat

Victor's words mean nothing to me.

I probably didn't hear them right over the swooshing sound pulsing in my ears that drowns out everything besides Avery.

I stare at him through the bars, desperate to understand what I just heard.

Canyon wants to do research on me?

He *could* send me home if he wanted to?

And Avery knew it?

Avery, who knew about my parents and why I needed to go back?

Avery, who stayed with me when I needed him? Who fought off the Ghosts for me?

No, I correct myself, that's not true. Not for me. For *Canyon*.

"You knew?" I breathe out the words hardly loud enough for Victor to pick up, let alone Avery.

"Noa, please listen, I—" He pulls his chains, leaning his body forward as if trying to bridge the distance that has sprung open between us.

He knew.

"Nothing you need to listen to, dear." Victor gently guides me away from the cell. "I know it's a lot to take in, but we'll help you—"

Avery roars and throws himself into the chains. "Don't you dare get her involved in your messed-up illegal activities. She's not your—"

"Neither is she yours," Victor calmly responds, the hand on my shoulder reaching over to the other one and drawing me close into his side. "It's a pity, Noa. Canyon and his pets are the number-one enemy of this world, and probably of yours just the same." The fingers on my shoulder squeeze once before he turns me toward him. "Thing is, *he* might not want to, but *we* can still get you back home. Let me bring you up to speed, and you'll see exactly why we brought you here."

"Noa, please don't listen to him," Avery begs me. "He's using—"

"I wish they'd program some common sense into these Sentinels," Victor murmurs, leading me away from the cell. "Really."

Avery throws himself into the chains again, trying to pull himself lose but to no avail. "You son of a b—"

"Cursing won't help, either." Victor wiggles a single finger. He grips my shoulder a bit tighter so it's difficult for me to keep looking at Avery, who rages inside that cell, his eyes blazing, doing everything he can to break free. A trail of blood runs down his wrists, courtesy of metal against human skin.

Automatically, I feel sorry for him—until I don't.

He knew.

He would have delivered me to research.

Something cramps up inside my heart, wilting, withering away.

"Let's go," I hoarsely whisper at Victor.

So we do, and I don't care where we go.

At all.

Victor takes me away from an infuriated and yelling Avery back to the spooky hallway. He leads us through several more of them, none in any better shape, until we reach a set of double doors.

Non-automatic. Like at home.

If my life depended on it, I couldn't say how we got here. All I see in front of my inner eye is the shock on Avery's face when Victor told me about Canyon.

I wonder if I looked similarly terrified.

With one hand on the doorknob, Victor stops and looks down

on me. He isn't quite as tall as Avery and also way more lanky, but he still towers above me—to nobody's surprise.

"You'll meet everyone. I know… I know it's a lot to take in, but please bear with us, okay?" He gives me a small smile, an honest one, while he searches my eyes. "You'll see how important it is. Make up your own mind."

Make up my own mind.

Right.

Everything I know in this world I know because somebody told me about it. I'm a stupid blank slate in this universe, and I'm so easy to manipulate, it's ridiculous.

I believed Canyon.

I didn't like him quite that much, but I believed him.

I believed Avery. I *trusted* Avery.

And look where it got me.

Still, I nod at Victor.

Apparently, that's all the confirmation he needs before he opens the door to a large room—more of a hall actually. It mirrors the same style of this whole place, which makes sense, given we're still underground. The ceiling is curved, but way higher in here, almost like in a church. That's probably why they have even more unshaded lightbulbs hanging from somewhere higher up, bathing the big, oval table in the middle in soft yellow light that throws shadows down the faces of the ten people around it.

All of their faces light up when I walk in as if I'm the balloon artist at a preschooler's birthday party.

Right.

On the far end of the table, a woman rises from her seat and walks toward me with quick strides. She's maybe in her late thirties with olive skin and long, sleek black hair that flows down her back like a living being, moving with every step she takes. Commercial-worthy.

Only when she's standing in front of me do I realize I've stopped somewhere between the door and the table, frozen to the spot. Too many people for me. Too much attention.

The woman doesn't mind my hesitation. She pulls me into a tight hug when I'm close enough. I feel her smile next to my ear, despite me stiffening under her hug.

"Welcome, Noa. We're so happy to have you. All will be well." She says it with such conviction, I almost believe her right there.

"Uh, th-thank you," I stutter, relieved when she releases me and keeps the smile. I'm not a hugger. Never was. Last time my parents hugged me was in elementary school. I think. With Andrew, they were different. He was always touchy-feely, and—

"Why don't you have a seat, Noa?" the woman asks, gesturing to a free chair right next to hers.

"S-Sure." Way to go sounding confident. At least I hold my head high as I walk after her to take my assigned seat, ignoring everybody's stares. Doesn't mean my face isn't burning, though.

Once seated, the woman folds her hands in front of her on the table. "Again, welcome, Noa. My name is Tonya. I'm the lead for this Haunted House. We're a small group, and these are our senior members." She points at everybody, starting with Victor on her left. "There are about forty of us total in this group. You've met Victor already; he's my second-in-command. Then we've got Kyle, Lacey, Shannon, Tomar, Hudson, Lucinda, Terry, and Shaniqua."

Each of the people introduced smiles at me and lifts their hand for a short *hello*. None of them seem much older than Tonya, and I'd go as far as to say they're all under forty. They're all dressed in black, some of their clothes patched up, but all clean. Kyle and… Terry, I think, have bruises on their faces. I wonder if they were there when Avery—

I drop my gaze to the table.

Not thinking of him right now.

Tonya finishes the introduction. "I know you must be curious. I'll be as thorough as I can, but feel free to interrupt me if you have any questions, okay?" She gives me a smile that's almost maternal. "We're the Ghosts, and *au contraire* to what you might have heard, we're not the enemy. Quite the opposite. We are the only ones standing between a totalitarian government and the people of Terra, and, quite frankly, also the people of Earth."

It echoes what Victor said earlier. Maybe they truly can cross over. I sit up straighter.

"As you might have noticed, our society differs from yours. The split-off happened during World War II, when in our universe Hitler was killed, while in yours he continued his warfare. We had less of a recovery time and more of a change of heart in regards to globalization and common strategies against war after the near-miss of a devastating world-wide destruction. For a while, all was good as the world grew together, at least until some of us realized we were living in a golden cage and on the back of others: Earth."

I tilt my head to the left. "What do you mean?" Looking at Terra, it's pretty clear they're so far ahead of us we're probably not even on their radar in terms of technology, even though they know about us.

Tonya takes a deep breath. "Well, this part isn't easy, and I would like to apologize upfront for what we, as a society, have done to you. Believe me when I say the Ghosts have been working for over fifty years to rectify the situation." The sad smile on her face turns serious. "Decades ago, two of Terra's most famous scientists discovered a way to cross between universes, between Terra and Earth, to be exact. Since then, the government has had researchers and others cross over and come back, and…" She pauses, looking down at her folded hands. "And they've been using Earth, Noa. For nearly five decades." She stares into my eyes, waiting for me to understand what she's saying.

"Wait, using Earth? How do you use Earth?"

"Research," Victor says. "They're doing research." He works one hand over his hair, adjusting his ponytail. "Human Behavior— inducing a mass panic by setting fire inside a club. How do subjects react to severe, life-threatening events? Metabolism—duration from exposure to addiction for intravenous drugs. Environmental—rising CO_2 gasses and the resulting compensation by plants. Marine Biology—adaptation by marine animals to toxic substances. Need more?" He huffs drily, but I'm still not getting it.

"So, what, they studied that? I'm sure so do we. I mean, those kinds of things are in the newspaper on any given day." In fact, it's almost all the news is made of.

Victor opens his mouth, but Tonya is quicker, covering my hand with hers. "That's not it, Noa. What Victor is saying is that we research those things on Earth. *After* we made sure they'd happen."

She watches me intensely for my reaction, her brown eyes serious. "Do you understand? *We* made this happen. *We* pushed diesel engines and discredited alternative forms of energy. *We* made sure your society thrived on single-use products that would end up cluttering the environment to see how long degradation would take and how nature would adapt, if at all. *We* were the ones who set fire to clubs, sent suicide bombers, or influenced politicians to push the proverbial red button so we could evaluate human behavior during crisis. *We* developed those drugs, using your population as a study group, reaping the benefits and making good use of them here on Terra." She swallows. "Do you understand? It was all us. All of it."

It's dead quiet around the table—so quiet, the gears turning inside my head must be audible.

"That was… Terra?" Horror colors my voice.

One of the others, Shannon, I think, answers. "Canyon turned Earth into one humungous petri dish. Tonya didn't even tell you half of it. Have you ever wondered why your prisons are full? Why so many people apparently disobey the law?" She laughs once, devoid of humor. "Well, that's because at least half are not from Earth; they are ours. Our criminals, shipped over to Earth to spend the rest of their most likely short natural lives there, leaving us with an intact and peaceful society that has the lowest crime rate since the beginning of records." She scowls, crossing her arms in front of her.

I'm completely petrified. All of that… All of that was Terra? We've been dealing with problems that weren't even our own, that were made for us to do research on us like guinea pigs?

I fall back into my chair and absentmindedly twirl my nose stud. "I don't know what to say." I have no words. None.

Tonya nods. "It was difficult for all of us to accept as well. We don't want to be the perpetrators responsible for the damage to your universe. We're all brothers and sisters, only separated by one single event that split our timelines."

A single event that equaled drawing the loser card for us—on many levels, apparently.

"How?" How can all of this have been staged? How could they do what they said they did without us noticing?

"Easy," Victor says, tipping off point by point from his fingers. "We first entered Earth decades ago, when you were vulnerable, right after WWII. We inserted our men high up, into leading positions. Silent infiltration. We made sure they got to where we needed them." His expression turns from disgust to complete seriousness, making him look much older. "It needs to stop, Noa. Earth is sliding down a slippery slope that won't be easy to stop as it is, but if Canyon continues…" He drums a silent rhythm onto the table. "We need to make a change. Terra needs to be stopped before it's too late for Earth." His green eyes burn with intensity. "And in the end, you're the one we've been waiting for, Noa."

I lean back as Victor leans forward.

"I know you want to go home. To us, you're the savior we've been waiting for. The one who's going to save Earth. It's you, Noa."

He nods as if to verify the bomb he just dropped on me.

"Help us defeat Canyon, and we'll get you home. Tit for tat."

CHAPTER THIRTEEN

Rough Times

"'Tit for tat?" I squeak. I didn't hear that right. Yes, everybody's eyes are on me, hopeful and expecting *something* of me, but that doesn't mean I heard that right.

They want me to help *defeat* Canyon. A Minister. So that I can get home.

"Are we sure about that?" I'm clinging to every little bit of hope there's been a mistake made somewhere. "I mean, Canyon said he needed more resources to cross me over, and after I helped him—"

Lucinda rolls her eyes and snorts. "He wants your help? Not for crossing. For re-election, yeah, because an Earthling crossing over to us is a threat right there. Your presence will be enough to give him the push he needs for re-election as president, and let's be honest, that's all he wanted since his co-president died and the executive power was taken from him." She falls back into her chair and crosses her arms.

Tonya covers my hand with hers on the table. "Exactly. He wouldn't send you back. You know too much. But he can—and will—use you for his own gain. But for us, you're the one who will help us win this battle, Noa." She squeezes my hand.

Yeah. There goes my hope for an auditory flaw.

And that's when my brain turns off. Simple as that.

Any moment now, the doom that always accompanies the raspy breathing and uprising panic must come. I can't *fight* with them. I'm not who they're looking for. I'm a stupid kid with panic attacks from a different universe who wants to go home.

Home.

A breath hitches in my throat and comes out like a choking sound. In a moment, I'll be rocking in a corner, I know it. Then they'll realize I'm not even able to fight for myself, let alone for somebody else.

Tonya looks at me full of hope, but I don't see it. "You're going to lead us through this. Finally, we have a fighting chance."

There is that word again, *fight*. I can't fight, I—

Everybody around me is talking all of a sudden, bombarding me with questions or information I can't process, until eventually Tonya picks up on my state of mind.

"Quiet, everybody!" she yells, and miraculously the voices stop. "Victor, take Noa to rest. We can adjourn and meet later again." The hand covering mine squeezes it again. "Take your time. I know it's a lot."

I feel myself nod and follow Victor out of the room. The excited chatters and whispers start up before I have the door closed behind me.

For the second time in fewer than thirty minutes, I don't know how I got from one place to another.

I walk the cold hallways wherever Victor directs me to, I turn when he tells me to, but I'm not truly present in my body. I must have gotten lost somewhere between Avery's betrayal and Victor's revelation that I'm supposed to save the world.

Correction: *two* worlds.

Neither of which I knew needed saving by me until ten minutes ago.

They can't have meant what they said. How am I supposed to—?

I heard them throw out words like *crossing over*, *adjustments*, and *home advantage*, but that doesn't explain anything to me, and I've got to say, my interest in *Terra—the Basics* is limited at this point. I feel like I got more than I bargained for already.

Victor opens the door to my room and enters first. He flings himself onto my bed on his back.

"Oh, dear." He crosses both arms behind his head. "Looks like we went a bit too rough on you, huh?" He sticks out his tongue at me while I close the door. "Should have taken it easy. I take it saving worlds usually isn't on your resume?" His cheekiness breaks me out of my shock.

"No, not until now, apparently," I say, unsure what to do with myself now that I'm in my room and blissfully panic-attack-free.

Victor pats the bed next to him. "Come here."

Uh, on the bed? That Victor is lying on?

The moment stretches until Victor rolls his eyes and sits up, tapping the bed next to him again. "There. Sitting. I don't bite, you know?"

I blush and keep my eyes downcast at the floor while I shuffle to the bed and sit down next to him—with twenty inches between us at least. *And* my hands folded in my lap.

Victor turns toward me, one leg half-crossed in front of him, and inadvertently bumping his knee into mine. I don't think he notices it, but I do.

"Look," he says, leaning his upper body back and supporting himself with his hands on my bed. "It's a lot, I get that. But we've been waiting for you since Canyon made crossing over almost impossible for us."

"How can you have waited for me?" Seriously. It feels like I'm in a bad movie.

Teenage girl, we need you to save the world with your special powers!

Yeah, sure. I have a free slot on my schedule tomorrow around lunch. Would that work?

"Well, technically not *you*-you, but somebody from Earth. I don't think we've ever had somebody cross over on their own, and Canyon doesn't bring Earthlings over. He adheres to a strict no-crossing policy for your people since all information he needs can be gathered in your universe. That way, he doesn't contaminate Terra." He frowns.

Contaminate Terra. "So I'm contaminating your world right

now?"

Victor pushes off and takes my hand that's been picking off lint from my pants. His skin is smooth and soft, missing the little bit of roughness of Avery's palm.

Avery, who sold me out.

My fingers twitch in Victor's, who completely misinterprets the movement and slides his fingers between mine. "According to Canyon, yes. See, that's the thing. Most Terrans don't know about Earth. It's a well-kept secret, and believe me, had you come out anywhere else but in the Reunification Building, you would have been thrown into a research bunker right away and never have surfaced again. Everybody working at the RUB and Bellevue Palace is government. Everybody knows about Earth, and everybody knows that if they speak a single word about it to civilians, they'd be gone. And I mean *gone*. Shipped off to Earth to never return, problem solved."

He traces a vein on the back of my hand, but I'm too distracted to be bothered by it.

"They don't know?" I ask. How can they not? How do you keep something that huge a secret? Somebody is bound to spill the news eventually, and… That's when I understand.

"So the Ghosts… you're the ones who know. That's why he's hunting you."

Victor gives me a quick thumbs-up before his hand cups mine again. "You got it. We're the only ones who know, and we're the ones nobody believes. We're the crazy ones, the terrorists disturbing peace on Terra."

"But the people who work for the government, they must know they're doing something wrong. They can't ignore what they're doing." Jeez, George was right with all his conspiracy theories.

"But it's all okay," Victor fake-argues. "It's only one small universe. There are countless others where the same people don't get researched on, where things went differently." He snaps his fingers like a magician. "To Canyon and his people, Earth is a copy of Terra they can use as they please. As if you had two books, exactly the same. One copy you treasure and take care of, the other one you doodle in because it's okay, it's only your backup copy."

My head swims with the news. Earth is the backup copy.

Only it isn't.

"But we're not the same," I whisper, my mouth suddenly dry. "It's not like we're a duplicate. Maybe we were at one point, but… it's been decades. Things have changed. People are alive in our universe who aren't in yours, and vice versa." I'm proof of that, it appears. "It's not like you could justify messing with one population because oh well, we've got more of exactly the same where we come from."

Victor's eyes sparkle at me as he gives me a mischievous grin. "You're catching on quickly. That's why the Ghosts exist. We'd like to free you from us, and us from universicide."

"Universicide?" Is that what I think it is?

"If Canyon continues the way he does… We don't think Earth is going to recover. It doesn't matter if other Earths will split off, unharmed. For this Earth—your home—we're the one chance it has. Every universe counts. Every single life in them does." He carefully lays my hand down on my thigh, caressing over it once.

Excuse me? Tad too personal here. I scoot back, creating distance.

Victor gets the hint and stands up. "Well, and on that bombshell, I'll let you get some sleep. Tonya said to let you rest anyway. I… I'll pick you up later. I'm pretty sure you're gonna have more questions then." He walks out, closing the door quietly behind him.

Alone.

I don't know what time it is, but my body is exhausted, and so is my mind. I'm at the mercy of others to bring me home. Everybody wants a piece of me for their own more or less obvious reasons. The Ghosts are upfront about it, which makes me feel at least a tad better, but Canyon… he pretended I could trust him only to ship me off to research.

I stare at the door Victor closed behind him. What did he say? *We never had anybody cross on their own.* Now it's my fault? I didn't do anything, I just…

I squeeze my eyes shut, pinching the bridge of my nose with my fingers. It must have been those stupid machines that sucked me right over and made me a play-ball in all of this. Had I known, I'd never have come near the Reichstag on my side of the Universe. Or maybe I would've pushed Kevan over first.

I rub my sleeve across my eyes, wiping away the little bit of moisture starting to form.

Quid pro quo is really starting to wear me down, and the hits keep on coming, one after the other. Not only am I stranded here, without my parents or any means to reach them, I'm also trapped in the middle between good and evil, or at least between wrongdoers and potential do-gooders—who knows? Obviously, I'm not an expert in judging people, or I would have never started to trust Avery.

To *like* Avery.

I let myself fall backward onto the bed, my hands blindly searching for the blanket.

My whole life I've been alone, or so I thought. Andrew and I were never that close, and my parents aren't the cuddly type. With me, at least.

It took getting thrown into another universe to realize what being alone truly meant.

Curling into a ball under the covers on top of the blissfully non-adjusting and quiet mattress, I cry for the first time since my life was uprooted and thrown into chaos.

I cry until I run out of tears, yet I can't stop.

So I cry and cry until I fall asleep, images of my parents and Avery dancing in front of my inner eye.

CHAPTER FOURTEEN

Eye-Opener

When I wake up, the lights are still on, but the chair next to my bed is pulled closer. Somebody dropped a set of black clothing similar to the Ghosts' outfits on it. For a moment, I wish I still had my old clothes, the ones I left in the Reichstag. Not that it mattered much, but I don't want to wear what Canyon provided, and neither do I want to turn into a Ghost. It would be too much of a sign that I'm with them when I haven't even digested the news yet.

Still, I get dressed and transfer all my nose studs into my current pants' pocket. At least the new clothes are warm. I need all the help I can get against the chill that had taken hold of me since I woke up here after my abduction. Or rescue. Or whatever.

Not even five minutes later, Victor announces himself with a knock at the door. "Thought you might like some food?" He opens the door wide for me, pressing a soft hand between my shoulder blades as he guides me through. I speed up a bit, and he drops it.

"You were out for quite some time. Terry got some food ready; he's the one responsible for that." He gives me a quick onceover. "You okay?"

"Guess so." In truth, I'm so hollow, a gust of wind could knock me over. While, yes, I slept, I only dreamed of Avery. Completely ridiculous and pathetic, but apparently, my subconscious mind has decided it needs to work on his betrayal some more.

I huff to myself. Betrayal.

How egocentric of me.

Nothing about Avery's actions was about me. It was all his job.

Victor chats away good-naturedly, apparently satisfied with my monosyllabic grunts and answers.

We enter the same room as before, only this time, there's food on the table. Everybody has a filled plate in front of them. They dig in, their conversations never fading. I can't tell whether this is breakfast, lunch, or dinner, because there's a bit of everything, from cereal to sandwiches to soup and meat. Reminds me a bit of a meal in the great dining hall during medieval times, especially with the high ceiling and spooky lighting.

Tonya gestures to the spot next to her, chewing on what looks like a turkey leg.

"Here." The guy next to me slides a plate filled to the brim over to me.

"Thank you… Hudson." If I remember correctly. Hudson smiles and gives me a thumbs-up. One hundred points to Noa for remembering a name.

For a while, I focus on eating while listening to the animated chatter around me. Every bite makes me feel better—well, my body. Everything else… I don't think about.

Eventually, Tonya pushes her plate away and claps. "Feel free to continue eating, but I'll go ahead and get started." Opening a satchel that hangs from the back of her chair she pulls out two items. "Kyle and the others brought this from the pod"—she holds up a flat, black piece of plastic, maybe the size of a small lighter—"and took this from the Sentinel." The black box she places on the table I remember only too well.

Rough hands on mine. "It won't hurt," he says.

I bite down on the inside of my cheek.

"Now, I accessed the GeneScreen and sent the information to Galileo but haven't heard back yet. The pod's program disc, we were able to unlock ourselves, but I'm pretty sure it was compromised during the attack. I was able to extract three more destinations we didn't know about before, but it would require confirmation before

we can act on it." She taps the plastic disc. "Interesting, though…
This thing here insists the pod was going to Forreston, Illinois, not
to Chicago, but then we know from Leiva she was supposed to go
to Chicago." Tonya nods at me.

Yeah, *she* was. For *research*.

I look down at the table and play with my napkin.

"No matter what, I would like to get the discussion going on
how to get Noa back to Earth, and how to set our plan in motion."
She looks around the table, waiting.

Me, I would like to focus on the part where we get me back
home. My tit for tats have a history of not working out for me so
well, a pattern that I'd like to break. No, that I *need* to break.

Shannon lowers her glass. "That's all well and good, but before
we get our hopes up, we need to make sure the basics are covered.
We all know Canyon. We all know what he likes to do." She looks
straight at me, raising a suspicious eyebrow. "You're not inked up,
are you?"

"Inked up?" Like, tattoos? I almost laugh out loud. Clearly, they
don't know me, or they're buying into the tough girl vibe the nose
stud gives off, even though today it's a harmless single drop-shaped
glitter stone.

Like the tears I've been crying.

Pathetic.

Shannon shrugs. "Well, if you're asking, you're probably not—"

"She isn't." Victor's cheeks take on a reddish hue. Everyone
looks at him.

"How do you know?" Tonya asks.

"How do you think?" Victor snaps. Tonya raises her eyebrows
higher and higher until Victor's blush deepens. "Well… when she
came in, she was unconscious, so I… I checked. Yes, I checked.
Happy now?" He glares at Tonya but ignores me.

Which is good, because I can only imagine what *checking me* would
entail.

My face burns with heat. He *checked* me—how far did he go?
Underwear? *No* underwear? My stomach cramps into a fist and

squirts bile up my throat. "You—"

"Look, it was just a quick scan. I promise I… behaved."

My mouth drops open. *Embarrassed* isn't even a strong enough word. Mortified. *Humiliated.* Mad.

Victor scratches the back of his head, his face the color of a tomato as he squirms in his seat.

Whatever he did, he didn't enjoy it.

At least that's something.

I snap my mouth closed again and take a deep breath. All things considered… I shoot a glare at Victor that's meant to kill, but I don't say anything. Priorities.

Tonya sighs. "*Thank you*, Victor, but next time, you will have a chaperone."

Or I'll cut off his hands.

Victor keeps his eyes downcast, nodding.

"Anyway." Tonya taps the table twice. "Usually, the first thing Canyon would do is ink you up, meaning giving you a deep tattoo with a very complex heavy metal ink that serves the sole purpose of prohibiting you from crossing back over. Like an anchor. This metal, vinculum, disrupts the wavelength needed to create a connection between the two universes. It makes it impossible for someone to cross, no matter in which direction. Canyon has a specialized facility somewhere in Paris, Earth, to produce this stuff. Send over the Terrans he wants to get rid of, ink them up, and keep them on Earth forever. Problem solved, especially since some of the metal is absorbed, so good luck trying to laser your tattoo. Great stuff, that vinculum." Her voice drips with sarcasm, and oh my god, prison tattoos serve a purpose? At least some of them? With the distraction of Tonya's revelation, the burn in my face slowly lessens, as does the sting of Victor checking me out while I was unconscious.

Then I remember something. "Is it black stuff, with a green shimmer to it, like mother of pearl?" That's what was in my cell and in Canyon's office. I had wondered about the strange stuff but hadn't paid much attention to it in the grand scheme of things.

"Correct." Tonya nods. "Vinculum tethers you to the world you receive it in. Nasty material; we've lost quite a few people on the other side because of it, thanks to Canyon." She frowns again, but something else catches my attention.

Click.

"Tethered? You said it *tethers* you to the world?" My heart makes a silly little leap powered by a sudden faith I didn't know I had.

"That's why they call it tethering somebody when they ink you up." Victor focuses on a hangnail rather than on me.

"Tethering," I breathe.

Tethering.

The world seems less dark than a moment before as my brain tries to add coincidences and oddities that might be neither.

Forreston, Illinois. Not Chicago.

Fingers tapping onto the pad inside the pod. "Chicago Ministry pre-programmed. Are you sure you want to—" A grumpy push of a button to silence the computer voice. "Code and new destination accepted."

I feel a rush of hope and the knowledge that while I may be stranded for now, I'm not alone.

I'm not fighting this alone.

"Avery." The word leaves my mouth like it's the solution to all my problems.

I remember it so clearly. Toshi chewing out Avery for not following orders, Avery saying it wasn't right. "He didn't want to tether me," I whisper barely audible, my heart leaping up like a frog during spring.

"What?" Tonya tilts her head.

Of course, none of the others are following my train of thought, and how could they? How could they know Avery is on my side and probably has been there all along?

My face splits into a wide grin. "Avery. The Sentinel. He never—"

A sudden harsh knock at the door interrupts me, mainly because the person knocking doesn't even wait for a reply. The same man Victor and I met at the bottom of the stairs down in the dungeon bursts through the door.

Uh-oh.

"Tonya," he rasps. Working to breathe, the man bends over and rests his hands on his knees to get some air into his lungs. "The Sentinel—"

Victor is already up on his feet. "What?"

The man wheezes, then pushes out his next sentence. "He's torn himself off the wall. He… He's taken a hostage."

Victor groans while the room erupts in nervous whispers. "Whom did he take?"

As if it mattered. Avery would beat any one of them with his hands tied behind his back—or to the wall, it appears. I've seen him fight Leiva, a trained Sentinel.

"Pearson. He has Pearson. And…" Another wheeze. "And if he doesn't get to speak to *her*"—he points at me—"he will tear off Pearson's fingers one by one. Or something like that."

Victor groans again. "Damn it. I like Pearson." He shoots a quick look toward Tonya, confirming something before he addresses the wide-eyed man again. "Is he still behind bars?"

The man nods heftily.

"Good. Then we still have an advantage. We're not giving in to his *requests*, and we need to get Pearson out, or he is as good as dead. Get the narcotics ready and—"

I jump up and push my chair back before my mind is officially made up. "No," I shout, already sprinting for the door. "We'll give him what he wants."

The rest of the leadership gang stares at me open-mouthed as I dash past them, but I don't care. I can fix this. For all of us.

"Noa, wait!" Victor yells as a chair topples backward and crashes to the floor.

I don't wait. I know I can fix this—I *need* to fix this. My feet hit the broken concrete so fast, I barely keep from stumbling and falling twice before I'm even out the door, but I don't slow down.

Victor grabs me by the arm, trying to slow me down. "Where do you think you're going?"

I twist away and keep running down the hallway. My memory comes back little by little, each step a bit more until I turn around the corner into the first hallway I ever set foot in inside this Haunted House. "The dungeon, of course." I hiss. "You're not knocking him out again. He's on our side."

A harsh fake laugh comes from behind me, slightly cut short. "You're not serious. What makes you think that?"

I reach the door to the basement. If Victor overpowers me now and takes me back, I will have lost. So will Avery.

I spin around and face him, searching his eyes for a little bit of doubt about Avery, or at least a little bit of trust for me—trust that I'm not completely off my rocker. "He didn't tether me, Victor. Canyon gave him the order, and he ignored it. Even after a superior chewed him out for it, he didn't do it." I pause and catch my breath. "He said it was wrong." Somehow, it seems a bit too personal to tell this last part, especially because I only discovered it by eavesdropping myself, but it's paramount Victor understands. "I don't think he's a danger to us."

Victor stares at me open-mouthed. "You mean that. You really do," he says, clearly flabbergasted, as if I'd just declared the world flat.

"Yeah, I do." And with that, I open the door to the basement, take a deep breath, and walk down the stairs. My legs melt into pudding from the short sprint and the anxiety of seeing Avery again, now that everything has changed.

Four wide-shouldered men block the view in front of Avery's cell, and frankly, none of them look too friendly, although their scowls can't possibly match Avery's.

"I said *move back* or this one pays for it." Avery growls and tightens his hold around his hostage's neck. Pearson's neck.

Pearson squeaks once, then coughs.

Victor curses once. He pushes himself past the other four men, only to be held back by one of them before he all but storms into the cell. "You bastard," he hisses at Avery, "you cunning, stinking bastard. Haven't you done enough damage already? If you hurt Pearson—"

"Back off and get me Noa," Avery barks. He can't see me yet

hidden behind all those big guys, although I'm right there.

I'm right here.

Victor tears himself loose from the guard. "I'll have you—"

"Let me." I push past the men and place a calming hand on Victor's arm, interrupting him midsentence.

After a quick look at Victor the guard opens the door. If he'd closed it any faster behind me, he'd take off my butt with it. With every step into the cell, the sweat drops on Pearson's forehead grow bigger and bigger. No kidding he's nervous.

Not me, though.

Not Avery.

The closer I get, the more he relaxes. Well, relax in an Avery kind of way. His fists aren't balled quite so tightly, the muscles in his jaw not bulging quite like crazy anymore. This isn't easy for him, but we have to work with what we've got.

I stop right in front of him. "Avery." I grasp his burning hot hands and gently push them down, away from Pearson's throat. "I'm here." I keep pushing until they loosen enough so that Pearson can take a deep breath in.

Eventually, he lowers his gaze to meet mine. "Are you okay?" It's a soft murmur, full of hesitation and wariness, but so low, nobody besides me will hear the edge to it.

"I'm fine. They only wanted to talk."

"They can do that with me next to you."

"I guess they're not big fans of Sentinels."

"The feeling is mutual." He growls. "And I really don't like to be restricted." He shoots another glare back toward Victor.

I chuckle once. "So you decided to throw a tantrum to get out of here?"

To his credit, Avery blushes the slightest bit. "A very adult tantrum. I threatened to tear his head off, one vertebrae at a time."

So not the fingers. Vertebrae. "Very adult." I roll my eyes, but I can't hold back the smile that's forcing its way through everything that's happened.

For a second, Avery closes his eyes, and when he opens them

again, the amber shines just as warm as when he kept vigil at my bedside, after Leiva attacked me. "Well, it worked, didn't it?"

Yeah, it did. And that's not all.

"I know what you did," I say quietly. "You didn't tether me."

Avery blushes for real, sucking in his lower lip. "You know?"

I nod. "I heard you and Toshi." If I expected him to get mad at me, he doesn't.

"I couldn't do it," he whispers hoarsely with a sad smile on his face. "I always follow orders, Noa. I always do. It's what brought me to where I am, despite what I am. But this time…" He blows out a harsh puff of air. "I couldn't do it."

I give his hand a squeeze. "I know." That's why I suddenly feel so light, so alive and free.

"Victor," I call out over my shoulder without taking my eyes or hands off Avery, "I'd like Avery with me, please."

The silence that follows is so complete, I wonder for a moment if I turned deaf.

"You're kidding me," Victor says from somewhere behind me. "Canyon's pet? Him?"

Avery's gaze on me does not waver.

"Yeah," I say. "Him."

CHAPTER FIFTEEN

The Other Point of View

"And you're sure I don't need to do anything else with it?" I wrap the bandage around Avery's chafed wrists. His skin has definitely seen better times. Much better times. Turns out that while his body is stronger than the average human's, his skin will tear just the same. While he was able to pull the iron chains out of the wall instead of his wrists off his body, his skin didn't do so well. Would be nice if they had a nurse here, but as it is… the Ghosts are mostly self-sufficient.

Avery keeps his eyes trained on me taking care of his wounds. "It will heal. Quickly."

"An Aug?" It would make sense, making your soldiers not only strong, but giving them faster recovery.

"Not in the sense that you're referring to, but yes. Genetically altered. A benefit of being a Sentinel."

Speaking of being a Sentinel… "Avery? Why didn't you tell me you weren't going to bring me to Canyon?" I could've gotten him out of the cell sooner. I wouldn't have doubted him.

He flexes and curls the fingers on the hand I'm wrapping. The pause before he answers is so long, I begin to wonder if he's going to ignore my question. When he finally speaks, his voice has dropped to a whisper.

"Because I was telling myself if I didn't say it out loud, I could ignore what I was doing. Blame it on… something. Temporary lapse in judgement. Anything but a well-informed decision, because... I don't defy orders, Noa. That's not me. I obey. I stick to the rules. And yet I couldn't bring you to Chicago and hand you over to Canyon's men. I couldn't." The last words are barely audible.

I smooth out a wrinkle in the dressing. "Thank you for that. Would've really sucked if they locked me away."

Pause.

"Yeah. It would've." The expression on his face is unreadable. Chills erupt over the skin of my neck, bringing with them a tingle all the way down to my toes. Did he mean because he would've missed—

"Because Canyon would have never let you leave." Avery curls his fist once more, then relaxes it.

Oh. Right. I mean, of course. Duh. I crank my neck. "Uh, where were you going to bring me anyway?"

His breath hitches. "To my brother."

My gaze flies up to his. "Your brother?" I mean, I know that he had a sibling, or else he wouldn't be a second child and First Class Sentinel, but...

"He lives in Forreston, Illinois. It was worth a try." I feel his stare on my face, which must be burning from his proximity. A gentle finger taps my nose stud. "You changed it again."

Lightning zips through my skin and settles inside my heart, stealing my breath.

The pause I need to compose myself is longer than any of Avery's. "You... You noticed?" I find the little piece of jewelry and twirl it. The tear needed to go. It didn't feel right for today anymore, and the exchange only took three seconds at most, done while Victor released Avery from his chains. I opted for my tiny silver feather— for freedom, for feeling light, for taking flight. I thought it appropriate.

A tiny smile tugs on the corners of Avery's mouth. "Of course," he says so matter-of-factly, my chest cramps up.

Of course.

He looks up toward the door of this small, improvised nurse's office at the scowling figure watching every single move we make. "He doesn't trust me."

Victor hasn't left our side since I took Avery from the cell. I can practically feel him stare a hole into my back, glaring at us. Well, at Avery, mostly.

I shrug and finish the dressing. "I don't know if I trust him completely myself, so there we go." I murmur to keep Victor from picking up on it. I hesitate for a moment. "They… They say they can get me back, Avery. All I have to do is help them."

I'm a bit blurry on the details, unfortunately.

His gaze flies back to mine. "So the rumors are true? They truly believe Terra is harming Earth in some kind of big experiment?"

I tear a piece of medical tape off a roll. "You don't think it's true?" Maybe I'm too naive, too gullible. Maybe I *want* to believe somebody else is at fault for our own shortcomings.

Avery stares at my hands holding his. "I don't know anymore," he whispers. "I used to be sure of so many things… so many things that have gone up in smoke over the last few days."

"Same here," I whisper back. "Same here." The amber in his eyes shifts to a warmer tone. I've only seen a handful of First Class Sentinels so far, but they all had golden eyes, probably a feature that comes with the job. Even if not, Avery's eyes are the most beautiful I've ever seen.

"Are you guys done yet?" Victor, still leaning on the doorframe, crosses his arms. "We've got stuff to do, you know, like, saving a world or two."

Torn out of the spell that had me, I clear my throat and turn Avery's large hand over in mine. Gotta make sure I got all the scrapes and cuts, right?

"We're done." No reason to prolong the inevitable.

Victor pushes off the frame. "Let's go. He'll be fine."

Avery slowly pulls his hand out of mine. "Thank you." His fingertips graze over mine in what must be an accidental touch. Doesn't mean it doesn't send sparks all the way down to my toes.

"S-Sure," I stammer, swiping a strand of hair out of my face.

Victor leads the way to the conference room. Noisy chatter seeps through the doors—until we enter the room and everybody's attention is on us.

On Avery.

It's so quiet, I could hear a needle fall.

Tonya jumps up, her chair toppling over behind her. "Victor?" It sounds more like an order for an explanation than a question.

Victor rolls his eyes and sighs, gesturing at Avery. "Everyone, meet Canyon's pet—"

"Avery," I say in a loud voice, then push out from behind the two guys. "His name is Avery."

A muscle in Victor's jaw twitches. "Everyone, meet *Avery*. Avery, meet the Ghosts."

Avery nods curtly. "Pleasure." I'm not sure he meant it seriously or not, but I don't pick up on any sarcasm. Maybe that makes it extra-sarcastic.

Terry huffs. "The Sentinel? What the hell, Victor?"

Ten pairs of eyes glare at us.

"Yes, the Sentinel," Victor says with an eyeroll. "If we could please get over the shock and back to business, that would be just wonderful." He points to the chair I sat in before I stormed out. "Noa… Avery. Sit." In a move that's surprisingly thoughtful given his obvious dislike of Avery, Victor pulls a chair from somewhere and puts it next to mine, placing Avery between Tonya and myself.

Three minutes later, he has explained Avery's presence, and while everybody is a bit more relaxed, that doesn't mean they'd look at him friendly.

Quite the opposite.

Tonya scoots a little bit away from Avery, creating distance. "You're Canyon's First Sentinel, aren't you?"

Avery nods. "Yes."

"You're the one who kept us from getting the Rhodium transport the other week. We could have used that for farming."

"It wasn't yours to take."

Tonya cocks her head. She keeps her eyes trained at Avery, silent for the longest time. Neither of them blinks. "I don't trust you."

"And I wouldn't expect you to," Avery replies calmly, "but what would you like me to do? Pledge my loyalty? Obviously, that doesn't mean much, or I wouldn't be here." His tone carries a little bit of a bite.

Tonya nods, cool eyes sweeping over Avery, as if looking for weaknesses. "And exactly that is my problem with you. A Sentinel who defies orders? How am I supposed to believe that it was your decision to not bring her to Chicago, and not Canyon's order from the get-go? You could be part of his plan to find our group, to take us down. Bait to infiltrate the Ghosts." She glowers at him.

"You're overestimating the importance of your single group," Avery replies, still keeping up the stoic mask of unaffected calm. "And you're welcome to keep me under supervision."

"Oh, we will," Victor adds. "We'll make sure you're on our side, PBM."

Avery stiffens while some of the others take a sharp breath in and the room's temperature drops by several degrees.

After a pause that seems too long, Avery looks straight at Victor. "I'm sure you will." His tone is icy, his hands clenched and hidden under the table, the veins on their back bulging.

PBM? Did Victor just call him a nasty name?

Tonya taps her pen on the table in a distracting fast rhythm, her eyes narrowed to slits. "Okay then. This is what we'll do." She points at me. "Noa, he is your responsibility. Right now, we're your only chance of getting home, so if that's what you want, you keep an eye on him."

Of course. There's always a condition I have to adhere to. Not that I mind this one, but still.

Tonya points at Victor. "Victor, regular precautions should be sufficient, mainly because I assume that if this is a trap, it's already snapped shut and we're too late anyway. Everybody, no killing him in his sleep. If what he says is true, he's stuck with us for sure and might actually be of use."

Murmurs rise up around the table, some angry and harsh, some quiet and soft. Overall, I'm glad nobody seems to think I'm unfit for the job, mainly because I don't want Avery back in a cell because they don't trust him.

Victor holds up his hands. "Quiet, guys. I know this isn't ideal, but we have a plan, and we're not going to let one single Sentinel derail it. Focus, please."

And just like that, the whispers die down and the stares stop. Avery relaxes a little bit, meaning he doesn't sit quite so straight anymore. Tonya twists in her chair and pulls a thick bundle of papers out of her messenger bag, unfolding them in front of her. My breath gets stuck in my throat.

"Business, people. Canyon has at least five portals to Earth that we know of. This one here"—she points to a dot on the map, somewhere around the Chicago area—"is closest to where we are, which means it's the one we'll use. Time is of the essence."

"Use it for what?" Avery asks. He's a bit behind the curve.

"To cross to Earth," Victor answers, regarding Avery coolly. "We cross, we get the evidence of Terra's involvement and destruction on Earth, we come back, and we show the public what has been done to other humans in our name. They'll finally see we were right all along."

He raises a challenging eyebrow at Avery, as if daring him to say something else. Avery remains unimpressed. "Evidence, I see. So you truly believe Terra enslaves Earth."

Victor jumps up from his chair. "Watch it, Sentinel. You know exactly what's going on—everybody does! You know Terra can cross over! You know we're doing research there. You know you were made to recognize and fight the army that Canyon fears but will never come!"

Avery leans onto the table, calm and completely in control, the exact opposite of Victor. "You are right, yet completely wrong. Yes, I know we can cross. Yes, I know we're doing research there. No, I don't think we're enslaving Earth. No, I don't mind being prepared for an attack that might never come." He tilts his head, waiting for Victor's reply.

"Ha! How typical of a made-to-order pet! Of course you would be siding with them, you—"

"That's enough." Tonya holds up her palm at Victor, then glowers at Avery. "You too. You're a guest here, and while I'm allowing you free speech, I won't have you question our values."

"So much for free speech then," Avery says, but then drops it and leans back into his chair, for my taste leaving me way too much on display for Tonya next to him. "One more question, though. Assuming you make it through to Earth, you get this evidence, and against all odds, you make it back through another portal to Terra, what do you plan to do with it? You're still only the Ghosts. Nobody is going to believe you."

A self-assured grin crosses Tonya's face. "They will. They'll believe everything they see if the evidence comes from one of our own, a Terran implanted on Earth so deeply, he has the power to influence over half of what Canyon needs." Her eyes take on a little glint. "What better proof could we have than the accessed memories of an augmented Terran on Earth?"

Listening to Avery, Tonya, and Victor makes me feel hot, then cold, then hot again. Everything is way over my head, yet here I am, trapped in-between and only understanding half of it.

"I can't access somebody's Augs," I say, my voice annoyingly thin. "I wouldn't even know how to recognize a Terran." Or how to approach him.

Hey, sorry, could I ram a USB stick or something into the back of your skull and I promise I'll be gone again?

I doubt it's going to be that easy.

Tonya points a thumb over her shoulder at Victor. "Well, you'll have Victor with you. He's responsible for getting the data and making sure that everything runs smoothly from our end, but we need you to get through Earth without complications. Imagine how stranded you would be in Terra without a guide. Either of us would stick out on Earth like a sore thumb, and we can't afford to lose any more people."

Okay, while that sounds minimally better, I'm still a bit unclear about the details. "And… whom exactly do we need to track down?" Not that it makes much of a difference.

Looking at the map in front of her, Tonya finds a blue, hand-drawn circle. "Robert Dunnam at Meyer Industries."

My mouth drops open. Not what I wanted to hear.

"Robert Dunnam?" *The* Robert Dunnam, founder of Meyer Industries and the biggest entrepreneur on the whole East Coast, if not the entire country? The one who owns factories left and right and turns everything he touches into money? The one who got elected Illinois junior senator last year and intends to run for president next term? *The* Robert Dunnam?

Completely unaware of my rising panic, Tonya nods. "Correct. Our research has shown there is only one Robert Dunnam in Chicago on Earth."

Her naiveté is so out of place, I laugh.

This is doomed, right from the beginning. "Getting to him is impossible." I shake my head. "He's the most famous man in all of Chicago. I won't be of help to you. Yes, I'm from Earth, but I'm a teenager. What am I supposed to do? Ring his doorbell? Get past his security and simply ask to see his Augs?"

This is ridiculous. I could very well be asking to meet with the President of the United States, although that might actually be easier.

"Victor will take care of that part, you—"

Avery huffs loudly.

Tonya turns icy. "Anything you would like to add, Sentinel?"

Avery straightens up again, holding her eyes. "Are you sure you want to know? Because there are actually a couple of things on my mind right now."

Tonya puts her pen onto the map in front of her, keeping it exactly parallel to the paper's lines. "Please, be my guest. And while you're at it—and while I still don't trust you—I'll give you a chance to prove your new loyalties to us."

Avery's eyebrows lift all the way to the top of his head, making Tonya smirk ever-so-slightly. She knows the ball is in her court, and she's gearing up for an ace.

"Get us into the facility that houses the portal. I know you have access to it," says Tonya.

Avery shakes his head. "What makes you think I'll do that? That's a big favor you ask."

"Not so much a favor. A necessity. We need to cross, you need a place to stay. You defected. We would lose more people taking the portal by force, and you wouldn't stand a chance alone if we set you free. Not if you like your mind, that is." She taps her temple and pauses. "Plus, there's the little fact that you went against orders—*presumably* went against orders—to get her away from Canyon. If you truly developed something like a conscience, you know it's the right thing to do."

I really don't like being referred to as just *her*.

Avery lifts his chin up. "Just to be clear. Nothing about this is a good idea. Getting into the portal with an access code is doable, but crossing might not be. It might be a one-way street no matter what. And once you hit Earth, he"—Avery jerks his chin at Victor—"will have no way back and three days at the most with the way rejection is going. Three days of pain and misery, unless—"

"We have a one-directional Bridge, and we will have a modulator," Tonya says.

That gets Avery's attention. "Really? A Bridge? Illegal for the last fifteen years and notoriously unreliable, but all right. *And* a modulator. Curious. Then why don't I see one on Noa?" He looks pointedly at my wrist and back at Tonya, who blushes.

"Because we'll steal it in the portal on our way to Earth," she says.

"And because for Earthlings on Terra, the rejection is presumably way less than for Terrans on Earth. By our calculations, she should have at least two years before the symptoms set in, and for another two, she could survive with medical care. We're not like your people, like Canyon. We don't condemn anyone to death by imprisoning them in a universe that rejects them." Victor hisses from across the table. "Maybe you shouldn't talk about things your simple mind is obviously not made to understand."

Symptoms? Wait, what symptoms? *Survive what?* My head turns back and forth between Avery, Tonya and Victor, like in a three-way tennis match I can't make sense of.

Avery chuckles. "A simple mind it might be, but also one trained by the Sentinel Forces." He looks around the table. Some of the Ghosts radiate open hostility, but most are mainly curious. This must be the best show they've gotten in a while.

Avery nods to himself once. "Do you know what's going to happen when—or if—you come back with your evidence? Because I do. There are only two scenarios, and neither one is looking good for you." He counts them off his fingers. "One. Your evidence is negligible and Canyon ignores it, and unfortunately so does the general public. You don't gain one inch, and all of this was for nothing, including potential casualties."

The room is dead quiet. Despite being the new guy and the quote-unquote enemy, Avery has them under his spell, Sentinel confidence and all.

"Two. You get exactly what you wanted, though that is very unlikely, and start informing the general public. As soon as Minister Canyon realizes you're a threat, the Sentinel Forces will change from basic control-and-containment to active pursuit. He'll not only discredit you like he does now, he'll activate the Sentinel Forces to Code Green, and we *will* hunt you down."

"*We.*" Victor layers the word with implication as he crosses his arms in front of his chest.

Avery ignores it. He looks around at everyone watching him. "If you think you have it rough right now, it'll be nothing compared to what happens when we go to alert status. Nothing. That's what the Sentinel Forces have been trained to do. We will hunt you, find you, and destroy you one splinter group at a time, and not only the Ghosts. Every person buying your story will suffer the same fate. Every riot will be broken down with force, all dissent will be drowned as soon as it arises."

He looks straight at Tonya. "You go public with convincing evidence, and I guarantee Canyon will strike back without mercy to keep Earth a secret. That is the contingency plan. The Sentinel Forces will not hold back, no matter if Ghost or civilian." He pauses, making his next sentence exceptionally clear.

"What you're suggesting is homicide on a grand scale."

CHAPTER SIXTEEN

Bad News

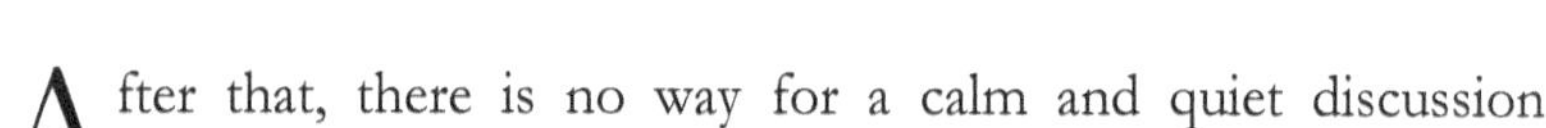

After that, there is no way for a calm and quiet discussion anymore.

Words and curses fly high and low until eventually Tonya has enough and breaks up the assembly, sending everybody off to calm down and postponing the meeting until tomorrow morning at 6 A.M.

As soon as she says the word, the others storm out, leaving Avery and me in the room, with Victor across from us. Victor, who can barely hide his disgust.

"Well done, Sentinel," he snaps. "Should have left you behind bars."

Avery stands and straightens to his full height. "You should have never attacked our pod," he counters, regarding Victor coolly from above.

Victor jumps up, his hands balled to fists. "If your government didn't—"

"Guys!" I'm the last one up, my hands out like I'm trying to separate two fighting toddlers. "Let it go. Seriously, let it go," I repeat again for emphasis, and when neither of them picks up their bickering, I breathe a sigh of relief.

"If you don't mind, I could use some rest. It's been a long day." And my catnap didn't help. At all.

Victor bites his tongue. "Sure." He leads us out of the conference room, down the hallways toward where my room is, then opens

128

another creaking door across from mine. "Your room. Don't break anything. There's no way out of here, not even for you."

Avery steps past Victor, holding the door open. "Wouldn't leave without Noa anyway." He says it so casually, it takes me a full two or three seconds to process it before something flutters up inside my chest and stomach.

Butterflies.

Fluttering, dancing butterflies.

I never knew they could take flight in somebody's stomach for real, but it turns out they can. Not even Victor's strained silence can bring them to settle down. Instead, they make me feel light, like when I found out Avery was on my side.

Throwing one last glance at Avery inside his room, I sneak into mine and almost close the door in Victor's face.

His hand catches it just before the impact. "Hey, I… I wanted to make sure you're okay… with everything." He follows me in, leaving the door slightly ajar behind him.

I fall into the chair he pulled next to my bed when I first woke up here.

He's asking if I'm okay with everything, but *everything* encompasses so much, I don't even know how to answer that. I blow out a puff of air and decide to answer to the part of the question he probably meant. "I guess I am. What other choice do I have? I need to get back to my parents, that much is clear. If you're my only chance…" Tit for tat.

I play with the little silver feather. Whatever I need to do to get back home. There's no other option. After being taken from Canyon and held by the Ghosts, I doubt the Minister would take me back in like a long-lost daughter. Not after everything that Avery said about hunting the Ghosts down, or people who spread information about Earth.

An idea hits me. "Maybe Avery should join us. He could help, and maybe he could stay. On Earth. Away from Canyon, I mean." My face warms. But come on: two birds, one stone. The Ghosts get help, and Avery doesn't need to fear being caught by Canyon.

Victor lowers himself to sit on the corner of the bed, a much more restricted approach than last time when he threw himself onto my mattress. He's giving me *that* look, the look I hate, because I've gotten it way too often in my life already. It's the expression people wear before giving bad news, like *your brother just died*, or *your parents have cancer.*

He sighs through pursed lips. "You really don't know, do you?" His face is full of pity, and it's making my stomach sour.

"Don't know what?"

"Tough to say where to start. Well, first of all, he can't come with you, at least not for long. Even if we got a modulator for him, they run out of power cells after a couple of years, and then he'd be dead pretty quickly because we wouldn't have any means to keep up the supply."

So the modulator really is *that* important. "You need a modulator to keep the universe from rejecting you?" Sounds like a bad cancer treatment.

Victor nods. "Yup. It's different for you here because our universe hasn't been sensitized against Earthlings yet, but Earth...." He shrugs. "Earth doesn't like us quite so much anymore."

And Avery wanted to make sure I got a modulator, first with Canyon, then with Toshi, and now with the Ghosts.

The butterflies all lift up at the same time, soaring high.

Victor swings his legs around so that he faces me. "And... I don't know what else is going on, and I'm going out on a limb here, but..." He smiles at me carefully, but then turns serious. "He will never reciprocate, Noa. Never. He can't. Whatever you might hope for, it won't happen. He's wired differently, he's programmed to be alone. Do you get what I'm saying?"

A sharp pain slices my chest. "He—"

Victor leans forward, laying one warm hand on my knee. "That's the way they make 'em, Noa. I'm surprised this one developed something close to a conscience, but feelings..." He shakes his head, and all the butterflies sink down to the pit of my stomach. "Feelings won't happen. That's why you don't get involved with a Sentinel. It doesn't happen. You stick to unmodified humans. There are better options than him."

Something drops to the floor outside my room and I jerk.

Victor squeezes my knee once for emphasis before he gets up. "I'll pick you up tomorrow morning. Sleep well, Noa." He gives me one more tight nod, then heads out, his blond ponytail swaying behind him. I stay rooted to my chair in the middle of the almost dark room, stunned into silence.

"He will never reciprocate."

Never reciprocate, as in… I don't know, as in what? My mind knows the answer already, but my heart hasn't yet digested the news. *"He's programmed to be alone. Feelings won't happen."*

I work on a dry swallow, my tongue's movement against the roof of my mouth like parchment over sandpaper.

It's not important and it shouldn't bother me. Not at all.

Yet I feel like somebody pulled the rug from under my feet.

No. It doesn't bother me.

I don't know why I'm reacting like this, I—

I swipe away the one tear that threatens to roll down my face.

I'm good.

I just need to be home.

CHAPTER SEVENTEEN

Still Good

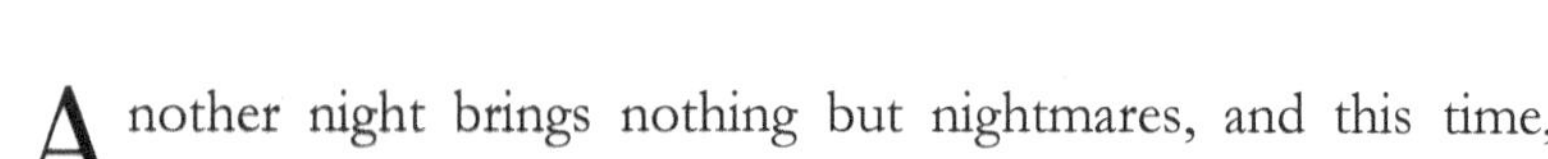

Another night brings nothing but nightmares, and this time, they're so bad, the third one makes me jerk up with a little cry. Yeah, I keep myself awake after that.

My subconscious had a blast bringing me back home, only to rub it in my face how badly my parents were doing.

I know they must be devastated, losing me so shortly after Andrew. Confused. Hurt. What if they thought I ran away from them because I couldn't stand them being sick?

Or maybe they're not thinking anything at all, a tiny voice whispers, that thought, the worst of all.

I'm dressed already in a black Ghost-outfit that has seen better days, but I'm still lying on the bed, staring at the curved ceiling and yellow light above me, when a knock on the door tears me out of my thoughts.

"Come in," I call out, fully expecting Victor to waltz in here, throwing himself onto my bed or whatever.

Instead, it's Avery.

And seeing him hurts, though it shouldn't.

"Good morning, Noa." His deep baritone resonates through me, and a couple of those butterflies respond by showing weak signs of life.

I swallow hard and ignore them. "Hey, Avery," I reply, sitting up on the bed. "Sleep well?"

He leaves the door open and shrugs, his hands stuffed in his pockets, for the first time almost looking his age and not like the soldier he is. He said they took him from his family when he was six. Soldier training instead of kindergarten. It shows.

"Not much," he says, looking around the room like it was the most interesting thing in the world. "Guess I'm not used to not being on the job."

Which would be my fault then. If it weren't for me, he'd still be with the Minister, for what that's worth. I was just too busy being miserable to notice what he did for me.

I swipe that annoying strand of hair behind my ear and slide off the bed. "You know, I don't think I've ever thanked you." The closer I get to Avery, the more the amber in his eyes seems to shine, and the more I pick up on his typical scent, something very Avery-specific with a hint of… sunshine. With that thought, my face warms and I really hope I'm not blushing.

Sunshine. *Really, Noa?*

I clear my throat. "So, thank you. For not delivering me to research. For not tethering me. For—"

"No need to thank me." He shakes his head.

I've stepped so close, I have to crane my neck to look up to him. He's broad-shouldered anyway, but from my perspective down here, he looks like a giant. A bit of stubble has grown on his face, emphasizing the high cheekbones and giving him a rugged look. Not that he needed it. The little bruise on his face is still there but much fainter already, proof of his enhanced healing abilities as a Sentinel.

Ex-Sentinel.

His lips quirk up into the hint of a smile, and only now do I realize I've been staring. A stab of something shoots through my stomach, like lightning, making the butterflies flutter up once before they fall dead to the ground again, killed by the memory of Victor's words.

He won't reciprocate.

Then why is he looking at me like this?

One-Mississippi…

Two-Mississippi…

Three-Mississippi…

And still he holds my eyes captive.

I take a deep breath. "Avery—"

"He's right."

"What?"

"Victor. His 1-0-1 on the secrets of Sentinel life."

"His—"

"Yes. He was right. Sentinels are made to stay alone. That's how we serve our world best. Minimizes distractions and keeps our priorities straight." He hesitates. "My life… My life is a boat built for one, Noa." Avery keeps his eyes straight ahead. If I heard a hint of bitterness, I don't see it in his face. He'd make a robot envious with his composure.

"A boat for one?" Victor was right, and Avery will never—

The door flies open with a bang. "Rise and shine!"

In an instant, Avery's eyes lose the softness they held a moment ago and take on that dangerous shimmer I saw twice before: once in my room against Leiva, and once against the Ghost in the tunnel. His body tenses and his muscles bulge, his jaw tightening.

"Beautiful day," says Victor as he walks around Avery, his blue eyes like the sky, his shoulder-length blond hair loose and falling down the sides of his face like a perfect frame.

My heart hammers, but it has nothing to do with Victor.

"Good morning, Noa," he says with a smile. Avery gets a cursory glance. "PBM," he adds like an afterthought, and it sounds considerably less friendly.

Then his focus is back on me. He doesn't see Avery's jaw tighten even more. He doesn't see the way his whole body added another layer of tension.

I do.

Victor completely ignores Avery and wraps an arm around my shoulders.

"Today is going to be a great day. Lots of planning how to get you home. Excited? Yeah, me too. We're going to be an awesome team over there. Earth, wow. Can't wait!"

He gives me a smile and wink and leads me away from Avery, shooting the shortest of annoyed looks at him. "Let's go. Breakfast, then planning."

"But—" I twist back to Avery, whose whole posture radiates a struggle for restraint.

"No *buts*. Great day. I'm telling you. *Great* day."

He steers me out of the room, chatting about today when all I want is to go back to Avery and continue where we left off, and, while I'm at it, apologize for what Victor said, whatever it meant.

"You know, I'm so glad it's you who crossed over." Victor's thumb smooths over my shoulder in little circles.

"Me?" I roll my shoulders in, but Victor only holds me closer.

"Yup, you. I don't think you know, because why would you, but I'm one of the few people actually born in the Resistance. I was born a Ghost." The pride in his voice is obvious.

"Oh, uh, cool." I'm probably lacking enthusiasm, but Victor doesn't pick up on it.

"Indeed. But that also means everybody else is way older. In fact, you're the youngest person to be with us since…" He leads us around the last corner toward the same conference room we've been in before. By now, this maze is starting to make sense to me. "I think since I was ten or eleven. Usually, people don't leave the warm nest the GU has built for them until they can see a bit more clearly what's going on, maybe in their thirties or forties. And usually, it's guys, so… Well, you being you is a double-plus for me."

"Uh, awesome," I add lamely. So I'm the catch of the day for him?

Avery snorts. Victor's hand tightens.

"Anyway," Victor continues extra cheerfully, "I figured tonight we should celebrate our upcoming trip to Earth. You, me, dinner. Whaddaya think?"

Now, I'm not an expert, but I'm pretty sure I know in which direction this is going, and it's not one I want to take.

"I didn't know you had fancy restaurants down here," says

Avery, his voice cool, saving me from providing an answer to Victor's question.

Victor whirls around so fast, he almost shoves me off-balance. "You have something to say, *PBM?*"

The moment the switch is flipped is so obvious to me, I wonder how Victor can't see it, how he can't bring his hands up to protect himself before Avery slams into him and both of them are pressed against the wall, Avery's forearm pushing into Victor's throat, cutting off his air supply.

"Indeed, *Ghost,*" Avery hisses back at a frantically struggling Victor. "You watch what you're saying—to both of us—or I swear, you will have to make your trip to Earth with three extremities instead of four." He leans in close for a lingering angry stare, then pushes off, leaving Victor coughing and gagging. Avery brushes off his palms on his sleeves, as if he'd dirtied himself. "Glad we talked that out." He opens the door next to a bent-over and wheezing Victor.

"Noa?"

Now, I could make sure Victor is okay. I could help him up and scold Avery for hurting him.

I *could.*

Instead, I walk through the door Avery holds open for me.

"Thank you."

And it's not only the door I'm talking about.

CHAPTER EIGHTEEN

Not as Planned

Needless to say, the atmosphere is quite icy during our morning meeting.

While Avery is his usual business-self, Victor scowls at him from across the table with murder in his eyes. It takes him at least two hours to calm down to a more sociable and less annoying attitude. In the beginning, Tonya throws confused looks from him to Avery and me, but then lets it go, ignoring Victor's bad mood.

I'm more than glad for it.

Our discussions about getting me home have me on edge already. Maybe the fact that I'm supposed to help Victor basically assault one of the best-protected men in Chicago has something to do with it.

I squirm in my seat, listening to all their planning. It's clear they've been over this many times and only need to modify it to fit me.

"We should make our move as soon as possible," Tonya adds. "We have Noa, a plan, and the means to pull it through. Every day we wait, we risk Canyon's Forces catching up with us."

"Shouldn't be a problem," Shannon says from across the table. "Two days at the most. That way, we get everybody in position to get us into the facility, and then *this one*"—she nods at Avery—"can disable the alarm and buy us a bit more time. That is, unless you're telling me you can override the system in fewer than two minutes by now." She throws a pointed glance at Victor, who scowls and rolls his eyes. "I'll take that as a *no*." Shannon sighs.

Tonya drums her fingers atop the table. "Noa, are you clear about everything? Do you feel comfortable with it?"

I pull one hand out from under my thighs and tug on my stud, the little owl. Feeling comfortable isn't quite how I'd describe it. More anxious, nervous, with a hint of panic—panic without the usual attack, which is a blessing in and of itself.

"Kind of," I answer honestly. "I'm just a little nervous." A little very much. If not for the proverbial carrot of going back home dangling in front of my face, I might actually be rocking in a corner somewhere.

I get soft and warm smiles from everywhere around the table. Throughout this meeting, I caught one or the other of them looking at me when they thought I didn't notice, but I did. And it made me feel very... on the spot. Like something actually depended on me, and it does.

Can't say that makes me happy.

Tonya smiles at me warmly. She has this maternal aura of caring around her that in my world would make it impossible for her to be the leader anywhere. Too warm. Too soft. She'd be overrun by men who'd all use her as a stepping stone on their way to the top. Not here, though. Here, she's boss.

"Don't worry. Victor trained for this all his life. He'll get you through the portal and through the mission, and then you'll be rid of us. As long as you get him out of the city after you fulfill the mission and to somewhere remote where he can trigger the bridge and cross back home without risking detection, he'll be fine."

I've come to learn that everything about crossing between universes is as complicated as I expected it to be: wavelength, five-dimensional coordinates, adjustment for temporal and spatial drift—point is, lots of calculating and processing power is needed to connect the universes and open a rift between them. That's why every portal has two computer consoles associated with it, one incoming, one outgoing, to divvy up the necessary math and physics for crossing in their assigned direction.

The bridge Victor is going to use is an emergency portal—an *illegal* emergency portal—and it comes with its own set of problems. For one, Canyon has sensors and jammers in satellites all around Terra that make it impossible for anyone on Terra to open a bridge to Earth. That's downer number one: can't sneak home via bridge. I have to enter a portal and do it under Canyon's nose.

For another, the moment Victor uses the bridge to cross back to Terra, Canyon will know about the breach thanks to his orbital scanners. That's downer number two, and while it's not quite my concern at that point, it's still annoying and dangerous for Victor. Hence, he needs a remote place to cross to give him a head start fleeing the Sentinel Forces.

Tonya winks at me. "And when the mission is done, you'll be the only person on Earth who knows why things look brighter for you."

All around the table, faces light up—only to fall the moment a loud *boom* resonates throughout the whole room from somewhere indeterminable. Screeching sirens follow not even two seconds later.

"Shit!" Victor curses. "Water!" He jumps up. "Everybody, up, up, up! We need to get above ground. *Move!*" His last word is for me, thrown at me like a whip that's getting my butt off the chair.

"What—?" Left and right from me, the Ghosts are up and sprinting toward the door. Only Avery stays next to me, much calmer than the rest, his head slightly tilted to the left, his forehead scrunched.

"Water!" Tonya calls out, grabbing me by my sleeve. "We're beneath a lake. The ceiling must've broken. If we don't get out—" Her wide eyes tell me all I need to know. The air gets too thin to breathe. Soon, there's not going to be any left, and we'll all drown.

I take a wheezing breath, about to run after everybody, when Avery holds on to my arm.

"Stop." His voice is loud and layered with command—and it's working. Almost everybody freezes, their heads turned toward him, their eyes wide, their breaths cut short.

"This is a coal mine?" He looks straight at Tonya. A coal mine?

How did he come up with that? I figured we were in some kind of huge church basement, curved ceilings and all, until they mentioned a lake.

Tonya sucks in one panicked breath. "None of your—"

"If you want to get out of here," Avery snaps, "you answer my question. Is this a coal mine?"

Tonya's jaw tightens. She still doesn't trust him. "Yes," she mutters, not happy to divulge that information.

Avery nods, satisfied. "Main shaft plus air shaft, I assume?"

"Yes."

Victor grabs her by the arm. "Stop it, Tonya. We have to get out or—"

"Exactly," Avery says, louder. "Why do you think I know this is a coal mine? Because you're not the first splinter group to hide in one. We're trained to flush you out with minimal damage to our troops. Literally. The water? That's us. It's either water or gas, depending on the mine. We're working under the assumption you won't expect a Sentinel attack without visible Sentinels. Flee the mine, and then we can pick you off one by one, no harm done to our Forces."

Tonya's mouth drops open and so has Victor's, his fingers still twisted in Tonya's shirt. "You're kidding me."

"I wish." Avery's face takes on a grim expression. "But this is how we work. Do you have—"

"How *you* work? Way to inspire trust, *Sentinel.*" Victor makes a rude hand gesture, and Avery rolls his eyes.

"Do you have a visual, I was about to say. Feel free to confirm. In not too much longer, the first group of Sentinels is going to enter the mine through the air shaft and arrest everybody who thought they could make it down here."

The alarm keeps blaring, and as if to verify Avery's words, water starts flowing in from under the door, spreading over the floor in no time like a living amoeba extending its tentacles. While logically, I know the water isn't rising too fast, the gurgling and splashing as it works its way into the mine sends my heart rate up into unknown dimensions.

Tonya and Victor exchange looks. "No. No visual. We stay low-tech to avoid—"

"To avoid detection, I know. And mostly it's working," Avery says. "But once they're down here, they'll scan for life signs, and they will find you without the protective layers of earth above you to drown out the signals. To speed this up: Do you have a Vac?"

She hesitates for a moment, the gears inside her head working visibly before she answers. "Yes. *Yes*, but it won't fit all of us. It was never meant for evacuation. We built it ourselves, it's rudimentary. Three tubes, and—"

"*Shut up*," Victor hisses at Tonya, his voice barely audible over the screeching of the siren and sound of rising water. "It's a trick, he's only going to use it against us, he—"

Tonya shakes his hand off, ignoring him. "What do you suggest?" She takes a shuffling step through the already ankle-high water toward Avery.

"There is no winning scenario right now," Avery says. "The moment they found us, we were doomed, but if we play it right, there is a way out. For some." He looks pointedly at me.

"For some?" Victor growls, "What about these guys? You think we're going to get you and her out of here and leave our own people behind? That's—"

"Exactly what you need to do." Avery stops him by taking a menacing step closer to Victor, his shadow drowning out all light in front of him. "You can't save everybody, and you don't want to. The majority of your people are fleeing through the air shaft and the main shaft as we speak, giving the Sentinels the Ghosts they've been looking for. The leaders have to take the VacWay."

Terry pushes past Shaniqua and Shannon, water splashing off his feet. "We're supposed to use our friends as *bait*? As *distraction*?"

"Yes." Avery stands his ground, not the least bit intimidated by the older man. "If you want to get out, that is."

Terry's eyes blaze as he turns to Tonya, pointing an accusing finger at Avery. "We can't trust him—obviously not. He is one of them, and what he's suggesting—"

Victor cuts in, his eyes narrowed to slits. "Terry's right. We'd be crazy to listen to him. It's all a big trick. Never trust a Sentinel."

Other voices chime in, siding with Victor. Somebody opens the door and screams out in surprise when a whole wave of water gushes into the room, bringing the level up to my calves.

I'm pretty sure I'm not the only one whose throat is about to close off.

The room erupts into almost immediate panic.

"Air shaft, *now!*" Terry yells, waving an arm while sprinting toward the door. Three or four of the others follow him right away, while the rest are visibly torn between following Terry or listening to Avery.

Tonya frowns once and curses under her breath. "Never thought I'd say this, but he makes sense. It's our only chance. If we don't give it a try, we've lost this battle already, and with that, the only option to get an Earthling to help us."

She throws a calculating glance at Avery. "Worst that can happen is that he's lying and the Sentinels know about the Vac, but then the outcome will be the same. We'll still be caught. Victor"—she looks straight at him—"lead the way."

For the longest of moments, Victor doesn't react at all. He looks back and forth between Avery and Tonya. "Fine," he eventually grumbles through clenched teeth.

Everybody falls back into action, like a TV un-paused. Somehow, my hand ends up in Avery's as we run out of the flooded conference room into the equally overflowing hallway. Instead of going right as I always did, Victor takes a left, the water splashing off his legs as he runs.

I take a quick look over my shoulder. Not many of the leaders are left: Tonya, Victor, Shannon, and four others, some faces filled with barely controlled fear, struggling to breathe like the water's already over our heads.

And it's not going to be much longer until it is.

Somewhen during the last corners we took, a current developed.

Thanks to its pull on my legs, it becomes more and more difficult for me to run. The hissing and bubbling of the rising water is so loud, it drowns out all the heavy breathing and fills up every corner of my mind.

Eventually, we arrive at yet another room, but the freezing water is already above my knees, giving me goosebumps. Avery's hold on me is much stronger than before, as if he wanted to make sure I didn't get swept away.

Another *boom* resonates throughout the mine and everyone ducks.

"We're running out of time," Avery calls over the sound of the rising water. "Faster!"

It's not as if anybody really needed encouragement at this point.

The wall in front of us has three little Hobbit-hole tubes, much smaller than the ones I've seen before, much less sophisticated-looking. Still, my heart leaps up when I see them.

A way out of here.

I don't want to be back with Canyon.

I only want to go home.

In the furthest corner of my mind, I realize my chances of doing exactly that have just been severely reduced, but I don't acknowledge that thought.

I need all the levelheadedness I have to not start panicking for real.

Tonya hits a red button next to her pod labeled *Emergency*. I agree with her. If this doesn't qualify, nothing will.

The instant the doors hiss apart, the pod floods to the chest level of the seats. This won't be a fun ride.

"Shannon, Lacey—with me, Tomar, Hudson, Shaniqua—take the second. Victor, you stay with them. Third pod."

I hear the message as clear as Victor does. Watch them. Watch *him*.

Everybody scrambles to get to the pods. Tonya's takes off with a swoosh before we have ours even opened. Tomar and Hudson enter theirs before Shaniqua hits the red button on the wall outside the tube and the doors snap shut, nearly taking her arm off.

If we don't speed it up, there won't be air to breathe inside the pods.

Victor pushes the red button on our pod and squeezes himself through the opening doors. "Come on. It's tight already, we—"

"Well, well." A condescending voice comes from the entrance of the room. "Leaving so soon?"

I spin so fast, I make myself dizzy, but I get only a glimpse of the person standing in the doorway before Avery is right in front of me, shielding me.

Tall, strong build with amber eyes that can't hold a candle to Avery's.

"Holloway," Avery growls. "Trying to get promoted?"

The other Sentinel laughs lightly, as if holding all the cards. "Already have been, McTighe. Took me about ten seconds to see you went rogue with her. How long have you been working with the Ghosts, huh? Canyon should never have advanced you so quickly, and you know that. You're not made to handle power." The playfulness is gone, replaced by a coldness that sends shivers down my spine.

Holloway comes closer, forcing Avery to step away from the tube, leaving Victor alone in it—Victor, whose face is as pale as a sheet. He sees me look at him and carefully waves at me, trying to get me to sneak over and into the pod with him, but Holloway catches the movement.

"As much as it pains me to let one go…" He racks up his arm and throws something at the tube, at the red big button.

Victor knows what's going to happen before I do. "No!" he yells, but it's too late. The doors zip closed and the pod shoots away, taking a wide-eyed Victor with it.

And with him our last hope to escape.

Holloway grins. "Whoops. Didn't wait for you, did he? Gotta love an emergency override." He takes another step forward toward Avery. "I recommend you come with me, McTighe. We can do this the easy or the hard way, but no matter what, I'll take her with me at the end of the day." He jerks his chin at me, and together with the ice-cold water all the way up to my mid-thighs, it makes me shiver.

"In your dreams, Holloway," Avery shoots back, already in a fighting stance, ready for an attack, and not a moment too soon.

With a grunt like a wild boar, Holloway shoots forward through the resistance of the water, aiming a kick at Avery that would've thrown a lesser man through the room. Avery deflects it with his leg, delivering a fist to Holloway's face that smacks his nose with a *crunch*.

I squeak behind him when blood splatters from Holloway's face, mixing with the water around us.

"Still not better in hand-to-hand combat, are we?" Avery taunts. "Should have graded you lower on your last test. You were always the weak one."

Holloway wipes the blood from under his nose but doesn't waste any time. With another growl, he's on top of Avery. Water and fists fly, knees ram into soft targets, bone hits bone. Soon I don't know whose blood is tainting the water red.

The current forces my back into the wall between two tubes. Thanks to the pressure of the water, I can barely budge. How Avery can move so quickly with the water that high is beyond me, because I'm paralyzed, and not just by fear.

Holloway gets one good kick in, splashing water high and driving Avery back and into the wall, his side hitting the concrete with a *thud* despite the water softening the velocity.

Avery slams his hand into one of the red buttons and pushes off the wall, all but throwing himself into the fight again.

Holloway takes a casual step back and pulls a short little device out of his pocket, holding it up high.

Avery freezes in mid-motion.

A nasty smile turns Holloway's face into a grimace as he points the device directly at Avery.

Avery lifts his hands up above his head, the apple in his throat moving up and down once.

Whatever this thing is isn't good.

"Don't, Holloway. You know what it'll do." While Avery still sounds like he's in control, that small device has changed everything.

It's given Holloway the upper hand, and they both know it.

"Do I look like I care, McTighe? I'll be restored, so what? You won't, but it's not as if that'd make me shed tears at night."

Avery keeps his hands up and stare glued to Holloway. "We both might drown."

"A risk I'm willing to take. The squad is close."

Something passes back and forth between them, something I can't interpret, but nothing of it is reassuring.

Not the way Holloway holds the device, arrogance dripping off of him even more than the blood from his nose.

Not the way Avery doesn't take his eyes off Holloway's thumb hovering over the one little button.

Not the way the water gurgles around us, rising by the second.

We're losing.

A wheezy breath leaves my throat, cut short by an unexpected bump of something heavy against my knee underwater. More out of reflex than anything else, I reach for it. Both men are fixated on the other. Neither of them picks up on my slow move behind Holloway.

At a snail's pace, I lift a short, thick stick out of the water, maybe the size of a kitchen paper roll.

The thing Holloway threw at the red button.

I grab it harder and turn it in my hand—and it springs into action without a sound, a two-foot extension shooting out of each end. It's the same kind of stick Avery used down in the tunnel when the Ghosts attacked us.

I have a weapon.

And to my surprise, I don't hesitate at all.

I lift the stick up high above my head, and before Holloway can pick up on the movement behind him I've cracked its end over Holloway's skull. The vibration of the impact reverberates all the way down my arms, yet I don't drop my weapon.

I'm not helpless.

I rack it up again and bring it down on his shoulders. This time, Avery has caught up with me. Making use of my distraction, he leans sideways and snaps out his front leg in a roundhouse kick to

Holloway's head.

"Ngh." Holloway grunts and stumbles backward, his eyes losing focus and glassing over. The device drops out of his hands and into the water, and Holloway collapses into a sitting position, stunned, but still not quite unconscious.

Avery sucks in a harsh, raspy breath…

And then storms toward me, tackling me like a football player. The impact drives the air out of my lungs and drops the stick from my hands because I need them both to cling to Avery.

"This will suck, but hold on! Hold your breath!" And with that, he throws both of us into the opened Vac Tube—the tube that's *filled with water* up to a third of its diameter, but without a pod.

Without a freakin' pod.

Avery smacks the red button on the way inside with the precision of a machine. Water splashes everywhere, entering my mouth and nose. Damn it, I—

There is no time to sort myself out, no time to think, no time for anything. When exactly Avery wraps his arms around me from behind to force me into a curled-up fetal position, or when he coils himself tightly around me, I don't know.

I only know that one second life exists within certain rules and regulations—and then the laws of physics have been revoked.

There's a short tug on our bodies, a short moment of confusion from this rather strange sensation—and then, *slurp*, all air around us is gone, a vacuum left in its place that lifts us up and sucks us away from Holloway and the mine.

And it does so with a force I never thought possible.

The vacuum whips us around like toys in a tube we weren't made for. It throws Avery against the walls countless times, every impact shattering my teeth and rattling my bones like I was the one taking the punishment, not him.

I scream, yet no sound leaves my throat.

The vacuum is relentless.

Soft waterdrops turn into hard, stinging needles that assault us from all directions. They race us to the finish line, although I'm not sure we'll ever make it. All air has left my lungs, long been sucked out by the vacuum. My eyes are about to pop out of my skull, my eardrums bulge and threaten to burst, and my whole body is on fire, hotter than the sun.

We shoot forward at a speed nobody should be able to survive, yet Avery keeps me safe.

All my thoughts circle around the need to breathe and the pain shooting through my body, from the inside to the outside and vice versa. Somewhere deep inside my mind, I wonder how Avery does it, how he can take all the punishment without letting go, because he never does.

He holds on to me no matter how hard we get thrown into the sides of the tube.

He holds on to me even when my vision turns cloudy.

He holds on to me when my grip on his arms begins to slip.

The last image in front of my inner eye is that of Avery pulling my arms closer into our twisted ball of extremities, the veins on the back of his hands swollen.

Then everything turns black.

CHAPTER NINETEEN

Out

Waking up sucks.

Before my mind has a chance to register what's going on, it's assaulted by pain.

My body burns on the inside, every cell on fire and screaming.

A moan leaves my throat and it sounds nothing like me.

"Shh," a soft voice whispers next to me. "It's going to be better any minute now."

Something cool presses against my neck and discharges with a hiss. "It's the third injection. It should do the trick."

I moan again, but this time I'm at least sure I was the one making that sound. I raise a hand to my head, relieved that my body still responds to my commands, although it's a rather clumsy movement.

Like the volume being turned down, the pain eases a bit, or at least enough that I can tolerate opening my eyes.

At first, I can't make sense of it because I'm looking up at the stars, but I'm sure I'm not outside. It's warm, I'm on something cushioned, and—

"Hi." Victor's grinning face leans over me, almost giving me a heart attack. "About time, my dear."

He takes the hand that's on my forehead and weaves his fingers between mine. "You're lucky you're in one piece—though it's a pretty beaten-up piece." His grin widens.

I pull my hand out of his and find armrests to my left and right

149

to use to push up. "Shut up," I rasp, the effort of sitting up robbing me of my breath and patience.

Victor supports my back, his hand between my shoulder blades. "Easy there. The dizziness is going to last a while."

"I'm not—" Ugh. I take it back.

He chuckles. "See? Here, drink." He hands me a bottle of water, and I take a sip. It feels heavenly cool gliding down my throat, as if my body had been sucked dry by our trip through the VacWay.

The VacWay.

"Where's Avery?" If I'm feeling like this, how bad must it be for him? He was the one shielding me with his body, what if—

"The Sentinel is fine," Victor says dismissively. "Protected from his own stupidity by conveniently altered genes. He's up front already. Doesn't want to rest until we get this baby to our destination."

Up front? This baby?

Only now do I take a look around. "A bus?" Is this… the Terra version of a bus? The size would be right, maybe a tad wider than a regular school bus, maybe a tad shorter as well, but the overall size is comparable.

That's where the similarities end, though.

Where a school bus would have rows of seats, this bus has maybe ten single seats, all comfy-looking, covered with blue fabric, including armrests and headrests. Some of them are reclined all the way back, like mine was, someone asleep in them. I recognize Shannon's hair, but most are empty.

And speaking of windows: wow.

It's already dark outside, but the view… is spectacular. The roof is completely transparent, which is why I thought I was outside at first. The windows are also larger than any I've ever seen, reaching almost all the way to the floor.

It's like riding in a bus made completely out of glass.

Victor squats in front of me. "Yup. Our very own SF Transporter. Pays to be prepared."

"Huh?" That didn't make any sense at all.

Victor's smile widens. "Our backup plan. It's a transporter that belongs to the Sentinel Forces. Well, *belonged*, until we got a hold of it a couple of months ago. It's our best way for making an emergency exit from the VacWay. The Sen… *Avery* had us destroy the Vac when you guys were out, but it still would only have been a matter of time until they figured out where the tubes led to, and from there on…" He shrugs. "Couple of scans from orbit, and we'd have been discovered. At least the SFT keeps unwanted eyes out."

I throw a pointed look at the transparent ceiling and sides. "Uh, you sure about that?" I feel rather on display in here, despite the dark outside.

He chuckles again. "Yes. This baby comes with a whole lot of cool features. It's made for the Sentinel Forces, so security is high up the list. The walls are transparent from inside, but outside, it looks like silver. It also keeps us from being scanned. All the stuff that usually annoys the heck out of us when we're trying to take the Sentinels down is now playing to our advantage. Can't say I dislike it." He wiggles his eyebrows. "Wanna come up front?"

Victor's hands on my back and elbow support me until I'm up to standing, more wobbly than anything, but still standing.

I really should stop making it a habit to get knocked out every other day or so.

Carefully, we weave our way through the scattered seats. Victor nudges one or two of them out of the way. They glide over the floor like on wheels and stop right before they'd bump into something or somebody else's seat.

Tonya sits on the right at the front, Avery on the left. The front looks pretty much like what I'm expecting from a bus, complete with steering wheel—only that nobody has their hands on it.

"Guys," Victor says by way of greeting, pushing between the two seats and squatting. "Noa is awake."

They swivel around in their chairs, Tonya with her trademark warm smile, and Avery—

"Holy cow, Avery!" My jaw drops open. "Is that…?" Is that from the vacuum? His face is bruised, his eyes bloodshot red, and even with the little bit of movement he had to make to turn the chair around, it's obvious he isn't at a hundred percent. Not even close.

I step around Victor before Avery has a chance to respond. "Shit, Avery…" I grasp his cheeks in both hands, careful not to hurt him even more. Those bruises… holy cow, they're swollen and raw. I trace my thumb over his cheekbones—and Avery's eyes widen. A little jolt goes through his body, and he jerks his head away from me.

I drop my hands like they were burnt.

"You, uh, you look horrible," I say weakly. *Way to go, Noa. Way to be inappropriate.*

A tiny smile creeps up his face. "Seen a mirror lately?"

A mirror? Because—

Oh. I shift my gaze to my reflection in the front window. That would be what he's talking about.

Although I took the least amount of punishment in that tube, I look like I took the brunt of it. *Nice bruises, Noa.*

"Aw, crap." I grunt. That's never going to heal.

Tonya places a hand on my arm. "Don't worry about it. You'll be as good as new in a couple of hours. The antidote against vacuum disease takes a while to correct the damage done." She pushes down onto my arm. "Sit. We've got to talk."

Victor reaches behind him and pulls one of the seats right into the back of my knees so I all but fall into it. The cushions automatically adjust to my body like the ones in the Berlin-pod did. I sink into the soft material that wraps itself around me. All tension leaves my muscles. Nice when the pain tunes down to bearable.

Better.

Then finally, after escaping through a VacWay without a pod, and after waking up beaten and battered, reality catches up with me: no, not *better.* Screwed up. Completely screwed up.

"How are we going to cross now?" I whisper into the ambient noise of a soft engine humming and people softly snoring in their seats behind us. "We're screwed."

The Sentinels stormed the mine before we could make our move, and now… now we're not only fugitives, but homeless fugitives, for all I know. My chances of ever seeing my parents and home again have dwindled down to negative numbers.

A shadow falls over me from behind. "We recapping?" Tomar brings another chair with him. The five of us sit more or less in a circle, with Avery pressing a couple of buttons in his fancy-looking cockpit before he swivels back around.

"Guess so." Tonya points at Tomar. "Might as well make use of our time and bring Noa up to speed."

Up to speed? What did I miss?

Tomar nods and leans forward in his seat. I'd say he's the oldest of the bunch, even including Terry, who is probably now in a cell somewhere, guarded by Sentinels. "We're not screwed, Noa. We're ready. You are ready." He nods at me.

"I am?" I don't feel ready. At all.

"You are." Victor reaches over and taps my knee once. "Nothing has changed."

"Depends on the point of view." And from mine, things definitely have gone downhill quite a bit.

Tonya crosses her legs. "You're right, but we were about ready anyway before we found you. The plans have been in motion for years."

Motion-shmotion. That doesn't change a thing. "But—"

"But we're out of a home base?" Tonya points her thumb over her shoulder in the direction we're coming from.

I nod.

"It doesn't matter," Tomar says. "We have others. If we don't act now, we can forget about it. And yeah, then you're right, then we're screwed. But we need to pull through, or our chance is gone."

"He's correct," Avery says. "It won't take long for them to get the information from the Ghosts they captured. A day at the most. By then, all portals will be secured even more tightly than they already are, and getting you home will be almost impossible."

I pick up on all sorts of things from his short comment: that he's looking at me again without the almost-panic in his eyes from when I held his face. That he's emphasizing getting me home, instead of the Ghosts getting their plan done.

Most of all, though, it's that he referred to the Sentinels as *them*.

It's the first time he's called those in his former life *them*.

I sigh. Thanks to me.

"Let me guess," says Victor, his tone sarcastic. "You're still suggesting using the Chicago Portal?"

Avery nods curtly. "Correct. We can't use the one you planned on because that's the one the captured leaders will know about, and therefore the one the Sentinels will secure the most. Chicago, on the other hand—"

"Is the biggest freakin' portal we have right after the Hub!" Victor shouts. "Getting into the Number Four Portal was difficult enough, but getting into Canyon's main portal in the middle of Chicago, that's—"

"Exactly what we need to do," Tonya says. "He's right, and you know it. You just don't like it."

Victor grumbles something between his teeth, not gracing her with a reply of any sorts.

Tonya sighs and counts off her fingers. "We have a Sentinel. We have a truck to get us in. We have an Earthling." She nods at me. "And I doubt you're going to get any more ready than you already are, Victor."

"Well, yeah, you're right about that," Victor mutters under his breath. "You're also right it doesn't mean I have to like it."

I'm not so sure I'm liking it, either. "So… wait. Chicago? The biggest portal? Isn't that… risky?"

"See? Even Noa gets it." Victor opens his palms to the ceiling as if waiting for some kind of divine intervention.

I try to be not too offended by the "even Noa" part.

Tonya swivels left to right in her chair. "Noa, don't worry about it. Avery is our key. He has reprogrammed the truck to give us cover and he's the one to get you into the facility as research subjects. From there, you'll quote-unquote escape and make your way to the basement and the portal, cross over while he distracts the guards with a search for you in the upper levels, and then *boom*, the two of you will have crossed over."

Did I hear that right? "So Avery is bringing us in as prisoners?" I look at him for confirmation, a tiny blush visible under his bruises, if I'm not mistaken.

"It's the only way."

"The only way, my ass," Victor grumbles, but Avery ignores him.

"Victor," Tonya growls, but Victor only rolls his eyes.

Tonya turns toward him. "This is our one and only chance, and if we don't take it… I don't think Galileo would let us live that down. Ever." She smiles wistfully.

Right. Galileo. Archimedes. Newton. Whatever.

"Whatever." Victor echoes my thoughts and stands. "Come on, Noa. Let those two work on how to best get us killed, and we'll catch some Zs in the meantime." He takes my hand and pulls.

I don't budge. "I'll stay some more." My desire to join Victor for whatever is down in the negative on a scale from one to ten.

Victor won't take *no* for an answer, though. "Aw, come on, don't leave me hanging here." He pulls again, this time more forcefully.

"Victor, I—"

"Let her go." All of a sudden, Avery is between Victor and myself, filling out the space between the seats completely.

Victor drops my hand, then freezes. "Careful, *pet*." He growls, his bright blue eyes turning icy.

"Or what?" Avery snarls back, never moving away from his protective position in front of me. "I would like to see you try something, *Ghost*. Please don't hold back, because even after ninety seconds of vacuum, I'll still beat the crap out of you."

Tonya clears her throat. "Avery."

"I'm not the one who started it," Avery says in cool tone, searching around behind his back for me with one hand, like he did during the ambush. This time, it's only Victor and not remotely as threatening as the Ghost attack, only—

And then it hits me.

He isn't defending me because I'm in danger.

He's defending me because he's my friend.

Avery is my friend, even after such a short time.

He's standing there, eyes blazing at Victor, body protectively positioned to cover me.

My *friend* worried about me.

I guess I'm so slow to recognize it because I haven't had a real friend in forever, not since Kevan turned on me in eighth grade. It's impossible to have a real friendship if all anybody sees is the weird girl with the piercing and the panic attacks. Nobody takes the time to get to know *that* girl.

Nobody but Avery.

Avery did, and sometime during the last days, we became friends—and maybe we were right from the beginning, when he saw a person in me, and not just a prisoner.

"Thank you, Avery," I say quietly, my hand sneaking up into his.

Unlike when I touched his face, he doesn't twitch.

He squeezes my hand once and then lets go.

"And to be clear, Ghost," he growls at Victor, "you screw up anything on Earth and get Noa into trouble, and I'll find you and make you pay for it, no matter which universe you're hiding in."

With that, he sits in the driver's seat again, checking the blue luminescent controls as if nothing happened.

I get one short glimpse at Victor's narrowed eyes and tightened jaw before he turns on his heels and struts down the truck toward a seat in the back.

"That went well," Tonya comments drily.

I let my head fall against the chair's backrest.

How I wish I could take Avery and leave Victor here.

CHAPTER TWENTY

Moving It Up

Two hours later, we're about ready to go and I'm a wreck.
The ache that burned inside every cell of my body when I woke up has lessened significantly, leaving only a slight sting with every move, but that's the only improvement.

At least when I woke up, I was blissfully unaware of my predicament, the fact that in mere minutes, Avery is going to drive Victor and me into the lion's den as his prisoners.

"Who says he isn't going to hand us over on a silver platter to get back into good standing with Canyon?" Victor hisses at Tonya for the umpteenth time, not even trying to keep his voice down.

"Nobody," Avery answers instead of Tonya. He straightens his new black Sentinel uniform he retrieved from one of the drawers hidden under a retractable mid-vehicle table, the same one that's now up to hip level and stretching from the front of the Transporter to the very back. Tomar moved all chairs close to it like for our mission prep.

"But if you think Canyon will let me continue in the Sentinel Forces after I redirected his pod, you're mistaken. No story could be watertight enough. You lose trust, you're out." He tugs the little silver pendant and leather necklace under his shirt and out of view. "Reprogramming the transporter and my ID is only going to get us so far." He taps his forehead.

What's a convenience for his job now bites us in the behind. One

157

look at him and any First or Second Class Sentinel will know who he is and that he's wanted—the exact reasons why Ghosts refuse to get the Augs that would make them show. With Victor's help, Avery overrode part of his ID, but it's a makeshift patch that won't hold up for long or against any closer inspection.

I really hope it doesn't have to.

There's a knock on the door, and Tonya opens it to Lacey, her arms full with water bottles and snacks.

"Here, guys." Lacey drops her bounty onto the table in the middle. "Say *hi* to your uncle, Hudson, and thanks for keeping the garage stocked."

Hudson grins at her from the other end of the table, giving her a thumbs-up. "Comes in handy to have family in high places, huh?" He grabs a pack of snacks and opens it. "If the Sentinels ever find out we used it, though, he won't be able to cover for us."

"And I wouldn't expect him to," Tonya replies from somewhere half under the table, strapping some kind of toolbelt around each of Victor's ankles, then hiding them by pulling the legs of his pants over to cover. "We're lucky he's pro-Ghosts, despite being high up in the government."

Hudson nods, chewing. "'Xactly."

I play with my heart-shaped nose stud. I didn't really plan on putting this one in, but… it happened. I've worn it maybe twice. I never had an occasion to before.

Avery gives me a soft smile. "Nerves getting to you?"

Nerves? More like an extreme case of anxiety. The old me would have curled up somewhere and given herself over to a panic attack, but since I got thrown into the Terra-Universe I've apparently put on my big girl pants.

Thank whomever for small favors.

"Kind of," I reply with a little frown. It's not so much the part where we all but break into the portal, Victor shortcuts it, and we travel back to Earth—it's the part that comes after.

The part where I don't have Avery to look after me.

It's not that I don't trust Victor. I do trust him that he wants the best for Earth, for the Ghosts, for their project, and that he's going to do all he can to pull this off.

But I trust Avery more.

We both sit at the table across from each other. For a moment, it feels like his stare lingers on my piercing, but I doubt it.

"All right, guys." Tonya claps her hands together, drawing everybody's attention. "We're set. Shannon, Lacey, Tomar, Hudson—we'll go and connect with one of the other splinter groups. Lacey, you got your contact lined up?"

Lacey nods. "Done. Meeting point and procedure cleared, and… I'll give you details later." She shoots a careful glance at Avery. I guess it's another case of we-don't-trust-the-Sentinel, or a wise precaution, in case we get caught and spill the beans.

And to be honest, it's quite high up on the list of possibilities from where I'm coming from.

Tonya lifts her eyebrows at Victor. "You got your gear?"

"Yes, ma'am, all tools for overriding their system right here and double-checked." Victor taps a hand against his lower legs on each side. "Got the one shirt-integrated backpack with the hoist system we have, for an emergency outbreak through the ceiling, and I even put a beautiful red bow around it."

Tonya rolls her eyes. "Bridge?"

"As if I'd ever leave without it."

"Good. Remember to take a modulator. Once you've crossed back to us, find a VacWay and give us the spike through the power system. We'll monitor it around the clock until you're back. I wish we had two emergency hoist systems, but we don't. Noa, you've got to stay close to Victor. He can get you out with his if needed be, and he knows how to fight." I hear what she doesn't say: *You don't. You have no clue how to fight your way out of there without him.* And no offense taken, she's right.

Tonya looks at Avery. "Any questions from your end?"

All eyes turn to him. "None." He shakes his head. "Once we're in, we don't have much time. I would say a maximum of five minutes. I will keep them distracted, but there's only so much I can do. At one point, the cat is going to be out of the bag, namely once you have activated the outgoing portal. Then it depends on you to cross as quickly as possible, or you will be caught."

There went my last bit of optimism.

Avery sighs. "You will also have to make sure you're not triggering the alarm or the lockdown before the portal is ready. The Sentinel override code is 39893. You should punch that in as soon as—"

Victor sneers from the other side of the table. "A Sentinel override code? Why have we never heard about that? All of a sudden, there's a convenient code that'll prevent the alarm from going off? I'm betting it's more of a convenient failsafe for you, alarming your former colleagues, so you can get back in their good graces."

The atmosphere shifts around the table. All eyes fall on Avery. Maybe Victor isn't the only one with that suspicion.

"It's a *Sentinel* override. We don't make it a habit of announcing it to the general public," Avery comments drily.

"Really." Victor drums his fingers on the table, cocking his head to the left. "I don't trust you, *pet*."

"Well, the feeling is mutual, *Ghost*," Avery says coolly, "but if you want to cross, you better remember the code or you're going to be running out of time really fast."

Victor nods, fingers never breaking rhythm. "We'll see."

Tonya clears her throat. "Okay, then. I guess we're as ready as we can be. Avery, we're going to give you exactly until 5 P.M. If you're not at the extraction point, we're considering you either caught or… well, that you switched sides on us." At least Tonya has the decency to look embarrassed while she's accusing Avery of playing double agent.

"Understood." Avery looks unbothered by the accusation.

"Also," she says, pushing a bag over to Victor, "you might need this for authenticity. It's from the Transporter's lockers."

Groaning, Victor catches the bag. He reaches inside and hesitates for a moment. "Tonya, I—"

"Give it to him."

Victor rolls his eyes but pulls out a stick and a gun of a size that's more-than-impressive. Even in Victor's hands, it looks large, and Victor isn't small by any means. He bends over the table and carefully lays the weapons down in front of Avery, keeping one hand on them.

"I really don't think we should give you a staff, let alone a gun, pet. It goes against the grain, really."

The corners of Avery's lips move up the slightest bit. "Believe me, Ghost, I know what you're talking about. As it is, I'm very much tempted to shoot you right in the ass." He meets Victor's hostile stare head-on.

Somewhere down the table, somebody giggles, joined a second later by another voice until everybody around the table is grinning—well, everybody besides Victor and Avery. And me, for that matter. I think I lost that ability the moment we initiated the countdown for crossing back over.

Tonya pushes back her chair. "Everyone, let them get ready. It's time. Noa?" She waves me over and presses a button that retracts the table back into the depths of the floor under our feet with a small hiss.

"I wanted to thank you for doing this." She grasps my shoulders in both hands and squeezes. "I know it's tough and feels dangerous, but Victor has everything under control. Soon, you're going to be home, and soon, your world will be safer again."

I wish I shared her optimism. Still, I nod. "I hope so. Thank you for getting me back." Although the whole plan still leaves a sour taste in my mouth.

Her smile widens. "Of course. Unfortunately, we couldn't get Galileo in to meet you. Our founder. The Sentinel attack took that from us." She sighs. "And I was so looking forward to meeting him. None of us ever have. It's rare anybody gets to see him. Security reasons, you know?"

"Oh, okay." Galileo is a real person, all right. Not that I care. I met with a minister, and how did that work out for me? The more I stay under the radar, the happier I am. Remnant of my upbringing, I'd say.

"Anyway. Good luck with crossing over, good luck with the operation, and… well, have a good life." She pulls me into a tight hug.

"You, uh, too." *Awkward.*

Tonya lets go of me and gives me a short nod before turning to Victor, who's making his way over to her, his arms spread wide already.

I need air.

The Ghosts I pass on my way to the transporter's doors pat me on the shoulders and whisper encouraging comments that I don't hear.

I step out into the dark of what must be a completely empty underground parking garage, with nothing but emergency lights on and an eerie feel to it. My steps echo on the sparkling clean, shiny floor that looks more like the frozen surface of a lake the way it reflects the reddish emergency lights high up in the ceiling.

For a moment, I imagine I'm back home, in a regular good old parking garage somewhere in a shopping center, on my way to George and Elaine, but… well, the glow-in-the-dark lines dividing the parking spaces kind of ruin that fantasy for me. Too fancy for Earth.

"Need a break?"

I clutch my chest out of reflex, startled by the voice from behind a pillar.

"Jeez, Avery! You're sneaky, considering your size." My heart hammers under my hand like crazy. It probably doesn't know yet the little scare here is nothing compared to what's about to come.

Avery chuckles quietly and pushes off the pillar. If it weren't for the little bit of greenish glow from the floors and reddish overhead lights, I wouldn't see him at all in his black uniform.

"Being sneaky is a class they teach in Sentinel school."

I wouldn't be surprised. Gives hide-and-seek a whole new perspective for young Sentinels.

He works a hand through his hair and drops his voice with the next question. "So… are you okay with everything?"

Me, okay with everything? "That might be stretching it a bit," I whisper. "I mean, I'm glad… no, I'm more than glad that I have the chance to get home, but there are so many things that can go wrong, and then—"

Avery grasps my arms at the biceps and holds them tightly. "It'll be fine. I'll take care of everything on this end, and honestly…" He takes a deep breath, his voice no louder than a whisper. "If Victor does anything fishy when you're on Earth, you drop him. You run. You vanish. He has nothing on you once you're there. You know that, right?"

I nod. It's not as if I hadn't thought about it before, but it feels wrong. Using them and then vanishing. *They're using you just the same, tit for tat*, a voice in the back of my head argues.

I look up into Avery's amber eyes. It must be the light, but they almost seem like they're glowing, their deep golden color even richer.

I swallow. "Thank you, Avery."

For getting me away from Canyon. For having my back. For bringing me back home. For being my friend.

His hands on my arms slide up and down once before he holds me even more tightly.

Avery takes a step closer, so close, the tips of our shoes almost touch. I have to crane my neck to keep looking at him.

His thumbs do a short quick circle on each of my upper arms, making me twitch from the onslaught of a million butterflies lifting up at once. The air heats around us, my throat dry and my heart hammering worse than before.

"Uh, thanks for everything, I mean. For helping me. And for helping them." I stutter to fill the silence.

Close. He's so close, and he—

No.

His life is a boat for one, as he said. And I'm leaving for Earth.

We never had a chance, not even in my wildest dreams.

His thumbs move in another circle over my arms. "I'm doing this for you, not for them." He whispers so softly, it's hard to hear despite him being so close. His Avery-scent is everywhere, surrounding me, cocooning me. "None of what I believed in, of what I was taught, was true, and I still don't know what is. But no matter what, you need to get back home and away from here, be it from Canyon or the Ghosts, it doesn't matter."

His gaze holds mine, neither of us looking away.

Maybe I'm imagining it, but something passes between us, something that wasn't there before.

Something that never will be, either.

I force myself to swallow, but it doesn't help against the worsening dryness in my throat.

How do you say *goodbye* when you know there's not a chance in the world you're ever going to see the other person again? When you know you owe them big?

I suck in my lower lip and bite it.

"I'll miss you," I whisper softly, then I push up on my tippy toes.

Before I can chicken out or give Avery time to react, I have my arms wrapped around his neck and my body pressed against his.

He takes a short breath in and stiffens. For a second, I'm afraid he's going to push me away, but then he deflates, a harsh sigh leaving his throat before his arms go around my shoulders, and he returns the hug.

We stand there for a long time, our arms wrapped around each other, unmoving.

If I was waiting for him to say he'd miss me too, it's in vain.

Avery stays silent.

CHAPTER TWENTY-ONE

Unexpected

Not even two hours later, we're on our way to the portal, driving through a Chicago completely unlike the one I grew up in.

Almost all traffic underground, Canyon said on that day that feels like ages ago. I never knew how much traffic—or the lack thereof—could change the face of a city, but with only a few Sentinel transporters or private vehicles out and about, this is not like my Chicago. At all. Never mind the streets are also smaller, cleaner, greener, and generally way better maintained than at home. That only adds a minuscule part to my general inability of orienting myself in Terra's Chicago.

I'm getting dizzy from my head swiveling left and right while my brain tries to align my internal map of the city with where we're going.

And it's not working.

At all.

Almost a century of differences pile up right in front of me, driving home the point that this is exactly not that: home.

I thought I'd feel closer to my parents by being in the same town as them, but I don't. Seeing a skyline that is anything but Chicago… it widens the gap I already feel way too much.

After a while, though, I think I recognize a pattern: buildings from before the middle of last century might still be the same—remodeled, but still there—while everything built after… is different.

Willis Tower? Gone.

Or rather: never built.

When Avery drives us past where I think the Sears-now-Willis Tower should be, there's a huge white structure in its place, like a golf ball cut in half and buried in the ground, the same type I saw from Canyon's office in Berlin. This one, though… it must be four times as wide as the Willis Tower, and almost half as high, if not more.

"What is that?" I breathe against the window, all but squishing my face against the cool glass. The blueish glow from my handcuffs reflects in the window.

"An LC." Victor shrugs, checking his fingers and pushing his cuticles back, the only movement he can make with his hands cuffed.

He's still miffed from when Avery pinched him when he put on the cuffs. Mine are loose, moving around my skin, while Victor's… well, I did see the glint in Avery's eyes when Victor twitched.

"LC?"

"Living Complex." He looks up. "Wait, you don't have these?"

"You mean, like a high-rise apartment complex?"

His only response is an eyebrow going up.

I sigh. "Many people living there, every family has their own apartment?"

"Kind of. Thousands of people live there. School, work, shopping. It's all in that one LC. They're tight communities, which happens when you almost never leave your LC."

I frown. "Why wouldn't you?"

Victor's smile turns icy. "Because the Government prefers people in their assigned LCs. Easier to control. Less chaos."

"Oh." So that's why it's so empty here. What I know as busy six-lane roads are narrow two lanes, framed by trees and bushes. Everything is in pristine condition, and now that I know why it's so empty… No wonder it's all intact. I remember Canyon's words from when I had just crossed over: Almost all traffic is underground besides Sentinel Forces, which today… is us.

I stare out the window at the white golf balls everywhere. "So what happens if you leave?"

"You can leave. But people don't. Not much, anyway. The VacWay brings you anywhere you want, so why go outside? It's all part of protecting the environment," he adds, sarcasm dripping from his words.

I take it things are much more complicated on Terra than I gave them credit for so far.

Avery takes us through downtown and toward the lake—I think. By now I've given up keeping track; it's no use.

Silence settles over us once again, but this time it feels heavy.

I might make myself think this is like home, but it isn't.

Crossing back over has to work. It has to.

"Get in position." Avery's cool and controlled voice pierces the silence. He keeps both hands on the wheel this time, looking like the model for professional Sentinel behavior.

Victor and I hurry to our seats across from each other, our handcuffed wrists resting in our laps, our heads down, our shoulders slumped over.

We have to look the part.

I throw a glance out of the window and almost choke on my next breath. "Is that…?"

"Adler Research Facility." Avery doesn't look back at me. "The location of the Chicago Portal."

The Adler Research Facility. Or the Adler Planetarium, depending on the universe, apparently.

My mouth drops open as I stare. One of my fondest memories of us as a family is from a night under the stars here with Andrew and my parents. Elaine and George were still healthy, and we all slept under the planetarium's star skyline, together with dozens of other families. I had a blast—well, after I got over my panic attack when we entered the planetarium. I don't do well with busy confined spaces.

Avery pulls up right to the front of the building that's painted in a brilliant white compared to the concrete-beige in my world. I'm pretty sure on Earth there would be stairs leading to the main entrance, but on Terra, there's a wide curved gate made of material similar to our SF Transporter.

Avery slows and the window on his left rolls down automatically.

"Two Ghost subjects for sub level B," he calmly announces to the Second Class Sentinel guarding the entrance. Another Leiva. There are definitely too many of him running around for my taste, but then, the attack from a couple of nights ago still has me biased, no matter if it turned out we were on the same side after all.

"Of course. One moment, please." The Second Class places his palm against the outside of the truck, and I jump when the walls shimmer and turn translucent, allowing his eyes to fall straight on me.

I drop my gaze and make sure to look beaten, battered, and afraid, which is absolutely not a difficult goal to accomplish.

Honestly, I don't have to *play* a prisoner. I feel like one, thanks to a completely different Chicago and the handcuffs. They might be fancy without a lock and instead programmed to react to one of the standard Sentinel Augs, and they may not have a chain connecting my wrists together, but I'm still handcuffed. Every time I move, some kind of magnetic force holds my wrists in place. The slim bracelets emit a slight blueish glow—mesmerizing.

I keep staring at the cuffs, trying to ignore the Sentinel inspecting every inch of our vehicle from the outside. While I'm at it, I force myself to at least *appear* calm because on the inside, I'm anything but. Fake it until you make it. We're going to be fine. We get in, Avery takes care of the guards, Victor knows the way, I stay close, he overrides the portal, we step through and stay close together on the other side, I take over.

Right. Take over.

Sure.

Easy-peasy.

Uh, that reminds me: Where are we going to end up on Earth? Also here, in the planetarium? I almost roll my eyes. I'm such an idiot. I should have asked. What if… What if we're somewhere I can't get us out of? A locked room? What—

No. Terra is actively using this portal, which means it must be inconspicuous for them to travel through, or they would've been detected already.

It's not much, but it makes me feel better.

The Second Class checks our transporter. He does a thorough job: Here and there, he squats down to get a better look, one hand always glued to the vehicle's side. I could swear Victor's breathing gets raspier the longer the Sentinel inspects us.

"All cleared. You may pass," he says eventually, pressing his palm into an indentation next to the gate.

"Thank you." Avery pulls inside.

Victor exhales sharply, the blueish glow from his cuffs throwing jittery shadows across his lap. At least I'm not the only one close to freaking out.

Avery drives us straight ahead into a large, wide area with white floors and high walls, topped off with a high glass ceiling somewhere above us. He stops in front of three pillars that rise out of the floor, flashing red.

From here on, all the wheels need to fall into place, or we willingly entered the lion's den without a way out.

Avery jumps out of the transporter and walks around to the side. The door opens after a press of his palm.

"Out. Both of you." His stern, strict voice catches me off guard and makes it clear how much he's softened over the last few days. Avery is always so on guard, I didn't notice it, but now in retrospect, it's obvious. Standing in front of me is the Sentinel he was when he kept the Second Class from choking me, back in my cell. Canyon's First Sentinel. He's back to who he used to be before I took that from him.

"Move it. I don't have all day." He makes room for us as Victor and I step out. Once we've cleared the transporter, Avery draws a pattern on its side with one finger. The door closes and the vehicle slowly rolls backward toward the exit, the red flashing pillars in front of it retreating into the ground a mere three seconds later.

Fancy.

But now our getaway options are limited.

"Follow me." Avery presses a button on his belt, and a pull on my cuffs strong enough that I have to follow it drags me after Avery.

The doors straight ahead open as soon as Avery approaches them and close behind Victor, who's taking the rear. While the first area looked less than a research facility and more like a reception area, this part reminds me much more of the Berlin Reichstag, or better, the Reunification Building, than I'd like. People in white coats walk back and forth, carrying supplies I can't identify or if they don't, they stare down at their wrists or back of their hands, lost in thought. Handy, these Augs. The only people not dressed in white coats are the Second Class Sentinels.

Avery ignores every single one of them, and so do we. I keep my eyes trained on the ground as much as I can because if I don't… I'm sure I'll give us away. As it is, I'm having a hard time controlling my breathing because of that ginormous elephant sitting on my chest, the pressure of what's at stake almost gluing my feet to the floor.

It's not only about me getting home, it's about saving a world. Or two.

After three or four bends in the hallway, Avery stops in front of a large door that, for a change, doesn't open automatically. Only the short hesitation before he places his hand on the reader gives it away. We're here.

Victor shuffles to get himself in a better position.

My breath hitches in my throat. If—

The doors hiss apart and Avery enters, the tug on my wrists pulling me along.

"Excuse me, sir. This is restricted ac—"

The Second Class can't finish his sentence due to Avery ramming his hand into the other man's throat. Coughing, he collapses and turns limp with one hit of Avery's stick, courtesy of the transporter's supplies.

Avery hooks the stick back in his belt, taking two quick strides to reach the wall that looks like one single ginormous touchscreen.

Victor whistles through his teeth. "Nicely done, pet."

Avery ignores him. He checks the information displayed in different areas on the screen. "All as expected. You know your way?"

"Sure do," says Victor.

"I need a minute." Avery presses his palm against the screen, the image under it changing to a control panel. Like an artist drawing an elaborate picture, Avery swipes and taps at the screen, completely focused on his task.

"I have cameras offline for seven minutes from now. Access to all doors granted. The portal room is empty right now, but remember, that can change in an instant if you don't use the override."

"Sure," Victor says with an eyeroll.

Avery shoots him a cool glance. "I mean it."

"Yeah, me too. Now these, please." Victor stretches out his hands to Avery and wiggles them in front of his face.

Avery looks at me instead and presses a button on his belt. My cuffs stop glowing, open up, and fall to the ground.

"Hello? Here, please." Victor shakes his hands even more.

Taking his sweet time, Avery teases his finger around the button and pushes it, releasing Victor. "You have five minutes. Make them count."

"Got it." Victor nods, rubbing his wrists. "Let's go." He grabs my sleeve and pulls me with him toward the door at the right side of the room.

"Avery—" I stumble after Victor.

"Go." A small smile plays around his lips. "Go," he repeats, more urgently.

"Come on, Noa! Move it!" Victor hisses, yanking me with him like a pig to slaughter. He doesn't even stop to grab the two white coats from a hook on the wall.

For one last time, I look at Avery, return his smile—

—and Victor pulls me through the sliding doors and into the hallway, thrusting one of the white coats he ripped off the hook into my arms and sliding into the other.

Goodbye, Avery.

"Thirty meters straight, then left, third door on the right, then twenty more," Victor mutters.

I focus on following him.

Well, that and trying to not run into anybody or look suspicious. Mostly, I try really hard to ignore the rising panic that feels way too familiar with its pressure on my chest and not enough oxygen in the air.

Not going to happen.

Not going to happen.

I was good for the last couple of days. I'm gonna be fine now.

We turn the first corner, then see the third door already parting for us as soon as we approach it.

Avery. That must be Avery helping us from the control room. A warm feeling spreads through my chest, chasing away at least a little bit of the rising panic. Knowing that Avery is watching makes breathing easier.

I can't find cameras installed anywhere, but that doesn't mean there aren't any. They're much better hidden than on Earth.

We keep on walking briskly through the hallways like everybody else, our steps echoing as harshly as our breaths, the tails of our white coats flowing behind us.

Another turn, another door that miraculously opens, and another hallway, this one almost empty, with only one woman walking around a corner and away from us.

Then another door. Jeez…

"This is it," Victor rasps, cranking his neck, taking the step forward that triggers the mechanism and opens the door under Avery's watchful eyes.

I don't know what I expected, I really don't.

It wasn't this.

It wasn't the dome.

The portal is located under the planetarium's dome.

On Earth, I'd expect rows and rows of chairs here, but this… this is an empty space beside the portal in the middle of the room. At this point, I've got to admit: I did expect something fancy. Cue

Stargate, cue the Guardian of Forever, and the portal doesn't disappoint. Like a huge omega, it forms a wide, more than human-high circle, a computer console connected to either end of the omega's feet via thick cables bolted to the floor. Terra's flag, the atom with circling electrons, embellishes the top center of the portal, and I could swear there's a hum in the air.

"I've seen this before," I whisper. The Reichstag, Terran side. Up under the dome, in the madman's laboratory—only there, the portal was filled with blueish energy zapping from one side to the other.

Victor ignores me as his eyes scan over the portal "We made it."

And the second we step in, panic hits me straight in the face.

Holy cow.

Like a switch flipped, my body isn't strong enough to keep me upright anymore. Forced down by powers I can't comprehend, I bend over, supporting myself with my hands on my knees. Something is wrong here, very wrong.

Victor doesn't notice. He's already checking the controls on the left of the Omega, probably the outgoing console, although right now it could be a rocket launching station and I wouldn't care.

If I thought I couldn't breathe before, *this* is where I become wheezy.

If I thought my heart was hammering before, *this* is what a true techno-rhythm feels like.

Oh, please no.

Not now. Not *now* of all times.

I'm not sure I can make it any farther. The old, familiar sense of doom is back, crushing down on me like a ceiling losing its support. My breath catches in my throat, and not from the run, but from fear.

From panic.

I did so well over the last days. Why now?

Pulling on all the self-control I have, I straighten up and make it over to the portal, although I don't know how. The edges of my vision blur together, something colorful lurking behind the haze, threatening to jump at me if I move the wrong way.

My throat is so tight, breathing is hell.

Victor pulls up the leg of his pants and removes one of the tools.

"Let's get this party started," he whispers, entering commands into a little, thin plastic sheet before he carefully lays it down onto the console, his movements cautious and controlled.

My hands shake so badly, I wrap them around my body to keep them still.

This is bad.

I try to fight it, to push it down, but it's the worst it's ever been.

I *know* something bad is going to happen. It's palpable in the air—

And I'm the only one feeling it. I know that as well.

Victor is completely unaffected and oblivious to me almost losing it. He enters command after command, focused on his task. "Come on, come on," he murmurs impatiently. "Why isn't this working? It's supposed to—"

"The code?" I rasp, one hand on my throat as if it could help me breathe. "Did you enter the code?" Avery's Sentinel code.

His eyebrows scrunch together, forming a V. "Of course not, why would—"

Deafening screeching, an alarm so loud it physically hurts. *"Unauthorized access. Unauthorized access. Unauthori—"*

Both of us jump.

"Shit!" Victor curses. He drops the cautious approach and instead hammers commands into the touchscreen. "Shit, shit, shit."

No kidding. Out of nowhere, another layer of doom presses down on me, drowning me on dry land, pulling me in and under, confusing my senses.

Part of me sees all seven doors leading into the domed room open at once, sees dozens of Second Class Sentinels spilling into the room and racing toward us, sees all of it, sees all the Leivas... Yet neither of these images holds anything against the uprising panic that grows inside my mind.

The Sentinels scream commands I can't understand in this chaos of alarm, shouts, and ringing in my ears.

"Oh, fuck, fuck, fuck, I can't open the portal." Victor's fingers fly faster and faster over the screen, but it's no use. It's not going to work. "Noa, behind me, quick, maybe if I—"

He throws one last panicked glance at me before three Sentinels come running straight at him, their arms stretched out, their faces distorted into angry masks.

"Shit!" Victor curses. His hand fiddles with something under his lab coat on his prison uniform's waistband. "Noa, come on! Give me your hand—"

The first Sentinel jumps forward, and only with a quick duck and roll is Victor able to evade him. He grunts but is back on his feet in no time.

"Noa—" Victor gives a quick look from me to the Sentinels and back, his eyes too wide in a pale face. "Fuck. I'm sorry, Noa, look, I'm sorry, I reall—" He swallows the rest of his sentence as he pushes a button on his belt and a rope of sorts shoots out of the back of his shirt. It hits the domed ceiling with a *clonk* that's surprisingly still audible in this cacophony of noise. Not even a split second later, Victor gets jerked upward at a speed that jackknifes his body an instant before the Sentinel's hands can close around his throat.

Like in slow motion, I see myself taking a step toward him, one hand outstretched, waiting for him to take me with him, to get me out. I'm fighting gravity itself to move my body, but I don't get far.

Something big slams into me from behind like a truck, tackling me to the cold floor, almost crushing me under its weight. I scream out once as the impact snaps my head into my neck and then forward onto the hard floor, momentarily stunning me.

"Not so fast, *Ghost*," hisses someone into my ear.

Large hands yank me back to standing again, strong fingers digging into my skin. A second Sentinel is there, and a third, and a fourth, until I'm surrounded by a sea of Leivas. One of them grabs my hair and pulls my head back. Their favorite move.

Above me, glass splinters and rains down on us. A lone blond figure pushes out from the dome, running down its slope. Somebody yells for a hunter team, but still, the figure runs out of view.

There's more yanking on my hair.

"Are there more? Tell me, Ghost, or this is not going to be pleasant." Spittle hits my face, but it doesn't register to me.

Their faces hover right above me, to my left, to my right, all around me, yet they're blurry and overshadowed by something else, something with more colors, something that can't be real.

Somebody cries out in pain behind me, a sound so odd, I can't make sense of it.

There's another yank on my hair. "Now, Ghost!" A fist hits my stomach with the force of a grenade. Pain explodes in my center and clouds my vision even more than it already is.

I shouldn't give in—I should fight, I *know* that, but still, I plunge deeper and deeper into the sinkhole my mind opened for me, pushed down quicker by every yank on my hair, by every shove to my body. Every punch that hits me ignites a new agony on my insides, adding physical pain to the already existing torture my mind unleashes on me.

This is it.

We failed.

I'll never get home, and Earth will never—

Commotion somewhere behind me, Sentinels crying out, bodies dropping to the floor, a loud growl, bone hitting bone, grunts—

—then the grip releases my hair, my hands are free, then—

"Noa, quick! Can you walk, we—*crap!*"

Another grunt, another body dropping, more screaming and yells from farther back, all drowned by the screeching sirens and blood swooshing through my ears.

Like in a trance, I see another group of Sentinels storming through the doors, forcing Avery backward and me with him, his body protectively in front of mine, one hand feeling for me behind him—a hand that shines into my darkness like a beacon of hope.

I take another step back, accompanied by another tightening in my throat.

"Give up, McTighe," somebody hisses. "We outnumber you. There's no way out. We—"

The voice drones on, but I don't hear him.

With every step backward and closer to the portal, my world narrows down to the hand that I reach for, the edges of my vision that tatter and tear, the noises that swell up and down—

A vortex opens beneath my feet.

The last thing I feel before I'm swallowed by a darkness that weighs heavier than anything I've ever felt before is Avery's hand in mine—then, there's nothing.

Absolutely nothing.

CHAPTER TWENTY-TWO

In Deep

“   which demotes Pluto to a dwarf planet these days, but • • • that doesn't make it any less fascinating. If your weight was one hundred pounds here on Earth, you would only weigh seven on Pluto, because its gravity is only one fifteenth of ours. Pluto's orbit is also—"

Stars above me, something heavy on my chest, the monotone droning of a voice, and the distinct feeling I'm missing something.

Somebody giggles.

More giggles and whispers.

The weight on my chest starts to move.

"We know that because of the Hubble Space Telescope, although Pluto is so far away, that the images are—"

The giggles and whispers get almost excited.

"Excuse me for just one second."

The sound of a microphone being cut off, steps, surprised murmurs—and suddenly a face right over me, replacing the image of a red planet.

"Out," the figure hisses. "This is inappropriate behavior. I give you ten seconds before I call security."

What?

The weight on top of me groans.

What—

Avery?

Everything shifts and clicks into place.

Earth.

This is my universe.

This is home, the Adler Planetarium—in the middle of a show, with me and Avery—

"Ten… nine…" The older man's face is upside down, but its frown is not.

Avery groans again, a sound the man does not like at all.

"Completely inappropriate, sir. This is a show for children. Now get out!" He lays one hand on Avery's shoulder, trying to pull him up and off of me by his shirt.

With ultrasonic speed, Avery thrusts his arm up and grabs the man's wrist while he twists his body on top of mine. Within a second, he faces up, bending the man's joint into an unnatural position. The man yelps out and drops his weight to accommodate for the sudden pressure on his wrist.

"Who are you?" Avery growls with a slight slur. "What—?"

Around us, the whispers grow shocked and louder, more urgent.

I push against Avery's back from below with both hands. "Avery, it's okay. Let him go. We need to leave."

The man whimpers, but Avery keeps his hold on him, his head jerking from left to right, taking in the situation and trying to make sense of it.

And I don't think it's working.

"Avery." I try to push free from underneath him, but that man is heavy. "Avery, let go. Get up. We need to—" I grunt. It's almost impossible to get at least part of my body out from under his weight. "Trust me, Avery. *Go.*"

Maybe it's my words, maybe it's the realization kicking in that things have changed, but mercifully, Avery releases the man and jumps to his feet, much more a warrior than the lover the planetarium's employee wanted to chase off.

I scramble to my feet. "Sorry about that. Lapse in judgement. We're out."

Open-mouthed, the man stares at me, and he's not the only one.

By now, the whole auditorium has realized the true show is not up on the dome's ceiling, but down on the floor, in front of the projector and narrator's area. People in the back stand up to get a better view of the two stupid ones who apparently decided to make out during a show about... Pluto or something.

Yeah, right.

Making out. Rather making our way out of Terra, a miracle I can't believe happened. The portal must have—

Doors open behind the man, and for a moment, I expect Sentinels to barge in, but it's only another suited employee.

"Again, so sorry." I drag Avery with me by his hand, as far away as possible from anybody with a planetarium's nametag on their chest.

Avery stumbles after me as we pass the countless aisles of seats, kids about middle school age in every one of them, grinning ear to ear over our interruption.

Finally, we reach the doors and spill into a quiet area illuminated in purple, with smooth plastic-covered, curved, and irregular walls, like the inside of an alien's spaceship.

I come to a dead stop. Avery bumps into me from behind.

No sliding doors, no sparkly floors, no scientists in lab coats.

This really is Earth.

My heart makes a silly little leap, only to sprain itself from the exertion. We're no better off than before, if not worse. Avery is here with me, not Victor, and while I'd prefer the Sentinel over the Ghost any time of day, he isn't prepped as Victor was. How are we going to—?

Around us, the purple shifts to blue, and Avery crouches out of reflex. The next moment, though, he stumbles and almost drags me down with a tug on my hand.

"Avery, you all—?"

I turn to help him up, and for the first time since he came for me, I look at him.

And he doesn't look good.

He's much paler than normal, and everything about him that

seemed normal in the Terraverse screams not normal in this universe.

His height, stature, amber eyes, uniform, gun, stick—you name it.

Despite the confused look on his face, Avery oozes danger, and while that might be a benefit for his Sentinel duties, on Earth, that's not a good thing. People have been pulled over by cops for less.

Gently, I push him against the wall, and to my surprise, he lets me. "Stay here. Don't move. Wait." I hold up a hand like ordering a dog to stay, and it does the trick. Avery nods, his gaze roaming over the walls, probably trying to make sense of any of it.

Without waiting for much of a reply, I open the door to the Sky Theater again, sneaking in as fast as possible. I'm sorry, guys, but we're kind of desperate. I drop down into a crouching duck-walk along the wall behind the last row of seats. There's a superhero backpack behind one of the seats, wonderful, and a jacket about my size behind another. Even better.

That makes two.

Come on, there must be something at least remotely Avery's size. The United States have the worst obesity numbers ever, and this is the one place everybody wears a size medium? Finally, I find a large black jacket that won't be perfect but will do the job. Keeping my bounty close to my chest, I sneak out of the theater undiscovered, finding Avery exactly how I left him.

By now, that's starting to freak me out a little.

"Here. Take off your gun and that stick-thingy. Put them in here." I zip the backpack open and hand it to him. We're lucky nobody saw that gun and freaked out. "And then put this one on." I throw the jacket to Avery, who catches and holds it in a daze.

I've never seen him this out of it.

"Avery. Hey." I take him by the shoulders. "It's okay. We're on Earth. I know you're confused, but we have to get going. Trust me and follow my lead, okay?" My eyes bore into his until I'm sure he understands what I just said. Waking up in a different universe must be confusing for him, as it was for me. At least nobody is trying to choke the life out of him.

After an eternity, Avery nods and slides his arms into the jacket. "Gun," I say, pointing at the backpack.

Avery drops the gun into it, then shakes his head. "Not the staff." He shoves it into an inside pocket of his new jacket.

A weight drops off my chest. Staff, stick, whatever. At least he's talking.

I sigh. "Fine. Keep it hidden, though. It's not really standard attire here." Neither are our outfits, patched up as they are. We stick out like a sore thumb, and that can't happen, for many reasons, like Earth police or Terrans coming through and finding us.

Oh, crap.

That's a distinct possibility. Maybe not now during daylight, not if Canyon's policy is to keep Terra a secret, but later.

We better hurry.

"Come on." I take his hand again and ignore the warmth that shoots up my arm the second my palm touches his. I only hold on to him because I need to keep him close, that's all.

That's all.

I lead us down the blissfully empty walkways, following the exit signs. Around us, the walls twist and turn, changing colors every couple of yards. Avery's head swivels left and right, especially when the first video presentation pops up on one of the pinkish walls next to us, triggered by our approach. He suppresses it, but I do pick up on the short twitch, as if he wanted to drop into a fighting stance.

All I can do is walk faster and squish his fingers between mine, willing him to follow my lead.

Finally the lobby, finally the exit. For a moment, I remember everything in white, the Sentinel Forces Transporter standing in front of us, but that's back in a different universe.

I open the doors and pull Avery outside—and he stops dead in his tracks.

In front of us is Chicago, *my* Chicago, in all its beauty, a grey skyline against a grey sky, rays of sunshine breaking through here and there.

"What… What is this?" Avery breathes, his hand nearly crushing mine.

"Chicago," I say, "the Earth version."

No time for sightseeing. I take the stairs down to the walkway that will bring us away from Northerly Island and closer to the city. Closer to home.

Closer to my parents.

And that's where the problems begin. I can't waltz in there after having been gone for several days, can I? I mean, the school is going to have the police involved, my parents will have to notify them, and… well, then there's Avery, who's now stranded in my universe, without the failsafe return option Victor had. We don't have a bridge.

I stop. "Shit."

Avery tenses next to me. "What?"

"Nothing, but…" I lead him to the side and toward a bench between two large planters with a great view of the skyline. "We have to brainstorm."

"Agreed." At least his voice has a bit more of its usual strength by now, and while I slump into the bench, he stays ramrod straight, assessing our surroundings.

I guess you can take the Sentinel out of his duties, but you can't take the duties out of a Sentinel.

"Relax," I say, tugging on his uniform until he leans into the backrest. "You're drawing attention." We're definitely not alone here. Lots of people decided today was a great day to visit the planetarium. Staying under the radar starts now.

"Well, first, welcome to Earth, Avery." I smile at him, but he only raises an eyebrow over a face that's way too white. "This didn't work as planned, did it?"

"Not quite," Avery says quietly. "But at least neither of us is in Sentinel custody."

Neither of us, nor is Victor. Avery doesn't say it, but the look on his face shows his displeasure about that loud and clear.

"I know," I answer in a voice barely over a whisper. "Thank you for that."

"I didn't—"

"You did. Without you, I'd be with them right now, and not here." Such a close call. I wonder how Victor did it. I mean, I didn't see a blue glow, which I assume is the active mode of the portal, but still. I shake my head. "Somehow, Victor must've activated the portal, or it wasn't inactive and we must've been closer to it than I thought—"

"I don't think that's it."

My eyebrows shoot up. "You don't? How else did we cross?"

"I'm working on a theory." His brows crunch down into a V. "What did you feel before you passed through the portal?"

Panic. Chest-crushing, breath-stealing panic with a touch of end-of-world-feeling.

I scratch my temple. "Uh, nothing much." I shrug. "The usual." I can't tell Avery about my panic attacks. I couldn't stand seeing the same look in his face that I saw in Kevan's or anybody else's. "Why?"

"Like I said, working on a theory." The corners of his lips quirk up the slightest bit, but his eyes take on a new intensity, like he's caught me lying.

I suck in my lower lip. "Okay… well, until then, let's focus on all the other stuff, like where do we go from here? How do we get you home? Can we still complete the mission?" Not that I'm looking forward to that part, but… I don't think I could ignore what I learned and keep on living my life as if nothing happened. I can't unlearn what the Ghosts told me, and neither could I live with myself if I pretended it didn't matter.

He studies the people passing us by. Most don't pay us any attention at all. Maybe here and there, somebody looks at us like people look at other people, in passing by and without any special interest.

"Fascinating," he murmurs, shooting a glance at me and then back at the passersby.

I punch him lightly in the shoulder. "Focus, please."

"Hey! I am focused." He rubs his shoulder as if my little nudge had any kind of impact on his muscular build.

"Okay, then, first question: Can we still get the information the Ghosts want?"

That definitely gets his attention. "You really want to do this?"

"Well, that wording is a tad too strong, but I think we *should* do it. We should get that, and then… I don't know. Maybe take it from there, depending on what we find?" I can't forget the words Avery said to Tonya: *"It's homicide on a grand scale."*

Avery sighs. "It's going to be difficult, if not impossible. To get to the level of planning the Ghosts already had in place…" He shrugs. "Weeks, if not months, that is, if I can get the materials I need to build an access for his port…" His gaze drops to the grey concrete ground. "If not impossible, but it's going to be a close call."

Weeks. Months. That's not making things easier. "I can't stay hidden for that long. Most likely, they're searching for me already. Maybe even here in America, although I got, uh, *lost* in Germany. Sooner or later, somebody is going to recognize me, and that's going to open a whole new Pandora's box of problems. Plus, and this is the real kicker, I don't have any resources."

His eyebrows scrunch together.

"Money," I say. "All I had, all my credit cards, all my stuff, is still in my suitcase somewhere in Germany. Or back here by now, who knows? Not that I could use the cards without alerting authorities, but still. Point is, we're stuck." And speaking of. "But the one stuck the most is you." I gently nudge him. "How are we going to get you back?"

The muscles in his jaw tighten. "For that, I'm also working on a theory."

I chuckle softly. We're so screwed, it's not even funny. "Okay, then. So it seems to me, the first thing we need is time. Resources second. Third… more theories." We need a home base. Period. The problem is, we only have one option, and that… will take some lying. Quite a bit of lying.

I close my eyes. Oh, boy, I can't believe I'm about to suggest this, but… it's not as if we have much of a choice, and if we're doing this, it needs to be watertight. Well, aside from the obvious holes in the story, but hopefully their anger at me will make them overlook that.

Clearing my throat, I look down at my hands. "I have an idea. We go to my place. My parents… are going to be sick with worry anyway." Even sicker than they already are. "I tell them I ran away from the field trip because… because I met you." My face heats up like a lightbulb.

Avery's head whips around. "Me?"

His eyes are about to burn a hole into me as it is, so I stare at my folded hands instead. I literally can't take the heat.

"Yeah. I apologize, blame it on teenage hormones, introduce you, and tell them some kind of story that will convince them to call the cops off my case and to not call the cops on your butt for… whatever." It's sweltering hot here, despite sitting in the shade on a cool afternoon. "Then we hope they let you stay, use our apartment as a home base and come up with a new plan."

It sounds easy enough, but it's anything but. There are tons of holes in my alibi. Besides the logistics of traveling and having made it to the United States without my passport or money, let's talk about the first thing George and Elaine are going to latch on—me, coming home after days of being gone without a word, and worse—me, with a… boyfriend? My parents are going to go nuts. I frown. Another disappointment on the already long list they probably have of me.

Avery stares at me for such a long time, I wonder if he's still too shell-shocked from the transition to get what I'm hinting at. Finally, he clears his throat. "That… uh, that sounds like a plan." He shuffles his feet under the bench. "Or we could play it by ear, depending on the hypothesis regarding your disappearance."

"Oh. S-Sure, of course." I swipe a non-existing lock of hair out of my face. Yeah. He's right, they'd never buy Avery was my boy—

"I mean, it's… it's a good plan, but for all we know, they could assume you've been kidnapped. So all I'm saying is to be vigilant and adapt, and…" He coughs into his shoulder. "Well, anyway. Knowing the Sentinel Forces, there will be a retrieval attempt soon—"

Wait, what? "Retrieval attempts?" That doesn't sound good.

Avery nods. "Yes. If they're not sending somebody through a different portal as we speak, they will send them through the planetarium once it's safe to cross."

"But they won't find you." Because Chicago is big. How could they, right? We're totally safe.

Avery inclines his head. "Eventually, they will. Standard procedure is to scan for Terran life signs, then check them off one by one. A remnant from times when Ghosts were crossing actively back and forth. If we're lucky, it will take them a few days, but at some point…" He stares into the distance. "We should take that into consideration. We might… *I* might have to go and hide."

Nuh-uh. It doesn't fly that way, incoming Sentinels or not. "Not *you*. If at all, both of us."

"I won't—"

"Yes, you will. You don't know anything about this universe, and I'm not about to let you walk into trouble. You watched out for me on Terra. I'm watching out for you on Earth." It's non-debatable. I wouldn't want it any other way. Maybe it's my personal tit for tat, and one that I'm much more comfortable with than any of the others before.

He narrows his eyes at me. "It could be dangerous."

"I don't care." Goosebumps pop up all the way down my back, spreading to my arms and legs.

He keeps staring as if looking for something, and with every second he doesn't blink, the goosebumps rise higher.

"Okay," he says eventually. "We're in this together."

I let out a shaky laugh. "Together." It sounds good.

Together.

CHAPTER TWENTY-THREE

Terrans

The trip through Chicago to my home is like bringing a toddler to town for the first time in their life.

Avery doesn't know cars—well, he knows the principle, but he's never seen six lanes crammed bumper-to-bumper during rush hour.

He's never smelled the fumes of congested streets, never heard the noise of a busy city life, never pushed his way through masses of people on the sidewalk, and never smelled cigarette smoke.

"Why would people do that?" He coughs wide-eyed after somebody blew smoke right into his face. "That can't be good."

He stops at store windows, looks into restaurants, and almost pulls out the staff when a nearby bus honks.

Something tells me he's not the biggest fan of my version of Chicago.

Because we don't have any money, we have to walk for several miles to get home. It's too risky to jump on a bus or the 'L' without a ticket. I've driven this very route countless times but never walked it before. And why would I? You don't walk. Half the time of the year it's too hot; the other half way too cold.

The closer we get to my apartment, the slower we go. We've been on our feet for a good two hours already, and while Avery isn't the quickest right now, neither am I. I want to get home so badly… yet I don't.

Facing my parents after what I did to them… well, it's not high up on my list. I know how their faces are first going to light up when they see me, and then fall when they see Avery and realize what I did.

Running away. With a boy. A *man*.

Every once in a while, I can't help but check him out as he walks next to me or stays a tad behind to look at something he's never seen before. Avery is… no boy, that's for sure. Sentinel genes and the couple of years he has on me made sure of that. So maybe I shouldn't consider the head-over-heels-in-love excuse. Maybe we should go with Avery saving me from kidnappers. One look at him and nobody would doubt that story—only it would involve more police than we'd feel comfortable with.

Eventually, there's no turning back anymore. "We're here." I shield my eyes against the sun going down behind our high-rise building. The twenty-third floor, second window from the corner. My room.

"Here?" Avery looks up, one hand shielding his eyes.

"Yup," I say. Nothing left to do but to wipe the sweat off my palms and punch the entrance code into the pad that will open the door to the lobby. "Ready?"

"I'll follow your lead, and… well, stay in the background for now."

While my parents will probably kill me over what I've done. Terra owes me. Big time.

The elevator arrives, and I open the door for us. Luckily, we're in alone because Avery fills out the tiny cab pretty much to the brim. After I press the number 23, the doors close, and with a little jerk, the elevator whisks us up.

"Whoa!" Avery reaches for the wall to stabilize himself. "The floor! It's moving. What—?"

I really don't want to laugh—I don't. But right now, he has the most adorable confused look on his face as he's trying to figure out what's going on. So yes, I giggle. A bit.

Avery shoots me a dirty look. "Not funny. Why is the floor… Wait, is this a transport tube?"

"The thing you took me up to Canyon at the Reichstag? Yeah,

kind of, only here, I know how it's working."

He deflates. "Okay. For a moment, I was worried there. Why don't you just use magnetism or a vacuum?"

Yeah, why don't we? "No clue. It's a cabin in a shaft pulled up by thick iron ropes and a motor."

That does the trick and Avery relaxes visibly, contrary to me. The higher we go, the more my stomach contracts and forces bitter bile up my throat.

The doors open into our hallway.

Is it bad that I'd rather run and cross back over to Terra than ring that doorbell right now?

He squeezes my shoulder. "You'll be fine. They're your parents. I'll take all the blame, and then…"

Exactly. And then?

I reach up and squeeze his hand back. "Let's do this."

My heart hammers like crazy inside my chest, each beat reverberating in my skull as if it were an empty drum. I don't hear anything besides the rhythm of my heart that's way too fast to be healthy.

There we go. Number 2319 at the very end of the hallway.

I blow out a big breath through pursed lips. Let's hope I at least have the guts to face them. What if they're worse because of me, what if—

I find the bell and ring it.

I imagine Elaine getting up from her favorite spot on the couch. She works herself to standing like it was a task too difficult to handle. Then she fishes for her cane and shuffles around the coffee table and George's chair, hoping whoever rings the bell will wait until she makes it to the door.

In my mind, she's entering the front room, when indeed I hear soft steps and the typical *click-click* of her cane.

"My mom," I whisper, my throat dry and raspy.

There's a swiping sound of the locking chain being removed, and then the door opens.

"Hey, Elaine," I whisper, raising a hand for a silent *hello*.

The door opens wider, just like my mom's tired eyes.

"Noa? What—?"

That's all she can say because Avery leaps in front of me, pushing me back so roughly I cry out and almost stumble. With one impossibly fast movement, the stick is in his hand, springing to full size a split second later.

"Stay away from Noa," he growls. *"Terran."*

CHAPTER TWENTY-FOUR

Truth, Hidden

My gaze darts back and forth from Avery—coiled, tensed and about to burst—to my mom, her jaw dropped, her hand slowly sliding off the doorknob without her noticing.

I try to push past Avery, but he keeps one hand out to stop me. "Stay back," he growls, his eyes never leaving my mom.

"Avery, she… It's *Elaine*. This is *my mom*, Avery!" What the heck is wrong with him? It's my mom!

My mother lets go of a big breath before she takes an equally big one.

"Sentinel," she says, opening the door wider. "Why don't we talk this through?"

Sentinel?

My mother knows Avery is a Sentinel?

How in the world…?

For the longest of moments, none of us moves.

Not Avery, watching Elaine like a hawk.

Not my mom, looking so much more vulnerable than ever.

Not me, trying to make sense of the scene unfolding in front of me.

Eventually, Avery lowers his staff but keeps both ends of it extended. "That is acceptable."

"Well, then." My mom steps aside, making room.

"After you," Avery says tensely. "Noa, stay behind me."

"But—"

"Behind me."

A small tired smile plays on my mother's face as she turns around. "Noa, please close the door behind you."

"Please close the door behind you?"

Hello to you too, Mom.

Elaine leads the way through our narrow and dark hallway past the room that used to be Andrew's, still full of all his stuff. Not a single item has been moved unless to clean around it.

She opens the glass door to the living room.

"Honey, what—?" George chokes on a breath the moment Avery steps into view. "Sentinel," he croaks, visibly trying to not lose his wits.

"Terran," Avery says by way of greeting with a slight nod, staff still at the ready in front of him.

There it is again. Terran? George and Elaine… both *Terrans?*

That can't be! I must've heard it wrong. It doesn't make any sense at all. Those are George and Elaine, born and raised in Chicago, with absolutely nothing out of the ordinary that would make them Terran.

"Noa, what… How…?" George tries to get out a complete sentence, although mainly his mouth opens and closes, like a fish out of water. He can't decide whether to stare at me or Avery, so it looks like he's having a seizure.

My eyes sting. "Yeah, those are good questions, George," I whisper. Not the reunion I imagined. Not even close.

Elaine walks around the coffee table and drops into her seat on the couch next to George. The cushions in her back are still messed up from when she got up a minute ago. I bet they've been sitting there all day, like they did every day since they became too sick to do much else.

I swallow hard.

"Sit," Elaine says, gesturing to the two comfy chairs across from her and George.

"I'll be standing, thank you," Avery says, the poster boy for politeness if it weren't for the wide stance and staff held at the ready. I fall into my usual chair next to the window, weak knees and all.

"Terran?" I ask them. "You're from Terra?"

Does that mean I'm a Terran? Andrew? What else don't I know?

George closes his mouth, his lips pressed into a tight line. "You're talking about things you don't understand, Noa. You—"

"Oh, I understand it just fine," I snarl. "I understand there are two connected universes, because I've been there. I understand they're connected through portals, because I've been through them. I understand people in Terra are slightly different from us, because I've seen them. And—"

All that's missing is the audible *click* to accompany my sudden understanding when all the little tidbits fall into place, forming an image I don't want to see.

I look up at Avery. "Do they show?" I circle a finger around my forehead. Regular Terrans don't know about Earth, the exception being prisoners sent here for their sentences, and... Ghosts.

Ghosts who don't show their implanted IDs, as Avery explained to me.

"No." He shakes his head.

I suck in a sharp breath of air. "You're Ghosts. Both of you are Ghosts."

George and Elaine... Ghosts? It doesn't make sense, and yet it does. Their distaste in anything government. Their desire to be independent. Their lifelong quest to stay under the radar.

Ghosts.

Elaine and George exchange a glance like I've seen them do a million times. Then Elaine sighs. "Yes." She looks up at Avery next to my chair. "I was wondering if you'd ever catch up with us."

"I'm sure at this point the Sentinel Forces know about your presence on Earth." Avery throws an odd, pointed glance at Elaine's wrist. "But the Sentinel Forces don't make it a habit of hunting down single fugitive Ghosts. There's no need for it. Not with the portals and bridges under control."

Elaine huffs. "Canyon must be so proud of himself, stranding his fellow Terrans on Earth. I'm surprised it took him so long to send you. And still, you're almost too late." She leans back into the cushions at a snail's pace but keeps her cane in her hand.

Avery points at it. "If you don't mind, let's have this somewhere else." He steps forward and takes the cane from my mom. "Nice work." He nods and lays it down onto the windowsill.

"Thank you," Elaine says past clenched teeth.

Nice work? What is that cane other than a cane, and—

"I want you to release Noa," George says, sitting up straighter. "She has nothing to do with any of this. Let her go." There's a slight shake to his hands, but he still holds Avery's gaze.

"What makes you think I'm holding her against her will?" Avery asks calmly.

George huffs just like Elaine, something so typical for my sarcastic parents, I almost tear up. "A Sentinel at our door after our daughter disappears. What other conclusion is there to draw? I'm surprised you still brought her here, but since she isn't—" He stops himself right there, his hand covering his mouth as if to stop the words from pouring out.

"Go on," Avery says. "You were about to say?"

"Nothing," George grumbles, earning himself an angry glance from Elaine.

Avery stays quiet for a moment, his head tilted to the side, assessing my parents. "I'm definitely here because of Noa. But then, *she* isn't Terran—or is she?"

Both my parents stay silent.

"Is she?"

Silence. Silence that's so thick I wonder how I can still breathe. What is he saying, that—

"Probably not," Elaine whispers eventually, focused on something on her lap.

My world goes up in smoke with these two words.

A wheezy breath leaves my throat. "What does that mean?" *Probably not?* My parents are Terran, depending on if it's a matter of genetics or location of birth, shouldn't it be an easy yes or no, and not—

I stare back and forth from Avery to my left and my parents in front of me, none of their expressions reassuring.

A cube of ice forms inside my stomach that grows with every strained second of silence that neither George nor Elaine look at me.

"That's what I thought," Avery eventually says evenly. "What about… Andrew?"

"Yes," Elaine breathes, tears in her eyes. "Terran genes and Terran born. That's why…" Her voice breaks. "That's why he died."

Excuse me?

"What?" I almost fall off my chair. "*What?*"

"It might be time," says Avery, his voice quiet. "She should know."

I should know *what?*

George lays a hand on Elaine's leg. "We wouldn't have had much more time anyway. Considering the recent development…" He nods at Avery. "The Sentinel is right, no matter how this ends. She needs to know, hon."

Elaine drops her hand onto George's and holds it while bending to the right over the armrest. She opens a drawer of the small wooden stand she has next to the couch. Usually, she keeps her knitting stuff in there, but this time she pulls out something else.

"Remember this?" She lays a bracelet out on the table in front of me I know only too well.

"Of course." I'd worn a similar one for the longest time until Kevan made fun of me, somewhen shortly after my first panic attack. All of us have one—or rather, *had* one. Andrew, George, Elaine, and me. Our family bracelet, a small silver chain with a coin-like center piece that's decorated with a symbol George always said meant peace. I loved that bracelet when I was young, and I hated it when I grew older. It made me look weak in front of Kevan, a symbol of my attachment to my parents, like I was still a kid and carrying the proof of it right around my wrist.

Needless to say, I dropped it and never wore it since.

I reach for the silver bracelet and pick it up. The back of the coin has been cut open. Wait—little circuits, electronic components. "What is this?"

Avery puts his hand on my shoulder. "A modulator."

My gaze shoots up to him. *This* is a modulator? The very same thing Avery asked Canyon to give me? All these years I was wearing a modulator and never knew it?

Elaine takes the bracelet out of my hand again. She sets it back next to the three other ones she took from the drawer.

"The Sentinel is right. These are our modulators, Noa. Terrans need them to adjust to the Earth Universe, or else..." She shrugs. "Well, or else we won't survive for long."

An uneasy sensation blooms in the pit of my stomach. "Then why aren't you wearing yours?"

George gives me a sad smile. "Because they all broke eventually. They're not supposed to work forever, you know? And we were never meant to stay for that long."

Ice spreads through my veins. "Oh my god," I whisper. "That's why Andrew died. The modulator, it... it..." It broke, taking the only protection he had against the Earth Universe from him. It was never cancer. Not for him, not for Elaine, and neither for George.

It was always rejection.

That's why there was no therapy that worked. That's why they never tried.

Elaine takes in a raspy breath. "Yes. His broke first, so I gave him mine, and when we found out you had stopped wearing yours for months... and you were fine... we used it for him, and the others for spare parts."

I remember that day. I got sent to my room without dinner that night, officially for lying to my parents about the bracelet, but now... Now I see it under a different light. Nobody should have been that mad because I didn't wear a stupid bracelet, not unless they thought I could've died without it.

I blink twice. "How come I'm doing fine without the modulator? Was I... Was I born here?" It would make sense, wouldn't it? Born in this universe, aligned with Earth. Born in Terra, aligned with them.

Elaine stares at the modulators. "Things aren't always what they seem, Noa." She squeezes George's hand, who sends her a small smile she doesn't see.

What am I not getting here? Avery rubs my back, reassuring me this is real, although it feels anything but.

Elaine stays quiet. She stares ahead without blinking until eventually George sighs and closes his eyes for a second to collect himself.

"Noa, it's complicated. Elaine and I… Yes, we were Ghosts. It feels like a lifetime ago, but once upon a time, we fought the good fight to free the people of Earth and the people of Terra from a tyrant who calls himself Minister—President at that time." He throws a careful glance at Avery, probably expecting a backlash that doesn't come.

"One day, we got instructions from Galileo personally. All three of us were to cross to Earth. Andrew was still a toddler, mind you. That's why we were chosen. A family was more inconspicuous for the job, they said. We were supposed to meet with an Earthling, get a package, and cross back to Terra, only…" He pauses, leaning forward while playing with the corner of the tablecloth draped over the coffee table. "Only we didn't expect the package to be a baby girl or the bridges to be closed that very same day, leaving us stuck on Earth with Andrew… and you."

I hear what he says, I definitely do, but it doesn't make any sense. They are my parents, they—

"We don't know much about you from before, Noa," George continues. "And when we found out we couldn't cross back over, we only had one choice. We settled, expanded our covers, and raised you and Andrew as well as we could, all the while always keeping on the lookout for anything Terran—options to cross, Sentinels, other Ghosts… but nothing happened. Nothing happened for over fifteen long years," he whispers, that sad smile still there. "Not even when the modulators broke, and our Terran life signs should've been detected on their scans. Nothing happened."

Without Avery's hand on my shoulder, I wouldn't be sure if I were dreaming or not.

George and Elaine… are not my biological parents.

That's why I'm tiny, while they're not, why I'm blonde, while they're not, why I always felt off, while Andrew didn't.

That's why.

I'm waiting for one of them to say they're sorry, for one of them to say they love me no matter what, for one of them to do *something*, but both my parents stay silent.

They stay silent for so long, I wonder how they cannot fill it with a simple sorry, a simple apology, or at least a simple smile.

Nothing.

Never has it been more obvious the balance between us is off—has been off forever. Me, trying to get them to love me, them tolerating me, or maybe liking me. But loving me?

No.

After an eternity, George clears his throat, looking up at Avery instead of me.

"So what now? You take us into custody and bring us back to Terra? Or do you throw us into jail here, like you did with countless others of our people, leaving them on Earth to rot and die?" His voice is too soft to hold much of a sting, but still, a little bit of rebellion is hidden in there.

Once a Ghost, always a Ghost, no matter how sick. The same can't be said about being a parent, apparently.

"Neither," Avery quietly responds.

Now it's my parents'—*George and Elaine's*—turn to look flabbergasted for a moment. "What?"

"Things aren't always what they seem." Avery flicks his wrist once. The two ends of the staff retreat into the handle that he carefully lays down next to Elaine's cane on the windowsill.

Elaine finally looks at me with tears in her eyes. "I never wanted it to be this way," she whispers. "We kept it from Andrew, and we always wanted to keep it from you too, because…" She finds a small smile for me that does nothing but open an abyss beneath my feet. "Because we always thought you both would die before any of this would happen."

Avery squeezes my shoulder so hard, I have a hard time not moving away.

My mother sniffles once. "Because it was Galileo himself who gave us the order, we figured you were Terran, but… you can't be. Andrew died within months without the modulator. It would've been the same for you after you stopped wearing your bracelet. The only reason George and I are still hanging in here is because our bodies slowly adjusted to Earth over the years with a working modulator, and because we're adults. Our cells are more static and don't divide as much anymore, which so far has saved us." And condemned Andrew. The look on her face says it all.

I drop my face into my hands, hiding behind them from the truth that stares at me like a spotlight. All the little differences between us that didn't mean much compared to the one true difference: George, Elaine and Andrew reacted negatively to the Earth Universe, while I didn't.

Three Terrans, one little Earthling.

"Noa," Elaine says, her voice breaking. "I'm… I'm sorry."

Now she says it—and it doesn't do anything for me. I laugh out loud into the hands covering my face before I let them drop. "Sorry? For what? For lying to me about being adopted? About the cancer? About where you're from?" All my life I've felt off in this family, off in my own skin like I was pressed into a mold I didn't fit into. Be quiet, don't get noticed, do as you're told, if there's trouble, back down. All my life, I've been trying to live by their rules, trying to be a good daughter, yet it never worked.

It was never me.

It was them all along.

"Noa—"

"No." I hold up a hand. "I don't want to talk about it. I—" I don't know. I need to come to terms with my life being torn away from me and twisted beyond belief. "I need a moment."

I jump out of my chair and storm out of the room, leaving behind Avery and the two people I thought were my biological parents.

CHAPTER TWENTY-FIVE

More Tit for Tat

My room looks exactly as it did when I left here, but it's not as if I expected anything else. Well, maybe. Andrew's room still looks the same, and he's been dead for over a year. *But then, he was their biological son, not the daughter they never wanted,* a nasty voice inside my head adds.

It was always different for him, and while we never spoke about it, I'm sure he felt it.

I felt it for sure.

I stare out the window into the illuminated night sky that does nothing to calm my mind or to ease the sting of life on my soul. Not like it normally did. Whenever Kevan teased me. Whenever I fought with my parents. Whenever I was too weak to stand up for what I wanted, instead taking the easy way and agreeing.

Agreeing.

I'm beginning to hate that word.

The door behind me opens and closes, and even if I couldn't see Avery's reflection in the window in front of me, I'd know it was him. My parents… *George and Elaine* wouldn't come in here. They never do.

Even in the reflection, Avery looks out of place in my room decorated for an Earthling teenage girl. Thanks to my status as a nut job, I never had anybody over at my place, let alone a guy. Seeing Avery right here, how he turns around his axis, most likely more in search of secret hiding places, escape routes, and other Sentinel-related stuff rather than to see how I'm living… it feels completely unreal. Even more so when he steps behind me, so close that I can feel the warmth radiating off him.

Our eyes meet, amber on turquoise, my white-blonde hair in the reflection shining so much brighter than his black.

Blonde hair.

"Who are my parents?" I whisper at the image of him. My biological ones. Why am I here? I'm not who I thought I was—not my parents' biological daughter. I'm somebody they picked up. An Earth package babysat by Terrans. "Who am I, Avery?"

Avery stays silent for the longest time. His breath warms the back of my head. "It doesn't matter where you come from, Noa. It only matters where you're going. You heard Victor call me a PBM, didn't you?"

I raise an eyebrow. How could I have not? "Yeah."

He sighs. "I once told you all second born children are recruited to the Sentinel Forces, remember? I told you they're altered in utero, their genes modified to make them fit for their duties, and then taken away from their families at age six to begin their training." He pauses. "I might have chosen to omit a few details."

My head tilts to the side. "Like what?"

"Like not all parents making their second pregnancies public. Some try to defeat the one-child-law. They keep their child secret and hidden. They deliver at home or with the help of pro-family midwives. They all hope to be the ones to beat the odds, that they're going to be the one family who gets to keep their second-born child." Another pause. "It never works out."

He adjusts his stance, as if he needed more stability for what he was about to say. "When the government finds these children, they're still taken away, and they are still modified. It's never as thorough and never as… *good* as the in utero treatment, but it serves its purpose. Still, those kids rarely reach the full potential of in-utero modifications, leaving them lagging behind their peers during training and lagging behind in life when they're older, oftentimes making them the runt of the SF. Do you know who they are?"

The way he tells the story, there's only one conclusion, only one answer to the question. "You?" I whisper. "Is that what 'PBM' stands for, like—"

"Post-Birth Modification," Avery answers. "It's an insult that implies stupidity, being less than you could be. A derogative term that hits the core in every one of us."

"But you're nothing like that, Avery. You were best in your class, you rock the whole Sentinel-thing, you—" I stop myself before the blush on my cheeks becomes too noticeable. *You rock that whole Sentinel-thing. Way to go, Noa.*

The corners of his mouth pull up the slightest bit. "I worked hard for it. I didn't take *no* for an answer. On the day I was taken for modification…" I hear him swallow behind me. "I was only six years old. My parents had hidden me for all my life, living in seclusion in rural Iowa. Well, the day they came for me, my mother took me aside. She told me it didn't matter what life threw at me—it only mattered how I dealt with it." He fidgets with something under his shirt, maybe the necklace.

"She said in a couple of years it wouldn't matter where I came from, only where I was going. As long as that was my path, the path that I chose, I was doing well."

Oh. I see his point. "Was she right?"

He pulls his shoulders back. "For the longest time, I didn't think so. Life changed. Memories changed. But recently… recently I've been thinking I might understand what she said to me. Maybe. I'm still working on a theory." The tilt of his lips spreads higher.

"You like your theories, don't you?"

"I do."

For a while, we look at each other in the window, our eyes part of the illuminated night sky and somehow connected by a fate neither of us chose.

"I wish I had known sooner," I whisper eventually. It would have made all the difference. I could have lived with being adopted, but living like I was a foreign body in a family that I thought was rejecting me for no reason… that stung.

"They did what they had to," he replies softly.

"I know," I whisper back. "But all this time, I've been thinking they might come around if only I was a better daughter. I've been trying to get back to them, and…" I shrug. "I don't think they even care." That thought hurts more than it should. We were never that tight to begin with, so why does it bother me?

"They do. All parents care, no matter what the circumstances. Yours… had quite unfortunate circumstances stacked against them."

"That's one way of putting it." Terra, Earth… It's all a mess. "Why did Canyon destroy the bridges? I mean, he trapped all Terrans here, and they're still his people."

The question answers itself the moment I ask it. They're Ghosts. Like with anybody else who doesn't abide by Canyon's laws, the solution to the problem is shipping them off to Earth. Out of sight, out of mind.

Avery stays quiet for a moment. "Your parents aren't the only ones. The Sentinel Forces suspect hundreds of Ghosts were trapped on Earth when we disabled the use of bridges." He crosses his arms behind his back in his typical stance of attention. Only the softness of his voice belies the image of a soldier ready to fight.

"As to the reasons why, I can't offer you facts, only an opinion. During the time the bridges were closed, I was still young, before my training. We had many unapproved crossings at that time, so many that the SF and Canyon feared discovery by Earthlings. From what we were told, Ghosts were endangering the safety of Terra and needed to be stopped. So within a month or two, bridge destructors went online, searching for the specific wavelength bridges give off, finding and destroying them. In fewer than two weeks, we spanned a net that covered Terra completely. Wherever a bridge was energized, we'd know about it within a couple of seconds, and we had a team there within minutes."

"Minutes?" How many people do they have for these forces?

"Minutes," Avery says. "It was a matter of Terran security." He pauses. "We didn't know, Noa. None of us know how it is here." He nods out of the window. "All we know is that you're dangerous to us. We're made to recognize you, the enemy. All we know is what Canyon wants us to know. We're kept in the dark. Everything is a lie." The apple in his throat moves up and down when he swallows, his voice barely a whisper. "I think we should do all we can to complete what the Ghosts set out to do. We need to free Earth from Terra."

"We need to free Earth from Terra," says Avery, the Sentinel. The man who was made for the exact opposite, who lives for his duty in more ways than one, and who has risked everything since he met me.

And I'm whining about my parents.

Perspective, Noa.

"You might be the first Sentinel to ever say that, Avery."

A shy, sad smile shows on his face. "I've always been wired a bit… differently."

I turn around, my shoulder brushing across his chest. Craning my neck, I look up at him, the little bit of stubble adding a slight shadow to his pale skin.

"We're both pawns in a game played by others, aren't we?"

Avery looks down at me, the deep breath he lets go mingling with mine. As if it only now realized how close we are, my heart starts hammering like crazy. If it thought it could make up for the drop in blood pressure that came with the jolt of electricity shooting through me, it's mistaken.

In less than a split second, the world narrows down to Avery in front of me like I zoomed into a picture on my phone. Everything about him stands out in way more than 20/20 clarity. The long lashes fanning his cheeks. The stubble on his face. The irises made of amber, with little clouds of darker gold mixed in.

So much is going on in those amazing eyes of his, so much more than I expected. I—

Avery's pupils widen and gloss over before he takes a step back.

The connection between us withers away into nothingness.

Avery focuses on something above my head, all business.

"It became a game played by us the second we found out about it, Noa. And now that we know the game, I intend to play it."

I can't tear my gaze away despite the distance he created. A shiver runs down my body—no, not only down my body. Through my freakin' heart too.

"My life is a boat for one."

I cross my arms in front of my chest. Silence hovers, and it's heavy.

Avery chews on his lower lip, then takes a step back and points toward the door. "The premise has changed. The *game* has changed the moment we found out it was played. We might have been the pawns in the beginning, but now that has changed too. There are two Ghosts sitting in your living room. Ghosts equal information until proven otherwise, and information is key if we want to win this game against Canyon."

He looks at me again, and the eye contact charges me with a rush of energy.

"Payback starts today, Noa," he says. "Tit for tat."

Tit for tat.

All of a sudden, I'm back in school, at Kevan's mercy, trying to fit in where I never did. I'm back with Canyon, being manipulated into his psychotic schemes. I'm back with Victor, getting me to join the Ghosts.

I subconsciously ball my fists.

Nothing in my life I did because of me, or because I wanted to.

I was too busy trying to please my parents, trying to please everybody else.

Too busy to fit in. Too busy agreeing with others.

I stand up straighter.

I'm not the person I thought I was, in more ways than one. I'm done playing by somebody else's rules.

It's time I build my own life, and it's time I stop giving up.

A small smile finds its way onto my face.

"Tit for tat," I repeat after him. "Tit for tat."

CHAPTER TWENTY-SIX

Truth, Out

Talking to my parents about what happened in Germany and then on Terra is both a relief and scary at the same time. On the one hand, I'm proud to tell my story, proud to show what I've been through, proud of what I tried to achieve together with Victor, but on the other hand, it's completely surreal to hear my parents discuss everything I say like the Ghosts they really are.

They interrupt me so often, I barely have time to finish a complete sentence.

"The Reichstag? But it's only an outgoing portal there, the Reunification Building—"

"She should have never been able to cross, and—"

"I told you she shouldn't have gone! Did they pull her over to get to us, is that—"

If it's not their bickering, it's a question, or a comment, or something.

And it's getting on my nerves.

Walking back into the living room and talking to them is much more of a victory demonstrating my maturity than they'll ever know. I wouldn't say I'm friendly, but at least I'm not openly hostile, although I'm starting to change my mind on that.

"Canyon met with you personally? Twice? Why would he—"

"Oh my God. Tonya? She was still a teenager last time I saw her. How is she doing?"

If it weren't for Avery standing next to me—not quite as much at attention as before, but still radiating calm in his typical wide stance, his arms crossed behind his back—I would've lost it already.

For the umpteenth time, George cuts through my story. "I'm still not getting it. How did the Sentinels crack down on us… on the Ghosts… I mean, on *you* so quickly at the portal? No offense, your Sentinel Forces are good, but…"

"None taken," Avery says, much more evenly than I still could at this point. "I assume it's because—"

George flails. "And how did you cross back when—"

Elaine shakes her head. "I'd rather like to know how they could get that far if the SF got to them so quickly after Victor triggered the alarm since—"

"Guys! Guys! Stop it!" I lift my hands up. "Let Avery answer, for heaven's sake!"

"Avery?" George asks, a confused look on his face.

"Him." Elaine nods at Avery next to me. "The Sentinel."

George's brows scrunch together. "Oh. The Sentinel is… Avery. All right. All right then. *Avery.*"

I roll my eyes. Could they *be* any more awkward?

Avery sighs.

"As I was trying to say, the Ghosts recently tried to intercept one of the SF transports to the Main Hub," Avery says. "After that, we upgraded to High Alert. I'm assuming the SF responding so quickly to the alert has something to do with that attack upgrading our Alert Status."

George scoots forward on the couch. "That's unusual, I'd say. We… The Ghosts do this all the time. It's the only way we get supplies. What did the transport carry? Weapons? Information?"

Avery shakes his head. "Nothing of importance, from what I know. Chemicals. Mainly Rhodium for the research projects at the Main Hub."

All color leaves Elaine's face. "Rhodium?" She gropes blindly for George's hand on her left.

"Yes, we resent more the day later that made it through. Why?"

George waves. "What about drysillium?"

"That will be delivered on the 24th together with research equipment, which is why the SF will stay on high alert until the delivery, as I was told. Why?"

My parents simultaneously sink back into the cushions as if they'd practiced that move in tandem for a perfect execution.

George turns his head to face Elaine. "So he's finally doing it."

My mother closes her eyes. "We expected it sooner."

"Not true," George says. "Galileo always said it was a possibility, but we never truly thought Canyon would do something of this magnitude…" He rubs his free hand over his almost bald head.

Avery stiffens. "What exactly are you referring to?"

"Yeah, I'd like to know that too," I add. They're freaking me out. I've lived with them my whole life, at least for as long as I can remember. They were devastated over Andrew's cancer diagnosis— almost destroyed by his death—but they never looked like this.

Hopeless.

George's lower lip trembles. "I… I don't know how to say it." He laughs sarcastically. "Hell, there is no good way of saying it. He…" He blows out a big puff of air through pursed lips.

"Galileo always warned us of this. Rhodium and drysillium are compounds used for research or farming and nothing on their own, but combined…" His voice breaks at the end. "Canyon has finally had enough of Earth's humans. He's planning on unleashing both toxins into Earth's atmosphere, where they're going to combine into a DNA-specific poison." He swallows. "A poison that kills humans within minutes. In less than a day, all human life will be gone from Earth. We have until the 24th—three days until Canyon is going to kill us all." George looks at us with eyes full of pity. "Unless you can stop him. The survival of humanity rests on you."

The next time my mind has something close to awareness, Avery and my parents are already in the middle of a full-blown discussion while

I hold a glass of water I vaguely remember Avery getting for me.

"If he hasn't already transported it via the main hub, that's our only chance," George shouts, pushing himself up from the couch.

"I agree, but rushing in will do nothing for us," says Avery, much calmer. "In fact, it will destroy all our hopes to prevent this."

"We must keep him from transporting the drysillium to the Earthverse. Once he has both substances here, all he needs to do is send small portions of it through the Hub to all of Earth's portals, and *boom*, goodbye humanity." George makes a dramatic explosion motion with his arms, narrowly avoiding knocking Elaine in the face.

Avery nods. "Again, agreed. Our best—"

"You have to cross again and destroy the drysillium. It's the only way. No drysillium, no toxic gas," George says, his face so pasty and sweaty, I wonder how he's still standing. As it is, he sways quite a bit. Not a good sign. I take a sip of my water and spill a drop. Stupid shaking.

Avery thinks for a moment. "No."

That gets their attention. "No?" George repeats it as if he hadn't heard it correctly.

"No," Avery says. "Destroying the drysillium on Terra will only make Canyon aware of our plan and more careful with the next transport. We can cut him off once, maybe twice, but a third time is highly unlikely. If he wants to get the drysillium to Earth, he will. Unless…" He pauses and raises an eyebrow. "Unless there is no portal."

George and Elaine's eyes widen. "What… What are you suggesting?"

Avery coughs a couple of times until it turns into a spell that racks his body and forces him to take a quick compensatory step forward when his weight shifts.

"Here." I scoot aside and tap the wide armrest of my leather chair. "Sit." He's been awake much longer than I have, and I'm dead tired already. And I wasn't the one fighting our way out of the portal.

To my surprise, Avery hesitates only a few seconds before he takes me up on the offer. I scoot a little to give him more room.

"As I was saying, we need to keep Canyon from doing this once and for all. I'm suggesting we make sure he won't be able to bring anything to Earth ever again. I'm suggesting we take down the Hub."

George falls back into his seat on the couch. "Take out the Hub?" he repeats, flabbergasted. "That's… almost impossible."

"Almost," Avery says, "but not completely."

Elaine shakes her head. "Security, the sheer size of it, and we only have three days—"

"Three days are enough to get there unnoticed. We—" Avery coughs some more. I gently poke my elbow into his ribs and offer my water to him.

He takes a sip and keeps it in his hands. "We have a difficult situation, but also several advantages. One, Canyon doesn't know we know about his plan. Two, I am a Sentinel. I should be able to get into the Hub. I do have a few tricks up my sleeve, no matter what's happened the last few days. Three, I destroy the Hub, or at least the central incoming portal, but leave the outgoing ones intact for Terrans stranded here to get back to Terra."

He takes another sip. "Two birds, one stone. Going for the Hub ensures no drysillium being delivered and no toxic gas produced, and it also ensures Canyon's research on Earth is over, at least for a considerable amount of time. That should give the Ghosts the edge they've been looking for."

I feel like I skipped part of the conversation that flows around me as if I weren't even there. "Wait, what's the Hub?" Portals, I get, but the Hub?

"You don't need to know—" Elaine starts, but Avery waves her off, turning slightly toward me on the chair's armrest.

"Earth has dozens of portals connecting it with Terra. They all have two separate PCUs—Portal Calculation Units, or consoles. One for incoming, one for outgoing—and each requires its own calculations to open the connection between universes. Now, because all universes are in constant flux due to the events happening in them, they drift apart and… let's just say, their coordinates change."

I think I get that part. "Because with every new big event, the differences become bigger, and the paths split more and more from each other." I've so got this.

Avery nods. "Correct. To keep crossing between the same two universes is an extremely difficult task requiring a massive amount of calculations, and that's what the Hub is for. All portals are connected to it. It's the one overruling authority they get their coordinates and data from. The portals themselves are nothing more than mechanical constructions executing what the Hub is telling their consoles."

"So if we destroy the Hub, the portals are useless," I say. Makes sense.

"Correct again." Avery nods. "I leave the outgoing one intact and destroy the incoming one."

He says it like it's no big deal.

"How would you do that?" George asks. "We have supplies, but no explosives, nothing that would—"

"The staff," Avery simply says.

George's mouth forms a little "o."

"In self-destruct mode," Avery adds. "All four buttons pushed—*boom*."

George and Elaine exchange a hopeful glance. "You really think you can do that?" Elaine asks carefully.

"Yes." Avery sounds a hundred percent sure of himself.

"Alone?" Elaine raises an eyebrow.

A short hesitation. "Yes."

Now wait a second. "Not alone," I say, looking up at him. "Not alone." I can't believe I'm saying this. I can't believe I'm not shutting up and letting them do their thing—the Terrans, a Sentinel and two former Ghosts, but…

Avery shoots me a stern look.

"Noa—"

I hold up a hand that, to my own amazement, only shakes a little bit. "No, Avery. Remember? Your universe, your rules. My universe, my rules. I'm sorry, but you don't know squat about Earth. If you want to make it to the Hub, wherever it is, you need me." I know

I'm reaching with that statement, but I have to.

I'm not staying behind.

I meant what I said right after we crossed to Earth. We should continue the mission—*I* should continue it. While I didn't want to be sucked into any of this in the beginning, this has become my war, just like it has become Avery's. None of us chose to be soldiers in it, yet here we are. None of us chose the path we found ourselves on, yet we can't walk away from it. It wouldn't be right—especially not with humanity about to be wiped out.

For the first time in my life, my presence can actually do something good, and I refuse to think about the consequences. At least for now.

"You and me," I say. "We're in this together. Remember?"

"Noa is right," Elaine says, pointing to the window. "When we first came here, we almost blew our cover several times, and we were prepped by Galileo and the Ghosts. You have no such advantage, and you look much more like an outsider than we did. No offense."

"None taken," Avery replies stiffly, still looking at me with this mix of annoyance and respect. I choose to only see the latter.

"Then it's a deal," I say, rubbing my hands together. "Now on to the details." The sooner we leave the topic of my involvement behind us, the better. Moving on like nothing worth mentioning happened.

George rubs his chin in thought. "Noa could actually be of help. You might get into the Hub without problems, but I'm thinking even the Hub will have been updated on you going rogue. Noa could be the excuse: you've suspected she was with the Ghosts and played along to uncover what was going on, and now you've captured her, bringing her to justice."

I raise my hand, like in school. "We kind of did that fake-prisoner thing already. It's how we got into the Adler planetarium." Fool me once, shame on you, fool me twice...

George shakes his head. "Who cares? They're not going to leave Canyon's First Sentinel and their fugitive standing in front of the Hub and not let you in. Either they're going to buy your story, which will give you the element of surprise, or they won't. But they'll still take you in. The latter would be inconvenient, especially for Noa, but it serves the same purpose." Spoken like a true Ghost.

Avery turns the glass of water in his hands. "Agreed. A cover. If we enter the Hub together, we also have better options for distractions, no matter the final scenario. But I need a plan for Noa. What if she can't hide and gets caught as soon as I have crossed over? What if they decide the sparrow in the hand is better than the pigeon on the roof and send her through the portal back to Terra? With the incoming portals destroyed, she would be stranded. No way back." Avery gives George a challenging look.

Oh. Right. There's that.

George cocks his head and one eyebrow. "Then you better make sure she's safe before you cross, Sentinel." He says it as if he needed to remind Avery of his job description.

"Insufficient." Avery crosses his arms in front of his chest, a gesture reminding me way too much of a million and one discussions I've had with George and Elaine—that all ended with me in a similar defensive posture.

George sighs and massages the bridge of his nose. "Okay. Look. What about this as a backup plan? Elaine and I will call in a bomb threat to the Hub to the Earth police for the time when the drysillium should be delivered. If you took out the portals, it will never arrive. Hallelujah, we don't need them. If Noa is safely out and on her way back, we don't need them either, double hallelujah. But if you failed and it arrived, or if Noa was caught by the Terrans, the police are her option to get herself out of there. Scream for help, point to the drysillium, damsel in distress, etcetera, etcetera. The police free the poor kidnapping victim and return her to her worried parents. The drysillium gets confiscated, done."

Avery's lips press into a thin line. If I had to guess, I'd say he's seeing the same error in logic I am: What if they already threw me into the portal before the police arrived? Then I'd be SOL. What if there are Terrans in the police force? Then they—or their superiors—would know about the drysillium and could still use it eventually, and it would be Earth that's SOL.

And I'd be on said SOL-Earth, knowing the end was going to come soon.

I guess failure is not an option then.

Something cramps in the depth of my gut. Going with Avery means facing the same risks George and Elaine did when they crossed to Earth. Granted, George and Elaine chose this kind of life while I stumbled into it, but still. I sit up straighter. "I think it's a risk I'm willing to take. Avery," I add, because let's be honest, he's the one needing convincing. Not my Ghost-parents.

He tips his head to the side. "But—"

"No, really. I think we have to have our priorities straight, and if it's one life against all Earth…" Kind of no contest.

George nods. "Good assessment. And the Sentinels are going to be busy defending the portal. They won't care about one teenage Earthling if they have a First Class Sentinel attacking them."

Avery gives George a long, questioning look. "You better be right about that, Ghost. Because if possible, I'd prefer to keep Noa out of trouble and the overall damage to a minimum."

George rolls his eyes. "There are mostly scientists there, but the kind responsible for getting Earth into this mess. Couple of Second Class Sentinels. That should be it."

Avery's eyes turn hard. "Still. It doesn't mean their lives are worthless."

"Wow," George says, full of irony, "fate delivers me the one Sentinel with a conscience. How convenient."

Avery goes rigid.

"Uh, s'cuse me?" I offer a change of topic before this becomes exactly that kind of headbutting I did on a daily basis with my parents. For years. "Where is the Hub? That would be helpful to know."

My parents stare at me like I'm slightly behind the curve. Then Elaine slightly shakes her head. "Right. You wouldn't know."

I frown. "No, *Mom*, I wouldn't."

Elaine ignores the verbal slap or doesn't even register it.

Knowing her, it's the latter.

"Most portals are in populated areas with lots of people around. That's because of the overlap. The distance between universes is the thinnest there. We also have the best cover there when crossing back and forth between both sides."

The Reichstag. The planetarium. Okay, that makes sense.

"The Hub needs the exact opposite. It's sensitive to electromagnetic distortions and vibrations. It needs to be in a secluded area, in both universes." She adjusts her cane next to her. "It's north of Lake Superior in Minnesota, close to the Canadian border."

Avery releases a small sigh. "I assume transportation there is going to be as challenging as it is on Terra? No VacWay, no roads? Hidden deep inside the forest?"

"Someone paid attention during Sentinel Class, it seems," George quips, but it falls flat. "Well, uh, yeah, that's the point. Well hidden. Dirt roads lead up to maybe fifteen miles before it; the rest is a hike, there's no way around it." He frowns and drops his gaze to the ground.

"But," Elaine says, "we might be able to offer at least some help." She winks at George, and for one moment, I'm reminded of the old times, when they were still full of energy and we'd all play Monopoly or something, and Elaine would cheat in a blatantly obvious way to make Andrew and me laugh.

I swallow hard.

Maybe… Maybe not everything in my life was a lie.

George grins. "Right, honey. About time it gets put to use, I'd say."

"What gets put to use?" I ask.

Elaine shrugs. "Well, once a Ghost… You don't stop just because you're separated from your world. We always had hope, you know? Always hoped we could go back one day, that somebody would come for us."

The way she says it, with this sad undertone… That's when the pieces click into place for me. "Wait a second. You're not coming."

I'm not sure if I'm phrasing it as a statement or a question, because looking back at the last minutes, it's clear: this plan is only about Avery and me, not about them.

Elaine sighs. "Noa, we're useless at this point. Useless and a risk. Don't get me wrong. I'd love to go home, but even if we did, it might be too late for us. And by coming with you, we'd severely reduce your chances to complete the mission. We can't do that fifteen-mile hike through the woods, we can't fight entering the Hub—hell, we can't even run fast enough to get past the Sentinels." Her voice turns bitter.

I shake my head. So what? Then we find a different way. "But maybe we can—"

"No, Noa. We can't. We literally *cannot*. The best we can do is stay behind." She gives me a smile I recognize from about a million doctor's appointments. The fake brave one. "Honey, we knew we were going to die here. Nothing has changed for us."

Nothing has changed—I blink twice. A burning starts in my throat, one I can't swallow down. I mean, I knew they were doing badly. Andrew died, and over the last few months, it became clear neither George nor Elaine were going to miraculously recover. But knowing they could go home if things were different… it changes their fate from predestined and devastating to unfair and tragic. A giant difference.

They should've taken the chance when they still could. "Why did you never try to use the portals or the Hub to escape back home? To Terra?" They could've pulled it off when they weren't sick yet. They were fit. Strong.

"What do you think, Noa?" George's lips press into a thin line. "How were we supposed to sneak into a portal with two children? What if they caught us? For us, who cares, but for you and Andrew? Galileo gave us the responsibility of your wellbeing, and handing you over to Canyon was not in our job description—and neither was exposing you to rejection on Terra." He leans forward. "But at least we can help you from afar and hopefully make this mission a success. That's all that counts. It's all that ever counted. We are prepared.

Took us a couple of years to get everything we needed. Most of the things haven't even been invented here, so we had to be careful designing it, but we did it."

Elaine reaches over to the same drawer that held the modulators, searching for something.

"Here," she finally says, holding up a car key. "This is all we have." She puts it on the table in front of her. Unbelievable how both of them can switch from the topic of their impending death back to business. That's George and Elaine in a nutshell.

Avery's brows scrunch together. "A key? To what?"

I sigh. Okay, back to business it is. "And that's why you need me. It's a car key."

"Oh."

"Exactly." I look at my mom, maybe for the first time since I found out she wasn't my biological mom. "What's so special about it?"

"The car? Nothing. The gear in the trunk, that's a different story."

"Gear?" Avery likes that word, I can tell.

"Gear," George says. "Tools, equipment. Mostly Earth tools we adapted into things we remembered from Terra. It should help you on your way into the Hub and when destroying it."

"Excellent." Avery nods. "Excellent."

And just like that, the despair that had me—that had us—in its grip is gone, replaced by a tiny spark of hope that keeps growing the more we plan our way to the Hub and to defeat Canyon.

And the weird thing about it?

I can't wait.

CHAPTER TWENTY-SEVEN

Adjourned

I t's almost 9 P.M. when we finally adjourn for the night.
"The outline is there; the details need to wait until we all get some sleep," George says, yawning. The last couple of hours took their toll on both of my parents, not that Avery looked any fresher. Or me, for that matter. On our way out of the living room, Avery grabs his staff from the windowsill, and Elaine keeps her cane close before she follows us out into the hallway, the *click-click* of its tip on the floor right behind us.

I'm about to walk down to my room when she clears her throat.

"Noa, you can of course stay in your room; everything is as you left it. Sentinel, you can have the guest room on the—"

"I will stay with Noa." Avery stands straighter.

Elaine's brows knit together. "You—"

"This is not open for discussion," Avery says, completely quiet and at ease but still radiating authority. *Danger.* "You know very well they will start scanning for Terran life signs and check them off one by one. It's only a matter of time until they find me, especially with the two of you already on their list of Terrans on Earth."

George flinches. "They don't know about—"

"Please do not insult their intelligence. Your modulators broke years ago. I would estimate the Sentinel Forces would have known about you after their next scheduled scan. Do not mistake their inaction for anything but purposeful. They chose to let you be. In

219

your condition, you're not a threat *and* living the punishment they would've assigned to you. Death on Earth."

"We—"

Avery raises his voice over George's. "So during their next scan tonight they will notice another Terran signature with you, and after data collection and correlation, we will be red-flagged and ultimately searched. While I do expect this to take at least twenty-four hours and while I do not wish any ill on you, my responsibility is to Noa."

Elaine shakes her head. "She is still our daughter, and we do not approve of male overnight—"

I whirl around. I can't believe she pulled the mother card. "Elaine—"

George is quicker, pressing a careful hand on her lower back. "Elaine, it's okay. He's a Sentinel. You know nothing is going to happen. Nothing can."

That's all it takes to shift the atmosphere between Avery and my parents back to frosty. That one comment. What slowly had evolved into mutual respect over the last few hours is now an icy roadblock between them.

Avery pulls his shoulders back, holding his jaw tight and up high, staring at a spot right over my parents' heads.

"You're right, hon." Elaine sighs, completely oblivious. "You may stay with her, Sentinel." It's as dismissive as I've ever heard her.

Avery doesn't respond, and instead turns around and opens the door to my room. "Noa?"

I throw one last wordless angry glance at the people I thought were my parents and then follow Avery. As soon as the door shuts, I lean against it.

Alone.

Alone with Avery.

So… where do we go from here?

Avery stops in the middle of my room with his back to me, looking as lost in the situation as I feel. This is new. To both of us.

Walking past him, I draw the curtains in front of the window. "I'm sorry about my parents. They—"

He chuckles. "Are you apologizing to me for your parents?"

I blush. "Well, yeah. I don't know why they were so weird, Sentinel this and Sentinel that…" Plus, the whole thing Elaine just tried, separating Avery and me… "I didn't take them for being *that* disrespectful, you know?"

Avery picks up my little school bus from the shelf on his left, the one I made out of toilet paper rolls when I was in Kindergarten. He turns it in his hands, playing with the little wheels that will fall off one of these days.

"It's the office that demands respect, Noa. Not the Sentinel. Not the person," he adds, his tone bitter. "It's never about the person. Not as a Second Child. Even for our own families, we're a shame. A sign of their rebellion gone wrong. An embarrassment to our firstborn siblings."

He puts the bus back in its place, looking at it a bit longer, lost in thought. When he speaks again, his voice is soft, carrying an undertone I haven't heard yet.

"You know, on the day you crossed to Terra and I brought you to the quarters in the Bellevue Castle… you were the first non-Sentinel person to ask my name since I can remember. You were the first." He gives the bus a slight nudge to align it with the road I painted on a cardboard paper.

I was the first to ask for his name.

Seeing Avery with a toy I made when I was five or six years old, the same age when he was taken from his family and turned into a nameless Sentinel only because he was the second child… it tugs on my heartstrings. And it hurts. It hurts for him.

"Thanks for staying with me," I say, focusing on picking nonexistent lint off my jeans. "I… I really didn't want to be alone." I turn and give him a hesitant smile.

"You shouldn't be alone, Noa. For many reasons." Avery's deep baritone is back to his usual strength, echoing through my room like a gospel in church. "We crossed universes. You found out about your parents. We still have a mission to work on, and Terrans might be hunting us as we speak. You're not staying alone. Period."

He keeps his eyes on me with the serious intensity I'm used to from him… that, and something else, something softer, warmer, like always when I'm alone with Avery. It's as if he dropped his defenses a tiny bit more when it's only me, and it makes me proud.

A faint shadow falls over his face. "It's bad enough you insist on coming with me."

I deflate. "Avery, let's not talk about that." The more we talk about it, the more I get afraid of the fear. Right now, I can ignore it with every fiber of my body, but if I ever sit down and start to think about it, I know it will paralyze me. And that can't happen.

"No, actually. Let's."

Groaning, I walk past him toward my bed, squat down in front of it, and fish for the spare mattress I always have under it—the one I haven't used since Andrew died, and with him our sleepovers.

"I'm still coming, Avery. We said—"

"I know what we said, but that was under different circumstances. This isn't getting data out of a Terran's brain—this is an attack on the Hub." He traces a finger over the spine of one of my books in my shelf. "We have to get there in one piece, get in, destroy the right parts of it, and then you will have to get out again." His fingers stop right over my Harry Potter books, and he sighs quietly. "I don't know if I can protect you."

I pull a fresh blanket and towel out of my closet and walk over to him. "I think worrying over one single person isn't really worth mentioning anymore. We left that behind once we found out about Canyon's planned mass homicide."

"Still—"

I rest a hand on his arm. "I know you want to watch out for me, and I know you will, but so will I. For myself and for you. Teamwork, Avery. It's teamwork." I drop the blanket in his arms. "Here. You start in the shower and I'll get us some food, okay?" Because for one, we need to shower. That thought alone, of Avery in my shower, or of me in my shower and Avery next door, makes me feel all warm and weird in a good way. Nonetheless, a shower is a necessity at this point. For another, I'm starving, and if I am, he must be even worse.

Last but not least, I want to stop talking about the Hub. I don't want to risk chickening out. "And then no more of this. I want to pretend everything is just fine for as long as I can, okay?" I wink at him.

He chuckles. "All right. You win. But so you know, during the assault on the Hub, I'm the boss, no questions asked. Understood?"

I sigh. "Understood, and of course. And now enough. Food."

With that, I turn around and sneak out of my room, taking care to be quiet. I don't want to run into George or Elaine right now. I need… I need a break. Like I said to Avery, I need a couple of hours pretending everything is normal—that *I* am normal, and not a weird package raised by people from a different universe who're about to basically commit suicide trying to stop a homicide.

A heavy weight sets in my stomach.

Maybe I didn't quite think this through.

I tiptoe into the kitchen. At least this fridge I can open without Augs, and it's filled with stuff Avery should like. In the middle of choosing between cheese and sausage and then deciding on both, I realize this also is a first.

I've never raided our fridge before. Never. What a pitiful first sign of revolt, going through my parents' fridge when it's not dinner time.

I'm a daredevil, that much is clear.

On the way back with my arms full, my ears pick up soft voices coming from the living room. Warm light falls into the hallway through the glass door that's slightly ajar. I creep up and peer through the gap at my parents sitting in the same spot they were in before, Elaine cuddled in George's arms, his hand tenderly playing with her hair. Both hold tissues in their hands. Both sniffle.

As if rooted to the spot, I stay put, staring and intruding where I shouldn't, my throat dry with a lump that won't go away no matter how hard I swallow.

CHAPTER TWENTY-EIGHT

Dark Is the Night

During dinner, the tension decreases by several degrees to the point where I'd say we're having fun, mainly because we ignore the topic of our impending travel to the Hub. The food is spread out between us on the floor in front of the mattress, like for an indoor picnic.

Surprisingly, Avery doesn't eat much more than I do, or maybe it's the other way around and I eat almost as much as Avery. I'm ravenous.

"And then what?" I ask, taking another piece of cheese from the cutting board between us.

He shrugs. "Then Toshi decided I might be worth the extra effort after all and pulled me into the advanced program. Despite the fact a ten-year-old PBM just made him look like a rookie."

"He still took you?" I almost drop my cheese.

A grin spreads over Avery's face. "Yeah, and he told me if I ever pulled a stunt like that again, he'd personally make sure I'd be missing a couple of limbs." His grin widens, and I laugh out loud.

"So that's why you like to threaten to tear off body parts when you're angry." I laugh. He did it for the Ghosts back in Terra, and—

"It works," Avery says, wiggling his eyebrows.

Right, it works. "You're crazy, Avery." I giggle, trying to punch him in the shoulder, although I almost fall over when he moves out of the way. My clumsy move makes him laugh out loud.

That's when I realize I've never seen or hear him laugh like that.

A smile, yes. Mostly a small one.

A laugh? Never.

Never.

Not with dimples, with eyes alive and sparkling—not a true laugh that makes him look so much younger and almost careless.

Almost happy.

Avery raises a brow at me, his laugh winding down into a beautiful smile. "What?"

Heat rushes to my cheeks. "Uh, nothing. I…" I swipe a strand of hair that's come loose out of my face. "Nothing."

The smile still stays. My room is almost dark with only my little nightlamp on, but its soft light reflects in Avery's amber eyes, turning them into two shining orbs of liquid gold. Even if I wanted to tear myself loose, I wouldn't be able to.

I don't just *see* him. I *feel* him all the way down to my toes.

I feel him.

Avery doesn't move, and neither do I. I could swear the pulse in his neck speeds up like mine.

It's quite amazing how my body reacts to him being so close. A tingling sensation shoots through me every second he looks at me, butterflies are pulling off perfect looping formations inside my stomach, and every breath I take brings a whiff of shower gel, but mostly Avery's scent of sunshine.

Sunshine.

I bite on my lower lip.

Avery's smile softens. His gaze drops down to my mouth, or rather, to my nose.

"You haven't exchanged it in a while." He lifts a careful hand until his fingertip gently touches the little heart piercing in my nose.

He could have put a taser to my skin and it would have had the same effect. A short bout of dizziness, my heart tripping over its own feet—

—and my hand shoots out and captures his before he can pull it away.

I realize my mistake the second I make it.

The moment our hands touch, Avery freezes. In less than a second, the smile is gone, a myriad of emotions running over his face, only to settle on the mask he wears as a Sentinel.

He's up on his feet in no time. A look akin to… *fear* flickers across his face, gone as quickly as it came. The next moment, his back is to me and he's checking out my books once more. Terse silence stretches between us.

"We… It's late, Noa. We should probably get some rest. The next few days are going to be rough." His voice is calm. Only the hoarseness betrays it.

I let my hand drop. "Yeah," I whisper. "We probably should." I'm such an idiot.

How could I be so wrong? Is it just me? My stupid teenage hormones running wild? I thought… For a moment, I thought I saw something in his eyes, but obviously, I was wrong.

I stand and gather the leftovers of our food, throwing another glance at Avery standing tall, ignoring me.

Avery, alone in his boat for one.

Something cramps inside my chest.

I better learn to swim.

Getting ready for bed is awkward, but at least mercifully fast.

Avery falls asleep first on the mattress right next to my bed. His breathing turns regular about a minute after his head hits the pillow. I haven't even switched off my nightlamp at that point, and now I'm glad for it. The soft light is barely enough to reach the walls of my room and keeps most of it in darkness, but it's perfect to let me look at Avery.

He fell asleep on his back, his hands on top of the blanket, his lips slightly parted, and, for the first time ever, completely relaxed. The little bit of stubble on his face hasn't grown too much but still adds a shadow to his cheeks. His black, wavy hair may be a tad more messed than normal, but otherwise, he looks like he had a regular day at the office. A bit paler, if at all.

Being thrown into a different universe will do that to you, I guess.

Avery moves with a small grunt in his sleep. One hand slides behind his head, and oh, boy. Muscles pop out like Popeye's after a can of spinach. My heart misses a beat, ending up in a stumble.

His motion causes the top of his shirt to fall open the slightest bit. Something silver catches some of the ambient light—the necklace he keeps hidden so well. It could be a number eight, but since it's on its side… or rather, an infinity symbol, if I'm not mistaken. It's beautifully made, a bit thicker and sturdier, fitting for a man of Avery's size, but still intricately done, the thick leather necklace completing the look.

Avery twitches once, and it's so adorable, I want to reach down and touch him, run my fingers through his hair, or gently brush them over his cheeks.

Maybe down his chest.

Groaning inwardly, I pull my blanket higher and squish my eyes closed.

Dang it, I should be thinking about Earth, about Terra, about anything else but Avery.

Yet I don't.

I open my eyes again and roll onto my side for a better view.

I'm aware I'm catering to the whims of the pathetic here, but I can't help it.

I just can't help it.

For a long time, I soak up the image of a sleeping Avery, hovering like a creep, memorizing every detail of his face, and when I finally switch off the light, it still takes me a long, long time to finally fall asleep.

I wake to the sound of coughing, teeth clattering, and a body shaking.

I open my eyes, confused for a moment as to where I am until I recognize the familiar glow-in-the-dark stars I put on my bedroom ceiling right above my bed.

I'm home, and the sounds—

Avery.

I reach for the switch for the nightlamp while the other feels for Avery, finding a shoulder that rocks back and forth from chills.

"Avery? Hey, what—" The question gets stuck in my throat when the light falls onto him. Judging by the way he's shivering, the blanket doesn't do squat for him. Avery's curled up, facing toward me, his eyes squeezed shut as if that could keep the warmth inside his body.

He doesn't look good. At all.

"Shit, Avery." I squeeze his shoulder gently. "What's going on? Are you sick? What—?"

He opens his eyes, but it costs him—and that scares me. Avery is strong. He's a freakin' Sentinel, the best in his class, and a machine. He took out a platoon of Second Class Sentinels at the portal. He can't be lying here working his eyelids open as if they weighed a ton and looking like *this*.

"You're so pale," I whisper, brushing his forehead. "No fever." Quite the opposite. He's so cold, it reminds me of Andrew, when the cancer—

My mouth drops open.

No.

Not already.

It must be something else, a virus, or exhaustion. The swaying, his pale face, not eating much, it must be—

A small smile plays around Avery's lips, but it's pitiful.

"Rejection," he rasps between clenched teeth. "Earth doesn't agree with me."

No. No, no, no, this can't be happening. Not now, not already.

"Avery, no, it must be something else. It's too soon, too—"

He shakes his head. "No modulator at all, Noa. No time to become acclimated. Earth is sensitized, rejections—" He shivers again, harder. "Rejections happen faster now."

Tears spring to my eyes seeing him like that when there's nothing I can do about it. "But, Avery…"

"It comes in waves." He wheezes, his body racked by another bout of chills. "I'll be fine in a couple of hours."

Fine.

Not exactly *fine*.

And I know how he'll feel until then; I've seen it happen. I didn't know what it was at that point, but I've seen it happen.

I curse myself for not thinking about a modulator. For crying out loud, my parents showed me ours. It should have rung a bell.

It should have, but it didn't. I was too busy being sorry for myself to think of Avery.

"How long do you have?" I whisper hoarsely. A tear runs down my cheek.

"A couple of days," Avery whispers. "At the most."

Another tear follows the first. *"At the most."*

He reaches a shaking hand out from under the blanket and up, one finger carefully wiping away the tear.

"I'll be fine."

I catch his hand before he can draw it back, pressing it against my chest, for a moment afraid I made the same mistake as before.

This time, he doesn't pull away.

He lets me hold his hand. His skin is so cold. So cold.

I swallow hard against the grief that threatens to choke me. "Yeah. You'll be fine," I whisper back, willing fate to hear me, to listen to me.

I blow onto the hand that's like a block of ice in mine and completely still, as if he didn't dare to move it. Another shudder brings his body to a shiver and his teeth to clatter harder.

He's freezing.

"Avery," I say, massaging his hand in mine. "Scoot."

Before he can protest or I can change my mind and chicken out, I've glided down onto the mattress, my blanket still covering me.

"What—?" Avery's eyes go wide in his pale face.

I reach up for the light and turn it off.

"You need to be warm."

"I am—"

"You're not. Shut up." I drape my blanket over him and lift up one corner of his, working my way under it. Once I'm half under, half not, I stop. Uh, where do I go from here? Do I hug him? Do I kind of… I don't know, spoon him? I didn't really think it through. I—

A strong arm reaches around my waist, flips me onto my side, and pulls me in. A tiny squeak breaks free from my throat—and then I'm on my left, my back pressed into Avery's front, his body wrapped around mine like a blanket.

A freezing, shivering blanket.

He takes my hand, our fingers entwined. His breath on my neck is warm despite his skin rivaling an ice cube.

And me… I'm glowing. Wherever we touch, my body must be up to a hundred degrees. Whatever he lacks in warmth, I'm making up for the both of us. Whenever he shivers from cold, I shiver because of his body pressed against mine.

I pull his hand up to my chest right under my chin. My thumb draws little circles on the back of his hand while his scent cocoons me into a wonderful place I never want to leave.

Another chill runs down his body. Heaven and hell both are made from every little inch in contact with him. His hand is so close to my lips, so tantalizingly close… I could drop a kiss onto it. A tiny one. He wouldn't even notice.

I suck in my lower lip.

Yeah, and then? If he did, I'd destroy everything we have between us.

Avery is my friend.

I am his.

He lets me warm him because that's what friends do, just like he saved me when I needed help.

It's what friends do.

I pull his hand closer and tuck myself deeper into his embrace, willing my thoughts away from this dangerous road and back to my friend, who needs me.

Avery holds me like an oversized stuffed animal, shivering against me until the chills die down and we both fall asleep.

Finally.

CHAPTER TWENTY-NINE

Learning

The next morning, Avery looks worse. Even my parents notice. The confused glances they exchange speak loud enough, although they say nothing. And what are they supposed to say? Sorry you don't have a modulator? Sorry you're going to die soon?

I chew the inside of my cheek until it's raw.

Not going to happen.

This is reversible, right? As soon as he's back on Terra, he'll be better. That means he has to go back. As soon as possible. He has to get to the Hub, and through the portal back to Terra.

He has to.

Avery checks his staff and shoves it under the jacket Elaine gave him, courtesy of an impromptu shopping trip at night and twenty-four-hour stores. He still looks out of place, but not like he broke out of a facility somewhere.

"Are you sure you don't want to come?" he asks Elaine. "I could—"

Elaine shakes her head. "Thank you, Sentinel, but no. Like we've said, we've come to terms with our fate, and… we would slow you down. With us in tow, you might fail the mission, and that cannot happen. Watch out for Noa. That's all we ask."

Avery glances at me. "I will."

Says the man who needed help getting up from the mattress this morning.

George pats his back pocket. "No phone, right?"

"It's somewhere in Germany, George."

"Just making sure. We don't need to add the potential of Earth tracking technology to what the Sentinels can do." He sighs and hands me the key Elaine took from the drawer yesterday. "Good luck, Noa." He gives me a careful smile that doesn't quite know where we're standing after yesterday's revelations. "I wish it wasn't like this, and I wish…" He sighs. "I wish we had talked sooner. Better. More."

I take the key and pocket it. "Me too," I whisper, choked up. "Bye, George."

He pulls me into a hug like he always does, with a little rocking from left to right, only he holds me tighter than normal.

I get the same kind of hug from Elaine, the type that lasts longer than I'm used to with either of them.

"Stay safe, okay?" she whispers.

And then we're out the door, down the hallway and gone from the life that was mine for as long as I can remember.

Once out on the street, I throw one last look up to the twenty-third floor.

Somehow, it feels final.

It takes Avery and me about half an hour to arrive at the storage place that stores my parents' getaway car. It's a three-story building with bright red letters on its front: SuperStorage.

The outside of the ground floor is dotted with countless quote-unquote roller-gated storage compartments, the last one and farthest in the back being ours. I unlock the gate and slide it up under the ceiling.

"No way." My jaw drops.

No, they didn't. I expected a small, crappy car, just like our usual one, or maybe something environmentally conscious, like my parents would always insist on, but no.

A Hummer. A freakin' huge, black Hummer with tinted windows.

Avery raises an eyebrow. "This looks sufficient."

I laugh out loud. "Yeah, I think so, too. We're only driving up north to Lake Superior until we hit the location where we'll have to stop driving and start hiking. I'm not expecting us to go completely off-road." Or having to survive an explosion or something.

A Hummer.

Seriously.

No wonder we never had any money; all of it went into this baby here.

Avery shrugs. "Never hurts to be prepared." He takes a closer look at the car.

My parents must have thought the same thing because the Hummer is packed. The rear is filled with four backpacks, all of them stuffed with more or less the same supplies.

Four backpacks.

They obviously haven't been here since Andrew died, or at least they didn't check the supplies.

I rest a hand on the blue bag that would have been his—pink for me, black for my parents—waiting for some kind of connection to happen, but there's nothing.

Avery climbs in behind the wheel, inspecting the instruments on the dashboard.

"I can drive," I call to the front.

"Not necessary," he replies, turning the wheel in his hands. "I've got the tactical training in case of an emergency."

In case of *what kind* of emergency, exactly? Never mind, it's not my main concern: "You also have a bad case of rejection, Avery."

He glides a finger over the speedometer. "Not at the moment. I feel perfectly fine."

I roll my eyes. "Uh-huh."

Avery looks up at the car's ceiling, as if expecting instruments there, like in a plane. "Is this general access?"

"Huh? Uh, yeah?" I guess so. Somewhere buried in here is a tent, emergency food rations, money, and whatnot.

At one point, we'll have to sort through and make sure we have our ducks in a row, but for now, we need to make some headway.

I crawl up front to the passenger seat.

A Hummer.

Still can't get over that one. I feel like a child in this huge seat.

Avery places his palm on the steering wheel.

Then he takes it off again.

And puts it right in the same spot.

"Why is this not working?" He bends to the side and inspects the wheel from below, probably to check if something is loose.

"Why is what not working?" What is he trying to do there anyway?

"The engine," Avery says, dropping his hand onto the wheel again, waiting.

Oh.

He was trying to start the car, Terra-style. "Well, we've got the key." I pull it out of my pocket and drop it in the center of the middle console. "And then you push the button that says *start.*"

"Oh. All right then." Avery pushes the button—and nothing, besides frantic beeping from the car and a couple of red warning lights flashing up.

"What—"

"Put your foot on the brake."

"The brake?"

"The brake pedal."

Avery all but dives down, checking the pedals in the front.

"The left?"

"No, the—" Then I finally do the math. "Uh, Avery? Have you ever driven a car? One like this, I mean?"

He comes up again, his face slightly flushed. It actually makes him look almost healthy, compared to before. "No. Can't say I have."

I glance at the stick in the middle of the car. Not automatic. Of course not. Best theft prevention in the middle of Chicago is owning a stick-shift car.

I sigh.

"All tactical training aside, maybe I should drive."

"Out of the question, my training—"

"So what is this?" I point at the stick.

He opens and closes his mouth, studying the gearshift.

I unbuckle myself. "That's what I thought. Let's swap places. I'll teach you how to drive, and if it makes you feel better, you can tell me all about tactical driving."

I always wondered why George taught Andrew and me how to drive instead of paid lessons from a service. I figured to save money. All our classmates went to a driving school, learning in fancy Mercedes S-classes or something, while we had to suffer shifting gears in our old Volvo. Now I know. Four backpacks, four people knowing how to drive this beast.

I slide behind the wheel and adjust the seat and mirrors. Today is the last day I want to be stopped and pulled over for anything. Avery mimics me and buckles himself up, testing the belt for durability.

"Interesting," he says. "No inertia control, I take it?"

I push the start button and the engine thrums to life. "I don't think so." I rest both hands on the rim of the wheel and take a big breath.

We have two days and change to get to the Hub hidden somewhere north of Lake Superior and prevent Canyon from unleashing his poison onto Earth.

No pressure.

"Ready?" I look over at Avery.

"Always."

Well, that makes at least one of us.

Finding our way out of Chicago is easy, and so is the drive overall. It's still early and in the middle of the week, which means most traffic is on the other side of the Interstate, heading into the city. At first,

Avery is more than impressed by the sheer amount of cars, but it only takes five minutes of what I'd consider mild stop-and-go-traffic for him to become annoyed.

Guys.

Instead of waiting for him to hate Earth because of its traffic or to decide we're not worth saving after all, I teach him how to drive stick.

I tap his leg with my right. "Watch what I'm doing. Clutch with my left before I shift, choose the gear, slowly release the clutch, accelerate, done." Every time I have to switch gears—and in slow traffic that happens all the time—I explain what I'm doing, until eventually we make it out of town and onto wider open roads. Not much shifting going on there.

Avery is quiet. Quiet and pale.

"How are you feeling today?" I nudge him gently with my elbow. Considering we slept in each other's arms last night, everything is pretty un-awkward between us. Granted, waking up was... *interesting*, with him still cuddled into me, but at least without his chills. The moment I woke up everything seemed so surreal.

Me and a boy, spending the night together.

Me and *Avery*.

I have to admit that despite knowing he only let me come so close because he needed my help, I stayed still when I woke up.

I stayed still and enjoyed his body close to mine. Enjoyed his breath dancing down my neck. His fingers still between mine. The weight of his arm across my body. His heart beating inside his chest and against my back, first slow, then picking up speed, like his breathing.

I stayed still and memorized the feel of it for eternity.

Then he woke up and let go of me, but at least he didn't seem to be trying to get away from me as fast as possible.

Avery grunts and tears me out of my daydream. "Okay. I've felt better before, but considering what I heard about rejection, I think it could be worse." He throws a quick glance at me. "I wish we could have taken your parents, but as somebody trained to put the welfare of the many ahead of the need of the few…"

"I know," I say, keeping my eyes on the road, trying not to blink. "I know." He doesn't need to finish the sentence.

The inconvenient lump in my throat grows bigger, but I clear it. Distraction. I need a distraction.

"So, Avery?" I look over at him. His focus is more on the road and the irrationally moving cars around us than mine—and I'm the driver. He's definitely not used to Earth's traffic yet. "How did you know my parents were from Terra? Because they don't show?" I let go of the wheel with one hand and tap my forehead. "I mean, I don't either, and I expect nobody here does."

He shrugs. "Easy. They might look the same as Earthlings to you and they might not show because they're Ghosts"—he mirrors tapping his forehead—"but they emit a different wavelength than Earthlings. That's how I knew you weren't from Terra when I met you in the cell after you crossed. It's a feature of Sentinel Augs to recognize and defend Terra in case of an Earth invasion. We see Earthlings with a different halo than Terrans."

I laugh once, making a circling motion above my head. "A halo?"

His brows scrunch together for a moment before he gets it. "Huh? Oh, no, not like that. Your whole body is surrounded by an aura. Like an outlining. Terrans are reddish; Earthlings shifted toward the blue spectrum."

I look down my body, stretching out one arm in front of me. Can't see a thing, blueish hue or not. "So I'm covered in blue to you?" I wish I could see it.

Avery throws a quick glance over at me. "Actually, you're more a light pink."

"Pink?" Why am I pink?

"It suits you," he says completely calmly, yet his words light me up on the inside and the outside.

It suits me.

I suck in my lower lip and bite down hard. Nope, I'm not going there, I'm not going there, am *so* not going there…

Focus, Noa.

The cars in front of us slow down and I get ready to shift down one gear.

A warm hand covers mine.

"Let me."

He curls his fingers over my hand and around the stick, moving it down from fifth into fourth gear.

"Like this?" He keeps my hand trapped under his. Trapped and burning.

"Yeah," I all but croak, "like this." I hold on to the stick like a lifeline because if I don't, he'll notice the shaking.

"Third?"

I only manage a nod. It's amazing how all my mental faculties can be exhausted by depressing the clutch and Avery's shifting. The cars in front of us speed up again before we even come to anything close to a stop.

"Gas, right pedal," Avery says, observing my every move. "Now clutch. Fourth, or straight into fifth?"

"Fourth." My mouth is dry. "You're a quick learner."

"Sentinel Genes. And I need to. You're not driving the whole route. We have to make sure we keep our strength up."

I accelerate. "Well, then don't slack off. Fifth, please."

I keep my face straight while Avery shifts the stick one gear up, fingers around mine and the faintest sign of a smile on his face.

CHAPTER THIRTY

Rammed

We drive like this for hours that feel like minutes. Time flies when you're having fun, right? Comes in handy, because with the Hub localized so far off the beaten path, we can't take the freeway for as long as I'd like to. Instead we have to make our way up there by taking small roads through small villages. It means a longer trip and more gear shifting though, so hey, gotta enjoy Avery's hand on mine while I have it.

Still, once I'm sure Avery knows the basics of stick driving, I let him drive. Okay, I also wait until we have left the Interstate and continued on smaller roads without much around that he could damage if he did it wrong.

I needn't have worried.

Avery is a natural.

Of course he is because he practiced shifting gears with me. His Sentinel genes have nothing to do with that, right? That was all my teaching.

Yeah, right.

The moment he gets behind the wheel, he practically owns the car, now that he knows how it works. To be honest, it's a bit depressing for me because I almost killed our poor Volvo when learning to shift. The sound that the engine made when I tried to force a gear it didn't like… George always got all nervous when that happened, patting the car's dashboard like it was a horse needing some calming down.

Avery doesn't make a single mistake, and I need to remind him of his own words about keeping our strength up to make him give up the driver's seat again.

Over the last couple of hours, the scenery has changed around us. The busy city of Chicago gave way to more suburban areas, and then to a beautiful countryside with thick forests to the left and right of the small, barely two-lane road we're on. The last time a car shared the road with us was more than an hour ago. I'm not used to this kind of serenity and loneliness, but it's soothing in a certain way.

Avery's been quiet for a while, and despite him trying to hide it, he can't.

I hear the coughs. I see the shakes and chills. I see his arms wrapped around his chest, trying to keep warm.

And there's not a thing I can do about either of it.

"Avery—"

"I'm fine."

"Right," I grumble. "Obviously."

Ten seconds later, a coughing spell racks him and leaves him gasping for air.

"Crap, Avery, we need to stop. We need to get you warm." I'm sure we have mega-insulated sleeping bags in the back.

He waves a dismissive hand, still wheezing with his next breaths. "Keep going. I don't—" More coughing. "I don't want to lose any time."

"Well, damn it, and I don't want to lose you!"

It's dead quiet inside the Hummer. Avery's cough stops as if turned off by a switch. Even the teeth clattering is gone.

Instead, he turns toward me, his dark brows high.

Must focus on the road. Must focus on the road.

Never before has driving a car needed that much attention, and never again will driving a car need that much attention.

I don't want to lose you. It just slipped out. I didn't plan for it to happen, I—

I reach for the dials to my right and first turn on his heated seat, then the heater up to max, blasting him with hot air.

"Here," I murmur, "that, uh, that should help." I still don't look at him. The road is much more important. There could be… I don't know, a moose or something.

Avery stays silent for another minute or so. Something heavy hovers between us and weighs down the silence.

"I don't think I have much more than three days, Noa."

His voice is so quiet, it barely carries over the engine, yet it pierces it like a needle a balloon.

"Three days?" He can't mean that. I stare at him. Three days is nothing, it's—

Any response I might've had evaporates the second I fully take in Avery, white as a ghost, pushed back into his seat, all but curled into a ball to stay warm.

He looks like Andrew did at the end.

At the *end*.

I force myself to shake my head. "You'll be fine, Avery. We—"

"You know I won't. If we don't make it into the Hub in the next two days, I doubt I'll be strong enough to get us in." The apple in his throat moves up and down. "If I can't cross back, then…"

He doesn't need to finish the sentence. I can do the math.

"You *will* cross back," I say. Optimism for the win. "Of course you will. We enter the Hub, destroy the incoming portals, send you back, and then—"

"And then you'll be stuck in the Hub with them on high alert and your version of the Sentinel Forces investigating the break and entry, and your vandalism."

I throw a glance at the rearview mirror, staying closer to the right for the vehicle approaching from behind to overtake me.

"But, Avery, of course I'll blame it on the crazy man who abducted me from my class trip in Germany and took me to that facility. I'm a poor victim in all of this, you know?"

The idea of using Avery to explain everything about my disappearance and then our destruction of the Hub was actually George's. *"Two birds, one stone,"* he said, visibly having fun making a

Sentinel the bad guy. "We explain Noa's sudden disappearance from the Reichstag to the police *and* give her a reason to be at the Hub. And, more importantly, a way out that doesn't involve jail time."

The car behind us speeds up, probably intending to overtake us before the bend in the road.

"I know that's the plan, but I still don't like it. I don't like leaving for Terra not knowing what's happening for you. I can't abandon you like—"

A jolt shoots through the Hummer, catapulting us forward and into our seatbelts. I yelp out in surprise, while Avery only grunts.

Another jolt shoves the car to the right. The tires dig into the dirt strip and the sudden change of surface almost rips the wheel out of my hands.

I look at the rearview mirror.

The car—

No, it's another truck, possibly a Hummer, I wouldn't know, and it—

"Incoming!" I yell, bracing myself for another impact while stepping on the gas.

Avery turns around, trying to catch a glimpse of the crazy person behind us.

"A Sentinel," he hisses. "They found us."

"What?" I yell. "Here? In the middle of nowhere? How?"

"Faster with tracking us than I assu—"

Another bump into our vehicle. This time, I have to work hard to not lose control when we swerve to the right.

"Shit!" I scream, willing the car to go faster.

"Noa," Avery calls out, "we have to lose him. He—"

"How am I supposed to lose him here? There's no where to go! It's a freakin' straight road in the middle of nowhere!" No bends, no turns, nowhere to hide. We're doomed. A Sentinel hot on our heels, and Avery already sick from rejection, me driving. We're doomed.

He grasps my hand atop the stick shift.

"We're going to lose him. We *are* going to lose him. Do what I tell you, okay?"

"Okay," I wheeze. It's not as if I had a choice.

A short nod is all I get from him, then his attention is on the side mirror on the right.

"Ready. Hit the brake hard in three, two, one—*now!*"

I stomp the brake, throwing us forward into our seatbelts again.

"Accelerate!" he yells. "Faster, faster, faster!"

"I am!" I shout back. "This thing is heavy; it takes a while!"

Avery doesn't listen. He stares into the mirror, his lips moving silently. "Brake!" he yells again, and I slam on it.

This time, the Sentinel behind us isn't fast enough and rams right into us. It whips the truck's rear around, leaving us fishtailing and me gripping the wheel like a crazy person, trying to control our course.

"Hold it steady!" Avery shouts. "He's going to come to the side now."

I fail to see how that's any better. "What then?" I squeak. I'm not a stunt driver—heck, I barely know how to drive under normal conditions!

"Then," Avery says with maddening calm, "we'll push him off the road."

"What?" I scream. "You can't be—"

"Brace yourself!"

Not a moment too soon do I grip the wheel harder before the other truck slams into our left side, rocking me in my seat. I grunt from the impact, but there's no time to recover.

"Hold it, hold it! He's—"

Avery's warning turns into a choke when the Sentinel rams into us again, apparently trying exactly what Avery wanted us to do. The Hummer's right wheels hit the dirt strip and our back fishtails.

I scream out, frantically holding the wheel steady, but the Hummer is much stronger than me. Avery grabs the wheel, but it's too late. Even he can't overpower the forces at play.

The attacker takes his chance and rams into us again.

And this time I lose control.

Our front tires hit the dirt. The change in surface rips the wheel out of our hands and spins it uncontrollably.

He rams us from behind at exactly the right moment when we're vulnerable.

The Hummer whips around and gives in to the g-force trying to tear it down.

Avery screams while the world turns upside down around us. Metal screeches, glass breaks, sparks fly. The Hummer lands on its roof, metal scraping over asphalt until we come to a complete stop—

CHAPTER THIRTY-ONE

Sands

The silence is so complete, I fear I'm deaf.

Only after a second or two do I pick up on Avery's and my heavy breathing. My whole body is made out of pain, like a giant bruise. A ringing comes from somewhere—or it might be in my ears, I don't know.

A groan leaves my throat. Something warm runs up my face from my chin toward my eyes.

Up my face…?

Rustling, groaning, the sound of a seatbelt unclicking—and then a heavy body drops with another grunt.

"Noa?" Fingers feel my pulse.

"Huh?" I mumble, but before I have time to sort anything out in my mind, the hand is gone.

Glass breaking, more grunts, more rustling.

I force my eyes open against heavy lids. Blood… Blood stings in my eye. Why does it—

Oh, crap.

We're upside down in the overturned Hummer.

My daze evaporates, replaced by fear—white, hot, blinding fear. Another Sentinel.

A car door opens. Fast footfalls approach our overturned prison. I scramble to unbuckle the seatbelt, but it won't budge, it won't—

It gives in and gravity takes over. With a small yelp, I drop out of my seat and almost break my neck.

My vision still upside down, I look out of my broken side window. There, in the middle of the deserted road, stands Avery, bleeding from a small cut close to his hairline, but otherwise completely unaffected. No cough. No chills. No nothing.

Across from him, maybe four or five yards away, waits another Sentinel, as if he had all the time in the world. He's as tall as Avery, his eyes as amber-colored, and dressed in the typical uniform.

"McTighe," the other Sentinel snarls. One flick of his wrist brings his staff to life.

"Sands," Avery hisses back, moving into a fighting stance.

That's all the warning I get before they throw themselves at each other, clashing like two Titans in midair, a thunder-like rumble rippling through the silence.

Yelping, I shield my face as if it would do anything to protect me if the other Sentinel decided to go after me.

But as it is, he doesn't.

He focuses on Avery instead. Completely.

The two Sentinels assault each other like madmen. Sands wields his staff so quickly, its movements become a blur. More than once, it crashes down on Avery like a force of nature. Where is his staff? Why doesn't he pull out his weapon?

Sands aims to take off Avery's head with a huge strike. In my mind I see it connect, see it split his head open and finish him off.

Powered by reflexes and protected by luck, Avery blocks the attack at the last second.

A roar bursts from his throat as he yanks on the staff and throws Sands off-balance. But the other Sentinel won't be disarmed that quickly.

The one who controls the staff controls the opponent.

The fight picks up speed and turns into tugging and shoving for the upper hand on the staff.

Sands moves wrong—and the staff goes flying into the bushes thanks to an unlucky twist of his wrists.

Now neither of them has a weapon, and it evens the battlefield.

It doesn't make it any less scary.

If I hadn't seen Avery fight before, unaffected by rejection, I wouldn't see the subtle differences, but I do.

The fight is a blur of limbs, punches flying, legs kicking—and between this chaos of two bodies trying to defeat each other is Avery, getting almost as good as he is giving.

And slowing down.

Sands hits him with an uppercut under the chin that whips his head back. For the scariest of moments, Avery's eyes roll into his skull before he counters with an elbow to the other man's face.

That moment of weakness was all Sands needed. With a cruel twist to his mouth, he amps up the flurry of punches and assaults to a whole new level, as if Avery's stumble had powered him.

All Avery can do is defend himself.

Where first he landed punches, he now eats them. Where first he blocked attacks, he now can't anymore.

Avery is losing this battle.

And we all know it.

Sands' cruel grin is etched onto his face, every ounce of his attention on beating Avery. An especially forceful kick drives Avery backward, doubling him over.

Sands takes the opening and aims for Avery's head.

This isn't about winning.

It's about killing him.

Ice shoots through my veins, freezing my heart.

Another kick, another hit by Sands, a deep, guttural grunt from Avery that shoots straight to my heart and destroys the icy grip horror has on me.

Help.

He needs help.

The sounds of the battle turn desperate, at least Avery's grunting does. Sands, on the other hand, releases a malicious snicker right before he unleashes a spinning heel kick to Avery's head.

Avery whirls around and collapses to the ground.

From the inside of the overturned Hummer, I watch it in all

horrible, stark detail:

Sands standing with his back to me, snickering twice, still in his fighting stance and towering above Avery.

Avery on the ground, barely enough strength left to push his upper body off the asphalt, his eyes dull and dazed.

Sands' body tightening, readying for the final blow.

"No!" My shout pierces the silence. Not Avery, he can't—

Sands' head whips around toward me, a wide, evil grin on his face. "McTighe. Your little toy. A resilient little one." He spins back to Avery. Cold. Hard. "She'll be next."

Like in slow motion, he lifts his foot for a stomp kick to Avery's head.

It's going to crush his skull.

I know it.

I'm about to scream, to beg—but Avery is quicker. The light that just left is eyes is back. He lunges into the kick and catches it with his body, wrapping his arms around Sands' leg and pulling with all his weight.

Sands sways—and then falls from Avery's unexpected attack, a look of confusion on his face.

What Avery lacked in speed seconds ago, he makes up now, and then some. He pounces on Sands and pounds a furious haymaker into the man's chin.

Sands' head bounces off the pavement like a basketball. He goes limp as his eyes roll back into his skull.

Avery keeps his fist coiled and ready, hovering above the unconscious Sentinel until he's sure the fight is over.

Finally, he rolls off Sands onto his back, his chest heaving up and down like after a marathon, wheezing.

Me, I'm still trapped inside the truck, helpless, frightened and scared to the core.

For the first time since I all but threw myself at this plan, I'm not sure it was a good idea.

CHAPTER THIRTY-TWO

Aftermath

Avery kicks in the remains of the window to my left, scraping his boot around the frame to get rid of all the little glass chunks.

"Noa?" Avery squats. "Can you come out?" He reaches in toward me.

I draw my legs in closer to my chest.

I could come out. But I don't want to.

Because I sat here while Avery fought Sands. After Avery defeated Sands. All I did was sit here while he tied him up with whatever he could find in the gear George packed up years ago. During the whole thing, I wasn't moving an inch.

Just like I didn't when Sands was about to kill Avery.

Another silent tear runs down my face, following the tracks of the others.

I almost saw Avery getting killed.

"Noa?" Avery drops onto his knees, looking into my self-made prison. My butt sits on the truck's roof, the driver's seat cushion above me on the new ceiling, the steering wheel in the upper right, next to my head.

Tight, but safe.

Safe.

Nothing is safe.

Sighing once, Avery reaches in and peels my hands away from my legs until he has a good enough grip to help me out.

"Come on out. It's okay," he says so calmly, I almost believe him, but I know it's not okay.

Nothing is.

Avery helps me out and up, keeping both his hands on my upper arms as if afraid I'd fall.

"What's going on?" he asks.

"Nothing," I whisper. "Nothing at all." I don't look up. I can't see anything anyway. I'm crying too much.

His thumbs smooth over my upper arms, so soothing I can't help but close my eyes.

"Noa," he says quietly. "What's going on?"

I stare up at his pale face streaked with blood, but already much less bruised and swollen than right after the fight.

Sentinel Genes.

His amber eyes hold all the warmth and life I was missing when Sands was about to—

"He almost killed you, Avery." And I was watching it—and didn't do anything about it. For the first time ever, I wish I'd had a real-deal panic attack. At least that would give me an excuse, but no, I didn't. Not in the sense of what I'm used to, not the completely disabling doom, the mind-numbing sensation of *something* happening. No. I froze. That's it. No excuses. I froze. Not that I would've been able to do much, but… I don't know. I could've *tried.*

A faint smile pulls the corners of Avery's mouth upward. "But he didn't kill me. You were there." The thumbs keep up their circling.

I huff. "Me?" Big help I was, hiding like a coward.

"Yes, you. You were the one who distracted him when he was about to… well, let's not think about that."

"I didn't do it because I was distracting him." I cried out because I panicked. Not like normally, but still.

His thumbs keep working across my arms. "And it's all I needed. A little incentive and a little distraction. Check and check."

"But he could have killed you." Avery doesn't get it. He doesn't get the horror that shot through me when I thought he was going to be dead the next second. The feeling of doom, not like my panic attacks, but different, an event set in motion without an option to turn around. That Avery would die, right there in that very moment. "And I did nothing."

I didn't search for his staff, which he found with one quick look lodged between the visor and windscreen on the passenger's side. I didn't crawl out and attack Sands.

I froze.

"I'm not made for this." It's true. Whatever illusions I had: gone. I'm a coward, and Avery's death… would have been on me, as the first of many more to come: how would I have taken care of the Hub all alone, if Sands hadn't killed me right after taking care of Avery? Not at all.

Not at all.

Avery's smile widens, but his eyes turn sad. "You're not supposed to be made for this, Noa. Nobody is—well, besides Sentinels, and that isn't healthy, either. Look, I'm glad you stayed out of it, or Sands would have used you to his advantage. I know how we—*they*—think. He would have seized the opportunity and used you to get to me. Neither of us would have survived. Sands is a Hunter, a Sentinel trained to know their way around in the Earthverse and trained for tracking down targets. And once he finds them, he gets rid of them."

"Even more reason why I should have helped you." I can't let it go.

His chest shrinks with his sigh. "You did. He considered himself safe and thought he had won. A distraction was all I needed. We're an arrogant bunch, Noa. We're bred to fight, bred to win. There's almost nobody naturally conceived who can defeat us, strength- or skill-wise, and we know it. It's that arrogance that's our weakest spot, and you helped me remember that."

I helped him remember that. Well, I didn't do much else. Everything all seems too much: the pressure to save the world, or rather two of them, leaving my parents behind, getting Avery to safety, and not getting killed in the process. It all comes crushing down on me.

Without thinking, I throw my arms around his neck and hold on tightly. "I'm scared, Avery."

His body goes rigid under me. He takes a sharp breath in—and then peels me off of him, holding me out to arms' length.

"Fear is what keeps you alive, Noa. Never lose it." He drops my hands. "And now let's go. I've got the gear that's still useable, and Sands is as secured as he can be. We have a head start of maybe an hour or two. We need to get lost before the next one catches up with us."

He claps my shoulder once and walks ahead to the truck Sands came in, some kind of pickup, black, with scratches on its side from running us down.

When will I learn to keep my distance?

I rub a palm over my heart, an empty hole inside my chest that I have nobody else to blame for other than myself.

The next two hours are quiet.

Every couple of minutes, my eyes drift back to Avery. It happens without me thinking, and every time I catch myself, I get sucked in deeper and deeper into a world that consists of nothing more than Avery and myself. His presence is both the Band-Aid healing my soul's wounds and the salt poured into them.

Still, I can't take my eyes off of him.

He insisted he'd drive, and I let him. I don't know if I'll ever get behind the wheel of any car after *this*. One look at me and Avery probably decided that he was in better shape to drive than me, and I guess he's right. His face is almost healed already; only a couple of darker bruises still visible. The cut beneath his hairline is gone, and if we had had the time to wipe the blood off our faces, we might look almost presentable.

Not like we just got run off the road and one of us almost got killed.

I steal another glance at Avery. He protected me. Again. I didn't do squat to help him but yet he never called me weak. He never called me a coward. Quite the opposite.

I'm not sure I deserve that, but I'll take it.

Despite all my failures and shortcomings, he's still taking me more seriously than anybody ever has.

In a way, that's also pushing me more than anything else ever has.

And while Avery puts absolutely no pressure on me, I know I have to get better. For the both of us.

That fight... It was horrible. Maybe Holloway was equally vicious back in the Haunted House, but somehow, that fight lacked the finality of this one, the sensation of no way out, of losing everything.

Sands would have killed Avery without a second thought. Cold-blooded. It seemed so easy for him, as if they taught that in Sentinel Schoo—

Jeez. That's one scary thought. I hope they don't. But then...

"Uh, Avery?"

"Huh?"

"You said Sentinels were made for this, and... that Sands would *get rid* of his targets. Is that... Is that normal? Killing people?" Terra is losing bonus points left and right. No matter how advanced they are, killing people throws them back to medieval times.

"Normal for a Hunter, or normal for a good old regular Sentinel?"

"Either, I guess?"

He pauses. "Yes. Depending on the situation and threat level, we are taught to *eliminate the threat*. We're supposed to kill fast and painless and to not toy with our victi—opponents, but obviously, Sands hasn't read the manual very well."

Eliminate the threat... "That's quite the job description."

A muscle in Avery's jaw hardens. "We're peace keepers, Noa. And in order to keep the peace, the rights of some are negligible and people become expendable." It sounds like a quote.

Ouch. "Not my definition of peace keeper."

"Not mine, either."

I scoot in my seat to take a better look at him. "You didn't kill Sands."

Avery gives one shake of his head. "No."

"Why? He could come back. He could notify the others."

He kneads the steering wheel. "The cat's out of the bag. They know we're here. They can guess where we're going. If it's not him, it's somebody else. And… I don't want to be the killing machine they made me into, Noa." The way he says it, with this underlying hint of desperation, makes me realize I hadn't truly understood the cruelty behind the making of a First Class Sentinel.

He sits up straighter. "Sands doesn't deserve to die for following an order for a job he didn't choose. It's that easy. And while I may not like him, that's not a reason to kill him, either."

What did George say? The one Sentinel with a conscience? Maybe so, but it's what makes Avery Avery. That he kept his moral compass and is using it, not that Sands would take that into consideration if we met again. A cold shudder runs down my spine. If Avery hadn't been weak from rejection, we would have never gotten to this point to begin with.

The gears click into place, making me groan loudly. I'm such an idiot.

"What?" Avery asks, immediately alert.

I let my head hang. "We should've checked Sands for a modulator." We could have taken it for Avery. Not nice for Sands to leave him without a modulator, but then, that's what you get for trying to kill somebody else.

"I did," Avery says matter-of-factly, visibly relaxing. "He didn't have one. Neither on his body nor hidden in the truck."

"No modulator?" They had time to prepare. Why would he come without one and risk rejection?

"None. He must have only recently crossed through one of the smaller portals. Every hour spent here… Every hour makes it worse. It makes a difference."

No kidding. His wounds may heal quicker than mine, but at least

I have a healthy baseline to return to. For Avery, that baseline is sinking toward a complete body failure rather quickly.

And it's my responsibility to make sure that doesn't happen. Mine.

I'm tempted to put my hand on his leg but don't. "We'll get you back home, Avery." I mean it. We will.

Avery stays silent, staring at the instruments. He frowns. "There's a red light here, next to a box with a cord on it?"

Box with a cord? I loosen the seatbelt and lean over, trying hard to not have my body touch his, because… because I couldn't take it if he scooted away again.

One glance at the instruments is all I need. Life has cranked it up for us. "We're out of gas." Or we will be, in another couple of miles.

"Gas?"

"Stuff that powers this thing. Liquid gasoline. Benzene. Combustion engine?"

"And we're out of it?"

I lean over a tad farther, finding the dial for the distance remaining until empty. "In about thirty-three miles, we will be." Our Hummer had a pretty large tank plus an additional reserve tank for increased mileage, thank you, George. With that amount, we would have made it to our drop-off point, from which we'd have to approach on foot anyway to avoid detection, but Sands' truck…

"Meaning, we're going to be stranded in the middle of nowhere." Just great. Thanks, Sands, for not filling up your gas tank. Was that sloppy preparation or blinding optimism that he wouldn't need to chase us down very far? Probably the latter. Sands chose an automatic, which suggests at least some kind of thinking ahead. And it doesn't matter at all. We're still stuck.

Since we don't have a phone—and, to be honest, even if we did, we'd probably still have no internet connection all the way out here—I pull the map out of the little backpack we brought, searching over it until I have our approximate location.

Shit.

"We're already fifty miles away from the nearest tiny village with the potential for a gas station and we're going to end up approximately thirty miles farther south than we wanted to for our hike to start." Thirty miles. I have no clue. Is that something we can walk in a day? With Avery in rejection?

Avery frowns. "No towns? No way to get more… gas?"

"Nothing that's on here. We're so far out, people don't live here." Which is why this is more a narrow dirt road than anything else.

His lips press into a thin line. "Inconvenient news. Thirty miles will cost us two days in this kind of territory. And that's with us cutting through the forest."

He doesn't say it. We don't have those two days. And those two days could become three, if he deteriorates much more.

And if they turn into four, we're all dead.

I drop the map onto my lap, shoving my shaking hands under my thighs. "What do we do?"

Avery never takes his eyes off the road. "We deal with it."

CHAPTER THIRTY-THREE

Night Out

The truck gives us slightly more mileage than expected. After thirty-nine and a half miles, the engine starts to stutter, and once the engine dies, Avery pulls to the side.

We shoulder our gear; black backpack for Avery, the pink one for me. Everything we might need is stuffed into those two rucksacks—tent, sleep sack, food, etc.—and while it's heavy, it could be worse. Maybe it is an advantage after all to have paranoid Ghost parents who always expect the worst. I can picture George in the camping store, weighing tents in his hands, choosing the lightest one just in case he ever needed to flee from Sentinels.

If I ever see him again, I'll have to—

"Ready?" Avery drapes another torn-off branch across the truck's hood to make its hiding place off the street perfect. Nobody driving by will pick up on anything out of the ordinary thanks to the greenery of a little forest cloaking it. *If* anybody came by. It's a single-lane road that looks more like a dirt road than the real-deal. I can't imagine why anybody would drive up here, unless they were a hunter, and I mean the human kind, not the Sentinel kind.

I force my thoughts away from that slippery slope. "Yeah. Ready." I don't let my mind drift to any of the what-ifs, because to be honest, I'm not a great hiker. Or outdoor survivalist or whatever. Hiking to the Hub with Avery is doable. Making my way back into civilization without the Hummer—or any car—waiting for me... a tad more challenging. But again, that's a problem to worry about if we get lucky and destroy the portal. If not, me being stranded up here isn't going to qualify as a problem in the grand scheme of things. I'll probably die to the poison before I starve or freeze.

Avery takes the map, tracing our path cutting through the woods once more, and off we go.

The sun is already on its way down below the horizon, but we need to create distance between the truck and us before we settle for the night. We also need to get a head start because whenever they realize Sands didn't kill Avery, they'll send somebody else, and that person might not run out of gas like we did. So yes, covering distance is paramount. I can't say I disagree with Avery's assessment.

I don't want to be found by anyone, Terran or Earthling.

I want this to work out and be over, even if that means I'll never see Avery again. At least I'll know he's safe, just like Earth.

At least I won't have to look at him and wonder *what if.*

I chew the inside of my cheek while walking behind Avery. I wish I hadn't left my nose studs at my parents', but after the night in Avery's arms... well, I couldn't take out the heart. Not after he noticed it, not after he slept cuddled around me.

I couldn't.

Now, though... Now I wish I could swap it for something else. The teardrop. Maybe the black stone. Something other than a freakin' heart.

We hike through the woods of the Superior National Forest for at least another hour before it becomes too dark to safely continue. Avery picks a spot for us that's mostly flat and protected by trees and bushes. Without even looking at the instructions, he sets up the tent in no time.

I get the sleeping bags from the bottom of the two hiking backpacks and unroll them onto the self-inflating insulated mattresses. One for Avery, one for me.

The mood is somber and quiet. Neither of us is up for chatting.

The attack, the loss of the truck, and the pressure of what's at stake are working against us.

During our meal of dried fruit and pretty stale water rations, Avery's chills start up again. He tries his best to suppress them and keep me from noticing, but I still do.

Of course I do.

I still do.

I notice while he sits on a tree stump and almost spills his water.

I notice when he climbs into his sleeping bag next to me.

I notice when he turns away from me and curls up into a ball, his back toward me.

I notice.

I reach out for him, to tell him it's okay, to tell him I can help him, but I hesitate, my hand hovering right above his shaking shoulder. I don't have enough courage for another rejection.

We fall asleep without a *goodnight*, the distance between us much wider than an arm's length.

The next morning begins at a time I normally would consider to be night, and Avery is even less talkative than the evening before.

He has us pack and start walking in under ten minutes, and while I'm sure it has to do with our less-than-thrilling situation, I can't help but wonder if his bad mood has to do with me.

Because he doesn't even look at me.

He doesn't truly ignore me, either, but when he holds a branch aside for me to walk past or holds out a hand to help me climb over some kind of rock formation or broken-down trees, he doesn't make eye contact.

Not once.

And after a while, it makes me nervous.

What did I do? Have I said something that offended him? Was it the hug? I knew I shouldn't have done it, but I thought...

Yeah, think again.

Once the sun is up, Avery can't hide behind the twilight of early dusk anymore. *Something* is going on, or he wouldn't wear a mask of stoic neutrality that would make any Sentinel proud.

Nature does its best to impress us with an orange-red sky, birds chirping in the bushes, large beautiful trees everywhere, and a view people usually pay a lot of money for. It doesn't even register to me.

In fact, this peacefulness and serenity make the uneasy feeling in the pit of my stomach even worse.

It must be mid-morning already when I finally have enough. This terrain is difficult enough with its bushes, trees, tree stumps, rocks, uneven ground, and other nature-things that don't make for an easy hike. I don't need Avery's heavy silence to make it even worse.

Avery holds a large branch out of the way for me to pass, pointing at the ground as a means for me to notice the ant hill and to avoid it.

The moment he lets go of the branch and, like the last ten or twenty or thirty times, speeds up to take the lead, I grab him by the sleeve.

"Avery. What's going on?"

His whole body tightens with my touch.

I drop his sleeve. "What's going on?"

"Nothing." He cranks his shoulders back once and starts to hike away from me, his face the same mask it's been since we got up.

Well, I'm not giving up that easily. With a couple of jogging steps, I catch up with him. This time, I keep my thumbs hooked under the backpack's shoulder straps. He's on edge as it is; no need to make it worse.

"Nothing? Seriously? Because from where I'm standing, it looks like *something* is going on."

He ignores me.

"Avery? Hello? Aw, come on." I groan when he keeps looking straight ahead as if the trees need his undivided attention. "I'm sorry if I did something wrong, but at least tell me what—"

He stops dead in his tracks. "I dreamed last night."

Uh, okay. Not what I was expecting. Nightmares? *That* bad?

We're right in front of a big clearing, almost the size of a football field, covered with knee-high grass and wild flowers, a couple of bushes sprinkled far and in-between. It is beautiful, but I doubt Avery sees it with his fixed stare into the distance.

I clear my throat. "You dreamed?" That's my shrink's trick, actually. Not adding value to a statement, instead validating it with a question and waiting for more information because... he dreamed, so what?

"Yes," Avery says quietly, his eyes wandering across the clearing.

"So... is that why you're a bit off today? Bad dreams?" Maybe that's a side effect of rejection.

A small sigh leaves his throat, the kind that carries more desperation than any words could.

I put one gentle hand on his arm. "Avery?" I'm starting to worry about him. More than before, I mean.

The muscles in his jaw twitch. "We don't dream, Noa. Sentinels don't dream. I suppose the last time this happened to me was before I was altered—when I was a child."

My eyebrows shoot up. "You don't dream?" Isn't that the brain's way of dealing with new information, of processing it? Isn't dreaming vital for life? Or is that my teenage girl interpretation of science?

He looks down at my hand on his arm, and it's all I can do to keep it there and not pull away.

"We don't. While we're asleep, our subconscious runs through training scenarios and processes fights. It's one of the reasons Sentinels are so deadly—we never stop practicing, not even in our sleep."

How sad is that? No dreams, just fights all the time? No wonder Sentinels are so... intense.

"But, Avery, then that's great that you dreamed. I assume anything is better than training scenarios—no offense." I smile at him, but he's still focused on my hand on his arm, the one that I don't know what to do with.

"You're not getting it, Noa. We don't dream. I was altered to make it physiologically impossible. It can't happen, and yet, last night it did." He finally looks me in the eye, the amber in them so dark, it seems almost solid.

"I dreamed for the first time in over ten years. And it wasn't about Terra; it wasn't about our mission." He pauses, the intensity of his gaze rooting me to the spot. "It was about you, Noa. I dreamed about you."

My jaw drops open. Me? He dreamed about... me? What does that mean? Is that good? And if he can't dream, then why—

I shake my head ever-so-slightly. "But—"

"I know," he says, his voice carrying a warmth that lights up my soul. "With you... With you, it's different. The rules don't apply."

He puts his hand on top of mine, squeezes it once, then walks across the clearing.

I stare after him, stunned.

Avery doesn't dream. Yet he did.

Of me.

I watch him go, the strong frame that tries so hard to not let anything get to him, ignoring rejection and whatever fate throws at him.

I swallow dry.

He dreamed of me.

CHAPTER THIRTY-FOUR

Boat for One

The sun is on its way down, but still a good hour or so from setting. Avery leads us to a little clearing protected by trees and bushes on three sides, leaving the fourth open to a mesmerizing view of a small lake about fifteen yards below the little cliff we're on.

"We're done for today." He drops his backpack onto the ground. Apparently, we're still on a tight schedule because he doesn't waste a single moment. The tent is untied ten seconds later, and Avery busies himself setting it up, his back turned toward me.

Since the admission about his dream, his back has always been turned to me, and that made it a very, very long day.

In case I ever wondered, yes, it is possible to hike next to a guy you have a crush on and not really talk. Or make eye contact.

I let my backpack slide off my shoulders and groan. This day sucked. If I still had my studs, I'd put in the mad-face smiley, but as it is, I'm stuck with the stupid heart that does nothing for me but hurt.

It's not my fault he's dreaming of me, is it? I'm not the one who made him *not* able to dream either, or who made him Sentinel, or…

I kick a stone that's in the way of me unpacking my stuff.

None of it is my fault.

A week ago, I was in Germany, on a field trip, fighting off a panic attack, and now I'm here, stuck in a war between Earth and a world I didn't even know existed.

Stuck with Avery.

I look at him.

With a quick flick of his arms, then a couple of pulls and adjustments here and there, the tent is up. His movements are less fluid than what I'm used to, but he still radiates power.

After a while, I catch myself staring at him.

Correction. I'm not stuck *with* Avery. I'm stuck *on* Avery.

At least until he's back home and the spell is broken by the gap between universes.

I sigh.

Then I'll never see him again, and while I'll probably eventually get over him… I'm going to miss him. So yeah, I don't want him to ignore me until we send him home. I don't want to feel like I did with George and Elaine, the third wheel.

I pull my ponytail tighter and literally take the first step. Somebody has to. I walk over to Avery and reach for the backpack his shaking fingers have been unsuccessfully trying to untie for a minute or two.

"Let me," I offer.

For a moment I fear he won't, but after a short hesitation he gives in.

"Thank you," he says. Looking much more like an old man than a Sentinel at the height of his power, he eases himself to sit on a fallen tree.

I unpack our rations and water before I drop the backpack into the tent.

Deep breath.

This is Avery. Whatever is going on with him, he'll manage.

I sit on the large, knee-high stump next to him, my bones and muscles protesting the additional squat. Despite our relatively slow pace, it's been a rough day. The terrain is uneven and, well, wild, which didn't make for easy hiking. The weather wasn't too bad, but we still didn't make as much progress as we'd like, and now… now we're just spent. I was about to beg Avery to take a break when he found us this spot, and while I know that an early retirement from hiking today only means an earlier start tomorrow, right now I'm glad for it. Plus, the view of the lake from here is truly awe-inspiring. Soul-food.

Speaking of.

I open one of the vacuum-sealed camping rations and hand it to Avery. "Hungry?"

He stares at the food as if it was poisonous.

"You have to eat, Avery. I know you don't have much of an appetite, but you have to. We hiked all day, and tomorrow..." Tomorrow is our last day to cover some ground. If we don't make it at least somewhat close to the Hub, we won't have a chance to set our plan in motion, and then... bye-bye, Earthlings. And if another Hunter should catch up with us, I need Avery at full strength, or at least as close to it as possible. We've clearly established I'm no good in any fighting situation.

I gently rock into his body. "Come on. Here. A little bit." The moment I say it, I realize I sound like Elaine, trying to get Andrew to eat.

Avery closes his eyes. "I'll try."

For a while, we eat in silence. Birds chirp around us while the sun sinks lower and lower, bathing the lake below us in the most stunning array of pink and orange.

Avery picks at a couple of bites, but that's it. Mostly, he looks out onto the lake, lost in thought.

On the upside, though, the silence between us is different now. More peaceful. All day long, Avery gave off this vibe of underlying aggression that kept me at a distance and afraid to even approach him. Now it's a quiet serenity, and I can't say I dislike it.

Avery shudders. Another wave of the rejection. Without a word, I get up and bring his sleeping bag from the tent. If I wait for him to ask for help, I'll wait forever. I wrap Avery in the unzipped bag and sneak under it on his right.

And I ignore his body tensing when I scoot close.

"Why do you think Sands didn't have a modulator?" Distraction is key, or Avery will never relax. I tighten the end of the sleep sack to keep the warmth in. Every degree counts. And yeah. A modulator would have made all the difference for us.

"Because Canyon never expected him to return." He says it like it's the most logical conclusion of them all. And obvious.

"What?" I blink at him. "He can't send him over here, knowing he'll die for sure."

"Of course he can. Send him over, let him fight before rejection weakens him, and if he dies, so be it. He's a Sentinel. We'll send another one. We have hundreds of thousands more."

My mouth drops open. "You're not serious." Sentinel or not, cruel soldier or not, you don't sentence somebody to death like that.

"Oh, but I am." He keeps on looking at the sun that's already sunken halfway into the lake. A couple of ducks float on top of the water, searching for food. Somewhere a bird calls, but other than that, it's dead quiet. Still, Avery's voice only barely carries over the silence. "Some lives are worth more than others, you know?"

An icy fist gets a hold of my heart. "What… What do you mean?" He isn't implying what I think he is, is he?

Another bout of shivers runs through him, making his teeth chatter so hard, I want to mold myself around him to warm him, but… I don't.

"I mean that Sentinels count for very little in our society, Noa." He throws a quick sideways glance at me. "That's why sometimes I wonder who you really are."

I jerk my head back. "Me?"

"You. Canyon wouldn't send Hunter Sentinels for me."

"Neither would he for me." Why would he? To throw me in jail because I escaped from under his watch? To use me for his plan? Any other Earthling would do for that, and I think by now we're well past that stage in our interplanetary relationship; the whole killing-every-human-on-Earth-thing made sure of that.

"I'm not so sure."

The last glimpse of sun sinks into the lake, and with it, the temperature drops by a good ten degrees.

Canyon must be out for Avery. After all, his former first Sentinel betrayed him and basically kidnapped Canyon's Earthling, i.e., me. The thought that Canyon was after me is ridiculous, but I can see him going after Avery.

I take a deep breath, the clean, fresh air doing not much to clear my head.

Over the next few minutes, the darkness becomes deeper and more complete than what I'm used to at home. I'm a city girl; darkness is relative in a city with all its lights. Here, it's different. One by one, the stars come out, bright gleaming dots on a black velvety background. The moon shines barely enough to highlight the tiny ripples the wind blows across the lake.

The longer we sit, the further apart Avery's chills become until it's been at least ten minutes since the last episode.

The whole attack was the longest he's had so far. Andrew took months to get to this point.

Avery plays with the zipper of the sleeping bag draped over his shoulders. "When I was little, my mom used to take me up on the roof," he says quietly, looking to the sky. "She and my dad would bring out the telescope and we'd look at stars. August, my older brother, knew them all by heart. I was still learning. It's one of my fondest memories of home, one of the few I think still are correct and unaltered."

He leans closer, one hand extended, pointing up. "This one, the bright one. Auggie called it 'Polaris,' as they taught him in school. Me, always hidden at home, I usually simply called it nightlight, because it was so bright. I was young." He gives a crooked smile.

"I love it." A nightlight to guide you through the dark. It's fitting.

I feel him turn his head toward me and my heart skips a beat. If I turned now too, our noses would be touching. Our noses first, and then maybe…

I try to swallow, but my throat is too dry.

Damn overactive imagination.

"We had a flat part on the roof," Avery continues in a whisper. "My parents laid out a blanket for Auggie and me, and when they thought we'd fallen asleep, they got up and danced. Every time. No music, just them and the sky."

I could swear his eyes are burning into my skin. *Burning.* My heart pounds so hard, my chest hurts, and breathing is impossible.

Avery gets up. The sleeping bag drops off his shoulders into the grass behind us.

"May I?" He holds one hand out for me.

I stare at him wide-eyed, sure I must be dreaming this.

He gives a slight bow to his head. "May I have this dance?"

My gaze shoots up into his amber eyes, shining bright and more alive than ever.

"Yes," I whisper. My small hand fits into his larger palm as if it were made for exactly this purpose. The roughness of his skin is so familiar, it brings goosebumps.

Avery helps me up as if he was afraid he'd break me, then reaches for my other arm, positions it on top of his shoulder, and drops his hand to my waist.

A short gasp escapes me, one I had no chance to suppress, none at all. Under his touch, I'm on fire. And not only that: it spreads. Within seconds, my whole body burns. My heart beats frantically to keep up with the amount of oxygen my brain consumes trying to make sense of what's happening.

Then, Avery sways left to right, moving me along with him.

I think I'm going to faint.

"Avery," I whisper, surprised it's not just a croak, "what are you doing?"

He sways back and forth, turning us the slightest bit in the process. The corners of his mouth tilt up in a small smile, one that makes the amber shine like liquid gold, thanks to the moonlight.

"I'm making room." The apple in his throat moves up and down. "This is me… trying to make room in my boat for one."

His smile widens at the same time my eyes do, as if he knew what kind of fireworks he just lit up inside my stomach—the kind that don't start slow, but rather explode at the same time, shooting sparks everywhere.

Avery is making room in his boat for one.

With me.

For me?

Does that mean… I mean…?

My hand slides an inch off his shoulder despite the lightness of our sway, and that's when I make an executive decision, probably the bravest one of my life. Instead of drawing it back up into position, I glide it down his arm and feel over the muscles under his shirt.

I don't let go.

I don't stop.

I don't take the easy way out.

I look up into Avery's mesmerizing golden eyes. He watches my every move, his lips slightly parted, the pulse in his neck beating as violently as mine, that's for sure.

My hand finds his and pushes it farther onto my back as I step closer to him, bringing us chest to chest. A small, hoarse breath escapes him, and just when I think I overinterpreted what he said, he takes my hand, and, as if he had all the time in the world, drapes it around his neck, dragging his fingers down my arm like I did with his, until this hand too finds my hip.

At this point, I'm sure spontaneous combustion is going to set in anytime now.

Avery drinks me in with his eyes. Fleetingly, I wonder if he sees the fear—the fear that he'll realize I don't know what I'm doing—but then I pick up on the vulnerability etched into the lines of his face. It's the same for him. This is new, for both of us, and somehow, that gives me courage.

I raise my left hand up behind his neck, brushing something metallic behind his right ear that faintly registers as the same kind of port I saw on Leiva, but my focus is elsewhere. On Avery.

Together we slow dance to a beat only audible to us. We hold on to each other, neither of us daring to breathe.

Then, so slowly that I first think I imagined it, Avery glides his hands across my back.

It lights me up like a burning torch.

Lightning bolts shoot through my body. Avery's hands leave

burnt trails in their wake, yet I can't get enough.

I want more—more of Avery.

When I thread my fingers up into his hair, Avery closes his eyes, only to have them fly open again a split second later, burning.

No need for the stars above us. I have Avery.

Avery, whose hands do wonders to me, making me feel alive, whose gaze holds so much warmth, I wonder how I could never see them this way before, how he could hide it.

He slowly bends down toward me, hesitating only the slightest bit before his lips touch mine.

CHAPTER THIRTY-FIVE

Heaven

I never imagined my first kiss would be like this.

Something special, yes, maybe even extra special, but not like this. Nobody told me it could feel like the whole world stopped and restarted with every second his lips were on mine, or like I was spinning out of control, my body torn apart and healed at the same time, or like if I ever stopped breathing, this could bring me back to life.

Avery's kiss is all of that. And more.

At first, it's the gentlest touch of his lips on mine, like a question, an invitation—one I accept all too willingly.

My toes curl and my fingers dig into his hair, drawing him in. The kiss changes from innocent to completely mind-blowing in a matter of seconds. Like something was unleashed or broken free inside both of us. There's no holding back anymore.

I can't get close enough to him.

I push myself onto my tippy toes and press my body against his, never breaking the kiss, never slowing my hands' exploration down his neck, over his wide shoulders and down his back for as far as I can reach, all the while Avery does the same with me.

Heaven.

This is what heaven must be like.

He breaks the kiss and lifts me up by my waist, bringing us face to face. My legs wrap around his torso, although I'm too short to cross my ankles behind his back.

Our foreheads press together. I want to feel the warmth of his breath forever.

"Avery." My palms cup his scruffy cheeks. Every square inch of his face deserves to be touched, to be caressed.

"Noa," he whispers back. He drops his hands from my waist and slowly draws them over my butt until he cups it.

A little moan escapes me, and how could it not? I'm melting despite the cool temperatures.

Avery's lips pull up into a smile, a real smile, no holding back.

"I like that sound you make." He circles my butt with his fingers, making me shiver and push forward into him by tightening my legs around his waist. "In fact, I think I've been lied to my whole life." He gives me a small kiss on my lips. "They said it's nothing we're missing out on, nothing to worry about, only one less distraction in life." Another kiss, this time lingering a bit more. "They were wrong. *This*"—he pulls me in and lifts me up a couple of inches by my rear— "this is *everything*."

Before I can dissect what he means, his lips are on mine again, and this time, something is different. It's not the probing from our first kiss, it's not the hunger from the second round, no—this is something else. There's a depth to our connection that was always palpable right under the surface—and now it's out.

And it makes all the difference.

His kiss deepens, and his tongue glides over my lips, a sensation so unexpected, yet completely thrilling at the same time. I gasp into his mouth, and his smile widens under our kiss. His tongue seeks out mine, plays with it, and… time stops.

Nothing else exists besides Avery and me.

The stars above us, the moon and the nightlight watching over us, the lake with its birds and the trees standing guard around it— none of it is important.

Nothing is, besides him and me.

Avery guides me to the tent, holding me tightly, then lowers me onto the insulated mattress, his weight coming down on me, applying pressure in all the right spots.

Everything about his touch causes my heart to flutter and my lungs to fail. He runs his hands down my sides, deepening the kiss, his tongue finding new ways to play with mine.

My toes curl, and my brain kind of shorts out. Too much, yet not enough. Definitely not enough. Never enough. A breathy sound escapes me as my fingers curl into his shirt.

Off. I need it off.

I tug and pull, and his shirt comes off when Avery obeys my silent command and lifts his weight for barely long enough to get the job done.

Skin. Velvety, soft skin over a hard layer of muscles. I slide my hands over his arms, his back, his sides, dragging my nails. Avery sucks in a breath, then lets out a sigh. *Whoa.* A rush of sensations hits me all at once. That sound… It brings something right behind my navel to a dance before it coils lower and lower.

Avery's arms crush me against him, and I swear, there's no better feeling in the world than this. I let myself sink deeper and deeper into the quicksand that is Avery—because let's be honest, I knew from the get-go there was no escaping him.

It could be minutes, it could be hours, and honestly, it could be days that pass and I wouldn't know.

Avery and I kiss and touch until we eventually fall asleep in each other's arms, me cuddled against his chest, his heart beating a reassuring strong rhythm under my palm.

Tonight, there is no more shaking, no more rejection.

There's only us.

When I wake, it's still dark in the tent, yet I know right away that Avery is up. For the shortest of moments, I'm embarrassed about what we did last night—the kissing, the exploring—but the explosion of fireworks lit up by the pure memory of what happened calls me a liar.

Yeah, I totally enjoyed that.

And I don't regret a thing.

My head still rests on his shoulder. Actually, my whole body is still cuddled against him. At one point, he must have reached over and gotten my sleeping bag for us since his is still outside where we dropped it when things… got interesting. Avery's one arm is wrapped around me; the other rests folded behind his head. It's still dark, but I know how strong that makes him look, bulging muscles and all. After all, I saw it the night in my room, and I copped a pretty good feel of said muscles last night.

My cheeks heat up and I suck in my lower lip.

"You're awake," he whispers.

I nod into his shoulder. "Hi."

"Hi." His lips touch my forehead in the tiniest of kisses that releases the biggest of sparks. I curl my fingers over his skin, feeling something metal under my fingers. His necklace.

Avery's hand glides down my spine as far as he can reach and back up again, a move so completely unawkward, as if we've been doing this forever. For a moment, we lie silently and enjoy each other's presence. I play with the little metal charm, twirling it between my fingers like I usually twirl my nose stud.

"My mother gave it to me," Avery whispers eventually, his breath warming my hair. "On the day she came to say goodbye, when they'd altered me already and I was about to be shipped off to the training facilities. She turned me away so the other Sentinels wouldn't see it and pushed it into my palm. She… She looked at me, tears in her eyes, and I… I didn't understand it." His voice breaks at the end. "I didn't understand why she was crying, and that made it only worse for her. I stood there like a miniature Sentinel, her emotions nothing to me, and she knew. 'One day you'll understand,' she said, and then she was gone." His chest heaves up and down under me. "I've been wearing it ever since."

"And keeping it secret?" I ask. The way he's been protectively tucking it away whenever it becomes visible kind of made it obvious.

"And keeping it secret," Avery says. "We aren't allowed any

mementos from our previous lives once we're altered. Most of us don't remember our parents or where they came from, and most don't want to. We're made for battle. For war, in case it comes. Not for emotions. Not for *this*." His lips brush over my forehead.

I turn my head up to look at him. "But you're different." I knew that from the moment he got chewed out by Canyon for asking about a modulator for me, and even though I didn't know that word, I knew that this soldier had tried to do something for me—something that he didn't have to, and that for sure Canyon didn't appreciate.

"Maybe," he whispers. "Maybe not. Maybe we're all like me, but I'm the first to break out. I always remembered more than the rest, I'd like to believe."

We fall into an easy silence. I could stay here for hours, cuddled into Avery, ignoring the impending destruction of my world, but duty calls. Even the birds wake up to tweet and chirp, a sure sign it's soon going to be light enough to resume hiking.

"Ready for another couple of miles?" Avery asks, obviously coming to the same conclusion.

"I guess so." I sigh and unwrap myself from Avery, my body cold where it's not connected to his anymore.

In a little bit more than twenty-four hours, if all goes well, Earth will be saved.

Earth will be saved, but Avery and I… we'll be lost.

CHAPTER THIRTY-SIX

Lesson Learned

Although it feels like the burden of our plan increases with every step we take closer to the Hub, walking is much easier than yesterday.

That would be because of Avery. His hand in mine. His thumb smoothing over my skin. His smile whenever I steal a look.

I'm sure I'm wearing the same one that only falters ever-so-slightly when I think of tomorrow.

I push that thought away as far as possible.

Once in a while, I catch him looking at me just like I do at him. Avery's eyes are even brighter under the sunlight today, as if they had a little battery installed on the inside, making them shine like two tiny suns. For a moment, I consider that idea, then discard it. Even Terrans aren't going to be that crazy with Augs.

We've walked a good two-thirds of what we still need to pull off today when Avery makes us take a break, and I know exactly why.

Because rejection is gripping him. Hard.

For the last ten minutes, he's tried to suppress the shakes, the shivering, his knees giving in.

It didn't work.

My heart breaks for him, how he's silently rocking back and forth, shaking, teeth chattering, all but falling onto the tree stump when he can't support his weight anymore.

"It's getting worse," he rasps through clenched teeth.

I can see that.

And the only thing I can do is make it bearable. I pull out the sleeping bag and wrap it around his shoulders, then get my backpack and sit on one of the larger rocks close to the little stream he picked to sit near for our rest. I grab a pouch of freeze-dried spaghetti in tomato sauce. It doesn't sound like the most delicious meal, because who likes cold, freeze-dried spaghetti in tomato sauce, but it's better than nothing. It goes down easy. I use the pocket knife to pry the pouch open, glad I'm not amputating any fingers in the process.

Something rustles in the bushes. *Please not another mountain lion, like earlier.* So far we've seen two mountain lions, one moose, several rabbits, and tons of squirrels.

I drop the dry food-covered knife on the ground to wash later. "Avery, here—"

"Well, well. We meet again."

Not Avery.

I whip my gaze up. Avery jumps up and whirls around, his arms spread wide, keeping himself between me and—

Holloway.

There, at the edge of the forest, barely stepped out onto the large gravel that lines the bed of this little stream, is the Sentinel Canyon must've sent after Sands. The Sentinel who gives me nightmares.

All the wounds, all the bruises Avery gave him the last time we met have healed, and for a moment I wish they hadn't.

"McTighe." Holloway greets Avery with a nod of his head, as calmly as if they'd met at a coffee shop.

"Holloway," Avery says, and while it sounds almost equally calm, I hear the difference and strain in it.

So does the other Sentinel.

"Been a long journey, hasn't it?" he asks with a condescending smile, taking a step closer. "Rejection is such an ugly death, McTighe. You should consider yourself lucky Canyon sent me to relieve you of your misery."

"Didn't work out for Sands, Holloway. Don't even bother."

"Ouch, yeah, Sands. Looked bad when I found him." He flinches in mock empathy, but his eyes stay cold. "Don't get your hopes up for a repeat performance. Sands didn't have Canyon's fancy new Augs, and then you weren't as weak as you are now, McTighe. I could smell your rotting stench from miles away. And because I'm a nice guy, I'll give you one chance to surrender yourself and her, and you won't be killed." He shrugs. "Well, not instantly anyway. *She* goes back to Terra. You don't."

I suck in a sharp breath. There it is, the confirmation: they want *me* back on Terra. Not Avery. Why—

"Non-negotiable." Avery growls, dropping more into a fighting stance.

Holloway heaves an exaggerated sigh. "That's what I thought. Well, then don't complain I didn't warn you." He whips a staff out from his belt, the ends springing into action the same moment my delayed comprehension makes me realize what's going on.

Avery and Holloway are going to fight, and only one is going to come out alive.

Avery doesn't give Holloway the advantage of the first strike.

With a roar, he charges, ducking under the staff strike coming down at sonic speed.

I scream and jump back, almost falling over one of the bigger rocks in the riverbed.

Before Holloway can bring his staff back up, Avery is already too close for him to use it again. For a split second, Holloway seems surprised, but unfortunately, it doesn't make him lose speed. Holloway drops the staff to free up both hands.

I'm still backed up close to the river, watching in horror as the two Sentinels exchange punches. At first Avery is quicker, landing more hits than Holloway. Avery ducks, weaves, attacks, and counterattacks. He's so precise, Holloway has almost no chance to defend himself.

Almost.

Because the more punches he throws, the slower Avery becomes.

Rejection is getting to him, working against him.

Like a prophecy, his words come back to mind, spoken a lifetime ago: *"I came in first, him second."* Holloway is good. He fights like he had a modulator, unaffected by rejection. And whatever new, fancy Augs Canyon might've given him… They're doing him a favor.

I yelp when Holloway lands a kick to Avery's thigh strong enough to shatter a small tree.

Holloway's grin widens as if my terrified scream was exactly what he wanted, and from there on, the fight changes. Instead of attacking, Holloway keeps stepping back with Avery's attacks, defending as well as before, but all he offers in offense is an occasional punch.

What is he doing?

Avery gives it his all to break through Holloway's defenses, and more than once he succeeds, but Holloway eats every single punch as if it were nothing. Avery works twice as hard to connect, exhausting himself.

My breathing turns raspy. Cat and mouse. Holloway is playing Avery.

He's wearing him out.

Why go through even more trouble when all he needs to do is have Avery do the work for him?

And Avery does do the work. As well as he can.

By now, it's obvious even to me he's tiring out: his attacks slow, become sluggish even—but he doesn't give up.

I'm trapped inside my head, just like when Sands attacked. Useless. I don't think I'm breathing, or if I am, it must be so shallow that it doesn't count because it's impossible for my body to do something as ordinary as breathing while I'm watching a fight to the death. My vision narrows, and I'm all but waiting for the panic to set in, the feeling of doom, of hopelessness, but it doesn't come.

Instead, bright hot fear slices my soul in half—not my usual panic crushing down on me, suffocating me. This is different.

It doesn't make it any better, though.

A silent scream leaves my throat when Holloway decides to swat Avery's defense aside and punch him in the face, as casual as if out for a Sunday stroll.

Holloway is toying with Avery, and it breaks my heart.

With every punch that lands, every grunt from Avery, every missed counterstrike, my heart breaks more.

At this point, the fight looks like it's over already.

The moment I realize that, Avery must have too because he visibly pulls on all the strength he has, throwing his body forward so desperately, I know it's his last move. I know it.

The side kick would have ruptured anybody's stomach wall—if it had hit.

But it doesn't.

Maybe Avery is a tad too slow, and maybe Holloway is a tad too fast, but he deflects it easily, spinning Avery around. He barely catches himself with a grunt, off-balance for a second, but it's enough.

A gleam lights up in Holloway's eyes, and before I can even utter a single word of warning, a scream, *anything* that would get to Avery in time, Holloway charges.

He wraps his hands around the back of Avery's head and pulls him down while ramming his right knee up into Avery's face.

The *crunch* of the impact is enough to make me nauseous, but it's nothing compared to the brutality that follows.

Avery's head snaps back, blood streaming from his nose, his eyes rolling into their sockets, his body already going limp. But Holloway doesn't stop. The sneer on his face widens as he pulls up an elbow and rams it into Avery's face.

Avery's head whips to the left as his body collapses under him.

It's not enough for Holloway. Spinning, he aims another kick at Avery's head that only misses because Avery drops to the ground. He draws the leg in, coming to stand over Avery like an archangel about to unleash his version of justice.

My heart stops.

Avery lies on the ground, with barely enough strength left to lift his head.

Holloway lifts his foot for the final blow.

No.

Not going to happen.

Not going to happen with me watching.

I scream, more an animalistic grunt than anything else, and charge at Holloway, all rational thought gone, extinguished from my brain the moment Avery's life was fated to end under the sole of Holloway's boot.

Fear gives me a boost of adrenaline. I throw myself onto Holloway's back, my arms wrapped around his throat, squeezing as hard as I can. I only have one shot at this.

The Sentinel stumbles forward, caught off guard by my unexpected attack, but that's it.

He isn't gagging, he isn't choking, he isn't doing anything.

Besides laughing.

I cling to his back, trying to choke him, and all he does is *laugh*.

He reaches up and grabs my back, digging his fingers into fabric and skin, not caring about either as he yanks me forward so forcefully, I have no chance at all to keep my position. I fly off his shoulders and onto the gravel-covered ground like a rider off a bucking horse.

The impact drives all air out of my lungs with a wheeze. I'm more than aware I didn't exactly improve our situation. Not in the least.

I only made Holloway madder.

"Acting up, are we?" Holloway snarls. He takes a threatening step closer, his hands on his hips. Frantically, I try to scoot back, but the gravel gives way under my hectically pushing feet. I'm not getting anywhere.

"McTighe is rubbing off on you, and I can't say I like it."

I see the kick coming, but there's nothing I can do about it.

Like a bomb exploded inside my body, his boot buries itself into my gut, shooting hot pain into every single cell of my being.

Somewhere far away, Avery growls, somewhere Holloway laughs, but neither fact truly registers at all. At this moment, lying on the cold, wet gravel, I'm a hundred percent positive I'm going to die.

We are going to die.

Another kick, this time to my back, spinning me around twice until I come to a rest against same small boulder I used as a seat a mere couple of minutes ago.

Holloway laughs—no, *snickers*—as he picks his staff up from the ground.

"I thought it would be harder. McTighe, you're not even worthy to be called a Sentinel anymore. This? This was *weak*." He spits out the last word before he turns his attention to me. "And you, my dear, better watch out. There's more where this came from. Canyon didn't specify whether to bring you back dead or alive, and right now, I'm leaning toward dead."

His eyes turn dark and he steps closer.

With the last bit of power I have, I push myself back, a last effort to get away. My palm brushes over something cold, smooth, and dusted with food specks.

Holy cow.

Hope just threw me a bone—or rather, a knife. My heart leaps up inside my chest as I wrap my fingers around the heel of the knife I dropped a couple of minutes ago.

I only have one shot. One shot.

One shot, or we're both dead.

Out of the corner of my eye, I see Avery trying to push himself up, then sinking back down when his legs can't support his weight.

It's my turn to save us.

And there's only one way.

"Please," I squeak. "I'll do anything you want. I… I'll come with you. I won't cause any problems. *Please*." I don't need to work on making my words sound pitiful; it comes naturally at this point. For good measure, I curl up a little more to show I'm in pain. Also not much acting needed.

"Noa—" Avery grunts from his position on the ground.

"Shut up, McTighe," Holloway snarls. "The girl is making the right decision. At least one person here has some smarts, but then, I never thought you did anyway, *PBM*." The maliciousness he hisses those words with hardens something in me. I won't back down.

I won't.

"Get up," Holloway snarls.

"Can't," I grunt between clenched teeth. "Need help." One hand is still on my stomach where his boot almost broke me in two.

Holloway rolls his eyes but bends down toward me and extends a hand. "Little weak Earthling, I'm not carrying you the whole way to the Hub."

We're an arrogant bunch, Avery said. *There's almost nobody who can defeat us. That arrogance is our weakest spot.*

I take Holloway's hand and dig my heels into the ground.

I'm. Not. Helpless.

"No need to carry me."

I whip my right arm out from behind my back, my whole body adding power, using Holloway's pull on me to gain velocity.

His eyes widen, but before he can free a hand, my knife sinks into his body like warm butter.

A spluttering gasp comes from his throat as he clutches his chest in both hands, dropping me and his staff.

I land on my back, the new pain of the impact not registering. Holloway pulls the knife out. Blood squirts from the wound and runs down his front.

For a moment, he stands there, staring at the knife with an expression of complete surprise.

His fingers uncurl until the knife falls out of his hand and clatters onto the rocky ground.

Holloway drops forward onto his knees, his hands limp at his sides, his eyes wide and glossy.

Then, in slow motion, he keels over, landing face-first in the gravel with a *smack*.

Then, silence.

CHAPTER THIRTY-SEVEN

Dealing

For the first couple of miles, I'm the one to carry our remaining backpack. It's much heavier than before, courtesy of the supplies from two backpacks stuffed into one. The other rucksack was unusable after Avery cut off its straps to keep Holloway under control.

"One less worry," Avery said when his shaking hands tightened the plastic straps he cut off one of the backpacks around Holloway's wrists, pulling them so tight the other Sentinel's hands turned blue. "Even a First Class Sentinel will take a while to recover after you almost stabbed him to death, Augs or not."

I walk ahead, trying to keep up the pace. Distance. We need to put distance between us and Holloway. According to Avery, he'll be out for at least a day, shut down to recuperate, like a computer doing a reboot, but neither he nor I trust Holloway to act according to our expectations. I can't help but wonder if Avery thinks I should have… I bite my lower lip.

Whatever. I can't very well go back now and finish what I started.

Avery's breathing has become a bit less labored over the last couple of minutes, but he's still nowhere near where he's supposed to be, and it hurts to see him like that.

I hold a couple of bigger branches away from him so he doesn't have to. He's still more stumbling after me than walking. This bout of rejection might be almost over, but the beating he received from

Holloway… that will take a while to recover from, even for a Sentinel.

We both need a while to recover.

I only got thrown once and kicked twice, yet every movement I make sets my abs on fire. Even breathing hurts. After Holloway collapsed, I thought I'd never be able to move again, but then… It's surprising what high stakes and enough pressure can make a body go through.

How in the world we're supposed to storm the Hub like this tomorrow, I don't know. It seems so ridiculous right now, even more so than before. One Sentinel, one little Earthling, about to walk up against Canyon's power, destroying the Hub.

Right.

It was barely doable before, but now… I glance at Avery. Now our chances are cut in half, if not less.

I shake my head and hook my thumbs under the shoulder straps of my backpack. Must think of something else besides the impeding mass murder of a whole planet's population.

It doesn't work.

I can't help but wonder if it's going to be quick. Breathe in, maybe a short bout of pain—done. Or maybe not; maybe it's like suffocating from the inside, taking a torturous amount of time, with each person painfully aware of what's happening: that they're dying, and so are the ones around them.

Evil doesn't even begin to describe it. Cruel, maybe.

A small sarcastic smile plays around my lips. I won't have to worry about myself, though. Chances are, the moment I realize we failed and the toxins are here, I'll be in full-blown panic mode anyway, and my attacks usually do a pretty good job distracting my brain from what's going on around me.

Granted, despite more than one occasion of a full-blown panic attack, my mind's been only doing some regular, good ol' panickin', nothing special. Doesn't mean it's not going to happen, though. I won't give myself over to that illusion.

Avery stumbles but catches himself just in time. He hasn't said more than two words since we got moving, but the barely suppressed grunts of pain speak for themselves.

Holloway did a lot of damage to him, and I wish I had done a better job.

I wish I had done a better job.

I wish I had killed him.

A lump forms in my throat, one of the kind that makes breathing difficult and that only comes when I know something is wrong—and I know for a fact that it is: nobody should wish for somebody else's death.

I surely wasn't raised like this. Heck, I'm the little girl who tried to please her parents in every possible way. My one and only rebellion was the nose piercing, and even with that, I stayed civilized.

Still. I wish I had aimed better, and that thought scares me.

We keep stumbling through this forest minute after minute, hour after hour, until the sun starts to set. It's a mind-numbing routine setting one foot in front of the other, helping Avery with the branches and obstacles, not thinking about anything.

I'm giving it my very best to shut out the last hours from my thoughts. I don't want to think about the sensation of the knife sinking into Holloway's chest. Or about what's lying ahead tomorrow morning, or what's going to happen to Earth if we fail.

And I sure as hell don't want to think about what's going to happen to Avery and me if we succeed.

Nope. I'm not thinking.

And it helps.

It must be close to sunset when Avery finally leans against a tree, wheezing. "That's enough. I doubt Holloway will wake up anytime soon, and even if he did and tore himself loose that quickly, he wouldn't catch up with us—if he figured out where we are." He wipes a bit of sweat off his forehead. "A lot of ifs. I don't know about you, but I need to rest." He gives me a faint apologetic smile.

"Me too," I whisper.

We set up for camp in silence. It's easy tonight: the tent was too heavy to take, which leaves us one mattress and one sleeping bag.

We have to clear the ground of loose twigs and little broken-off branches before the surface is ready for the night, but the moss will add some extra softness. Sure, the other sites were quote-unquote better, but for one, it doesn't matter, for another, I don't need to ask: we're deep inside the forest, and even if there were a river or a lake, we'd want the protection from the trees. We want to vanish from view. Another reason not to bring the tent.

We prep for the night before it's too dark to see. I've already found a good spot on a fallen-over tree stump close by and unpacked most of our meager rations. After dividing up the granola bars, I take out another pouch of noodles and the knife that's clean again thanks to Avery rinsing off Holloway's blood in the river.

The moment my hand touches it, I freeze.

Cold metal in my hand. A little bit of resistance, then a sensation like a small pop, before the tip hit something hard inside his stomach.

I stare at the knife in my hand. When I held it… I didn't freeze. I didn't go into panic mode. All I did was cold-bloodedly execute a plan, even though I didn't do it properly. If he comes back… If Holloway comes back and hurts Avery again… that's on me.

"I wish I had killed him." It's barely a whisper leaving my mouth, so soft that it belies the severity of what I just said.

I wish I had killed him.

Avery sinks down to his knees in front of me, resting his hands on my thighs. "Noa—"

I shake my head. "How can I want to hurt him, Avery? He's still human, despite what he was trying to do. How can I wish to kill him?" I look up into his amber eyes. "What am I doing here?"

Avery's shoulders heave up and down with a deep breath. In the almost dark, the big purple bruise on the left side of his face isn't quite so prominent anymore, although I doubt it's gone already. At least he washed off the blood before we left.

"You're defending yourself and your… team," he says with a short pause. "That's how a soldier thinks, Noa. A soldier is always prepared to do whatever it takes to win, but at the same time, a good soldier should know when to stop. And you did."

Barely.

"But—"

Avery shakes his head. "No *but*. I know how you feel right now, but killing somebody is never the answer, no matter what others say." He hesitates for a second. "Killing isn't hard. You could have stabbed him again, and it might have done the job. It would have been easy. What comes after, though, that's hard. The guilt. The what-ifs. That's what nobody tells you about. It's what you will carry with you each and every day of your life. Nobody should take another human's life if they can help it."

I chew on my lower lip until it's almost raw, my eyes glued to his. They trained him to kill. They *want* him to kill. And yet here he is, telling me—little, innocent me, of all people—how it's the wrong way. It's opposite day in the parallel universe. "But what if—"

"See?" he says with a small little smile, a finger touching the tip of my nose. "You're doing it already. The what-ifs."

I frown. "Can't help it. What if he comes after us? What if—?"

"He won't. This wound will take him over a day to recover from, especially without any medical support. And the same I told you about Sands holds true. If it's not him coming after us, it's somebody else. The Hub surely is warned at this point, so it doesn't matter."

"But if they—"

"It doesn't matter. They're not going to fly in a squad to take care of a single Sentinel, weak from rejection. They'll expect us and be ready, so a surprise attack is out the window, but we didn't plan on that anyway. You see? It. Doesn't. Matter. What does matter is that we stay true to ourselves because losing what and who we are is not an option." He wraps his fingers around the charm around his neck and pushes up to standing, supporting his weight with his hands on his knees. "I don't know about you, but I don't want to talk about Holloway anymore. Never liked that guy." He winks.

"Can't say he's my favorite Sentinel, either." I give him a small smile. Avery's amber lights up the slightest bit, making him seem much healthier than before.

"I sure hope so," he whispers. That small sentence loosens the knot inside my stomach and turns it into sparks. He holds out his hand for me.

"Come here." With one quick tug, I'm up and pressed against Avery's chest. My arms find their way around his on their own. He cradles my head against his body while gliding his other hand over my spine. I flatten my palms against his back, cuddling deeper into him.

This… This is good.

More than good.

Life-affirming. A Band-Aid for my soul. Medicine that works.

I keep my eyes closed, imagining us somewhere other than on our way to the Hub. Maybe somewhere on a beach, or a pool. A normal couple.

I suck in a short, sharp breath.

A couple. I'm thinking of us as a couple.

Avery kisses the top of my head.

A couple.

A wide grin spreads over my face.

"Noa? Can I ask you something?" It's a whisper, but loud enough amidst the silence of the forest. He sighs silently. "When you crossed over from Earth to Terra, back at the Reichstag… what happened on Earth? How did you find the portal?" His hands stop moving across my back.

I stiffen. *Panic. The sense of doom, of something so bad about to happen, nightmares would have nightmares about it.* "I… I don't know." There was no portal that I could see, at least that I remember.

"You didn't see a portal, like the one at the Adler Research Facility?"

I shake my head into his chest. "No." I didn't see anything besides grey. I was too far gone.

"Okay," Avery says quietly, his hands resuming their movement. "Tell me what crossing over felt like for you."

Oh, dang. There's not much I want to talk about less than my panic attacks, but… It's Avery. Maybe this is the point where I trust him to handle my secret and not label me as crazy. Avery isn't like everyone else.

Deep breath. "I don't know," I whisper, squeezing my eyes shut. Here goes nothing. "I was kind of preoccupied with panicking." There, it's out. My big secret, it's out. I wait for my words to sink in, for him to realize I'm crazy.

"Panicking?"

I lift my shoulders once and drop them. "It's something that I do. Always have. There's no pattern to it; it comes out of the blue." And not even meds helped it. "And when the attack hits, I don't see or think clearly. Some go by fast, some take longer. When… When I woke up in your cell in the Reichstag, that was the longest one I ever had." And possibly the scariest one.

Avery stays quiet for a moment—so long I fear I've said too much. *Nutcase*, Kevan called me, and that was one of the nicer things he said.

Yet Avery's fingers keep brushing over my shirt.

"I see. But you didn't panic with Holloway, not down in the Haunted House, not at the river."

I huff. "I did panic, only in a different way. It wasn't half as suffocating as normally."

Again Avery stays quiet. Way too quiet.

I swallow hard. "It's the only time I turn crazy, you know?" I'm trying to make it sound lighthearted, but it comes out strained.

And finally Avery chuckles. "What? You were worried about me thinking you're crazy?" He peels me off his chest to get a better look at me, his eyebrows lifted quizzically. "Really?"

My mouth opens and closes without a sound coming out, and Avery laughs out loud.

"Well, you are crazy, but differently so. We're two people trying to keep one truly crazy man from killing a whole planet's population, we're talking about portals between worlds and rejection, and…" He shakes his head. "And you having… *panic attacks* is not even on the scale, from where I'm standing. Not even close."

"Oh," I say, my mouth still open. I didn't expect that.

Avery chuckles, the sound so deep, it reverberates within his chest and all the way into my body.

All the way into my heart.

Maybe twenty minutes later, we've had our meager dinner and freshened up. Avery's wounds look better, and since the last bout of rejection has worn off, he hopefully will have a couple of quiet hours ahead of him. He'll need it. We both do. I'm exhausted.

It's become completely pitch black over the last half hour, even more so than last night, courtesy of the surrounding trees with only a little bit of the night sky shining through. The moon is there, but compared to the camping spot above the lake, it doesn't do much to illuminate our campsite.

But then, it also makes it more difficult for others to find us, thank you very much.

Nearby rustling sounds like Avery climbing into the sleeping sack.

"Come on in," he whispers.

I picture him holding it open for me. Now, logically, I know that we only have one mattress and sack left. I know I'm climbing in there with Avery so we can both sleep and stay warm, but…

But I'm about to climb into a sleep sack to share it with Avery. There's not going to be much room. I'll be able to feel everything… heck, *he'll* be able to feel everything.

The thing is… I'm okay with that. In fewer than twenty-four hours, Avery will have either crossed to Terra and left me here, or the toxin will have killed me, and maybe even him.

There's not going to be another night with him, no matter what happens.

I step out of my boots and feel my way into the sleeping sack, which sounds easier than it is in the dark. I'd prefer to not make too much of a fool out of myself in the process, thank you very much.

Avery is quiet as I slide in and settle down on my back next to him. The fabric is stretched to its max with both of us on our backs next to each other. Only because I'm not really wide around the shoulders do we fit: Avery takes the room of one and a half people.

For a while we lie like this, next to each other, my side burning where it touches his. Neither of us says anything, and I wonder… I wonder if I should take his hand, or roll into him, or… Gosh, I'm so new at this, it's embarrassing. A one-time make-out session does not an expert make, or something like it.

"Tomorrow, you run." Avery's whisper breaks the silence. "Once I'm in, you run back. You put distance between you and the Hub. Follow the map, like I taught you. Find the road. Go home."

Home. I don't even know where or with whom that is anymore. Avery feels more like home to me than George and Elaine ever did. I guess my parents and I, we're complicated.

"Promise me," he says.

I nod into the darkness. "I promise." And I guess not dying from poison I'll find out if Avery was successful destroying the portal or not.

A gust of wind moves the trees around us and chases the clouds apart.

"There's the nightlight," I whisper and point up at the North Star, like Avery did last night. It's the only star easily visible, as cloudy as it is. He takes a deep breath and grips my hand. Our fingers entwine as if they'd waited to finally be close again.

Funny what this little touch can do. It drains all adrenaline, all worry, all fear, all the negative vibes, and fills me with light. I must be glowing where we connect.

"The nightlight," he repeats, and then again, softer. "The nightlight." A sigh leaves his throat heavy with the weight of the world. "Tomorrow… Tomorrow is going to be rough, Noa."

"I know," I whisper, gazing up at the sky. I don't want to think about tomorrow. I want to ignore it until it's here, and then… I don't know, then what? Keep Avery here? Not an option. He'd be dead within another day or two. Cross with him? Not an option, either, because then I'd be dead, only slower.

One way or another, tomorrow, this is going to end.

We end.

Avery's thumb draws soft little circles on the back of my hand.

I hear him swallow next to me.

"I don't want to lose this memory," he whispers hoarsely, and it carries something so desperate, something so vulnerable, it makes my heart hurt even more.

"We're not going to lose it, Avery." I squeeze his hand back. Never. No matter how old I get, I'll never forget him. How could I?

I clear my throat. "You know… every night that I look up at the sky and see the nightlight, I'll be thinking of you, and… maybe you'll be doing the same." I hope. It sounds cheesy, but it feels right. The North Star is connecting us, no matter the universe. That's what led to our first kiss. It'll always be special to me.

Avery rolls onto his side. He draws my hand up to his mouth and places a tiny kiss on my knuckles. A little shudder runs down my spine. Him, so close, his lips on my skin… He's driving me crazy, no matter how bleak the circumstances.

Ever-so-slowly, he sneaks his free hand up to my waist. I would like to thank my shirt for riding up, because Avery's rough palm on that little bit of skin sets me on fire. Even if I wanted to, I couldn't keep the gasp in.

Despite the dark, Avery's golden eyes burn into mine. Maybe they're Augged after all. I bet he absorbs every move I make, every widening of my pupils, every breath I take.

He rakes his fingertips over my skin, and nothing—*nothing*— could be better than this. My eyes roll back into my skull. I'm not even aware I'm squeezing his hand so hard a non-Sentinel would probably have bruises tomorrow.

"Noa," he whispers, "look at me."

Forcing my heavy eyelids open, I do as he asks, but hell, it ain't easy. It takes all the willpower I have to hold back and not push myself farther into him. His fingers continue their assault on my skin, setting it on fire, setting *me* on fire.

Another kiss for my hand, and this time his lips linger on my knuckles, quivering the slightest bit. His eyes must be even wider than mine, full of wonder, full of something warm and tender.

I never want him to stop looking at me like this. It makes me feel like I can do anything, as long as I'm with Avery. It lifts me up, pumps me full of endorphins, and leaves me stronger than before.

The apple in his throat moves up and down. "I want to remember," he breathes, his voice thick. "Everything."

"Me, too," I whisper back at him. I never ever want to forget about him, about this moment. Knowing him has changed me, and kissing him… it made me a whole different person.

He lets go of my hand and grabs the hem of his shirt. With a surprising grace, considering we're stuffed pretty tight in here, he pulls it over his head.

The moment the shirt is gone, I stop breathing.

It's not that the view is taking my breath away, because the little bit of light from the moon is barely enough to see his face, let alone his chest farther down, but the mere thought of him lying *this close* to me shirtless… It makes my heart stutter. Yes, we've been there, done that yesterday, but the fact that we're in the sleeping sack together…

As quickly as the shirt is gone, his hand is back to grasp mine. He flattens it against his chest right on top of his heart, trapping the little infinity charm under my palm.

"Whatever happens tomorrow, I… I want you to know that *this*"—he presses my hand onto his chest—"this is yours."

As if it wanted to agree with his words, his heart beats even harder under my touch. I curl my fingers into his skin. "Avery—"

"No, wait. Let me. Please," he adds before he pauses, glancing down at my hand over his heart and then back at me. "I've always been the odd one out, Noa. First a Second Child, then a PBM, then a PBM who actually turned out to be good at his job. And just when I had thrown all the ballast I carried from that overboard, you came along, reminding me again why my parents hid me from the government in the first place. You gave me the strength to rise and stand up for what I think is right. If it hadn't been for you, I'd still be Canyon's pet." His voice takes on a hint of bitterness when he uses the nickname Victor gave him.

"Maybe they did something wrong with my programming, maybe the gene sequencing was off when they did the PBM, but… I never fit, and it never felt right. Not until now."

He slides his hand down my arm all the way to my shoulder and then down my side until it finds the same spot as before, the crook of my waist. His gaze soaks up all the sparks that he set loose the moment his skin touched mine again.

"That's why I don't want to forget," he whispers again. "Never." The way he looks at me, as if he were drowning and I were the only anchor for him, it almost scares me.

"You won't." Something like this, it's impossible to forget. "And neither will I."

A small smile plays on his lips. "I know." Then he leans in, his lips almost touching mine. "I'm counting on it." His breath teases my skin—and then, in the softest kiss ever, his lips brush over mine.

An explosion has nothing on the fireworks shooting through my body. Maybe it's because we've kissed before, maybe it's because of Avery's little speech, maybe it's… I don't know. All I know is that in this very moment, there's nothing more important than Avery and me. Heck, nothing else exists.

He opens his mouth the slightest bit, his tongue searching for mine. The palm on my waist moves upward, my fingers dancing across my skin where he pushes my T-shirt higher.

I dig so hard into his chest, I'm surely scratching him.

Avery smiles under our kiss. "More."

My nails dig in harder, breaking his skin. Avery takes in a deep gasp. "More."

More? I can do that. In fact, it's all I want. I work my top leg over his hip and pull myself closer to him, connecting both of our fronts, chest against chest, body against body.

I feel *everything*. Every inch of his body pressed against mine, every heartbeat pulsing in his blood vessels, every shiver that runs through it and passes into mine as if it were my own.

His smile widens. "Good."

Then his lips are back on me, and my mind on nothing else but

Avery.
    Avery and me.
    Together.

CHAPTER THIRTY-EIGHT

Playing It Safe

That night is heaven and hell at the same time.

His kisses are heaven. His touch. Me pressed to him. All of that is heaven.

At least until rejection sets in. Then it becomes hell, Avery's and mine.

Yes, he's the one shaking through the pain and the cold. He's the one suffering on a physical level, but while my body doesn't hurt, my heart does.

I wrap my arms around him as much as I can, trying to warm him and at least get him through this, but I still feel utterly helpless—helpless and lost, because there's no winner in this scenario. No matter what happens tomorrow, we're going to lose one way or the other, and I'm scared. I'm surprised I made it this far without majorly freaking out, but just because it hasn't happened yet doesn't mean I won't.

If it doesn't happen when we're going all rogue on the Hub, it surely will when I see Avery step through the portal, knowing it'll be the last time I ever see him.

At least he'll be alive on Terra.

Here, he won't make it much longer.

I will myself to hold on to Avery, not only with my body and my strength, but also with my heart and soul. I hold him as tightly as I can until deep into the night, when finally his shaking dies down and both of us fall asleep.

When I wake in the morning, the sleeping bag next to me is empty.

Somehow, I know Avery isn't far. I roll onto my side, lazy and still half-asleep, my eyelids barely wide enough to let in the little bit of daylight that's pushing through the clouds and trees into the depth of the forest.

As if pulled in by a homing beacon, I find Avery sitting on a tree stump with his back toward me. He pulls something silver from the back of his head, but the moment he hears the rustling of the sleeping bag, he turns around. The most wonderful smile spreads across his face when he realizes I'm awake.

"Hey," he says so softly, it carries much more than a greeting.

Warmth spreads across my face. "Hey," I whisper back, and I hope it sounds the same to him as his greeting did to me.

Avery gets up and pockets something. He brushes his hands off his pants before he kneels next to me, one hand cupping my face, his thumb smoothing my cheek softly. "I like to watch you sleep."

I blush even more. "You do?" I feel like an idiot because I don't know what else to say.

He nods. "Peaceful." He takes a deep breath. "Unlike today is going to be." His jaw sets as he looks up to the sky. "It's still early and we're within thirty minutes of the Hub. I say we get ready and get this plan under way because frankly… we're running out of time." He caresses my cheek in a warm, rough hand.

I'm not sure if he's talking about Canyon's plan to poison all humanity, or rather his rejection getting worse. No matter which one it is, he's right.

I nod. "Agreed." As soon as I say it, my stomach tightens up in knots.

I guess our timeout from last night is over.

Avery looks at me with a sad smile, his thumb retracing the lines of my face. "Can you do me a favor?"

A favor? "Of course." Any favor. The time we have left is measured in hours and on one hand. Of course I'll do him a favor.

His chest rises with a sad sigh. "When we're at the Hub… I don't want you anywhere near the portal, do you understand? We'll get in together as discussed, and while honestly, I'd feel much more comfortable with you as far away from that whole place as possible, we need you to get in. Still"—he holds up one finger to stop me from protesting—"once we're in, you do as I say, and you get out as quickly as possible. Can you do that for me?" The sadness is gone from his eyes, replaced by an intensity that makes me squirm. "Please?"

"But—"

He covers my lips with one finger. "No *but*. Stay as far away from the portal as you can, okay? Do me that favor?"

That means I can't say goodbye. I can't see him cross over. I can't get one last look at him.

"Please?"

Not the way I imagined our farewell, but then, who knows what awaits us inside the Hub anyway? I might be busy fighting off Sentinels.

"All right." I nod and purse my lips against his finger. If it's that important to him, I can do it. I'm probably romanticizing the whole saying-goodbye thing anyway.

His shoulders slump forward, as if a weight dropped off them. "Thank you."

We sink into each other's eyes for another eternal second. Then Avery pushes himself up and holds out a hand for me. "Showtime."

Although we only walk for fifteen or twenty minutes instead of the thirty Avery predicted, it feels like an eternity, and I know exactly why: with every step I take closer to the portal, I feel it more and more. The panic. The doom. The sensation of an unspeakable danger that slowly suffocates me.

Of course, just as I predicted: when it becomes important, my panic attacks are there.

First it was nothing but the tiniest pull and twist on the insides of my brain, so small that I could easily ignore it and chalk it up to nerves, but the closer we come to the Hub, the more powerful it becomes. I still have it under control, but… I swallow. There's no predicting anything with this, and it feels way too similar to the major attack at the Reichstag.

Huh.

As if my subconscious tried to warn me the portals were there. My very own cosmic radar.

Right.

If I weren't busy keeping my wits, I'd think that thought was funny.

Avery holds me by the hand the whole way, once or twice glancing at me as if he knew what was going on inside my head, what kind of war raged between logic and devastation. It's impossible he picked up on it, though. I'm holding myself together pretty well, so far at least.

Avery stops, all but yanking on my hand to keep me from walking any farther. "There," he whispers, looking straight ahead.

I follow his line of sight. "What?" I whisper. There's nothing but trees, shrubs, bushes, and all the other plants we've seen all over the place for the last two days.

Avery tilts his head. "Right. You can't see it." The hand that doesn't hold mine taps his temple. "Sentinel Augs." He points to somewhere in front of us. "Three meters ahead of us, between those trees and most likely circling in a perimeter around the whole hub: a sensory force field."

My mouth drops. "A sensory force field?" What is that even?

Avery sneaks forward, taking me with him. He's looking for something—well, or assessing something Sentinel-style, or else his head wouldn't be swiveling left to right to check the thick underwood of the forest.

"A force field invisible to anybody but Sentinels. A security enforcement. The moment somebody runs into it, an alarm goes off. Sentinels like to be informed about incoming humans."

"I bet they do. Sounds appropriately paranoid to me." *Precautionary* sounds too nice, considering we're talking about Canyon's people.

Avery suppresses a smile. "It gets better. If need be, we can make this thing give off a short electric surge and the person is stunned. Gives us enough time to collect the intruder, and either take them into custody, or alter their memory and send them on their merry way when they wake up."

I whistle through my teeth. "You can do that?"

He shrugs. "Not well for most humans. Not well compared to Sentinels, at least." He pulls me over to a large tree, with berries hanging from it. "Here it is. Let the cover story begin." He places his palm on the trunk, though it looks like any other tree. Only I could swear I hear an almost silent hum that I didn't pick up before it stops.

Satisfied, Avery nods to himself. "There we go. I'm still in the system." He drags me forward until we've passed what I assume must have been the force field.

"Wait—there was a chance you weren't going to be in the system?" And what would we have done then?

Avery grins and lifts his shoulders, a twinkle in his eyes that makes him look young, almost boyish. "Well, I can always pass through being a Sentinel, and you…" He winks at me. "I could have thrown you over. Might have even caught you on the other side. I'm fast, you know?"

I'm not a hundred percent sure if he's kidding, but then his grin widens. I stick out my tongue at him as the most mature countermove I can think of in this moment.

Avery's grin fades.

He brings my hand up between us and plays with my fingers. The atmosphere shifts from playful banter to something much heavier, much more oppressing.

"Now they know I'm here, and that I have a non-Sentinel with me." His expression becomes even more grim. "This is the point of no return. From here on, it's our plan or nothing."

I can't exactly say his words ease the weight on my chest. In fact, breathing is rough enough as it is.

"Noa, I… I'd like to give you something." He reaches into his pocket and comes up with a black leather necklace with a silver charm dangling from it. Avery squeezes my fingers once and lets go, using both hands to slide the necklace over my head.

"Avery…" I look down onto my chest, the silver infinity charm resting right above my heart. "I can't accept it, I mean, it's the only thing you have left from your family, and—"

He cups my face. "And I'm doing exactly what my mother intended me to do. I want you to have it. I need you to have it. It's… part of me." There it is again, the sad smile, the one that makes me want to cross over with him, if it weren't so impossible.

My fingers brush over the cool silver. "Thank you," I whisper. This is not just any gift. It's special. "I wish I had something to give you too." Oh. *Idea.*

Reaching up to my nose I remove my piercing, shine it up once, and hold it out for Avery. "Okay, cliché, but I'm giving you my heart. Literally." I might say it with a joking undertone, but I mean every word.

Avery takes the little heart stud, turns it in his hands, then pockets it. "Thank you," he whispers. I've never seen more emotions flash over his face than in this moment. It makes me a bit self-conscious.

"It's not much—"

"You've already given me so much." He lowers his head until his forehead is pressed against mine. "If I could, I'd stay."

"If I could, I'd come." My answer is out in a heartbeat, and it's true. Nothing keeps me here. I'm still mad at Elaine and George for the deception of a lifetime. Yes, I'll go back home to them. Yes, I'll be okay, and we—them and me—will be okay eventually as well, at least on an interpersonal level, but the thought of going back to my life from before doesn't hold any appeal at all.

Not compared to the thought of staying with Avery.

My life only really began once I crossed over and soared to unknown heights with every single one of Avery's kisses and touches.

No, if I could leave with him, I'd go.

He kisses the tip of my nose. "But even then, I wouldn't let you. Canyon would be out for you, and I'm only one Sentinel against unlimited numbers. I don't like those odds."

He pulls me against his chest, the stubble on his chin scratching across my skin as if he wanted to physically etch himself into my memory.

I soak it all up. Avery's heart beating inside his chest, the warmth of his body, the sunshine scent… all of it. I open my mind to absorb every single piece of information I can and store it for later: the feel of his muscles under his shirt, how tall he is compared to me, how wide. The way his breath glides down my skin, leaving goosebumps in its wake, how soft his hair is.

I want to remember it all. For eternity.

Eventually, Avery pulls away. "We should get going. They got the signal already that we breached the perimeter. We don't want a search team on our hands." He swallows hard, holding on to both of my hands and looking at me as if he wanted to say something more. He leans forward and touches his lips to mine. His grip almost breaks the bones inside my hand. Still, his kiss is soft and tender, playful, a promise of more to come—only it won't.

I know what this is.

This is goodbye.

And it hurts.

"We need to get going," he whispers against my lips, but he doesn't move away the slightest bit.

I push myself up on my toes and harder against him.

Avery groans. "Noa…" He grasps my cheeks in both hands and carefully peels me away from him. I could swear his eyes are watery, but then he blinks and it's gone. He sucks in his lower lip and leans his forehead against mine again, another short moment of heaven.

"Thank you," he whispers, and before I can ask for what, he stands up straight, takes my hand, and gives it a slight tug.

Timeout's over.

CHAPTER THIRTY-NINE

The Hub

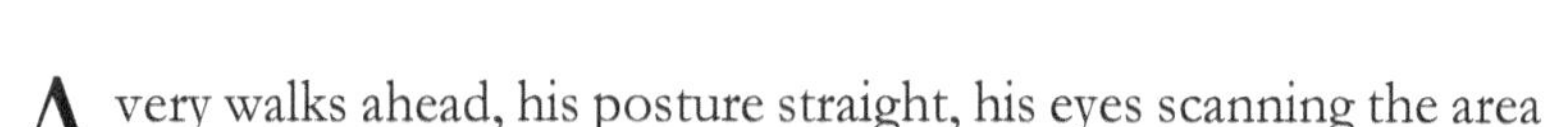

Avery walks ahead, his posture straight, his eyes scanning the area in front of us. A Sentinel in control.

Only the tight grip on my hand tells a different story.

After a minute or two, I can make out something in the depth of the forest in front of us, and predictably, the dread cranks it up to a whole new level. My body tingles in a painful sensation of pins and needles. The next hour or so is not going to be fun.

How I could stay so calm with Holloway I don't know because right now I'm already a mess. Maybe that's why Avery's hand is so tight around mine. At one point, it slides up to my wrist, changing from a lover's hold to the one of a guard.

And there we are.

After passing through an especially thick patch of bushes, we're out of the woods—literally, at least. All trees are gone, leaving only a flower-covered meadow, and, in the very middle of it, there's a building with a curved, large dome that covers the majority of it.

The Hub.

It looks like a smaller planetarium, only the colors are off. The olive-green shimmers depending on how the light hits it, probably some Terran way for camouflage.

Avery keeps up his pace. If I could, I'd dig in my heels and run the opposite direction. This building, the Hub, it's trouble. I feel it down to my toes.

Nothing good will happen here—and this is me saying that despite the fact that no Sentinel Forces come barging at us.

I chew the inside of my cheek. *Keep it calm, Noa.* This is the panic talking, nothing else. We have a good plan, it's going well so far, and everything will be fine. Avery will get home, nobody on Earth will get killed, and I'll… well, even my life will continue.

The Hub is quiet. No doors open, no cameras move in our direction, nobody steps out.

Nothing.

Still, I don't dare to look up at Avery or ask a question, mainly because I'm scared that if I did either, I'd lose it.

I'm *that* close already.

What if they don't let us in? What if they overwhelm us before we even set a foot in there? They'll probably take Avery back for some kind of trial and punishment, which means he'll at least be alive, but Earth… All seven billion of us won't be.

Drawing in a raspy breath, I almost stumble for the third time since we entered the clearing. Avery's grip on my wrist is the only thing keeping me upright—and then we're there. A nondescript, camouflage-green door without a knob. Avery places his free palm onto a seemingly random area on the door, like at the tree.

Not even two seconds later, the door becomes transparent at eye level, the face of a man I know only too well visible.

Leiva.

No, I correct myself immediately. Not Leiva. A Second Class Sentinel. Not Leiva.

"We have been expecting you," the Second Class says without any greeting, his eyes cold and not in the least inviting.

"Requesting entrance. I'm returning the prisoner who escaped from Minister Canyon," Avery answers crisply, nodding his chin at me. "Scan her."

The Second Class raises an eyebrow and then looks at me, the eyes roaming over my face completely expressionless.

"She is wanted," he says, "and so are you."

Avery doesn't even twitch. "Correct. A necessary distraction to fit in with the Ghosts and find out their plan. I have information for the Minister he will value."

The Second Class tilts his head, as if he just figured something out. "Two Sentinels have not reported in."

Avery sighs, as if he were dealing with a toddler. "They were uncooperative. You will find both of them unharmed within a fifteen-mile radius. I do not harm our own."

"I will have to take you into custody." Not a threat. A statement. And exactly what we want: a calm entrance. Not twenty Sentinels storming out of the Hub to overpower us.

"Of course." Avery inclines his head. "I'd expect nothing less. I am unarmed."

The Sentinel nods crisply, then moves away from the doors that slide apart. "You may hand over the prisoner." He points at me.

"No," Avery says, holding out a hand. "She is mine to deliver." I could swear he stands up taller. "I'm the Minister's First Sentinel coming back from a deep undercover mission, and I won't give up my charge unless told so by the Minister himself. Check your logs."

The Second Class stares into nothingness for a moment or two before frowning. "I cannot find any confirmation."

Avery huffs. "Insufficient answer, Sentinel. Recheck."

We both know he's checking in vain, but that's not the point. The point is getting in—and diversion.

"No confirmation," the Leiva lookalike says again, frowning. "I will have—"

Avery shoots forward and into the Hub, as if propelled by explosives. He grabs the Second Class' throat in one hand while yanking the Sentinel's staff from its holster, activating it with a flick of his wrist.

The Second Class grunts and claws at Avery but doesn't stand a chance. Lightning shoots out of the staff's end into the ceiling with a *crackle*. Sparks rain down on us as the blue charge crisscrosses overhead, chaining from one camera to another, leaving behind smoking black spots in the floor and walls.

Avery brings the staff down, retracts its ends back into the shaft, and knocks the struggling Sentinel over the head. The man's eyes roll back into his skull, and he collapses.

Avery steps over his unconscious body without hesitation. "Quickly now. If I wasn't fast enough, they might have seen me before the cameras dropped out."

I ignore the tightening of my throat and follow him. *Focus, Noa. This is important. Saving Earth.*

The problem is, my body is doing its best to distract me. My heart pumps to a wild rhythm inside my chest, and my lungs don't take in nearly as much air as they normally do.

Avery walks ahead through a narrow hallway until he stops in front of another sliding door. "Sentinel watch room," he whispers. "Behind that should be the access to the Hub."

He takes a deep breath, and for a moment I envy him for it because my throat is closing in on itself. He activates the staff, presses the panel to open the door, and charges in at the assembled Second Class Sentinels.

Yeah.

Showtime.

Avery is lightning on his feet.

I haven't seen him this fast and this alive and vibrant since we crossed over. Not that he's back to his old form—this is fighting on borrowed energy, but still, the four Second Class don't stand a chance. If that's what a prepared Hub looks like, they underestimated what kind of damage Avery can do when he's properly motivated, rejection or not.

I watch in awe as he disposes of every single one of them in fewer than thirty seconds, knocking them out like the first guard.

"Good." He breathes heavily after the last man drops. "I'm slightly offended they didn't call for backup. But alas, Minister Canyon will find out pride comes before the fall." His hands shake the slightest bit when he disarms them all, holding a staff out for me.

"You know how to defend yourself."

"But—"

"You did well the last time." He winks at me.

Despite the weight pressing down on me, I blush. Holloway had that thing pointed at Avery, back in the Haunted House, and…

Nevertheless, I take the staff. Better safe than sorry.

He strides over to a control station and checks the settings. "I've unlocked the doors leading to the portal room, but from here… I'm doing this alone." The look he gives me is sad and determined at the same time.

I bite my lower lip. "So this is where I leave and make my way back?"

He nods. "As planned. I've got my staff to destroy the console, and you need to head back. I don't want to rely on your parents calling the Earth police, nor on them getting you out of here. As planned, you stick to the map, you find the road, you wait for somebody who can take you home. Kidnapping story—done."

Sounds so easy when he says it like that.

Avery takes me by the shoulders. "Whatever happens, you get out of here. You don't run after me, and you for sure do not come anywhere near the portal room. Is that clear?" Avery is part boyfriend, part Sentinel, but neither part is messing around with my safety.

I suck in a harsh breath. Being here, in this room, four unconscious Second Class on the floor and Avery about to leave me… it doesn't exactly make breathing easier.

Quite the opposite.

His thumbs circle over my upper arms. "Bye, Noa," he whispers.

"Bye, Avery." I wish my voice were stronger. I wish I could hug him and hold him, and… we don't have the time.

We stare into each other's eyes desperate for one last connection, for one last memory.

Then he squeezes my shoulders and tears himself loose. In a couple of long strides, he's crossed the room and taken the other door out—and I'm left alone.

That was it.
Avery and me, we're over.
My hand creeps up to my neckline and finds the infinity charm.
I was right in the forest.
It was goodbye.

CHAPTER FORTY

Losing

I keep staring at the door Avery vanished through, imagining where he must be right now.

Probably already at the portal.

Probably already trying to destroy the incoming one.

Maybe he's even crossed back home already and is feeling better. He said it was *that* fast.

As much as that thought chases away the dark clouds, it can't completely banish them. It doesn't change that I'm sitting here, playing on an alibi that I don't care about at all, while I'd rather be somewhere else.

With Avery.

Footfalls echo in the hall a mere two or three seconds before they stop in front of the door, the same one Avery and I took to get into here. *Crap.* There's no time to run. I all but jump into that little space under the control panels where the chair used to be.

Not a moment too soon.

The door opens. Heavy steps fall in and stop abruptly. Two pairs of shoes. Black leather slippers and combat boots like Ave—

"Shit. We're too late. He's here already." A familiar voice. No. Please, no.

I freeze in my hiding spot. No way. Not now of all times. Not when—

"You," Holloway growls at the owner of the pair of black leather shoes. "Lock and guard the doors. Nobody escapes from here."

"But there's nobody else—"

"Oh, I'm sure there is. And I will find her. But first things first. McTighe." He spits out Avery's name. "Go to full alert. I don't care if Earthlings find out about us, I'll deal with the fallout later. McTighe and the girl are more important."

"But—"

"No but. I'm the First Class here and put in charge by Minister Canyon. I give the orders."

"O-Of course, Sentinel," the other voice stammers. "D-Do you need medical help? There's blood—"

"I'm fine," Holloway hisses. "The Minister Augged me to survive, so don't you worry about me, *scientist*." He spits it out like a bad word.

"Y-Yes, Sentinel. If it helps, I c-can send reinforcements with you, and—"

"No. All Forces are to stand down and retreat. Their job is securing the exits," Holloway snarls, already on his way to the other door, the one Avery left through. "We're old friends. We go way back. McTighe is weak. I will take him down myself." He stops for a moment. "He's not leaving Earth. Or if he is, it's in pieces." He laughs and strides out of the control room, leaving the other man rooted to his spot.

One second.

Two seconds.

Three seconds.

And finally the man blows out a heavy puff of air and turns on his heels.

The door closes behind him and I'm left alone, hidden between the wall, a trash can, and the office chair.

I never knew a heart could freeze in the face of unspeakable fear. Mine does. Right in midbeat, it stops with a shooting pain unlike anything I've ever felt.

Holloway.

How can he be back and well so fast after I stabbed him? How,

how, how?

What kind of freaking Augs did Canyon give him to recover like this?

It doesn't matter. Holloway is back, and now he's on his way to kill Avery. And then, probably me.

A raspy breath that sounds way too panicky, even to my own ears, leaves my throat. Clearly, Avery's gallant refusal to kill him has not changed Holloway's view of the matter at all. And now Avery is going to pay for his—maybe misplaced—sense of fairness.

He has crossed already, right?

He must have.

Another cramp inside my heart. What if he hasn't?

I clutch the staff he gave me.

Only one way to find out. It's not as if I could leave, locked-slash-guarded doors and all.

I rush out of my hiding place. The Second Class Sentinels are still knocked out on the ground the way they dropped. Avery was right. Nobody cares for them, not that it matters now.

Without hesitation, I jump up and dart toward the door on the left, the one Avery and Holloway took. I don't stop. I don't think. I run.

I sprint into the hallway, not questioning my luck when it's empty. With every step I take, the humming inside my chest gets worse.

Of course.

More panic.

More doom.

A wheezy breath leaves my throat as I almost lose my footing on the sparkling linoleum floors.

Can't fall.

No time.

No time to pause, no time to think.

I must reach Avery.

Must warn him.

As if pulled by a string, my body knows what to do and where to go. The worse the pressure on my chest gets, the more I'm sure I'm running in the right direction.

Toward the panic.

Toward *Avery*.

Maybe my body knows more than I do.

Despite the tight sensation and raw throat, I pump my legs for all they've got, because if I stop for only one second, I'm positive I'll run back, screaming. That's how bad the fear already is.

I speed around another bend and skid to a complete standstill, panting like crazy, yet moving no air.

The Hub.

I don't need a sign. It's obvious.

The large, sky-to-floor window stretching over at least thirty yards in front of me leaves nothing to the imagination.

It's big.

Much bigger than the portal we went through in Chicago. *Massive.*

The Hub looks like a crazy scientist's lab. It's at least twice the size of our apartment in Chicago, and the only thing I recognize is the Omega-shaped portal in the middle, an incoming console to one side, and an outgoing console to its other. The rest of the room is filled with scientific machines, metal tubes, wires, power cables, and other stuff I've never seen before.

And it scares the hell out of me.

Breathe, Noa. Breathe and focus, damn it. I shake my head twice to clear it, although the haze stays, clogging my senses and invading my mind.

Something moves behind the window.

I all but fly forward and press my nose and hands against the cool glass. Avery? Next to the portal, both consoles do their things, little electrodes blinking and displays lighting up.

Clearly not destroyed.

My breath fogs up the glass. Come on, Avery. Where—

Something large and heavy flies through the room from the left and crashes into the window right in front of my face.

I scream and jump back.

Before I've made sense of what's going on, a burst of blue lightning shoots through the room, hitting the window next to my face and dousing a ducking figure with sparks.

Avery.

Another lightning bolt.

Holloway.

With a roar I can't hear through the glass, Avery moves out of the way in the nick of time and charges Holloway, who keeps his staff up and a condescending smile on his face, as if this battle were decided already.

In mid-run, Avery extends his staff, using it like a lance, aiming for Holloway's midsection.

I act before I think. Like a madwoman, I dart toward the door on the right reading *DANGER: Do not enter without permission.* To my utter relief, it slides open for me, granting me access to the Hub.

But that's where my luck runs out.

With the first step into the Hub, a drop in temperature assaults me, like I stepped into a freezer. Against my expectations, my breath doesn't fog, but it hitches inside my throat, refusing to come out.

Haze, fog, clouds… The sensation of reality slipping, of falling without end, of losing my mind.

I shake my head and blink twice.

Not going to happen. I—

A guttural grunt followed by a crash breaks through my daze.

Avery.

Damn it, Noa. Focus.

Balling my hands into fists, I force myself to look away from the portal as Holloway lands a huge kick to Avery's thigh that makes his knee buckle under him.

A scream bursts from my throat—and both Sentinels' heads whip around.

Holloway's lips turn up in a satisfied sneer, while Avery's face drops.

Oh, crap.

The next three seconds happen in slow motion.

Holloway turns away from Avery, his eyes trained on me, ready like a panther before it leaps onto its prey. Caked blood stains the front of his black Sentinel uniform. I stumble back, but Avery is faster. Determination replaces the surprise in his eyes as he shoots forward and wraps one arm around Holloway's throat, bending the other Sentinel's back until he's on his heels.

"Noa!" Avery yells. "Incoming portal. Now!"

Holloway's hands fly to his throat to loosen the grip Avery has on him, but no such luck. Still, the movement is enough to make both of them lose balance and tumble to the ground, a mess of extremities and grunts. Both Sentinels fight for the upper hand, but their movements are edgy and less than fluent—and Avery is still slower than Holloway.

"Now!" Avery shouts again, and finally, I unfreeze.

I yank the staff out from under my waistband and dash around two bulky machines, hitting my shoulder on one of them while trying to cut the corner as fast as possible.

The incoming portal's console is right in front of me. *Thank you, Avery, for teaching me.*

I flick the staff once, bringing it to life. This is it, the brain that controls all crossings from Terra to here.

Something colorful scurries past my line of vision, accompanied by a whiff of disinfectant.

Another blink, another shake of my head, and the console is back in focus.

I'm losing my grip on reality, and that can't happen.

I lift the staff as high as I can and ram it down into the console. It sinks into the metal with no resistance at all.

A blue flash spreads out from its tip, like a hungry entity looking for food. Some of the lights and electrodes flicker, but it's not enough.

"No!" Holloway's roar bursts over the room, drowned out by more fighting sounds.

Faster. Have to—

The staff turns blurry in front of my eyes, but still I find and press all four buttons on it at the same time.

"Noa! Move!"

I hear my name. I hear the command.

Yet I don't understand it.

A high-pitched whine fills the air, louder than Holloway's grunting and cursing.

"Noa!" Choking cuts off Avery's cry.

The whine becomes ultrasonic, piercing my brain and—

Hot air blasts into me, lifting me up and flipping me like a toy until I hit something hard. All air leaves my lungs as I slide down the outgoing console of the other side of the portal. The burning scent of smoke wafts over and I cough.

"No!" Holloway howls. "You idiots! You destroyed it!"

As if the power I drained from the console had gone to Holloway instead, a roar breaks from his throat. He bursts out of Avery's hold and hurls him against the wall like the exploding console did with me.

For an instant, Holloway gazes back and forth from me to the portal.

And then he charges.

The cotton around my brain retreats enough to see the danger— to see the face that screams of hate and aggression, to see the blue glow and flicker at the tip of his staff waiting to be released and do its damage.

A tiny yelp bursts from my mouth, but I needn't bother because he isn't coming for me.

He's heading for the intact outgoing console behind me.

I scramble away, through the haze that has me, through the confusion, panic, and fear—

"No!" shouts Avery as he jumps back to his feet, leaping toward Holloway, trying to stop him.

But he's too late.

"You think I'm going to let you leave, McTighe?" Holloway yells, raising his staff. "This ends here!" He rams his staff into the console.

Sparks fly, metal screeches—and a second later, my world turns into one of blinding light and heat as the outgoing console explodes in a ball of fire.

Avery's roar is louder.

It pierces everything—the explosion, Holloway's scream as the shock wave throws him through the air—and my heart.

The outgoing portal.

It's gone.

There's no way out for Avery, or any of the Terrans.

With a grunt, Holloway hits the floor about a yard away from me. His hair is singed and his face covered in soot, but his eyes still carry murder in them.

And they're zoomed in on me.

In retrospect, I probably should have moved away the second Holloway landed. I probably should have kept my distance.

As it is, my brain doesn't really come up with any of those ideas, unfortunately.

Holloway's strong arms yank me off the floor and pull me up in front of him, like a shield. It takes me a second to realize what just happened, as if my brain were on time-delay. The sense of doom that's been present since we approached the Hub cranks it up to a new level, and for once it has a reason. Holloway's arm wraps around my throat. Such a simple move, yet it makes Avery stop in mid-motion in front of the portal, one hand raised for a punch, the other holding the staff, ready to attack Holloway.

Avery's breath comes out hoarse. It's the only thing I hear more clearly than the swooshing of blood inside my ears, or the pounding of my heart.

"Let her go," he rasps.

"Or what?" Holloway tightens his arm around my throat. "You're going to risk killing her to get to me?"

A muscle in Avery's jaw ticks. He clutches his staff so tightly, his knuckles turn white.

Holloway laughs. "I knew it. I knew you couldn't do it. You're weak, McTighe. Weak and faulty. I'll cut you a deal. Throw over the staff and I'll give you your little toy here." Another squeeze to my throat.

I want to shake my head, I want to tell him *no*, but Avery's decision is made quicker than that. He throws the staff over to Holloway, who catches it with the hand that a moment ago was still around my neck.

"Good boy," he coos. He plants his hand on my back and shoves me forward into Avery's arms.

The moment he catches me and moves me behind him, I want to cry. Part of me is so incredibly relieved Avery is here, alive, with me… but I know it's only fleeting.

The weight of the world still presses down on me, opening the gates of hell inside my mind, stealing my breath and sanity.

I barely have enough left to know we're done for.

Holloway has the staff, and he destroyed the outgoing portal. Avery is trapped here like everybody else. Holloway did exactly what we hoped to prevent—sentencing countless Terrans to a slow, painful death.

Including Avery.

Avery, whose chest moves up and down so fast, I'm afraid he's going to collapse. Despite his fighting stance and raised fists, we all know he's not going to survive another attack.

Or staying here.

"No way out, McTighe," Holloway says with a grin that's so cruel and crazy, it would scare me if it penetrated the haze at all.

As it is, it doesn't. I'm too far gone, too far down the rabbit hole of no return, trapped inside my mind and led down a path I've feared all my life.

Colors, scents, sounds—none of it makes sense.

The attack hits me full speed after it toyed with me for its own amusement.

"I'll make it quick. Maybe first her and then you. Or would you prefer it the other way around?" As Holloway takes a step forward, we take a step backward, only my legs won't do their job anymore, like two lazy pieces of equipment that stopped functioning. My whole body refuses to work, frozen and caught in a spell that rips this world away from me.

"You touch her," Avery says, "and it's the last thing you do, Holloway."

Everything blurs around the edges, everything turns fuzzy and frayed. The only thing I see as clear as day is Avery in front of me. Nothing else matters; nothing else is important.

My harsh breathing sounds foreign to my ears, almost as if I'm not in my body anymore, but an outsider, standing by. I raise a shaking hand to my throat as if it will help me, although somewhere deep down, I know it won't. It never does.

"We'll see about that, McTighe," Holloway says. "Maybe I'll keep you alive, barely at least, and then kill her in front of your eyes." He takes another threatening step forward. "Yeah, I'd like that."

Another step forward, and another one backward for us, bringing us closer to the lifeless portal.

The humming inside my chest triples—no, quadruples. My whole body vibrates, and to make it worse, my vision is almost gone. Only here and there do little specks of different colors poke through the haze and cloud, and they make absolutely no sense.

Anytime now, I'm going to fall apart, distracting Avery and costing him his life.

Somewhere in the fog, Avery's voice keeps me anchored. "Not going to happen, Holloway."

Another step back. My foot skims over something rough—the portal's threshold.

My heel touches down and—*boom*—everything changes.

Time freezes around me and clears my vision to way more than 20/20.

Like a curtain drawn, I *see*.

I see *everything*.

Colors, faces, noises—all so familiar and yet so foreign, all pulling me in, urging me to let go, to give in. The faint scent of a strong disinfectant hits my nose, like in a hospital.

Terra.

I see *Terra.*

I see the other side.

And it's calling to me.

Like in the Reichstag. Like in the Adler Planetarium.

Like my whole freakin' life and every freakin' panic attack.

Realization strikes like lightning. It was never that: never panic attacks.

It was always this pull on my inside, this connection, this bond, always the other side calling to me. It *was* a built-in cosmic radar.

The weight that was about to suffocate me lifts off my chest, and finally, I can breathe.

Gone is the sense of doom, the paralyzing fear, the suffocating panic.

My heart fills with relief. Amazement. *Wonder.*

I lift my arm, the movement foreign, as if it weren't my arm at all, but a stranger's. It looks the same, yet it doesn't. The fingers moving in front of my face have an almost translucent quality to them, as if they were half here, half in Terra.

Incredible.

A high-pitched whine followed by blue lightning bites the floor in front of Avery.

Cackling.

"No way out, McTighe."

Wrong.

Like in trance, I reach out for Avery in front of me. I'd find his hand even in the dark.

Anytime. Anywhere.

Our fingers connect, and while it might be a soft touch, its effect is anything but.

Avery's head whips around like a ball on a string, his eyes wide and alarmed—until he sees my face.

Then his expression changes to sorrow.

Deep, painful sorrow.

For me.

"Noa." His whisper holds everything. Heartache. Grief. *Love.*

He knows.

He knows what I just found out, that I'm… connected.

And it scares him.

But it doesn't need to.

A smile finds its way onto my face. "It's okay," I whisper back, my voice strange to my own ears.

Somewhere, Holloway growls, pushing a button on his staff.

Fast, heavy steps charge at us.

Avery's fingers entwine with mine as he holds my hand. His touch grounds me, giving me the strength I need.

Then I finally let go, give myself over to the forces of nature, and let the chaos reign.

CHAPTER FORTY-ONE

Crossed

Darkness slams into me like a truck and hits me square in the chest. My last breath of air is gone, vanished like all common sense, like all memory of what was and thoughts of what will be. I'm only a ball in a game too big for me, too violent to understand. My body is bent and twisted into unnatural positions threatening to break me in half, the brutality of it tearing a silent scream from my throat.

Scorching heat burns me at the same time freezing cold solidifies every liquid cell inside my body. There's no time for my confused brain to make sense of any of it, forcing it to do the only thing it still can: Focusing on Avery's hand in mine.

And it keeps me sane.

Then, unexpectedly, we hit cold tile floor with a vengeance, sliding across on our backs like somebody tripped us on ice.

For a moment, there's nothing but quiet, peaceful silence… until the loud howl of a siren screeches in the air, ending the illusion of peace. *"Intruder Alert. Unauthorized Crossing. Intruder Alert. Unauthorized Crossing. Intruder—"*

Even before I make sense of it, the hand that held on to me throughout the crossing is gone. Avery is on his feet, and not a moment too soon.

I scramble backward as quickly as I can, but even so, I barely get out of the way of the three Second Class Sentinels storming at Avery.

The first one to reach him dives in as if he had a personal score to settle.

I scream, afraid the three Sentinels will finish what Holloway didn't: killing Avery right in front of my eyes.

Yet it doesn't happen.

Instead of crumbling under the attack, a gleam lights up in Avery's eyes. He grabs the incoming Sentinel by his shirt and trips him over his feet, shoving him as far away from him as possible in some kind of Judo throw. The Second Class lands with a *thud*, stunned, but not disabled, and neither are the other two.

But Avery… Avery is on a roll.

Gone is the weakness, gone is the vulnerability and fragility that had him on Earth. This is the old Avery. The First Class Sentinel. Best of his year. Canyon's freakin' pet.

And he's a machine.

His movements are smooth again, like the trip through the portal recharged his batteries.

Another Sentinel runs in from behind. "Watch out!" I yell, jumping to my feet, a wave of dizziness assaulting me. I reach out and stabilize myself just as another hum starts to vibrate in my arm.

The portal.

I'm touching the *inactive* portal, and while I feel the other side lurking behind it—the doom, the panic, the danger—this time it doesn't choke me. Yes, it calls to me like an invitation, but it stays under the surface. How in the name of all that's holy—?

Something whooshes by, barely missing me before clattering against the portal and dropping to the floor.

I scream, my hands flying up to protect my face as a Second Class charges at me, his arms outstretched, ready to throttle me.

Only he doesn't even get remotely close because as fast as he is, Avery is faster.

Shrugging off two of the other Sentinels, Avery shoots forward and rams his massive body into the other man's. The impact tears both off their feet and throws them to the ground. Three or four punches later, the Second Class is knocked out and Avery springs to his feet again.

"Noa, quick!" He holds a hand out for me and drags me toward a door in the far corner of Terra's Hub.

Yelling and commotion erupts behind us, loud enough to drown out the blaring intruder alert.

"Crap," Avery spits, changing our escape route to more of a zigzag course—and the first lightning-shot hits one of the consoles we just passed. Sparks fly from it, the impact torturing the poor console to a high howling sound that drowns out my squeak.

"Faster!" Avery tugs me along and past him, so that I'm leading the way and setting the speed.

"Where to?" I yell over my shoulder, almost running into five or six thigh-thick pipes leading from somewhere to the Hub.

Another impact crashes somewhere on my right, more sparks, and more aggressive yelling and shouting from behind us.

"Door, eleven o'clock, weave through. We need cover!"

Indeed we do. The Sentinels behind us don't shoot to warn. I don't need any more incentive than that. Fear gives me a speed I never thought possible. I hit my hip against something hard a couple of yards before I finally reach the door and we spill out into a narrow white hallway without any doors or windows.

Just like on the Earth-side.

I stop dead in my tracks and Avery runs into me, the impact of his body propelling me forward a good couple of steps. He doesn't lose time and slams the door shut, smashing his palm against the frame, an intense look of concentration on his face as his palm lights up with the slightest blue.

"That should buy us a minute or two." He lowers his arm. "We need to get out. Run."

No need to say it twice. Something or someone crashes into the door we locked behind us a mere second ago.

Nothing better than that to give me wings. Our footsteps pound down the hallway like a whole Sentinel Force running, not just two fugitives trying to escape.

Trying to make it out alive.

"This is the Security Wing!" Avery yells. "Sentinel only. Special safety features. Can help us or can kill us." He pushes me toward the left at a crossing before I can keep on running straight ahead.

Something bursts open behind us. Loud voices and shouts spill into the hallway.

Avery curses again. "We only have one shot at this—"

Twenty yards in front of us, another door slams open into the wall behind it. Four Sentinels spill out from wherever, staffs extended and aimed at us.

Before my body has overcome inertia and stopped, Avery grabs me roughly by the shoulders, lifts me up like a child, and turns me around to face the direction we came from. In his best Sentinel manner, he keeps himself between the attacking Second Class Sentinels and me, ducking when the first lightning bolts hit the walls next to us.

"Shit! Run, Noa!"

My feet hit the ground and I sprint like never before in my life. My lungs burn, but it's nothing compared to what I'd feel if one of those charges hit me, I'm sure.

And it's not for lack of trying that they don't.

It's unbelievable sheer luck that keeps us alive. That and Avery directing me into an irregular zigzag course.

Deafening *bangs* accompany the stench of burnt plastic and blue energy crackling along the walls.

It only takes ten seconds for our luck to run out.

There's nothing special about this one shot of electricity, yet I hear it more clearly than the others. The click when it's released, the whine as it slithers through the air—and then Avery's grunt when it hits him in the back and throws him forward, propelled by an invisible force.

He hits the floor with a heavy *thud*, sliding across the slippery surface, momentum carrying him forward.

"Avery!"

The Sentinels never slow down. They recharge their staffs while running, the distance between them and us shrinking faster than ice in the sun.

No, no, no.

We were so close.

So close.

There must be a way out, we—

My hands wrap around Avery's outstretched arm and pull with all my power. We need to keep moving, but I can't lift—

For a moment, Avery is so limp, I fear he's out cold, but then a slurred and gurgled moan leaves his throat. He's awake. Thank goodness.

"Avery." We have twenty yards to go at the most. It's a long hallway, but still.

Like a switch in him flipped, Avery jumps up to his feet. For one frightening second, I fear he's going back down—swaying, his face way paler than normal—but no.

"Run," he slurs, driving me forward by my shoulder, and not a moment too soon. The shouting increases in intensity, and now that their prey is moving again, the Sentinels don't hold back anymore.

They resume fire.

I scream as one bolt sizzles past my head on the left, only missing me by a couple of inches. This is not going to end well.

Avery shoves me to the left around a bend in the hallway. "Catch up in five secs," he whispers under his breath.

While Avery opens a door on the left and leaves it open, I keep running across the slippery white floor like there's no tomorrow. We need to get away, but I don't have a clue—

"To the right." Avery steers me around another crossing of hallways. "Stop!" He yanks me back by my shirt, then palms us through yet another nondescript door. The footfalls get louder. It can't just be three or four Sentinels. There must be at least a dozen, if not more.

As soon as the next door opens, Avery steps through, pulls me in, and closes it silently. He presses his palm against it until it glows blueish, focusing on something only he can see.

"A Sentinel Emergency Control Room. Special security, but still we don't have much time." His breaths come out in heavy puffs. I'm not doing any better. Heck, worse. I lean against the cold metal wall behind me, my hands on my knees, gasping for air. My whole body feels like I was the one shot, not Avery.

Au contraire to me, though, Avery doesn't waste time. He turns, surveying the room, evaluating our options.

A Sentinel Emergency Control Room. It definitely looks technical, not quite as much as the Hub did, but it's still impressive. Massive screens cover one side of it from left to right and floor to ceiling, all dead and blank right now. Some look more like touch screen panels integrated into the wall, but that's all there is. No consoles, no computers, pipes, or whatnot. It's an empty room otherwise. But there, on the far end… is a window.

"A window," I whisper, out of breath. "Avery, a window!" A freakin' window at the end of the room, a window to freedom. Our way out. We—

"We can't take it." He chews on his lip, still scanning the room as if looking for something in particular.

"What?" My mouth drops open. Why can't we take it? "There's no way out otherwise; we *have* to take it!" Or we're trapped. It's that or the door—the door something heavy slams against the very moment I think about it. I jump and squeak.

Avery shakes his head. "It's what they expect. They'll know. They…" He looks back to me. "I'll get you out of here. Then I'll distract them, buy you time. That way—"

"No, Avery." I shake my head so forcefully, my already messed-up ponytail almost comes undone. "No separating. We're in this together. We can—"

He slams his hands against the wall on either side of my head. "Damn it, Noa! I don't have a choice!" He draws in a deep, shuddering breath and exhales roughly.

There's a banging at the door—like a hundred more Sentinels trying to break through, yelling behind that thin barrier that's surely going to give anytime now.

Avery flinches. "Shit." It's a muttered curse drowning in the noise of the assault.

His eyes meet mine and hold them for an eternal second. He bows his head and slouches.

"I don't have a choice." It's a whisper, yet it screams louder than the Sentinels on the other side of the wall.

As if to prove his point, something heavy and solid rams against the door from the other side, buckling it.

Avery balls his hands into fists. "We can't get out of here together. Separated, we at least stand a chance. You have to get out of here; that's the priority."

"Bullshit." The word flies from my lips without me thinking about it. "It's not about me, it's about us, and—"

"It *is* about you." The hue of his eyes deepens. "All of this." Avery places a hand over my breastbone, trapping the infinity charm under his palm.

"Avery—"

"No. I know the way they think, Noa. We do it my way and we have a chance, or we might as well let them in right now." He glances over his shoulder at the door.

A sinking feeling grows inside my stomach and spreads throughout my body, settling inside my heart and drowning it with lead.

I don't think *I* can make it alone, but maybe Avery can.

Because, let's be honest, I'm slowing him down. If we separate, he at least has a fighting chance.

I swallow heavily.

The air is too thick to take another breath, yet somehow I do. "Avery, I—" I can't bring myself to finish the sentence.

"I know." He moves his hand from my chest to cup my cheek, then tilts his head, and, as if we had all the time in the world, he slowly brings his lips to mine.

This kiss… it's gentle. It's desperate.

It's full of sadness, longing, and loss.

It screams of words never spoken, of hunger and despair. Of love.

This kiss is the chain that binds his soul to mine, no matter what. It holds a tenderness that sets me on fire and heals all my wounds, creating a want and need that goes beyond the physical.

More banging echoes from the door, then screeching, like metal being bent out of place.

Avery pulls himself loose from me. He sucks in his lower lip, like he was taking in every last bit of our kiss.

"Now or never, Noa."

"I don't want to." I'm whispering it like a belligerent toddler.

His response is a sad smile, the one I've seen too much of over the last week. "It's that or we both die in here."

I know. Alone he stands a chance. Alone he can fight for himself, without having to protect me. Alone he can make it.

"Okay," I whisper. It's either both of us getting caught, or just me, and then… It's better if it's me.

Avery jumps to action with my approval. He searches the metallic panels behind me, feeling for something. The noise coming from the right cranks it up a notch with the addition of some kind of banging tool that will undoubtedly eventually break through the door—and by the sounds of it soon.

"Gotcha," Avery says, his long fingers prying a corner of a metal plate loose before he puts his whole body weight into it. Groaning, he bends the metal out of shape.

What…?

A crawlspace behind it?

Pipes, electric conduits, like a maintenance duct, maybe wide enough to hide a child.

Or a tiny teenager.

The door bulges with a screech, sparks flying from it. Dozens of Sentinels scream louder in excitement.

Avery works the metal plate with all his strength. "In. Hurry." He grabs my arms and all but stuffs me into the narrow opening and tight space inside the wall. "You follow the yellow tube; that's a vacuum emitter, it leads to the VacWay. You stay right there, and they'll get you." He reaches in the hole, yanking twice on another cable that runs right next to it and ripping another one out. "There. The Ghosts should see that spike and come for you."

His fingers graze across my cheek so, so gently, it melts my heart. He taps my nose where the heart nose stud used to be, stealing a moment we don't have. So much needs to be said, so much needs to be done, but there's no time. There's absolutely no time.

I catch his hand before he withdraws it and place a kiss onto his rough palm.

For another second, our eyes stay connected. Neither of us dares to say *goodbye*—and then he's gone, bending the metal panel back in shape to hide me.

All that's left is a small gap right where he started peeling the panel loose, around my eye level.

Shit.

What if…? What if they find him now? What if he can't make it? A new level of panic hits me, but not the usual, the one I now know to be from a portal close by, but a different kind, one made out of worry. For Avery.

"Avery," I whisper against the metal, pressing a hand against it from the inside. I should get going, but I need to make sure…

I lean forward and peek through the tiny opening I have, just in time to see Avery kick in the window.

Good. He's almost out—

Only he isn't.

Instead of climbing out, Avery takes on a fighting stance right in front of the window.

What the—?

Crash!

The door bursts into a million pieces.

I jump inside my hiding spot, my forehead hitting the metal wall.

Oh, no.

At least fifteen Sentinels storm past me toward Avery, who's waiting for them, his hands raised, his mind focused. Ready.

"Run, Avery," I whisper, my fists balling. "Run, damn it."

But Avery does no such thing.

The first Sentinels attack, and Avery counters.

Their staffs come down with a force that would make lesser men crumble, but not Avery. Now that he's back in his universe, his counters are stronger, and within three or four seconds, this is a full-blown battle.

But no matter whose universe it is, Avery is outnumbered.

I swallow a scream when three of them attack simultaneously and he has almost no time to react.

Avery is the dove surrounded by crows, attacked without rules and without mercy, and the difference is obvious.

The Second Class hit to do damage. Avery counters to do damage control.

But it's not enough.

The first significant hit he takes goes straight to his midsection. Like a jackknife, he doubles over, a move that costs him precious time before he recovers.

Boom.

A second hit, this time a kick to the kidneys.

"Where is she?" one of the Second Class yells at him. "Where is she?"

Avery's glance darts to the window. "None of your concern, Second," he calls back at the other Sentinel, whose face spreads into a wide grin.

"Force One, back window, *now*! Fugitive is out. Search the forest! Force Two, change approach to take-in!"

Like a single being, ten or fifteen Sentinels move away from the fight toward the window, jumping out without even checking where they're going to land.

My heart leaps in joy. He misled them. Only ten stayed, if we're lucky—

We're not.

A swarm of bees couldn't be more coordinated than those Sentinels. Instead of attacking one by one or in small groups, they strike together.

No.

A hole opens up in my chest, cracked open when the first staff hits Avery with a sound I will never forget in my life.

I clamp a hand over my mouth, covering the silent scream I can't suppress because Avery is drowning in a sea of Sentinels.

They force him down to the ground by the sheer onslaught of bodies and weight.

The scene turns into bodies, limbs, no ups or downs, nothing but chaos—and Avery somewhere in the middle, lost.

Come on, *come on…* He must have a trick up his sleeve, he must, he—

One of the Second Class yells out in victory and my insides go numb.

"No," I whisper inside my prison, my eyes wide, a bottomless pit opening beneath me. "No, no, no!" This can't be happening, it can't—

I bite the backside of my hand to keep myself from screaming. I don't feel my teeth penetrate my skin because I'm glued to the scene unfolding in front of me.

Horror seizes me, growing out of proportion with every punch, stomp, knee, and kick to a grounded Avery.

He does his best to defend himself, but nothing to attack.

Nothing to get out.

One of the Second Class Sentinels unleashes a soccer ball kick that whips Avery's head around. His eyes roll back in the most horrible slow motion I've ever seen.

I scream into my hand. I scream and scream yet make no sound. My fingers claw at the metal, tears drench my shirt and drown my soul.

Fight, Avery, fight! Don't give up, don't—

Another kick lands on Avery's midsection with a force that could rupture a stomach, and this time they get close enough. One of them yanks back Avery's head by his hair and holds a knife to his throat.

My teeth draw blood on the back of my hand.

Avery… no. No, no, no. Please.

With three Sentinels holding Avery on each arm, plus the one controlling his head, they jerk him up to standing, keeping him supported or he'd fall. His face is bruised and swollen, one eye turning black already, and the way his knees buckle under him…

"Avery," I whisper desperately, reaching out as if I could touch him, as if I could help him, as if I could make him feel better. "Avery."

The Second Class in command steps up to Avery, regarding him coldly. "Avery McTighe, you are under arrest by the Sentinel Forces of the Great Union. The charges brought against you include conspiracy with the enemy and high treason."

Without waiting for a reply, he turns around swiftly. The others follow him in unity, hauling Avery along, his legs dragging across the floor.

Tears stream down my face. They drip onto the dusty ground beneath my feet, taking my will to flee, my will to live, with them. The edges of my vision grey, like the world has lost all its colors. The bottomless pit widens beneath my feet and threatens to swallow me whole.

And I let it.

I sink into it, waiting for the blissful numbness to set in and relieve me, but it doesn't.

Every step they drag Avery closer to the exit, closer to my hiding spot, the knife gets turned around once more in my heart, making it bleed until surely not a single drop of blood can run through my veins anymore.

It's all gone, bled out for Avery.

When they pass my hiding spot, none of them sees the faint sad smile on his face or the quick glance at the little part of an inconspicuous metal panel that's the slightest bit bent out of shape.

I do.

And it breaks my soul.

CHAPTER FORTY-TWO

Ghosts

By the time I dare to move, the back of my hand is bitten raw. The salty taste of tears in my mouth cranks up the nausea inside my stomach to a whole new level.

He knew what would happen.

The moment he hid me, he knew how this would play out. Avery never had any intention of getting out of here.

A bitter taste rises up inside my throat.

Maybe he even knew back in the woods. *"Stay as far away from the portal as possible,"* he asked me. Why? Because he knew I could cross us over? Because he knew what awaited him here?

Anguish wracks me, the events of the last thirty minutes destroying me bit by bit, taking my sanity and picking it apart until I'm nothing but a shivering mess.

I opened the portal. It was me. How did I do it? What did I do? Was I always that way? I rub my forehead, my skull pounding like I was the one who got hit by the Sentinels' staffs.

Avery.

I ball both fists and press them against my temple, willing myself to not lose it. If I hadn't come with him, if I hadn't followed him to the control room… But then Holloway would have killed him, and now—

Now Avery is where he never wanted to be again—with Canyon. What are they going to do with him? Conspiracy with the enemy and high treason—what does that bring you on Terra? Jail time on Earth is out the window. Regular jail time? How long?

My nails dig into my temples.

There's no question I have to get Avery out, but how? How can I? How could I? Get the Ghosts? I almost laugh out dry. Get the Ghosts to do what? To free Avery? How eager are they going to be to help a Sentinel?

I drop my hands from my face.

Well, they better be eager, because this Sentinel saved Earth, most likely Terra, and finished a mission Victor didn't even start.

They owe this Sentinel.

My jaw tightens. They owe Avery.

I straighten up from my crouched position between pipes, power conduits, and other ducts. I feel through the near darkness for a way out of here before my luck turns on me.

Luck.

Yeah, right.

It takes a considerable effort to squeeze my body sideways along the narrow passage. Like Avery instructed, I keep one hand on the yellow pipes, willing them to lead me out of here. For a moment, the guilt tunes down the slightest bit when I realize there's no way Avery would have fit through here: this maintenance passage is so tight, it fits me like a glove. He would have gotten stuck by now, ten times.

Well, the guilt only abates until I remember again that without me, he wouldn't even be in this situation. That's when the lump squeezing my heart to death is back, with a vengeance.

For the next thirty minutes, I flatten myself through the narrow, warm darkness of this maintenance shaft. The tightness releases when the walls open up to a wider tract, a bigger pipe leading from somewhere on my left to somewhere on my right, the three small yellow pipes I followed meeting another three bigger ones on the floor of this maybe shoulder-wide tunnel. Every twenty yards, a small sign on the ground glows in the dark, a yellow circle, in its center the schematic drawing of a tube with arrows pointing out from it in all directions: *Careful. Vacuum.*

What do I do now, besides hoping Avery was right and the Ghosts got the signal?

I hope.

And wait.

I curl up on the cold concrete floor, tears spilling from my eyes before I've even settled down.

And they won't stop until I fall asleep.

A gentle hand shakes my shoulder. "Noa? Noa? Hey, shh…"

I jerk awake with a jolt that would have mashed my head on the low ceiling if not for that same hand keeping me down.

"Easy. Easy. You're in the maintenance shaft. Hey."

"Victor?" I croak, my voice heavy from crying and sleep.

He switches on a little lamp attached to his wrist to shed some light into this darkness. He's dressed all in black, similar to when they stormed the VacWay and abducted Avery and me a lifetime ago.

"Yeah, it's me." He sounds grumpy. "What happened? Why are *you* back, and hell, why at the Hub? Could you have been any more inconspicuous—*not*, I mean? The *Hub* of all places? Did you at least finish the mission, or did the Sentinel—"

I all but shoot up to a sitting position, never mind hitting my head. "The mission? You dare ask me that before anything else after all that's happened? After you abandoned me at the portal? They would have taken me in if it hadn't been for Avery! You did absolutely *nothing* to help me; in fact, you refused to even listen to Avery's advice, and that's what got us into this mess in the first place!" I glare at him, my insides as tight as a coil. How *dare* he ask about the mission first. How dare he, after what he put Avery through.

Victor's mouth opens and closes. "Uh. Yeah. Well, I guess I deserved that." He scratches his head with the hand that doesn't have the flashlight on its wrist. "So, uh, why are you here and not on Earth, and where is the PB—" He clears his throat. "Avery, I mean?" His voice trails off when he sees my face fall.

"Noa?" Victor's hand squeezes my shoulder once.

"The PBM?" I whisper sarcastically, my voice thick. "He didn't make it out." A tear runs down my cheek, burning like acid on its way down.

Victor adjusts his body into the tight space so that he can see me better. His hand finds my chin, lifting it up. "What do you mean, he didn't make it out?"

What do I mean? I huff drily. "He made sure I got out of the Hub, and then the Sentinels got him," I say. "Boom, taken in, just like that." Including a beating that will replay in my nightmares for weeks to come.

Victor sucks in a sharp breath through his teeth. "Holy shit… Are you serious? No, well, yes, of course you are." He cringes at my glare. "So, Canyon got a hold of him?"

I nod. "Yup."

Victor curses loudly, and this time it echoes. "Not good. Not good at all. What is *wrong* with that PBM? Something was programmed differently in him, I can tell you that. Not that that's going to be any worry of ours after Canyon is done with him." He scoots a tad backward and away from me, angling his body and holding out a hand for me.

"Anyway, I'd like to chat and stay, but we've got to leave." He nods down to his right, and only now do I pick up on some kind of board that floats about an inch or two above the three yellow pipes.

My hand drops into his, but I don't follow its tug. "What do you mean, not any worry of ours?" I ask, my brows scrunched tightly. It sounded so dismissive, a typical Victor sentence, yet it gave me chills.

He tugs my hand again, but I still don't move. He sighs once. "Because the second they get all the information from him they need—and believe me, they're going to get everything once they access him, which, by the way, is why we *really* need to get the heck out of here—well, once they have what they want, they'll erase him. Blank slate, re-program, and they'll have themselves a brand-new, compliant Sentinel."

Victor lowers himself onto a type of boogie board floating a couple of inches above the concrete. "Noa, come on. Let's go." He pulls harder on my hand, but I'm frozen.

Frozen in horror.

"What?" I whisper, my stomach twisting into unnatural positions. "Erase him?" That can't possibly mean what I think it does.

"Standard procedure for errant behavior. He won't have any memories of what happened. If they're nice, they'll do a selective delete, only the last couple of weeks. If not, they start at point zero." He shrugs, like it was no big deal at all. Like we weren't talking about all that made Avery Avery.

"We *really* need to get going. If they started extracting information already, they'll know we take the VacWay maintenance shafts."

"No." I almost don't hear myself, but Victor finally stops pulling on my arm.

"What?"

"No," I repeat, this time with much more emphasis. "I'm not leaving. Not if that's what they're going to do to Avery." I shake my head and scoot backward, away from Victor. I don't know what I'm going to do, but I'm not leaving Avery alone with this, about to have his memory deleted. Everything about his life. Us. The little he remembers about his family.

"Noa—" Victor reaches for me again.

"No, I said!" I scoot back farther.

Victor cusses again. "Please don't panic, damn it! Not now, with the whole Sentinel Force dancing a cha-cha-cha above us!" He crawls toward me, reaching for my ankle, and only a well-placed kick makes him withdraw his hand.

Panic? I'm not panicking. In fact, I've never panicked in my life. I've only felt the other side bleed through. Maybe if I get to Avery, maybe I can get him back to Earth, maybe—

Victor shakes out the hand I kicked. "We don't have time. If they—"

"Exactly!" I scoot back farther, my legs frantically trying to get away from Victor and to find a way back up into the Hub. If they started already, I've got to make sure, I've got to—

There's a short pinging, a harsh bite into the back of my right shoulder—and then warmth spreads from the point of impact down my arm, then up my neck, engulfing my head like I'd stuck it into an oven.

"What…?" I slur, and then everything turns black.

Again.

CHAPTER FORTY-THREE

New Family

When I wake up, the world around me moves in short, bumpy little waves that do nothing to ease the nausea inside my stomach.

I groan and lift a heavy hand to my forehead.

"Shh, easy," Victor murmurs close to my ear. "We're almost there."

Almost there? Where—

Memories of the Hub, Victor, and his uncaring description about Avery's impeding fate come back to me.

My eyes spring open, staring right at a moving broken high ceiling and Victor's chest.

"Ugh." I grunt and buck my hips, struggling to get out of his arms and onto solid ground.

"Noa, wait, I—shoot, I'll drop you if—aw, whatever." Victor stops and lowers my legs to the ground, keeping a hand on my upper arm. "Better?" he asks, but it's more sarcastic than caring.

I press the back of my hand against my forehead. "Ow. What in the name of—"

Victor sighs. "Short-term sedation. Comes in handy when working in the Ghost industries. Usually, we shoot it at Sentinels, so, uh, this dose kept you out a bit longer than expected." He shrugs, the movement transmitting up my arm and cranking up the dizziness.

"You shot me!" Come on, seriously? "All I wanted to do is make sure we get Avery—"

"Yeah, about that. It's done, Noa. It was done when I found you. Unlike ours, their software doesn't need an alert mind. No matter that they beat him half to death or whatever, the moment they took him in, they hooked him up to extract as much memory-information as possible, and then click, delete, re-program. Done." At least he has the decency to sound apologetic with the last word.

Done.

My fingers wrap around the silver charm dangling from the necklace Avery gave me. How can they do that? That's almost like killing him—taking away everything that makes him who he is. How can somebody, *anybody*, with a conscience do that?

Victor drops a hand on my shoulder, patting it awkwardly. "Well, uh, we should get going. They're waiting for us."

"They?"

"Tonya and some others. Couple of the guys you know, and… well, if I'm not mistaken, we're going to have a high visitor today too." Victor leads me forward like a Sentinel would a prisoner.

Like they grabbed Avery.

Tears prick at my eyes. Maybe that's why I stumble and almost fall when my foot hits something solid sticking up from the ground. Only thanks to Victor's quick reaction do I not faceplant into—

"Where are we?" This is definitely not underground, not like the old Haunted House. Rays of sunshine dance through cracks in the dirty windows, and even the high ceiling isn't quite intact anymore, revealing glimpses of a blue sky. The ground under my shoes is covered with dirt, debris, old leaves, and…train tracks?

"An old weapons factory from the 1940s. Set up in a hurry to defend against Nazi Germany, and then not needed anymore when Hitler was killed and Germany lost. Like with everything else, Canyon likes to ignore the past, and that's fine with me. Gives us hideouts."

He points at the heaps of bent metal, rusted and eaten up by time and weather. "They left everything here—all their machinery. It causes a whiteout spot on Sentinel radar, hence it's perfect for us."

Victor leads me past assembly stations and broken-down tables toward a doorway without a door. It must have fallen off the hinges a long time ago, judging by the rotten state of its frame. Just before we're about to pass through, a wide-shouldered man steps out, his arms crossed in front of his chest.

"That her?" He gives me a cold look.

"No, Thatcher, it's somebody completely else. Figured tricking you would be fun." Victor rolls his eyes. "Yes, of course it's her. My goodness!"

Thatcher grunts once but steps aside. He isn't quite of Sentinel proportions, but still… scary big.

I squeeze past him and follow Victor into a way smaller room than the huge hall we came through, but equally dirty and broken down. The only difference is a long, oval table smack in the middle of it. That table is definitely from this side of the century, complete with those iPad-like devices on top of it and at the least twenty people seated around it. One of them gets up when we enter.

The light shining through the dirty, blind-covered windows straight ahead makes it difficult to see who it is, but then she's right in front of me.

"Noa." Tonya sighs and wraps me in a tight hug.

Somehow my arms go around her chest. Somehow I hug her back with way more force than I'd usually do. It helps.

She holds me almost like Elaine, and it makes me feel better amidst the sorrow.

Eventually, she pulls away from me. "While I'm happy to see you again, I can't deny it's surprising. The Senti… *Avery* I would have expected, you—not so much."

I force down a dry swallow. "Long story," I whisper hoarsely.

"I figured so. We need to hear about it. The way things went at the planetarium…" She shoots a glance at Victor, whose cheeks turn into tomatoes. "We have to come up with a new game plan—unless you tell me you got the intel from Robert Dunnam, but I assume the Sentinel's priorities were not ours." She gently guides me toward the table, everybody's eyes on me.

For a moment, I can't make sense of her words until it comes back to me: the mission the Ghosts asked me to do, the reason they wanted me to help them.

A small sarcastic laugh escapes me. Getting intel from Robert Dunnam has been the furthest on my mind since we crossed over and found out about the toxins. Who cares about Robert Dunnam? He's stuck on Earth like everybody else, thanks to Holloway, but at least he's a bad guy, so I don't mind. My parents, all the others… different story.

Tonya pulls out a chair for me. "What?" she asks when she sees my expression.

I let myself fall down into the chair that creaks under my weight and cross my arms in front of my chest as if that'd help keep myself together. "Robert Dunnam doesn't matter," I say, and the effect on the Ghosts around this table couldn't be any bigger. The two across from me jerk back as if I'd slapped them, and some others whisper to each other, shaking their heads and probably doubting my sanity.

Even Tonya looks taken aback. "Wait—but you wanted to help us with this. It's your planet—"

"Yeah, I know," I blurt out, my patience running thin. Every moment we spend talking about unimportant old plans, we delay working on a rescue mission for Avery. "And he won't be a problem anymore. No new orders, no new instructions, no new whatever. He's alone."

Tonya frowns and shakes her head. "Huh?"

I pinch the bridge of my nose. "Long story short: Canyon's plan was a different one altogether. Two toxins that when mixed would have killed all humanity on the planet, set within days of my arrival. A DNA-specific toxin. Once we found out about it, Avery got the idea to take out the incoming portals at the Hub, so it would be impossible for Canyon to send the second part of the poison. We wanted to leave the outgoing portals intact so Terrans could go back home when their modulators ran out, but… but there was this psycho Sentinel who destroyed the other one. So they're both gone… incoming and outgoing."

I keep my eyes trained at my hands folded in my lap. "So no, we didn't get the intel from Robert Dunnam, but it won't be an issue anymore because the Hub is down. The connection to Earth is gone."

Silence.

Somewhere outside these dirty, caked windows, a bird chirps. The wind rustles through dry leaves.

That's it.

Tonya swallows. "The... The Hub is down?" she repeats tentatively.

I nod. "Completely destroyed."

"You're sure?"

"One hundred and ten percent."

That's when the first laugh starts, bubbling out of a woman to my right, joined a moment after by somebody else, then another person and another, until everybody is off their chairs, hooting, laughing, hugging each other and clapping each other's shoulders. The whole room fills with sounds of happiness. People I've never seen before come by and pat me on the shoulder, or thank me, and it all feels so wrong.

Yes, I smile at them the best I can. Yes, I answer their questions the best I can. Yes, I confirm what I said over and over.

But no, I don't feel as happy about it as they do.

I should.

After all, we succeeded.

We saved Earth from Canyon.

We saved billions of people, sacrificing one to save them all... I shouldn't consider it a high price, but I do. Too high a price.

It takes the group of Ghosts at least ten minutes to calm down again, and even then Tonya has a hard time getting them to sit around the table and listen to my whole story, from beginning to end, as she says.

And it takes a while. I tell them about my parents-slash-former-Ghosts, our plan to take down the Hub, our trip there, Sands and Holloway. I tell them about Avery's rejection, and how he never stopped fighting, never stopped protecting me. At one point, my fingers cling around the infinity charm. It grounds me.

The only two parts of the story I omit is what happened between Avery and me, and how we crossed back to Terra.

"So the incoming console was destroyed already, and then…?" asks a new Ghost across from me, a man I'd guess to be in his thirties with grey streaks in his brown hair.

"The incoming console was what I took out while Avery kept Holloway busy." I move the charm back and forth between my fingers.

"And the outgoing console…?" he asks.

Well, that's where it gets a bit tricky. "It went so fast." I shrug. "We were right next to it, Holloway rammed in his staff, sparks were everywhere, the portal made a weird screeching sound, and the next thing I know, we're being sucked through." Kind of true.

"But how do you know that direction is dead too?"

Because I saw it on Earth. Because we would have been trapped if it weren't for my weird ability to sense the other side. "Because one of the scientists manning the Terran-Portal yelled it out and couldn't fix it while we were fleeing from the Hub." I lift an eyebrow at him. Could have happened that way.

Everybody nods around me or mutters sounds of understanding.

Tonya leans forward and places a hand on mine that's not playing with the pendant. "I'm sorry about Avery, but there's nothing we can do. Even if we got him out, he wouldn't be the same person who did all this for us. He'd be a blank slate, even more a Sentinel than before. There's no coming back from this, Noa. They've reprogrammed him. They've wiped him. He knew that was going to happen the moment he crossed over." She shakes her head. "No, actually. He knew it the second he defected. I'm sorry," she repeats again, more softly.

I blink once, then twice, trying to keep the tears at bay. *The second he defected*—the second he decided to help me. If it weren't for me, none of this would have happened, and Avery—

I close my eyes, willing the tears and the new wave of guilt away.

Tonya squeezes my hand in support.

"Thank you," I whisper, opening my eyes when I'm sure I'm not going to start bawling. "I wish—"

Out of nowhere, commotion starts at the door. Two large, muscular men in the typical black Ghost outfits slip past Thatcher and scan the room, one of them turning back into the bigger hall. "Clear."

The table breaks out in whispers, but Tonya's face spreads into a wide grin. "I believe our visitor is here," she says as she stands, pushing her chair back.

Before I even know what's happening, the two big men step aside to make room for two more people walking slowly into our room. The first one, slightly leading the way, I recognize.

"Tomar," I whisper. Although there's no way he could've heard me, he looks at me and grins, winking once.

It's Tomar and… a very old man.

A very old man who walks hunched over and supports himself with a cane, his other arm hooked into Tomar's for stabilization.

Canyo—

No, not Canyon. Relief floods my system. Of course it isn't Canyon, but somebody equally old. This old man has long, white hair pulled back into a ponytail, not Canyon's shorter 'do. White eyebrows too, suggesting he must either have been blond once, or be very old at this point. As soon as he enters, the murmuring turns quiet.

Every single one of the Ghosts stands up silently.

Wait, what—

Respect.

Everybody's eyes are on the old man, respect shining from all of them. Who—

"Come on," Tonya says. She takes me by the arm and pulls me out of my chair. "He's here because of you."

"Me?" Who is he—and why because of me?

Tonya drags me toward Tomar and the old man in the middle of the room. "Galileo." Tonya bows slightly, an expression of awe and surprise on her face. "It's an honor to meet you. I'm Tonya, the leader of this group. We have excellent news, we—"

"I know," the old man says with a voice that's much stronger than his frail body suggests. "I saw the spike and correlated the data. The Hub is gone. The portals are gone. A job well done," he adds, making Tonya blush.

"Well, it wasn't our doing. Our original plan failed. The praise for destroying the Hub goes to Noa and a Sentinel."

Galileo raises an eyebrow. "Is that so?"

"Yes," Tonya says, "and since you wanted to meet her before the mission already. This"—she steps aside, opening her palm toward me—"this is Noa."

The old man stares into my eyes and it's like a mirror. The same turquoise looks back at me, only framed by white bushy eyebrows and wrinkly skin instead of my younger face.

I tilt my head. Why does he look so familiar? Is it the eyes? Or…?

"Figuring it out?" he asks, amusement coloring his tone. "I'm sure Canyon did, or he wouldn't have tried to use you to get re-elected."

"Canyon?" What does he have to do with it?

"The same." Galileo nods, then looks past me. "You there, show her a picture of Claudine Gervais." Somewhere behind me, one of the Ghosts scrambles for a pad and almost trips over his feet when he brings it over.

"Here, sir."

"Thank you." Galileo lets go of Tomar, who checks on him with a short glance before he retreats to the table. He sprouts the same questioning look on his face I'm sure is on mine.

A gentle smile tugs on Galileo's lips as he looks down at the pad. "Claudine Gervais." He turns the screen so that I can see it.

The image hits me in the gut like an iron fist.

Two turquoise eyes smile at me, framed by long, white-blonde lashes and hair of the same color so thin, it can't do anything else than go into a ponytail. Her nose is small and similar to mine, and only her mouth a tad wider, but otherwise… otherwise, we're from the same mold.

"My real name is Mauricio Gervais," Galileo says, never taking his eyes off me, ignoring the sharp intake of breath from Victor behind me. "This is my granddaughter, Claudine."

He pauses.

"Your mother."

CHAPTER FORTY-FOUR

The Old Man's Story

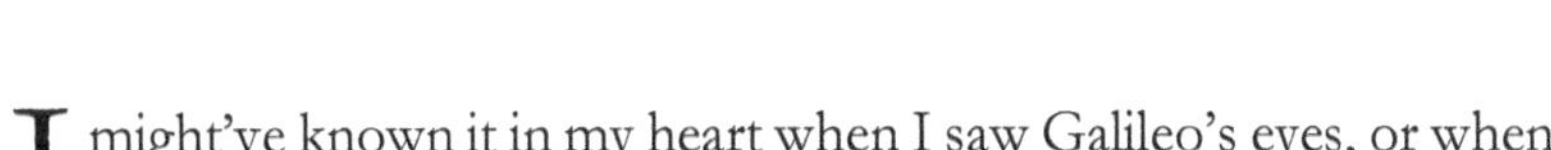

I might've known it in my heart when I saw Galileo's eyes, or when I looked at the image of a woman who could have been me in two or three decades, yet his words still come as a shock.

I'm barely aware of whispers around me, or Tonya asking if she heard that right.

All the Ghosts besides Victor and Tonya clear the room, then Tonya leads Galileo and me to the table.

My mind chases its own tail, trying to make sense of my life with this new information that just revealed itself.

I'm the daughter… of a Ghost? I'm truly Terran? But I lived on Earth, how—

A chair pushes into the hollows of my knees and I sit automatically. A large hand reaches for mine and holds it.

Tonya drums a nervous rhythm on the table. "So… the great Galileo is the even greater Mauricio Gervais, and Noa is your great-granddaughter," she says. "That's why you looked familiar. It's been a while, though."

Galileo smiles at Tonya. "Obviously. Dead men tend to avoid the public."

"They also change their appearances."

"A necessity if I wanted to stay unrecognized for Terra's benefit—and for my great-granddaughter's."

I blink twice hearing it spoken out loud.

I'm sitting across from my *great-grandfather.*

Tonya looks at me, then back at… Grandpa. "I should've seen it. But then… who expects *that*?" She shakes her head in disbelief.

Galileo straightens. "Nobody. But now, the time has come to drop the disguise. Galileo was a necessity born out of history and prevention. After Noa was trapped on Earth when Canyon secured all portals… I never gave up hope that my precautions would prove themselves successful as they did. I never gave up hope we'd find her again. Alive." A little twinkle plays in his eyes, and Tonya nods, as if that explained everything.

I look at the old man only separated from me by Victor, who's still holding my hand, his thumb gently moving in circles across my skin. I yank my hand away as if burned, rubbing it to clear the memory of Victor's touch and replace it with the memory of Avery's.

If he's losing his, I'm holding on to mine twice as strong.

I have to.

"Why didn't I get sick?" I ask Galileo as I push my chin forward. If I'm a Terran… Avery got sick immediately. My… parents got sick eventually, Andrew died. I pranced through life not knowing how extraordinarily lucky I truly was.

Galileo gives me a small acknowledging nod, followed by a sigh. "A very good question, my dear, but one that requires some explanation. I'm sure you know I founded the Ghosts decades ago?"

"Yes." It's the little bit of Terran history that I know, thanks to Tonya.

Galileo nods again. "Good. What you probably don't know is that Canyon and I… we used to work together."

My brows narrow. "Okay?" So he knows Canyon, maybe even dislikes him on a personal level. "In politics?"

The old man huffs. "Yes and no. It started in science. We're both old, Noa. Very old. If it weren't for the advancement of genetic research and modifications, neither Canyon nor I would be alive today. I'm well over a hundred, and while I may look weak, I can assure you that the important parts"—he taps his heart and then his head—"are guaranteed to work for another thirty years at least.

Anyway, I digress."

Galileo lays his cane on the table, leaning forward and looking straight at me. "During World War II, Canyon and I were… well, let's call it *recruited* by Nazi Germany. We were supposed to work on a new weapon to make Germany invincible. Canyon was a young student from America who got trapped in Europe when the war started. Me, I was a research assistant from Italy, also trapped, especially with Hitler's promise to find and kill our families if we didn't comply."

His eyes lose focus, as if he's gone back to the 1930 or 40s, back to World War II.

"Canyon and I, we are both physicists. Neither of us was thrilled to be working on a weapon of mass destruction in a secret research lab deep inside the belly of the German Reichstag. We did everything we could. We stalled, we sabotaged our own experiments at the sake of our health, but one day… one day I made an accidental discovery—I opened the first bridge." He regains focus, something new shining in his eyes. Guilt?

"We kept it quiet, but after we could reliably open up a connection with what seemed to be a parallel universe to ours, Canyon had an idea. We invited Hitler to present him with our ultimate weapon, and he came. That day, we had our closest friends with us, scattered throughout the Reichstag, ready and armed. We led Hitler into the Reichstag's science lab alone under the pretense of our top secret discovery, and then…"

He closes his eyes for a moment, pursing his lips. "June 23rd, 1940. We pushed him through the portal and closed it behind him."

My jaw drops.

"You sent him to Earth," I rasp. "We had four more years of war, is that…?" I don't even dare say it out loud. Is that is why… Is *that* why Terra's World War II ended so much sooner than ours? Because they sent their Hitler to our universe?

Galileo bows his head, which seems too heavy for his wrinkly neck. "Yes," he whispers. "Because of us. Because of me. I discovered the bridge; I discovered how to cross somebody. We sent

Hitler off. We didn't realize what damage it would cause. He was out of our hands, and we became heroes. As soon as he was gone, our loyal friends got us out of the Reichstag and we all hid, until it became obvious Hitler was gone. The Allied forces took over and brought a confused Germany to its leaderless knees within less than four days. The rumor of the weapon Canyon and I developed destabilized the Axis powers, and with the resistance movements rising up to the occasion all across Europe the Nazis lost. Everything was well, especially once it became known what Canyon and I had done. That's how the Great Union started—Canyon and me, saving the world with science." He huffs.

"We never spoke the truth to the general public. Only a few select people knew. To the rest, Hitler was atomized in a weapon we designed that later destroyed itself from the powers it generated, and that was it."

He turns the cane over on the table. "I was young. We both were young. We were asked to lead the Great Union, and of course we did. We never thought twice. It was so easy to make this world better." He uses his fingers to count off. "Make equality law to prevent another Nazi disaster. Make life better by offering Augs. Bring technology and science to everybody, no matter their upbringing or social status. We had the most brilliant minds working for us—to improve humanity. And for a while, it worked." He presses his lips together tightly.

"And then?" I ask, glued to every one of his words, the history of Terra—my history—spread out before me.

"Then I reopened the portal years later and saw what I had done," he whispers, his eyes full of sorrow. "We don't have the exact details, and maybe nobody has, but we do know that without our Hitler the war would have been over a few days after Canyon and I disposed of him through the portal. Days after our war ended. Because of us, of our wrongdoing, your war cost millions of lives more."

My mind spins from the enormity of the revelation. "How?" I whisper back, voice rough.

A heavy sigh leaves Galileo's throat. "A few days after we sent Hitler over Graf von der Schulenburg assassinated Hitler in Paris, France. For a moment, a handful of hours, the news of Hitler's death spread, and with it a single photo of his body—a very convincing photo. But then the Führer is back, mysteriously unharmed, and stronger than before."

His voice has lost almost all emotion.

"Our universes split the moment I sent Hitler through, and instead of the war ending after he was assassinated four days later, Earth had a backup Hitler, one just as eager to continue where the other one left off. And, without rejection at today's levels, he had ample time to do so."

His gaze drops to the table.

"I might have saved Terra, but I damned Earth."

CHAPTER FORTY-FIVE

New Hope

Stunned silence hovers like a blanket, covering the table and everybody at it.

For a full ten seconds, nobody says anything. Not Victor, not Tonya, and for sure not me. The hits keep on coming, and I can't say I'm handling them well today.

"Is… Is that why you founded the Ghosts?" Tonya offers a shy smile.

Galileo lets go of a deep breath. "Yes. Once Canyon began to reopen the portals in the early 60s to use Earth as a Petri dish, it became clear we were not on the same page anymore. I had to try to make up for what I did."

For the first time since our little meeting started, Victor makes a sound, clearing his throat. "But you died. I mean, you're Mauricio Gervais, one of the GU's double-Presidents until '96, when you died. That's why Canyon had to step down and become Minister of Science, because the office of the presidency was dependent on both of you governing."

"Well, the rumors of my demise have been greatly exaggerated," Galileo says, a twinkle in his eye. "I knew eventually Canyon would want me out of the way. I had turned into the conscience he didn't think necessary. Not when it came to Earth. As long as Terra was benefitting from our abuse, he saw no wrongdoing in exploiting another universe. Power, time, and fear of the unknown can change a man. Eventually, my security detail alerted me to an assassination attempt—and we let it happen. Well, we faked my death, and that was it. Mauricio Gervais died, and the Galileo-persona took over my life. It was only a matter of time until Canyon would've found out about my double-game, and this way I stayed a step ahead."

Galileo pushes the cane farther onto the table, folding his hands in front of him before he looks up at Tonya, then Victor, then me. "And right now, I need the Ghosts. Terra needs the Ghosts."

Victor shakes his head. "Why? Noa and the Sentinel took out the Hub. The portals are down. As far as I know it will be impossible to do the math for Earth's exact location at this point, since they have continued drifting apart from us since the Hub went down. Needle in a haystack. Earth is safe. We're out of a job," he says with an eyeroll.

"Quite the opposite. Your job has only begun," Galileo says, his voice more tired, as if he were at the end of a very long marathon.

Tonya throws a worried glance at Victor, then back at Galileo. "Why?"

"Because I have reason to believe that Canyon is about to open another portal to another, newer parallel universe. The signs were there all along, but now with the connection to Earth gone, I promise you he'll try to access another parallel universe."

Tonya sits up ramrod straight. "Explain."

"Canyon will fix the Hub. It won't give him Earth's coordinates, but he will be able to open a new portal. And you can imagine what that would mean."

Victor pulls in a sharp breath of air. "Are you saying that all of us would be in it, or a version of us? And that he'd use us like he used Earth?"

Galileo's eyes harden. "Correct."

I blink hard. It makes sense, yet… doesn't. "But if he is opening a portal to Terra, wouldn't that Terra be doing the very same? Opening a portal? I mean, right now, we are one and we do the same, because we haven't split yet." I press both my palms together and wiggle the fingers of both hands in synchrony. "Shouldn't then

Canyon be opening a portal in every universe, meaning, the others will do the same?"

"Also correct." Galileo gives me an approving nod. "If he opened a portal the way we did it in 1940. I assume though he won't, because that would mean that universe's Canyon would also have opened a portal, which would ultimately mean our Terra would also be invaded by another Terra because of the law of parallel actions. It's a risk he is unlikely to take."

My head is spinning. "So, what else is he going to do?"

"The portal technology has come a long way since 1940. He doesn't need to split off a current copy of us. It's less risky if he finds a universe that has recently split from ours, but is still close enough that we can still calculate its coordinates and access it, but also different enough that they won't even be thinking about an invasion."

Tonya's brow pull into a V. "Split off recently?"

Galileo points at me. "Multiple universe theory. Take Noa, as one of many examples. There are universes where she didn't make it back here from Earth. Where she never crossed to us in the first place. Where maybe even she wasn't born. Small changes, but they will have led to a different outcome in those universes. Canyon will access one of those universes, ready for our exploitations and not likely to strike at the same time."

"Heavens." Tonya falls back into her chair. "It's 1940 all over again. What does he want with a copy of us, I mean…?" Her voice trails off.

"Resources. Imagine a whole second modern Terra. He could get metals, supplies, raw materials… Everything we have less and less of. That was ultimately also behind his reason to utilize Earth."

"This is so short-sighted. What if the other Terra fights back?" Tonya massages her temples. "He could condemn us all."

A muscle in Galileo's jaw pops. "I do think Canyon has lost all rational thought when it comes to this. Illusions of grandeur, whatever you want to call it. I agree with you, there is no guarantee we won't be on the receiving end of this, but I also guarantee you,

Canyon will do all he can to come out on top."

Victor swallows hard. "What can we do?"

"Well, that depends on Noa."

All eyes shift to me.

"Me?" I squeak. Not again. I have nothing to do with this. I've done my duty and more. There's no way—

"Why Noa?" Victor asks. "We're well trained, we—"

"She has done enough already," Tonya adds, "I think we should probably—"

"Noa is the only one who can cross without a portal. To any universe."

That shuts everybody up.

"Excuse me?" Tonya turns toward Galileo, her eyebrows all the way up under her hairline.

"Noa is the only one who can cross without a portal," Galileo repeats. "It's what I was trying to explain to you in the beginning, Noa. I'm a scientist, a physicist. Your mother is a geneticist. You were… enhanced to feel out different universes and cross over to them, and if you did, to survive. Rejection doesn't affect your cells."

"It doesn't?" I repeat like a parrot. So many questions come to mind. Who's my dad? My grandparents? Are they all still alive? Why was I on Earth? Why—

"No. It doesn't. That's why you were on Earth when Canyon closed the portals—to test your viability."

Oh.

Galileo looks away for a moment, then back at me.

"We hoped you would become our ambassador to different universes. For peaceful connection and exchanges. To advance science, to better life for everybody. We never thought we'd need you to prevent a war, but…"

"But here we are," I whisper, my throat completely dry. Here we are—after I crossed Avery and myself over twice. "So I was right. When my mind blanks out and I see and hear things that aren't there… It's the other side calling to me?" It sounds ridiculous, but I've heard crazier over the last few weeks.

"Correct. You're picking up on Terra in areas where the connection is especially strong. Usually either where the bridge between the universes is thinned by a portal, or where we have a lot of connections to the other side."

Like at the Reichstag. There's a portal there. Of course at the Adler Research Facility and at the Hub I was standing right next to one, and then my other so-called panic attacks… it was all the other side calling to me.

And Avery figured it out before I even got close to it. A *pink* halo, not red, not blue. Ghost parents. Surviving without a modulator. Crossing without intention.

Yeah, Avery knew it way before anybody else.

A sharp pain slices my chest, and I hold my head higher in response.

Galileo leans forward. "And that's why we need you, Noa. I can't yet say how Canyon is going to play this, but I know while the Ghosts won't have a portal, we will have you. We'll have to do all that we can so Canyon doesn't enslave another universe. And we can't do it without you."

This whole situation screams déjà vu at a deafening volume. They want me to save something I didn't know needed saving with abilities I didn't know I had, nor how to use them.

"You should know that it will be dangerous, but the only way to evade the Sentinel Forces is with you and your potential." He measures me with a gaze.

Yeah, the Sentinel Forces… about that.

Besides the fact that I'm still not anything like a Ghost—not a fighter, not a daredevil—I don't want to see any Sentinel ever again.

Not a Leiva, a Second Class.

Not a First Class, with their amber eyes like Avery's, but still so different. So much less alive, so much less warmth in them.

No. It's too much. I don't want any part in this. If it's true what Galileo says, I could cross over to Earth on my own. I'm sure eventually I'm going figure out how to open a portal when I actually want to.

Being back home, maybe crossing my parents here first, then staying on Earth and far away from all things Terra… it holds a certain appeal.

A very strong appeal.

Because staying here would mean constant reminders of what I've lost. Of Avery.

A pang of sadness penetrates the numbness around my heart.

Avery…

Deep in thought, I play with the necklace he gave me, the metal warm from its resting place against my heart. Close to Avery.

Galileo leans forward, one hand reaching out toward me, his eyes trained onto my necklace.

"May I?" He raises a questioning eyebrow, waiting for my nod before he carefully lifts the infinity charm from my chest, turning it between his fingers.

"Interesting," he murmurs with a reminiscent smile. "I didn't know she still made them." Galileo looks at the little infinity symbol warmly before he gently drops the charm back onto my chest. "Who gave that to you?"

My jaw tightens. "My friend."

"And that would be…?"

I lift my chin up higher. "Avery."

"Avery. Of course. Of course it would come from a Sentinel, although I didn't expect it. Not after they improved their programming." He nods to himself as if it'd make all perfect sense. "What has he told you about it?"

I cock my head. "Told me about it? N-Nothing. He said he wanted me to remember him. He gave it to me before…" I try to swallow, but it gets stuck. I can't get myself to say it out loud.

Before they took him.

Galileo chuckles once. "Before they deleted him? A smart one, your Avery. He must trust you completely, or else he wouldn't have given you his memories." He points at my necklace.

Now wait a second. "His memories? What do you mean, his memories?" Like, a memento? It's not like this could actually be—

"It's a Memory Keeper." Galileo taps a finger to the bone behind his ear. "Useful only for humans with a port, so First and Second Class Sentinels. Invented in the early years of the Sentinel Program, when parents still clung to the individuality of their children, later banned, possession punishable with automatic deletion for a Sentinel and prison for non-Sentinels."

"A Memory Keeper?" I breathe, my fingers gliding over the cool metal, my eyes closing automatically, remembering how Avery gave it to me.

"Indeed. If he gave it to you, I assume he uploaded his memory for you for safekeeping."

Avery sitting on a tree stump, pulling something metallic from the back of his head.

Avery's memory. Avery's *memories.* Everything they took from him is right here, with me. I suck in my lower lip. It all makes sense now. Avery was always one step ahead of me, from the moment he met me. He knew what was going to happen when I was still clinging to illusions and plans that would never work.

He knew, like he did with so many other things.

My eyes fly open.

He knew.

He knew there was a chance.

"Can it be restored? Can he get his memory back with this?" I lean forward just like Galileo, my hand coming to rest on top of his, not even realizing this is the first time I'm touching my great-grandfather.

His smile widens. "Spoken like a true Gervais. Yes, dear, it can be restored. Everything that makes somebody's personality is saved on this. All you need to do is access his port and it will upload instantly."

My heart beats so fast, I feel dizzy from it.

I can restore Avery.

I can get Avery back.

"All you need to do is to access his port."

My hands start shaking as my mind races through my options.

"I hate to break up the pity party, but can we please go back to talking about how we can keep Canyon from enslaving copies of all of us?" Victor makes a circle in the air with his index finger.

Galileo's… *my great-grandfather's* smile is gentle. "That depends on Noa." He turns his hand around so our palms touch. "I know we're asking a lot of you. Again. You were supposed to be trained, to be prepared for this, but…" He sighs. "Alas, Canyon took that from us. We can't win without you, Noa. And even if you're with us, we might not keep Canyon from executing his plan. But with you on our side, we at least stand a chance."

Three people's stares rest on me, waiting. Expecting.

I draw in a breath of air that smells fresher.

Truth is, I should have more altruistic reasons.

I should be mostly concerned about Terra.

As it is, my priorities are different.

I look at Tonya, Victor, and, last of all, at Galileo.

"All you need to do is to access his port."

My decision is made.

He saved me more than once, and now I'm going to save him, tit for tat—no, not because of that, but because it's Avery.

"I'm in."

Tonya squeals once and throws her arms around my neck, almost strangulating me. Victor slaps my back like crazy, and Mauricio… Great-Grandpa… His smile widens, a twinkle in his eyes.

"I knew you were going to do the right thing." He watches my every move with the kind of attention that doesn't miss a detail. "Regardless of your motivations."

Neither Tonya nor Victor notice the little addendum, but I do.

Looks like my Great-Grandpa knows me pretty well already.

Because to me, right now, all that counts is Avery.

Only Avery.

Acknowledgements

Books are like babies: they start out as a tiny spark in the back of your mind, slowly grow and develop month by month, demand all of your time, give you sleepless, or at least short, nights, and need a plethora of support to get them out into the world.

Now, as a pediatrician I can handle the real-deal human babies, but the book babies… Boy, do I have people to thank for keeping this one alive!

To Lyssa Chiavari and Snowy Wings Publishing: Thank you for taking us under your wings and teaching us how to fly (done with the owl-analogies now). Snowy Wings is the perfect home for Noa and Avery, and I'm looking forward to continuing their story with you.

To Matt Cox: I'm at the verge of a heart attack every time I get a manuscript back from you, but so far I've pulled through unscathed and the stories have become the better for it. Thank you for keeping me honest!

To the team: Clare, Amy, Tandy, Dorothy, KimG—thank you for your patience and for answering all my millions of questions. I promise I'll learn and be less obnoxious next time. ;o)

To the First Responders: Sharon, Jen, Geri-Ann—thank you for being my guinea pigs and reading my stories, no matter which one. I'm naming you godparents to them!

To my family: Couldn't have done it without you. Thanks for tolerating my odd schedule, for having my back, and for taking all my quirks as they come. You rock! (PS: Dog—thanks for all the early-morning-hour-cuddles. Much appreciated.)

To my readers: Thank you for letting my stories be part of your life for a little while. To stick to the analogy, you're the book-baby's friends along the way, and I'm more than happy you came along for this ride! See you next time!

About the Author

Micky O'Brady is a pediatrician-turned-writer living in beautiful, dry Southern California with her husband and two critters (one son, one dog). Micky loves to write YA thrillers with a romantic twist, mainly because she wishes her life had been such an awesome mix of action and cute guys when she was a teen.

When she isn't up at around 3 a.m. (with a cup of tea, Earl Grey, hot) drafting stories she can't get out of her head, she can be found at a martial arts dojo, though maybe not at 3 a.m. She holds a 2nd degree black belt in Judo and a brown belt in Krav Maga, and is convinced every girl should know how to kick some butt.

Micky also is a firm believer in the healing powers of Nutella eaten straight from the glass and in the magic that can happen on a rainy day, as long as there are fuzzy socks and a cup of hot tea involved.

Her previous publications include a doctoral thesis and several medical articles as well as a medical book about emergency communication. None of them are as fun to read as her YA novels though. Her first YA-novel, THE PRESIDENT'S DAUGHTER, and its sequel TRIAL BY ICE, are published by Curiosity Quills and available through all major retailers, such as Amazon, B&N, Kobo, and Smashwords.

Through Snowy Wings Publishing Micky is the author of YA-sci-fi romance BETWEEN WORLDS, published in May 2020, and is happy to announce more novels will be coming your way.